ALSO BY JAYDEN THOMPSON

Diamond in the Rough

Stars in the Sky

Map made by Ink & Lore Maps

First edition
ISBN: 979-8-9924339-4-4

Age Rating: 15+

To my little brother, who may or may not have been taught a curse word because he was reading the manuscript over my shoulder during editing.
(Sorry, Mom)

TO STOKES ↑

THE CITY OF
LOCHRIDGE

Feet 60 180 240

1 ROOK MANOR
2 DAELIK HOUSE
3 SHERIFFS OFFICE
4 SILAS HOTEL
5 MEETING PLACE
6 SALTARE
7 THE BROKEN BOTTLE
8 BEACH HIDEOUT

TO THE GREAT RIVER ↗

THE BARTER STREETS

RAVEN TERRITORY

PROLOGUE

Once upon a time, Stella Rook lived in a fairytale.

Her fingers brushed along the keys of her piano. A song swept through the sunbathed parlor, drifting through the open windows and out into the garden beyond. Stella tilted her head back to let the summer breeze warm her skin. A few loose strands of her hair danced across her shoulders, keeping time with the music.

"Has anyone ever told you how pretty you are when you play?"

She glanced to her left, where Liam sat on the bench beside her, his blond hair gleaming gold in the sunlight.

"You're a sorry romantic," she mumbled, unable to help the heat that rose in her cheeks.

He grinned, showing off both dimples. "Me? Never."

Stella yelped as he threw an arm around her waist, tugging her close enough to press a kiss to her cheek. The movement jerked her hands off the piano, but she was laughing too hard to notice.

"Stop," she giggled.

He tweaked her nose. "Unfortunately, I have to." He glanced at the clock on the far wall. "It's late."

"No! Just stay here tonight!"

Liam gave a pointed look towards the sunset peeking through the open windows. "It's getting dark. My parents will be worried."

"They know you're here."

"They also know that your father has a hundred people who want to kill him and everyone else in this house." Liam stood up with a sigh. "I don't want my family to worry."

The mention of the feud sent ice creeping through Stella's veins. She didn't like thinking about it, didn't like dwelling on the fight between her father and the Daelik family. Stella had seen her fair share of violence over the years, but she didn't like to get involved, even if the rest of her family did.

She leaned her head against Liam's chest. "I want you to stay," she murmured.

He brushed her hair out of her eyes. "I wish I could, but my parents will be beside themselves if I get home any later than I already am." He poked her. "I'll make it up to you later. Deal?"

Stella sighed. "Deal."

Liam tugged her into a hug. Stella wrapped her arms around his neck, stealing every last moment she could get.

"I love you," she said.

"I love you, too," he replied. He stole a kiss and she grinned. Then he pulled her out the door and down the hall, trailing kisses down her neck all the way to the front door.

"Say hello to Tag for me," she called as he turned away. "I haven't seen him in a while."

He opened the door, frowning at the mention of his little brother. "He hates that nickname."

Her smile turned wicked. "All the more reason to use it."

Liam gave her a roguish grin to match and slipped through the door. Stella rushed upstairs to her bedroom. She flung aside the gauzy white curtains that hung over the balcony doors, granting her a view of her family's sprawling property. The house was surrounded by a wrought iron gate, a field of roses in between. Her mother's prized garden looked delightful in the dimming sunlight, but Stella's eyes were on Liam's figure as he strolled down the dirt path. He paused at the gate and turned, knowing Stella would be watching from the balcony as she always did. He plucked a red rose from the nearest bush and raised it towards her in farewell. Her smile softened as he turned away, tucking the rose into his shirt as he sauntered into the city proper.

Had Stella known that was the last time she'd ever see him alive, she might have insisted that he stay. She might have warned him about the danger waiting for him in the city, waiting to take his life in order to hurt her. She might have done a hundred other things to prevent what happened at nightfall, but at the time, she was as oblivious as he was.

Stella leaned against the balcony railing, playing with her hair as she gazed after him, basking in a fairytale that wasn't meant to last.

SHADES
OF
RED

CHAPTER 1

Blood ran between the cobblestones, forming small red rivers that made bile rise in Stella Rook's throat as she threw herself into the fray. She grabbed her cousin's arm, which was cocked back, ready to deliver another blow. Harvey snarled at her. Underneath him, the remaining Raven moaned weakly, his fingers clawing at the hand Harvey clenched around his throat.

"Enough," Stella hissed in his ear.

Harvey ripped away and punched the Raven again. He was taking his time with this one; three other Ravens laid a few feet away with their throats slit open. Stella ignored them as she lunged at Harvey again, this time securing his arm and twisting it behind his back in a move so quick he didn't have time to deflect it. Her lip curled in disgust as she felt how slick his arm was, coated in blood that was not his own.

"This has gone too far," she snapped, quiet enough that only Harvey could hear. "Father isn't happy, and neither am I. You need to follow orders if you wish to keep your place in this gang."

He twisted to glare at her. "You wouldn't kick me out."

Stella bared her teeth. "I dare you to find out."

Harvey glared at her for a long moment. Then he jerked out of her grip and stalked away, pausing long enough to spit on the Raven. Stella's amber eyes flashed as she glared after him, but a weak cough from the ground snagged her attention.

The Raven's face was a bloody patchwork of bruises, his arm fractured in multiple places. Stella didn't have to see the beginnings of the fight to know Harvey was responsible for the three dead men, too.

The Raven moaned, attempting to roll over.

"Dump him back over the border," Stella ordered her men. She jerked her chin at the corpses. "And take care of them, too."

They exchanged an irksome look at the blunt orders. Stella narrowed her eyes, and they rushed into action, dragging the Raven towards the border by his legs. Trespassers deserved punishment, of course, but Harvey Rook going all-out on Raven lowlifes would not ease the tension brewing in the Barter Streets.

Fighting back her frustration, she turned on her heel and stormed after Harvey. Her dark hair fell to the bottom of her ribcage, the curls swirling in the salt-tinged breeze. With her amber eyes and brown hair, she was a spitting image of her father. Harvey and his sister took after the Rook lineage as well, resembling Stella so much that people often mistook them for siblings rather than cousins.

She caught up to Harvey. Her hands itched to draw her gun, or better yet, punch him, but she kept her hands at her sides as she fell into step with her cousin.

Harvey's lips curled into a sneer as he looked down on her, amber eyes glinting in the midday sun. "Are you going to lecture me now?"

Blood coated his hands and face. He licked the back of his bloody knuckles with a sly smile. Stella kept her gaze firmly ahead as she drawled, "Are you going to quit beating up every Raven that crosses the border?"

"They know better."

"*You* know better. Daelik is winning the sheriff's favor because of your antics. We don't kill everyone who walks into our territory. It sets a precedent."

"I didn't kill him," he said smugly.

Rage flickered in the corners of her eyes. "Don't tell me that wasn't your intention."

Harvey examined his knuckles. "If you had let me finish, you would have seen what my intentions were." His eyes flicked to her. "I don't like it when people interrupt me."

"Father sent me," Stella said, crossing her arms.

He grunted and fell silent, toying with his prized hunting knife where it hung at his side. It was long and had a wooden handle with a leather grip, the tip of the blade curved just so. Harvey's calloused fingers curled around it protectively. Stella resisted the urge to take it away from him, knowing it wouldn't go over well if she tried. Her father was perhaps the only person Harvey respected. He was the one who took Harvey and Zoey in after the siblings' father was killed in the feud. Stella never cared for the idea of sharing her house with her cousins. Zoey was alright, but Harvey was… *twisted.* Something dark had taken root inside of him, and it had only grown worse over the years. She wasn't fully convinced that he wasn't rabid.

The wind picked up, blowing her hair into her face. A lone raven rode the breeze high overhead. Lochridge was eerily quiet for this time of day. Stella couldn't help but frown at the streets that were typically teeming with people, at the restaurants and shops and bars that now sat empty. These were the Barter Streets. They were usually flooded with customers, especially on a day like today when the sun was out and Lochridge wasn't trapped under the layer of clouds that always seemed to be present. Every business that operated in the White Roses' territory paid a tax to Marcus, who headed the gang, but their income would be low thanks to the bloodbath behind them scaring away customers.

Stella's features hardened. Harvey, however, seemed oblivious as he used his shirt to clean off his knife.

The cobblestone streets faded into a beaten-down dirt path. Stella turned on instinct, walking up the hill towards Rook Manor. The family didn't live in the city proper but rather on the outskirts in a beautiful farmhouse. Rolling green hills surrounded the property, the grass thick and luscious from the near-constant rain. As the cousins drew nearer, Stella could pick up on the intoxicating smell of roses. The source soon came into view: Evelyn Rook's prized rose garden, white roses sprinkled with reds and pinks, taking up most of the front yard. An intricate fence sectioned it off, thorny vines dotted with white blooms snaking up the wrought iron designs.

White roses. Evelyn's favorite flower and the namesake of their gang.

Two guards waited at the gate. They nodded at Stella as she breezed through, Harvey grumbling under his breath as he followed her into the house.

Her father's office was at the end of the hallway. Stella didn't bother knocking as she swept into the room. What she really wanted was to clean off the grime on her hands before it could stain her shirt, but she wouldn't have missed Harvey getting lectured for anything.

"I brought what you asked for," she said, sinking gracefully into the chair in front of his desk. Stella was born with the grace and beauty of a dancer. Even wearing nothing but a simple pair of dark trousers, knee-high boots, and a white blouse—which she noted with distress, had a bloodstain on the sleeve from where she'd grabbed Harvey's arm—she was breathtaking. It was her most useful quality, in her opinion; she could get men to ease their guards with nothing but a sly look, leaving them open for an attack.

Marcus barely glanced up as Harvey entered, kicking the door shut behind him. "Sit."

One word that carried so much authority. Harvey slouched in the other seat.

Stella watched her father stroke his beard. His once-dark hair was now streaked through with gray, though his whiskey-colored eyes were as alert as ever.

"I don't know what to do with you," Marcus said at last. Stella tried not to get too much satisfaction out of seeing her cousin squirm in his seat. "You disobey my orders again and again. How many times have I told you to let little things go? When a lowlife sneaks across, we give them a warning and move on. The only time we engage in a fight is if they start it. That rule has been in place since before you were born. It's the only thing that keeps any kind of peace around here, and you…" Marcus sucked in a deep breath. "You are hellbent on breaking that peace, aren't you?"

Stella examined her blood-splattered hands through the lecture. Her father's idea of peace was a far cry from the actual thing. To him, *peace* meant going a day without having to lecture somebody or get into a fight himself. Nevermind the daily skirmishes and rumors and dirty deals and brawls that happened all over the city because of the feud.

"What do you have to say for yourself?" he demanded.

Harvey let out an exasperated sigh that set Stella's blood boiling. "I don't know what to say, uncle. I saw a problem; I took care of the problem. Yes, it was a little messy, but it comes with the territory." He shrugged. "It's not a big deal."

"That's what you think," Stella snapped.

Marcus shushed her. "That answer is unacceptable," he said to his nephew. "Come up with a better one."

He shrugged again. "That's all I've got."

"I will not have you strutting around here, doing every damn thing you please," Marcus snarled. "The scene today will cut down on customers across the Barter Streets. I have enough on my plate already without you getting caught up in every disagreement that takes place in this city. Do you understand?"

To his credit, Harvey didn't cower. He straightened in his seat, his head held high.

Marcus studied his nephew for a few long moments. "That's the way it's going to be, then." Harvey didn't answer, but Stella didn't think Marcus expected him to. "Fine. You're on guard duty out front tonight."

Harvey exploded from his chair. "What? That's for scrubs!"

Marcus had already returned his focus to the ledger in front of him. "Guard duty for a week."

"You can't force me to," he snarled, bracing his arms on the edge of the desk. A lesser man would have cowered under the full wrath of Harvey Rook's murderous gaze, but Marcus merely eyed him with icy indifference.

"You will find yourself in a much worse position if you disobey me again," he said. "You have two weeks on the night watch out front. Do you wish to keep going?"

Stella smirked as Harvey stared, his mouth hanging open in a way that was almost comical. He was a mess, his white shirt untucked and stained red, his dark brown hair falling in his eyes, which were alight with fury. Marcus held his gaze until Harvey finally relented, shooting a glare at them both before turning on his heel. The door slammed shut behind him with such force that the lamp on the desk rattled.

Stella turned to her father. "He needs temper management lessons."

Marcus scrubbed his face. "What am I going to do with him?"

"It's not too late to put him down. It's what we usually do with rabid dogs."

He stroked his beard again, as if trying to rub away the streaks of gray. "Zoey needs to keep a better eye on him. She's the only one he'll listen to."

"Most of the time."

"Most of the time," he agreed. "His antics are getting to be a problem. Things with Daelik and his Ravens are bad enough without Harvey making it worse. And with the meeting coming up, we can't afford extra tension." He studied his daughter. "I know it's not exactly your place, but you need to keep an eye on him, too. Zoey has her hands full."

Controlling Harvey was most definitely not her place. Stella studied her father, his tired expression and rumpled suit, his jacket discarded over the back of his chair, and she decided it would do her no good to argue with him about it. He had already punished one person today. Stella didn't want to be next.

She sighed. "I better talk to Zoey."

"That would be a wise idea," Marcus agreed.

Stella left his office with a splitting headache and a gutted feeling in her stomach. She eyed the grand piano sitting in the corner of the parlor as she passed the open door. It was a beautiful day to play—with everyone out on errands, leaving the house mostly empty, the room was quiet, filled with the sunshine pouring in through the open windows. Her fingers itched to dance across the ivory keys, to lose herself in the music, but when she reached out to play a note, she cringed at the sight of the blood caked on her hands.

Stella's mouth twisted as she trudged upstairs, doing her best not to touch anything as she aimed for the bathroom. She nudged open the door with her foot and turned the water on full blast. Droplets splashed against the porcelain sink as she stuck her hands under the spray of scalding water.

"What happened?"

Her head jerked up at Zoey's voice. Her cousin leaned in the doorway, her cropped shirt riding up, baring a sliver of tan skin. While Stella's hair was long and fell in soft curls down her back, Zoey's was straight as a board, chopped off just above her chin. Her amber eyes strayed to Stella's hands and the blood now swirling down the drain.

"Your brother happened," Stella snapped, still scrubbing. "Three Ravens dead and another on the way. I thought you were supposed to be with him today."

"Something came up. Trystan took me to that new cafe on Hanson Street for lunch—"

She paused her scrubbing. "Trystan?"

12

"That guy I met at the bar last week."

"I thought you were still with Cal."

Zoey yawned. "We broke up two days ago."

Stella rolled her eyes and continued washing, focusing on a spot of red caught behind her fingernail. "Harvey is getting out of hand. Father has informed me it's now *my* job to deal with him."

Zoey winced. "No, forget that. I'll keep him contained."

"You always say that." Stella turned off the water with more force than strictly necessary. Her hands were now clean, her fair skin free of every red stain. She turned to face Zoey fully, folding her arms over her chest. "I'm not worried about Harvey getting himself killed. I'm worried about him getting *other* people killed. When I have to bail him out, I'm terrified that he's going to come after *me* in a moment of rage!"

Zoey chewed on her lip. "I'm sorry."

She pinched the bridge of her nose. "It's not your fault," she said at last. "You shouldn't be responsible for Harvey's behavior, either. But if someone doesn't keep an eye on him, he'll have free rein to cause all the trouble he wants."

She squeezed Stella's shoulder. "I'll talk to him. One of these days I'm bound to get through that thick skull of his."

That was as good as she was going to get for now. Stella grabbed her hand, squeezing it back. Zoey grinned at her, a wild, lopsided thing that had Stella grinning back.

"Now," she drawled, looping her arm through Zoey's, "tell me all about Trystan."

CHAPTER 2

The steady drip of blood matched his erratic heartbeat as Jordan Daelik stood over his prisoner. The Rose pulled at the restraints binding him to the chair, coughing weakly, his face darkened with bruises. Jordan's own knuckles were bruised and bloody, but he didn't care as he raised his fist again, delivering a swift but brutal blow to the Rose in the chair.

"I can keep this up all night," Jordan snarled. He grabbed the Rose by the front of his shirt and hauled him close. "Is Marcus Rook paying off sailors in the Red Harbor?"

"I don't know," he moaned.

A door opened. Jordan glanced over his shoulder to see his father walk in, his face severe as he leaned against the wall and crossed his arms, watching the spectacle before him. John Daelik didn't have a speck of dirt on him; his black suit remained spotless, his light hair slicked back, the only crack in his facade being the tie that was undone and left to hang around his neck. Meanwhile, Jordan was a mess. His sandy brown hair hung in his eyes. Drops of blood were splattered across his jaw and the bridge of his nose, contrasting with the warm tone of his skin. His dark sleeveless shirt was left untucked, a rip in one place where the Rose had given him a fight before he wrestled him into the chair.

John offered his son a tiny nod. Jordan's jaw clenched as he turned back to the Rose, who shrank back as the Raven heir gave him his full attention once more.

"I'm going to give you one more chance," he said, his voice low, guttural.

The Rose didn't answer. Jordan cocked his arm back again, prepping for another blow until he noticed the shift in the Rose's eyes. It was a tiredness, a meek resolve tinged with defeat.

Jordan lowered his arm as the Rose started talking.

"The sailors had a deal," he panted, his broken nose making the words hard to understand. "Old Rook wanted to keep 'em in line—"

"Did he pay them off?"

"He sent his nephew down to—"

"Did Rook pay off the rutting sailors or not?"

"Yes," the Rose moaned. "He's been paying 'em to not deal with the Ravens." Tears streaked down his face, his eyes glassy with pain. "I swear that's all I know, please let me go—"

Jordan released his shirt. "I'd wager you know more than that. How about we keep you around a bit longer and find out?"

The Rose drew in on himself, pulling at the ropes keeping his wrists and ankles tied to the chair. Jordan raked a scathing look over him before stalking over to his father, who gave him a nod of silent approval.

The two of them walked out of the room without a backwards glance, leaving the Rose bloody and breathless behind them. John's men waited outside, the sleeves of their left arms rolled up to reveal the raven tattoos on their wrists. "Take care of him," John ordered, jerking his chin at the room behind them. "Give him food and water but don't let him escape, or else I'll have your head."

The men scrambled to obey, leaving Jordan alone with his father. John scratched the stubble on his chin as he stared into the distance.

"I knew Marcus was paying off the sailors," he said at last, more to himself than to Jordan.

Jordan crossed his arms. "We all did. Now we prove it to the sheriff and let him deal with it."

The Red Harbor was neutral ground. It had been ever since an especially bloody skirmish scared ships from docking in Lochridge for a month. The sheriff was a raging drunkard that let the gangs do whatever they pleased most of the time, but where he put his foot down, Jordan had learned it was best not to test it.

Both gangs had members employed at the Harbor. If the Roses were bribing sailors to refuse work with the Ravens, that violated the neutral standings of the Harbor and meant the sheriff could take action. He wouldn't do anything *too* drastic; he would go easy out of a well-placed fear of the Rook family. But perhaps it would be enough to keep the Rooks in line for a while.

Enough to keep them out of Jordan's hair for a day or two.

"No," John said. "We don't have enough evidence to go to Schode. We need to handle this on our own."

A sinking feeling settled into Jordan's stomach. "What does that mean?"

His jaw worked. "If the Roses want to bribe the sailors, then we can bribe them right back. I want you to poke around the Harbor, see if you can find what kind of money Marcus is offering. If we match it, we can turn the tables on him."

Fighting fire with fire—John's preferred method of attack. Jordan glanced at the darkening sky. "Tonight?"

"In the morning. Bring Declan and Mateo with you. But make sure they don't get into any trouble tonight. Declan won't be worth a shit if he's hungover again."

His mouth twisted into a dry smile. "Duly noted."

"And be careful," John added.

"You're saying this like I won't see you again before morning."

"Probably not. I just got word that Harvey Rook went all-out against the western border patrol." John's storm-gray eyes darkened. "I need to deal with it, but it's liable to take all night."

Jordan let out a soft curse. No wonder his father was in a mood. Harvey Rook was a psychopath—a bloodthirsty monster that thrived on conflict. The Rook clan was tight-knit and undyingly loyal to each other, but even then Jordan had spotted them shooting irksome looks in Harvey's direction whenever he opened his mouth.

He was glad his father was taking care of it. Jordan didn't like the prospect of going against Harvey himself. He was a good fighter and an excellent shot, but even Lochridge's sharpshooter wasn't a match for a man known to lick the blood off his knife after he finished gutting someone with it.

"I'll leave you to it, then," he said.

The two of them exited the warehouse they had commandeered as an interrogation room and parted ways as soon as they hit the street. They were on the far side of the Ravens' territory, the warehouse strategically picked so it would be hard for the White Roses to initiate any kind of rescue mission. Jordan used his shirt to wipe the blood and sweat off his face as he turned onto a busier street. People stared as he walked past. Jordan was well known; as the heir to the Ravens, every member of the gang knew his face. The blood wasn't an unusual sight, either. He was the one sent to represent his father, the Ravens' enforcer dealing with the dirty work while John stayed behind running his business empire.

Jordan walked with his head held high, meeting the stares of everyone who dared to look at him. They shrank back, and he smirked. This was *his* territory. His gang. Every person in Lochridge with a raven tattooed on their wrist would answer to him once his father passed.

And one day, the White Roses would, too.

He wound through the streets, taking the long way around in order to sweep through his half of the city and ensure nothing was amiss. Eventually he found himself in front of the Daeliks' house. Jordan relaxed a little upon walking into his childhood home. It was far from a peaceful household, but at least he didn't have to look over his shoulder for threats like he did anywhere else.

Loud voices greeted him the moment he opened the door. It was lunchtime, and most of his family was in the kitchen. Jordan would have joined them had he not been a mess of blood and sweat and grime. He didn't want anyone to see him like this, especially not Lana.

He darted past the open doorway and up the stairs, all the way to his room, the steps creaking underneath his worn leather boots as he climbed the two flights up to the attic. He only had vague memories of his old bedroom on the second floor; his parents had converted the attic into a bedroom when Lana was born because the house was running out of room. Jordan didn't mind in the slightest. The attic was up and away from the rest of the house, just a narrow flight of steps and a creaky door at the end of the hall. The room itself boasted two small windows that overlooked the street below, one in front and one in back. He sometimes used the back window to sneak out—as long as you weren't afraid of heights, it gave access to the roof, and to the drainpipe on the far side of the house that Jordan shimmied down to escape.

The room was small, and he often hit his head on the slanted ceiling. A bed was shoved in one corner. A desk on the other side was laden with pencils and bits of charcoal and his thick sketchbook. The walls bore the evidence of his artwork, covered in all the sketches he'd done over the years, everything from portraits of his family to doodles of the Lochridge skyline to detailed drawings of the ravens that sometimes perched on the roof.

It wasn't much, but it was his space, and his alone.

And he liked it that way.

There was a knock on the door. It opened before Jordan could answer it, and Declan poked his head through, his dark green eyes narrowing on Jordan. "What have you been up to?"

"Get out," Jordan said flatly.

His cousin threw open the door and sauntered into the room, a glass of whiskey dangling from his fingers despite the early hour. Mateo frowned as he followed him in, taking in Jordan's clothes with a concerned look. Apparently he hadn't been as slick as he thought when he ran past the kitchen doorway.

"Interrogations?" Mateo asked, shutting the door behind him.

Jordan lifted a shoulder in a shrug. "Pa's orders."

Mateo leaned against the wall, disturbing the sketches pinned there. "He can't keep making you do that."

"Yes, he can."

"He shouldn't."

"That doesn't matter."

Declan's eyes darted between them, looking for a chance to insert himself into the conversation. "But did you find out anything?"

He peeled off his shirt. "Rook's paying off sailors to refuse to work with us. And Harvey just killed some of our men on the border. Pa's handling that now." Declan let out a low string of curses, and Mateo looked inclined to do the same. Jordan chucked his stained shirt into the corner of the room. "He's in a mood."

"So are you," Declan muttered.

Mateo huffed a laugh, earning a grin of approval from Dec. The two of them couldn't be more different. Declan was loud and bawdy, with messy blond hair and green eyes that glinted with mischief. Mateo's darker skin and hair were accompanied by a calm and collected demeanor that made him the most level-headed out of the three. Jordan was somewhere in between, dancing over the line between calm and chaotic on a daily basis.

"We're supposed to go to the Harbor tomorrow and figure out how much Rook has been paying the sailors." Jordan tugged on a fresh shirt as he elbowed past Dec and Mateo. They trailed him to the bathroom on the second floor. "If Harvey is there, I'm abandoning the mission. We should take this to the sheriff but Pa doesn't think we have enough evidence for Schode to do anything."

Mateo's mouth twisted as Jordan splashed water on his face. "That's not how it should be done."

Jordan slicked his hair back. "You're telling me."

He shut off the water and studied his reflection in the mirror. His face and hands were now clean, his hair dripping with water, but he was quick to turn away when he saw the tiredness in his eyes. "Maybe after we poke around the Harbor," Mateo mused, leading the way downstairs, "we can go to Schode ourselves. Pa won't find out until it's too late to stop it."

Declan frowned. "If we go to the sheriff ourselves—"

"Go to the sheriff about what?"

Jordan, Dec, and Mateo whirled to see Lana standing in the doorway to her bedroom. She and Jordan had the same light brown hair, but while Jordan's eyes were brown, hers were the same storm-gray Mateo and their father had.

Lana planted her hands on her hips. "What did the Roses do this time?"

Jordan flashed Dec a look, a silent warning not to say anything. Despite the sass, Lana's question was innocent. She was only twelve years old; Jordan had begun to worry about her more and more, hoping his father would spare her from the harsh reality of the feud for as long as possible. Marcus Rook had his daughter doing his dirty work at a much younger age. Jordan himself had been going to business dealings since he was eight. Most of the Daelik family was crooked and prone to violence, but Lana was sweet, innocent, her nose always buried in a romance novel like the one currently tucked under her arm. He was determined to keep her as far away from the inner workings of the gang for as long as he could.

Which is why he plastered a smile on his face and said, "Nothing. Just a little disagreement."

Lana's eyes narrowed. "Why do you need the sheriff involved, then?"

"To keep it from being a *big* disagreement," Declan drawled, slinging an arm over Lana's shoulders. "There's no reason to worry, Lanabug."

She scowled. "Stop calling me that!"

Jordan sidled up to her other side. "Never, *Lanabug*."

She pinched his arm. He pinched her right back, and she squealed, shaking off Declan's arm and darting down the hall. Jordan grinned and gave chase, squishing her into a hug so tight it could have cracked a rib.

"Stop it!" she cried, but laughter traced the words.

Jordan finally released her. "I'll stop calling you Lanabug the day you get bigger than me."

"But you're always going to be bigger than me," she whined.

He gave her a light shove. "That's the point." His eyes fell to the book tucked under her arm. "What are you reading?"

She held it out of his grasp. "None of your business."

He lunged for it. "Let me see it!"

"No! It's not like you *could* read it, anyway!"

"Hey!"

Lana hit him with the book and darted into her room before he could retaliate. Jordan smiled after her before turning back to Dec and Mateo.

"We'll talk about it tomorrow," he murmured, quiet enough that Lana couldn't overhear.

Dec nodded, drained the last of his whiskey, and sauntered downstairs for a refill. It was then that Jordan remembered his father saying Declan wasn't supposed to be drinking tonight.

Mateo must have read it on his face, because he raised both brows and said, "Good luck getting him to stop. You're not the only one in a mood."

"What's he upset about?"

"He and Dan got into an argument." His mouth twisted. "I was in my room trying to study and all I hear is them two screaming at each other in the kitchen."

Jordan tugged at the collar of his shirt. Declan and his father had never been on good terms. It was bad when they were kids, but he thought they were doing better recently.

Apparently, he thought wrong. "What about?"

"Dec hasn't been very forthcoming on the details."

That was his cue not to press the matter any further. "I see. How's your studying coming, anyway?"

Mateo smoothed his raven-black hair even as ire sparked in his eyes. "I swear, I can't get anything done around here. Every time I sit down to study, I get interrupted by someone. First it was Declan and Dan throwing hands, and then Pa had an errand for me to run, and then your mother called us all down for lunch." He scrubbed a hand over his face. "I'm never going to make it to a university if I can't scrape out the time to read."

"You'll get there," Jordan said, a weak attempt at reassurance.

Mateo gave him a rueful smile. "We'll see."

CHAPTER 3

The wind tore Stella's hair out of her braid as she stepped onto the Red Harbor. Sailors bustled across the docks, loading cargo onto ships and bringing in nets overflowing with fish. Beyond the Harbor, the ocean was a tempest of choppy gray waves. Thick clouds rolled in the distance, riding the wicked wind that blew towards Lochridge. By nightfall, rain would be pounding the cobblestones as one of the city's famous thunderstorms raged overhead.

Zoey clicked her tongue as she fell into step beside her cousin. "It's going to be a hell of a day, isn't it?"

Stella grunted in agreement as the wind picked up, stinging her nose with the overpowering scent of salt and fish. She had decided to make a good impression at the Harbor today by wearing a sleeveless white dress and sandals, her hair braided down her back, but the wind had other plans. It tore at the skirts of her dress and pulled at her braid. The storm looming in the distance promised heavy rain, and she could only hope her business was finished by the time it arrived.

Marcus' spies had reported an unusual amount of Raven activity in the Harbor ever since Harvey's stunt at the border the day before. While technically neutral ground, a lot of trades between the gangs happened at the Harbor. Plenty of Roses found work as sailors or fishermen here, and Stella didn't want to see that disturbed.

She glanced at Zoey. "Where do you want to start?"

Zoey ran a hand through her short hair, trying to smooth it, but the wind spiked it back up the moment she took her hand away. "We should head to the south end and work our way up. The Ravens do most of their work down there."

The wooden boards of the Harbor groaned underneath their feet as they walked across, dodging stacks of crates and loose nets. Stella's eyes picked out the telltale tattoos on several of the sailors, a flying raven encircling their wrists. Nothing she saw was out of the ordinary; Ravens were employed here as well. Many of them stared at her with open hostility as she breezed past.

John Daelik had been throwing around accusations that the Roses were paying off sailors to do their bidding. Stella initially passed them off as baseless rumors, but to her dismay, she'd found that her father had, in fact, bribed several of the leading captains who docked their ships in the Harbor, convincing them to restrict access to anyone bearing a Raven tattoo. That tidbit of information would have been helpful *before* Daelik caught on and the plan blew up in their faces. Marcus sent Harvey to scare the captains into submission the first time around, and now it was Stella's job to scare them again—and to keep prying eyes from poking around in places they had no business being.

"Did you talk to Harvey?" Stella asked, sidestepping a sailor.

"Not yet."

Her head whipped around. "Not yet?"

Zoey groaned. "I know he's been out of line. I'm working on it."

"Are you? Because if that's true, it's certainly not going the way you want it to."

She flashed Stella a dry look. "I know you're annoyed with him—"

"I'm a little more than *annoyed*."

"You're pissed," Zoey corrected, "and rightly so. I've tried to talk to him, but it's not as easy as it used to be. Harvey's not... *responding* like he used to."

Stella hissed under her breath. It wasn't Zoey's fault her brother was borderline insane. She *did* try to control him, but there was only so much one could do. "It shouldn't be anyone's job to follow him around with a leash, but something has to be done. You're the only person he listens to. Perhaps it's time for some tough love. Or else..."

"Or else?"

Stella smirked. "Or else, I'm going to fill out that application I requested to that military school in Westhaven. I think sending Harvey there for a few months would whip him right into shape."

Zoey snorted. "An asylum might be a better option."

A laugh escaped Stella, but it was cut short when Zoey grabbed her arm and dragged her behind a stack of crates, cursing under her breath.

"Rats," she hissed. "Thatcher and Half-Daelik, dead ahead."

Stella peeked around the corner to see Declan Thatcher and Mateo Daelik strutting down the docks. The pair alone was trouble enough, but she knew that wherever those two went, Jordan Daelik wouldn't be far behind. Sure enough, the heir to the Ravens strolled into view, his hands resting on his revolvers as he walked after his cousin and half-brother. All three wore black, the Ravens' color. Jordan's heavy boots thumped across the Harbor, and Stella's vision flashed red.

"What do we do?" Zoey breathed.

"We thank the heavens your brother isn't here," Stella snapped, pushing off the crates and darting after the Ravens. Whatever their business here was, it couldn't be good. She needed to send them away before they interfered with her plans.

"Daelik," she called, running after them.

He turned, brows rising as he took in Stella. "Well, if it isn't the little thorn in my side."

He ambled closer, a smirk playing on his lips. Behind him, Thatcher unslung his rifle. He didn't point it specifically in her direction, but it was close enough to set Stella's teeth on edge. Half-Daelik—the nickname Zoey and Stella had appointed John Daelik's bastard son—edged closer to Jordan's side, his gun halfway out of its holster. Jordan himself didn't draw his famed revolvers, but that meant little. Stella knew he could whip them out in the time it took her to blink.

"What are you doing here?" Zoey demanded, coming up behind Stella.

Jordan smirked at the two of them, even as his eyes scanned the surrounding area. "Where's your brother?"

A small part of Stella was pleased he feared the idea of Harvey being around, though most of her was glad Harvey wasn't here to cause more trouble than they needed. She crossed her arms. "Answer the question."

"Our business here is none of your concern," Declan drawled. "The Harbor is neutral. We aren't breaking any rules by being here."

"Are you sure about that?"

Unease flickered in his eyes, but Jordan called Stella's bluff with a soft snort. "We don't answer to you, Rook."

"Likewise." She angled her head. "It's interesting, though, that after you and your family made *such* a big deal about us bribing the sailors on the Red Harbor, I've been hearing countless rumors about the Ravens doing the same."

"Is that so?" Jordan dared a step closer. Stella's hand flashed to the pistol she wore, held up by a leather belt that cinched her dress at the waist, but he just chuckled and took another step forward. "I'm afraid I don't know about these *rumors*, little thorn."

With good reason—Stella had made it up on the fly, trying to swing the accusations back at him. Jordan came closer, until Stella was forced to tilt her head back to look him in the eye.

Jordan read her expression and smiled. "It's the ones with dirty hands who are always pointing fingers."

Gritting her teeth, she snapped, "What are you doing here, feathers?"

"What are *you* doing here?" he shot back, baring his teeth in a wicked smile.

She was going to kill him. She was going to pull out her gun and shoot this cocky little son of a bitch right where he stood. Her fingers wrapped around the handle of her gun, but before she got it fully out of its holster, Jordan had already drawn both of his revolvers and had the barrels pressed against her chest. Stella snarled as she held up her own weapon.

Jordan's dark brown eyes bore into hers, a silent challenge.

"Get out of the Red Harbor," she ordered.

"You're in no position to be making demands, little thorn."

"Little thorn?" She barked a laugh. "A new nickname, I see."

The barrels of his guns dug deeper into the fabric of her dress. "Better than feathers."

"You don't like that name, feathers?"

"I would watch your mouth if I were you," Jordan said, a soft snarl edging his voice. "I've got you outgunned. You won't walk away if you turn this into a fight."

Stella considered her options. Thinking straight proved difficult when Jordan had two bullets primed to go through her heart. He was Lochridge's sharpshooter; his skills were outmatched, even if it wasn't from point blank. His twin revolvers were famed in this city, and Stella was currently standing on the wrong side of them. She risked a glance over her shoulder to see Zoey leveling both of her pistols at Declan and Mateo. Thatcher still had his rifle, and Half-Daelik was fingering his gun, eyeing the Rooks warily.

Jordan was right, and she *hated* that.

Stella opened her mouth, teeth bared, prepared to spit out a venomous remark to put him in his place, but a voice from behind interrupted her.

"Drop your weapons, the both of you."

CHAPTER 4

Jordan Daelik glanced over to see Lochridge's sheriff pointing a shotgun at his face.

Sheriff Schode was an older man with muddy brown eyes and hair to match. Lines formed at the corners of his eyes as looked down at Stella, whose face was set in a grimace as she glared between him and Jordan.

"Now," he barked.

Jordan retreated a step, shoving his revolvers back in their holsters. Stella gave him a cool look before doing the same. Declan and Mateo came up on either side of him, shouldering their weapons as the sheriff looked them over.

Schode spat on the ground. Even from this distance, Jordan could smell the whiskey on his breath. "All of you know you ain't supposed to be fightin' around here, right?"

"We weren't fighting," Stella said dryly.

He laughed, but there was no humor in it. "I don't believe that for a second, missy. Git on out of here before I arrest you all."

Jordan crossed his arms. "We have business here."

The sheriff whirled, and Jordan once again found himself looking down the barrel of a shotgun. "You stay here one second longer, boy, and I'll pump you full of lead."

Jordan laughed and brushed the gun aside. "You wouldn't dare," he said, "not even on your drunkest day. My father would shred you to pieces and appoint himself as sheriff."

Schode lowered the shotgun, just a little. "I still want you to git out of here."

"Of course, sheriff," Zoey cut in smoothly, motioning to her cousin as she swept past. "We wouldn't want to cause you any trouble today, not before a big storm blows through."

Jordan clenched his jaw as she and Stella flounced away, earning an appreciative glance from the sheriff, who did indeed look worried as he glanced towards the gathering clouds. Likely the only reason he was out today, somewhat sober, was because of the storm. And now the Rooks had followed orders without a hitch.

They were sucking up to get on Schode's good side.

"Good day, sheriff," Jordan bit out.

He turned on his heel and stormed after the Rook girls, fingers itching to draw his guns. Declan and Mateo jogged after him. "What are we going to do?" Mateo asked.

"I don't know," Jordan hissed, "but I'm pretty sure it involves wringing someone's throat."

They'd talked to only three sailors and gotten zero information before the Rooks showed up and got them *kicked out of the Harbor*. John would be furious, and Jordan was sure he would be blamed for it. His hands curled into fists at the thought.

"You've got quite the temper, don't you?"

Jordan whirled to see Stella leaning against a lamppost, cleaning her nails with a knife. Zoey crossed her arms where she stood beside her cousin, her short hair whipped around by the wind.

"We're on Rose turf now, in case you were wondering," Stella crooned.

With a growl, Jordan retreated just a few steps, putting himself on the other side of the border and out of her reach. The wind howled through the buildings, not as strong as it had been closer to the shore, but enough to send the loose strands of Stella's hair swirling around her face. Her whiskey-colored eyes surveyed him with cool amusement.

He forced himself to relax, to smooth the irritation from his face and replace it with edged steel. The heir to the White Roses might drive him insane, but the worst thing he could do was let her know it. Her dark laugh already haunted his steps as it was.

To his extreme gratitude, Declan didn't seem to have anywhere near the problem with her as he stepped forward—still within the confines of the border—and said, "You're a weak suck-up, Rook."

Something like surprise flashed in her eyes, but it disappeared as quickly as it came. "Better than an uneducated drunkard."

"At least we didn't start the fight that got us kicked out of the Harbor," Mateo said.

"I said it back there and I'll say it again: We weren't fighting."

Jordan arched a brow. "We weren't?"

Stella tossed her wind-ravaged braid over her shoulder. "Are you insisting that a mean word is the same as a full-out brawl?"

"In this city, words have a tendency to turn into brawls."

"They don't have to." She kicked off the post and waltzed towards him. "But if a certain someone is known to have temper issues…"

Behind him, Declan snorted. "Does your ass ever get jealous of the shit that comes out of your mouth?"

Stella's eyes flashed to him. Dec gave her a cheeky smile in return, his finger hovering over the trigger of his rifle. On his other side, Mateo's eyebrow twitched.

Jordan stepped towards Stella, until the two of them were only a breath away, the border standing between them. "You should really get *your* anger issues taken care of, little thorn." Her eyes narrowed on the last word, and he grinned. "Now you know what it's like to have a less-than-pleasant nickname."

Her answering smile was saccharine-sweet. "If you think *feathers* is bad, just wait until you hear what I really think about you."

Jordan's smile widened. "You think about me? I'm touched."

The two heirs glared at each other until a crack of lightning flashed overhead, sending the ravens that swamped the nearby rooftops flying off in a frenzy. Declan cursed, and Jordan caught Zoey frowning at the sky. Stella's younger cousin wore her usual cropped white shirt, her tan arms covered with handmade bracelets. She caught Jordan looking and glared at him until he returned his gaze to Stella.

"It's a shame we have to cut this short," he crooned.

Stella's smile sharpened. "Yes, you have people to interrogate and Roses to kill."

Jordan's spine stiffened. His mind flashed back to the back room in the warehouse—not just the Rose he questioned yesterday, but a hundred other people he'd beaten until they were too exhausted to resist.

But his mind strayed to one in particular—the one he knew Stella was thinking about now.

Even though his mind churned, Jordan forced a smile to his face as he looked down on Stella. "You don't happen to have another lover for me to kill, do you?"

Stella's face went slack for a moment, then her expression came alive with anger—the exact reaction he'd been hoping for.

"Take it back," she hissed.

Jordan laughed even as his blood boiled with anger that wasn't directed at Stella. "What is this, primary school? I'm not going to *take it back*, Rook." He bared his teeth. "Come and make me."

Stella dared a step forward, looking all for the world like she was about to take Jordan up on his offer. But Zoey grabbed her cousin's arm before she could step over the border. Whatever Zoey hissed into her ear had her retreating a step, though both girls glared at Jordan with open hostility, Zoey's amber gaze tinged with protectiveness as she kept her hand on Stella's shoulder.

It wasn't wise to play with snakes, but that didn't stop Jordan from smirking down on them. "Too good to swing at me, little thorn?"

His attempt to lure her onto his side of the border for a fight fell on deaf ears. Stella tossed her hair over her shoulder as she fixed him with a haughty look. "I wouldn't want to mess up that pretty little face of yours. Your ego is already so fragile that I think a mark on your face would send it right over the edge."

"I'd like to see you try," he taunted.

Thunder echoed overhead. Jordan narrowed his eyes and Stella did the same. It wasn't until Mateo put a hand on his shoulder that he stepped away, still glaring at the Rooks.

"I'll see you at the meeting, feathers," Stella crooned, backing away as rain started to fall.

"I look forward to it," Jordan said sweetly, wondering if he could spit on her from this distance. In truth, he'd forgotten about the meeting. The sheriff had decreed that the heads of the two gangs meet for half an hour each month in an attempt to wage peace between them. Most of the time, the meetings weren't productive, but they could be entertaining. Like the time last year when Declan drank a bit too much before coming and used the opportunity to insult every Rose in attendance. Harvey Rook had leapt across the table and beat Dec into a pulp before they'd been able to pull the two apart.

Good times, Jordan thought wryly. He turned away, all too aware of Stella's eyes on him as he headed deeper into Raven territory. She unnerved him; perhaps it was the fact she shared blood with a murderous psychopath, perhaps it was that their fathers hated each other, but being around Stella Rook always put Jordan's teeth on edge. He risked a glance over his shoulder to confirm the Rook girls were out of sight before letting himself relax.

His mouth twisted. Good times, indeed.

CHAPTER 5

The rain hadn't let up by the time the following evening rolled around. Stella frowned as she stared out her balcony doors. Water pounded against the glass, each droplet making the leaves of the plants outside bounce up and down. She shivered as she pulled closed the cream-colored curtains, shutting out the view of the storm raging outside.

"I wish Father would postpone the meeting," she muttered, seating herself behind the vanity. She eyed the assortment of perfumes and brushes and oils and pins, finally settling on a wide-tooth comb and running it through her silky brown hair. A box overflowing with jewelry rested on the edge of the vanity next to a vase of pink roses, freshly picked from the garden. To the side, a massive armoire was just as full, dresses and blouses in various shades of white hanging within. "It's much too wet to be outside."

Zoey popped out of the armoire, her arms weighed down with an assortment of dresses and jewelry. "You're telling me. You should have seen Harvey come in from guard duty this morning."

Stella winced as the comb snagged on a nasty snarl, a parting gift from the harsh wind. Marcus had allowed Harvey off of his punishment tonight in order for him to attend the meeting. Stella thought it was quite unfair. Harvey had been ecstatic, however, his mood from the past couple days replaced with an unusually chipper attitude. He was sucking up to stay in Marcus' good graces, but Stella could only hope that his attitude would hold fast throughout the meeting so that he wouldn't cause any unnecessary tension.

She didn't have high hopes, though.

Zoey held up a short white dress that Stella forgot she owned. "How does this one look?"

Stella raised a brow. "For the meeting?"

"No, silly. For my date with Zane."

"Zane?" Stella choked. "I thought you were with Trystan!"

She waved a dismissive hand. "It was one date. I realized I didn't like him and called it off."

"And you already met someone else."

Zoey grinned and hugged the dress to her chest. "Well?"

Stella sighed and shook her head. The dress *was* Zoey's style—the white fabric would accent her tan, slender frame well. "It looks great."

"Perfect." She set the dress aside and picked up another one. "*This* one is for the meeting."

It was three inches longer and didn't reveal nearly as much. Stella nodded her agreement as she set her comb aside and joined Zoey by the armoire. All of her clothes were some shade of white or cream or silver. It wasn't an official rule that the White Roses had to wear white, but it was certainly tradition in the Rook household, just as surely as the Ravens wore black. Stella didn't own a single article of black clothing—none that anyone but Zoey was aware of, anyway. Some business called for stealth, and while Stella loved the purity of white, it wasn't suited for sneaking around in the dark.

But for now she focused on the dresses in front of her. She had a lot—she and Zoey had an affinity for clothes, though their styles were a touch different. Zoey opted for cropped shirts and dresses that didn't go below mid-thigh, outfits that would have been scandalous in any other city than Lochridge. Stella's clothes bore the same practiced elegance she walked around with, full-length lace dresses and blouses with billowing sleeves. Today she selected a cream-colored, halter-necked gown that hugged her curves. She pulled her hair into a sleek knot, leaving a few curls loose to fall over her bare shoulders, the dark strands contrasting with the light fabric.

She and Zoey stood side-by-side, examining themselves in the mirror as they pinned on earrings and necklaces and bracelets, borrowing from each other's generous jewelry collections until they both deemed themselves fit. Stella finished her look with a pair of heels, a brush of rouge across her cheeks and lips, and a small silver dagger that she strapped to the leg that wasn't exposed by the slit in her dress.

"Ready?" she asked.

Zoey smeared a final layer of red gloss across her lips. "Ready."

The two of them linked arms and descended the stairs. Harvey waited in the doorway, the first to be ready, for once. His hair was slicked back, one loose strand falling over his brow. He'd thrown a vest and tie over his usual dress shirt, and as he tucked a hand into his pocket, Stella saw that he'd even polished his watch. His hunting knife remained in its usual spot on his hip.

Zoey released Stella and flounced to her brother's side. "My, Harv, you almost look presentable tonight. What's the occasion?"

He glared down at her. "I will kill you."

Her red-painted lips stretched into a wide smile. "Not if I kill you first."

Harvey smirked. Zoey nudged him with her elbow, the only person who could do so without getting a knife in the gut. Stella's parents walked in right then. Marcus wore a white suit, a single rose pinned to his chest, his dark hair combed back. Evelyn looked like an angel beside him. Stella always thought her mother was pretty, with her auburn hair and hazel eyes, but tonight she looked especially so, wearing a lace gown with a pearl necklace so large it took an impressive woman to wear them. Stella had always held her mother to a high regard. She gave her the soft smile she reserved especially for her, and Evelyn squeezed her shoulder as more Roses piled into the living room. Some were aunts and uncles and cousins; others were close friends and acquaintances of the family; others still were just scrubs pulled for guard duty.

Marcus swept a look over the assembled crowd and nodded. "Let's move out!"

Carriages waited for them out front. Stella squeezed into the closest one with her parents, hissing as a few errant raindrops hit her before she made it inside. Marcus ran an approving look over her attire as the carriage lurched into motion.

Silence reigned for the entire ride. The meeting spot was at an old bar on the far side of town in one of the few areas considered neutral. Technically, it belonged to another gang—one so small and insignificant that Stella couldn't even recall the name, but whoever they were, they knew better than to stop the Roses or Ravens from using it.

Stella followed her father inside. A table had been set up in the middle of the room, the bar cleared of everyone but the attendees of the meeting. The Ravens were already there, taking up one side of the table, their own entourage standing behind them like an army of statues. As usual, they wore all black, symbolizing the bird their gang was named after. Zoey always joked it looked like the Daeliks were on their way to a funeral while the Rooks were headed to a wedding.

John Daelik sat in the center of the table. His wife Lillian was to his left; Jordan lounged in the seat to his right, wearing his usual sleeveless black shirt, his revolvers strapped to his hips. Half-Daelik and Thatcher sat at the ends.

Zoey tried to take the seat in front of Thatcher, but Harvey beat her to it, his eyes gleaming as they surveyed each other. The two had always had a weird rivalry, made worse by last year's brawl in this very spot. Stella eyed them warily as she settled into her seat opposite Jordan. While she sat upright, her legs crossed and her hands folded neatly in her lap, Jordan slumped in his seat, his long legs stretched out so far that she was tempted to give him a good kick to the shin. The Raven heir tilted his head, his brown eyes swimming with amusement as if he could read her thoughts. She hadn't been able to get yesterday's conversation out of her head. It had been stupid of her to bring up Liam, of course, but hearing Jordan jeer over his death had done horrible things to her mind. She hadn't slept well last night, her dreams plagued with memories of their last day together.

Her hands curled into fists underneath the table. One day she'd get her revenge. She hadn't forgotten Liam.

John reclined in his seat, his eyes on Marcus. The two of them studied each other for a long moment. Everyone else held their breaths as they waited to see who would speak first.

In the end it was John who broke. "We need to discuss the Red Harbor."

Marcus cocked a brow. "What about it?"

The picture of innocence. Stella fought back a snort as Jordan caught her gaze again. His hand drifted to the revolver at his side, a silent warning.

"You've been paying off the sailors in the Harbor to refuse business with my Ravens," John said.

There it was. The accusation, plain and simple.

"We've already been accused of that once," Stella said, picking at her nails. "If I recall, that particular conversation got all parties involved kicked out of the Harbor for the day." Her eyes flashed to John. "Do you really wish to continue?"

She wondered if the leader of the Ravens was going to kill her then and there, judging by the way his hands flexed, eager to draw his gun. Stella merely continued examining her nails. Lillian leaned over and murmured something to John that had him relaxing.

"We have proof that you paid off sailors," he said.

"Just as I have proof that you interrogated Roses so harshly that they would have said anything to make it stop." Marcus' smile was void of warmth. "Are you sure your information is reliable?"

John angled his head. "I didn't interrogate anyone."

The slight emphasis on the *I* had Stella glancing at Jordan again. For a moment, she was surprised to see his jaw clenched, his eyes fixed on his father in a manner that was less than pleasant, but the expression was gone so quick she wondered if she had imagined it. Jordan met her gaze again, his dark eyes narrowing even further.

Jordan was only six months her elder. They'd both been in their mothers' wombs when the fight between John and Marcus went from a disagreement over business ventures to an all-out war. Stella had been told the two of them used to be close friends—they'd grown up together, been as close as brothers. *Inseparable* was the word most people used. They moved to Lochridge together to seek their fortunes, but this city had a habit of twisting even the most respectable of men. All it had taken was a disagreement over finances, a trade gone wrong, and a rift formed between them.

Stella studied the two patriarchs glaring at each other over the table and wondered how people like them could have ever been friends.

She held Jordan's gaze. The two of them had been born into this— their fight was a continuation of their fathers'. A natural rivalry had formed between them from the moment they were born.

Rivalry might be too weak a word, though. Jordan had killed Liam three years ago out of spite, knowing good and well who he was and what he meant to Stella. She'd killed people on his side, too. They'd done countless deeds to bring the other down, make them suffer, watching to see which one broke first. So far, both held strong.

They couldn't kill each other—sure, there had been plenty of times where they had each other at gunpoint, where the pull of a trigger would have sent the other to their grave. But killing one heir would bring down the wrath of their gang. Stella couldn't shoot Jordan without John Daelik and the entirety of the Ravens hunting her down. The feud was all about balance. Disturbing it could have disastrous consequences.

The conversation droned on, a mixture of insults and passive-aggressive arguments that drove Stella insane. These meetings were pointless and often had the opposite effect the sheriff intended. She perked up as Marcus' voice rose to a shout.

"I won't stand here and listen to false accusations being thrown in my face," he snarled.

Declan Thatcher sat down his whiskey long enough to sweep a very pointed look over Marcus. "Technically, you're sitting."

The gaze of every Rose whipped to him. He only shrugged and knocked back another drink.

"Paying off sailors goes against the neutral standings of the Harbor," John snapped.

"And you've never bribed someone before?" Stella cut in.

"I don't see how that's any of your business."

Stella Rook was not a woman to be dismissed so easily. She leaned forward. "I don't see how it's any of *your* business to be throwing around accusations without proper proof, and yet here you are."

"There is proof," Jordan said. "Multiple witnesses informed us—"

Zoey stood up. "If you have so much proof, then how come Schode hasn't been involved?"

Jordan's mouth clamped shut, and Stella smirked. "If we really are bribing sailors, do you think flinging accusations at us is going to do a damn thing about it?" She bared her teeth in a smile. "If you've got proof, go to the sheriff. Otherwise, leave us alone."

His eyes twitched as she called his bluff. She didn't doubt that they had proof—after all, their accusations were fully founded. But whatever they had wasn't enough to convince Schode there was wrongdoing, meaning their hands were tied.

"Watch your tone," Declan growled at her. "You rats are liars and thieves."

"It takes one to know one," Zoey shot back.

Marcus flashed her a look, warning her to remain silent. "You will drop the accusations and leave the Red Harbor alone. We are doing nothing wrong by being there, but if you continue to spread these rumors, then *I* will go to Schode and tell him exactly where to find your interrogation room." He smiled. "The warehouse on Dawson Avenue, correct? My spies see your son coming out of there every other day, covered in blood."

There it was, the change in Jordan's expression. The slight narrowing of his eyes, the tic in his jaw, gone as quick as it came. Stella tilted her head as John rose from his seat.

"I do not take orders from men who cannot keep their word," he said, his voice lethally soft.

Marcus stood up as well, rising to his full height, though he was still shorter than John. "I am not the one who cheated on a deal." He cocked a brow at Half-Daelik. "Or on his wife, for that matter."

He might as well have dumped a bucket of ice-cold water over the Daelik family. Mateo flinched. Lillian looked down at her hands. Declan sat down his bottle with a resounding *thump*. Jordan drew his revolvers as he rose to his feet.

John angled his head. "I seem to recall that *you* didn't have a problem throwing around accusations and rumors when that happened."

He couldn't deny it. The Daelik family had never said Mateo wasn't pure-blooded, but there was no way he could be. He had John's gray eyes, but his darker skin and tar-black hair didn't resemble Lillian at all. He always had a habit of fading into the back during a conversation or fight, listening but not participating, forgotten by everyone until it was his time to strike. But now the attention had been brought to him too early. He ducked his head, letting his dark hair hang in his eyes.

Stella almost felt bad for him. His heritage wasn't something he could control, but it made for a fine argument that made every Raven in the room see red.

Marcus shrugged. "How can I trust a man who can't even stay faithful to his own wife? You have no proof about the sailors in the Harbor, nor do you have the grounds to accuse me of such things. You are a liar—"

"Says the man who forged my signature on that trade deal!"

"That's a lie just like this is!"

"I refuse—"

"I didn't—"

"You can't—"

"Don't—"

Stella shot to her feet as the meeting descended into a cacophony of shouts. Everyone sprang from their seats except Lillian and Evelyn, who met each other's gazes through the bustle. And Harvey, who had been slouched in his seat this entire time but now rose with a smile.

That was not good.

She grabbed Marcus' arm. "We need to leave."

He ignored her. "You're a filthy rat, John Daelik! A bastard, just like your son!"

"Leave that out of this," Jordan snarled back.

"I will *not*—"

"I said—

"You rat—"

Heavens above. Stella met Jordan's gaze in the fray, his eyes as wild and panicked as she felt. The guards on both sides moved in. If someone pulled a weapon, this would turn into a bloodbath.

The shouts grew louder, masking the sound of the door opening behind them. Stella only saw it open because she had turned her back to the table, heading for the door in what she hoped would be a signal to her father to do the same. But she stopped short as a man in a striped suit stepped through. His pale blue eyes surveyed the brawl breaking out before settling on her as a smile spread across his face.

CHAPTER 6

"Enough!"

Stella's voice cut through the shouting. Jordan wouldn't have listened had he not noticed the man standing in front of her. It was perhaps the oddest-looking person he'd ever seen. A green-and-white striped suit hung off his tall, wiry frame. His hair was such a light shade of blond it was nearly white, his pale blue eyes the color of ice on a winter morning. A dark green hat sat crookedly on his head. Stella gaped at him—and the man behind him, wearing all black, dark-skinned and built like a boulder. Jordan had no idea who they were, and the look on Stella's face suggested she didn't either.

Despite the bell that rang when he entered, despite Stella's shouted warning, nobody else noticed the newcomer, too consumed in the argument. Jordan drew a revolver, spun it around, and gave himself a half-second to aim before firing, all without ever taking his eyes off the strangers. The gunshot brought a halt to the conversation, and the strange man jerked back as the bell over the door shattered.

Silence reigned, and people gaped at Jordan and the broken bell now swinging from its chain. "Enough," he growled, jerking his head at the newcomers. "We have company."

Everyone twisted in their seats. Stella retreated to her father's side as the dark-skinned man—a bodyguard, perhaps?—drew a curved sword halfway out of its sheath.

"This must be the right place," the one in the suit mused in a nasally voice that grated Jordan's ears. He nodded at Jordan's side of the table.

"The Ravens." Then at the other. "The White Roses. My name is Silas Tradow, and I am pleased to make your acquaintance."

Marcus and John exchanged a look. Whatever argument they had with each other, they were able to put it off long enough for John to say, "This is a private meeting."

"Oh, I'm aware, but I was told this was the only time I could get the leaders of Lochridge in the same place." Silas adjusted the lapels of his suit. "I am a representative of the Stokes Workers' Union. My good friend Stephen Trace is the leader of the Union. His mission is to revolutionize cities and their economies to be more profitable for everyone involved. He has already revolutionized Stokes, Lionsville, Triet, Morninghaven, and Keya City. And now, he is interested in doing the same for Lochridge."

Jordan shot his father a look. *What is this about?*

John shrugged. *No idea.*

Silas continued, "We would love—"

"This is still a private meeting," Jordan interjected. "Third parties are unwelcome."

Declan cleared his throat. "Besides, I don't think you have the right people for…" He waved a hand in Silas' direction. "For whatever this is."

"Oh, but I do!" he said cheerfully. "Typically we go through the mayor of the town to arrange things, but I was very interested upon hearing that Lochridge has no mayor or one official that rules it. It's split almost perfectly in two, ruled by gangs—how very interesting indeed!" He stepped forward but stopped when everyone in the room pointed a gun at him. "That's a lot of weapons," he said, flustered now. "In any case, Mister Trace wants Lochridge next in line to be revolutionized. All employees of every business in the city will be joined under the Workers' Union, which will ensure each one has fair wages and hours. In return, we will make sure every business has the help they need to continue running. Anything that is unnecessary—shops that don't get customers, restaurants that don't see business, anything that is falling under—will be closed and replaced with a more profitable source of income." His blue eyes gleamed. "Mister Trace is especially interested in the Red Harbor, given its flow of traffic."

"The Red Harbor is neutral ground," Stella cut in. "If you're here to discuss ownership of it, we cannot help you."

Silas angled his head. "You must be Stella Rook. I've heard much about you."

Stella tensed under his gaze. "What is that supposed to mean?"

"I did my research before coming here." Silas offered her a warm smile to which Stella blanched. Her white dress hugged her tight enough to leave little to the imagination, and while Silas' gaze wasn't predatory, there was still an intensity to it that made Jordan almost feel sorry for her. "The heir to the White Roses. The sharpest woman on this side of the Great River. A beauty. A grace."

"One who will shoot you in the face," she said flatly.

Silas grinned. "Miss Rook, what if I told you that when the Union revolutionizes this city, the Red Harbor will no longer be neutral ground? There will be no more borders, no more fights between gangs, no more territories that you have no access to."

A murmur broke through the room. A gleam entered Marcus Rook's eyes—an expression that meant nothing good. "What does that mean?" Jordan demanded.

Silas tilted his head in the other direction. "And here we have the opposing side. Jordan Daelik, Lochridge's sharpshooter. I've heard a lot about you, too." Jordan didn't like the way he looked at him, either, but Silas laughed and carried on. "No worries. My offer stands for both gangs. All the research I have done suggests the two of you are evenly matched, locked in a standstill for the better part of twenty years. I've been told it is impossible to work with both, so I am here to offer a deal. An alliance between the Workers' Union and one of Lochridge's infamous gangs. Mister Trace is interested in revolutionizing Lochridge. All of you are interested in winning this war amongst yourselves." He shrugged. "I see no reason that we can't help each other out."

Jordan's hands slipped down to cradle his revolvers. Mateo caught his gaze and raised both brows, a silent question. He shook his head.

There was something off about this, a bizarre, feverish quality that had Jordan rubbing his eyes. Whoever this was, whatever this was… He didn't trust it.

Because if it was what he thought it was…

"What are you implying?" Marcus asked.

Jordan didn't like his tone. Didn't like the hunger, the lust, the greed in his eyes. Silas tilted his head with a smile. "I am offering help to one gang. The Workers' Union has a small army at their disposal. For our plan to work in Lochridge, there cannot be any friction or tension between its people—which means one gang must go." He glanced between them. "Mister Trace has not decided which gang he wants gone and which he wants to work with. That is why I am here—to observe both sides, work with each of you, and decide whether the Ravens or the Roses will be more beneficial to our cause. Once I have made my decision, the opposing side shall be taken care of immediately. We will work closely together to eradicate any tension and establish a booming economy in Lochridge."

He finished his spiel with a clap of his hands. Jordan gaped at him.

"By *eradicating tension*," he said slowly, "you mean killing off one of the gangs."

He shrugged. "If that's what it takes."

His mouth fell open. "You can't be serious."

Silas stepped closer. "That's the goal, isn't it, Mister Daelik? To win this feud? To see the other side dead on the street?"

"How soon will you decide?" John asked before Jordan could answer.

Jordan gaped at his father while Silas smiled. "I do not know yet. It will be a couple of weeks at the least. I'm interested in getting to know both sides."

Stella crossed her arms. "What if we aren't interested in working with you?"

Jordan could have kissed the Rose heir for having a shred of reasoning. Instead he settled on meeting her gaze for the briefest of moments. She tilted her head, her eyes dark.

Jordan recognized that look. She didn't trust Silas either.

"If the Roses aren't interested in working with you," John cut in, "then consider the Ravens eager to take up the offer."

What?

Jordan shot his father an incredulous look that went ignored. He turned to Declan and Mateo, searching for an ally, but both appraised Silas with raised brows. Jordan's mother was the only one who seemed put off by the offer, but Jordan suspected she was still upset after Marcus brought up John's affair.

Out of options, Jordan risked a glance at the Rooks. Marcus' jaw worked as he stared at Silas. Harvey and Zoey were appraising him with expressions that Jordan didn't like in the least. And Stella…

Stella was giving Marcus a warning look, which he ignored as surely as John ignored Jordan.

"The Roses are also interested," he announced.

Stella's eyes widened. Jordan felt a sinking sensation in his stomach. His gaze flickered to hers for the briefest of moments, the same confusion in her eyes that he felt clawing through his head.

Silas, however, flashed a grin around the room. "Excellent! The Workers' Union has grand plans for the city, and I look forward to working with both of you." He adjusted the sleeves of his suit. "I will meet with both of you individually to discuss the details, but I would like to sincerely thank you for your interest in working with the Union."

With a final smile and a mock bow, Silas turned on his heel and walked out the door, a bounce in his step that hadn't been there before. His bodyguard gave everyone a dark look before trailing after him.

"What the hell was that?"

John turned, his brows raising as Jordan stormed after him. He waited until the door to his office closed before saying, "If we didn't take the deal, then the Roses would have. Now we have a chance at getting him on our side."

"I don't *want* him on our side! Why should we trust someone we know nothing about?"

"I may not trust the man, but our best interest lies in him. If he helps us take out the Roses…"

Jordan gritted his teeth. "Either that, or he takes *us* out."

John leaned back in his seat. His eyes were cool, calculating, alive with the prospect of eradicating the Rooks. "I have full confidence that we will secure his favor. We outmatch the Roses in every way."

"They have more territory."

"And we have more manpower to make up for it. It won't take him long to see our worth."

Jordan wanted to scream. "This won't go our way."

44

His father glared at him. "It certainly won't if you keep that attitude. You are my heir. Act like it."

That was a slap to the face if there ever was one. "I am acting like an heir because I am looking out for the safety of our people. If something happens to the Roses, they can just slip back into the woodworks. But we are all marked." He held up his arm, brandishing the raven tattoo stamped on his wrist. "We can't just disappear. All they have to do is look for this mark, and they will weed us out. We are undertaking more risk than the Roses are."

John shuffled through the pages on his desk. "We will prove that we are better than the Roses. Silas will help us get rid of Marcus Rook and his family once and for all, and then we will dispose of him when he is no longer of any use to us." His gray eyes flashed to Jordan. "That is the plan. If you deviate from it, there will be trouble. It is alright for you to express concerns, but when we are in public, we are to present a unified front. Understood?"

His jaw clenched. "Understood."

"Good. Now get out."

Anger swirled through Jordan, hot and vicious, but he turned on his heel and stalked out. He slammed into Lana, who was eavesdropping behind the door, but he stepped around his sister and kept walking without a word.

Declan and Mateo waited for him in the living room. "Well?" Dec asked.

"We're actually doing this." Jordan's entire body was tense with anger. "He actually wants to make a deal with a bumbling stranger who has no business being in Lochridge."

Wanting to meet with both John Daelik and Marcus Rook in the same room aside, the man was unprepared for Lochridge. Jordan had spotted Silas getting into a *motorcar* on his way out. His wealth would make him an easy target for pickpockets and thieves. Even with the bodyguard looming over his shoulder, Jordan doubted Silas' diamond-encrusted pocket watch would make it to the end of the day. Silas himself did not appear to have the abilities of a fighter; to step away from his guard, even for a moment, could turn deadly for him. And heaven forbid he leave the motorcar unattended—thieves would loot it, smash the windows, and strip it for parts if he so much as turned his head.

Declan shrugged. "I don't know, Jordie. If he's telling the truth and actually has an army…"

"An army that's just as likely to turn on us than the Roses."

"You don't think we're better than the Roses?"

"Silas might think so. The Rooks are sophisticated—they live in a mansion and dress nice for every occasion." Jordan gestured to the three of them, wearing shirts with the sleeves ripped out. The only nice thing Jordan wore was the leather holsters that held his guns. Declan's hair was a mess, his eyes glassy from drinking. And Mateo… Well, Mateo strived to have class, but if tonight's spat was any indication, class didn't matter when everyone viewed you as the product of an affair. "The Rooks seem like Silas' kind of people, if you know what I mean."

Mateo bit his lip. "That's a fair point."

"But they're not *better* than us," Dec protested.

Jordan's lips twitched. "No, they aren't. But I'm still worried. Neither side should work with Silas. It doesn't make sense."

"What's done is done. Might as well make the most of it."

His jaw clenched. "I guess you're right."

Declan grinned and threw an arm over Jordan's shoulders. "*Of course* I'm right. Now come on, let's go have some fun."

"I think I'm just going to head to bed."

"Nope," Dec said cheerfully. "What you need is a drink."

"I don't—"

"If there was ever a time for a drink, I think it would be now." Mateo sidled up to Jordan's other side with a grin he knew meant trouble. "Come on."

His protests died on his tongue, and Jordan groaned as he allowed Dec and Mateo to pull him out the door. It was past nightfall, and Lochridge was alive. The streets bustled with people. The gambling halls on either side had their doors wide open, and shouts and cheers could be heard from within, drunken patrons stumbling in and out. Many of them bore tattoos. It was no secret that the Ravens liked to have a good time— while the Roses opted for classier establishments to fit their upmarket lifestyle, the southern half of the city was littered with bars and brothels and too many casinos to count. The Ravens were loud, disorderly, and chaotic, drowning in liquor and gambling debt. Jordan didn't always approve of the trouble his people got themselves into, but he liked to think that living wild and free made for a better atmosphere than the stuffy posh environment Marcus Rook shoved down his gang's throat.

The trio ignored everyone as they passed through the crowds. It wasn't long before they entered a lively bar in the heart of the Barter Streets. Declan went straight for the table in the corner with cards and bourbon. Jordan didn't enjoy being drunk, not in the way his cousin did it, living in a hazy state all the time and ignoring his problems. But even the Raven heir knew how to have a good time, and as he and Mateo slid into a booth by Declan's table, he ordered a round for the three of them and knocked it back without mercy.

CHAPTER 7

"You cannot be serious."

Stella stood in front of her father. Marcus was taller than her, forcing her to tilt her head to look him in the eye, but that didn't stop her from glaring at him.

"Last I checked," she hissed, "we didn't trust bumbling businessmen that crashed our meeting and gave us an offer that seemed too good to be true."

Marcus crossed his arms. "If we didn't take it, Daelik would have."

"Which is no doubt the same reasoning they used. You should both call this off."

"Are you kidding? We have a chance to get rid of the Ravens for good."

"*If* Silas is telling the truth. Where would someone like him get an army?"

"Not him. The Workers' Union." Marcus scratched his beard. "I've heard of them before. The details are sparse, but they did a lot of work in Stokes. Completely changed how things worked there." He shrugged. "You saw Silas. His motorcar. His clothes. He has money—where did it come from if not this Union?"

Stella planted her hands on her hips. "I still don't trust him."

"Which is why we don't let our guards down. But we are taking this deal, and we are going to win over Silas." He nodded at her. "He already praised you back there. Keep it up."

Stella's face flushed. She hadn't appreciated being the subject of Silas' gaze. She was used to flaunting her beauty to her advantage, but something about Silas' ice-colored eyes had rubbed her the wrong way.

"We shouldn't do this," she said softly. "I got a bad hit off of him."

Marcus brushed her shoulder. "Don't worry, Stella. I have a handle on this." He winked. "We're Rooks. We always come out on top."

And with that, he disappeared into his office, leaving Stella alone in the hallway.

Sunlight flooded the parlor, bathing Stella's skin in warm light. Her hands flew across the keys of the grand piano. A haunting melody flowed from the instrument, beautiful and intricate, each note echoing through the sun-bathed house.

She let the music flow through her, sweeping her into its song and away from her thoughts. She was dimly aware that Zoey and Harvey stood in the doorway, holding a whispered argument she didn't want to know the topic of. Her cousins met her gaze from across the room. Harvey sneered at the music. Zoey smiled lightly and gestured for her to continue before dragging her brother out of the room.

Stella tilted her head back, her fingers finding the ivory keys by memory. The piano was her comfort. She started lessons at the tender age of nine, her aunt being an excellent musician. The ability to create something so richly beautiful with just a few strokes of a key was bewitching to her.

Liam had loved it when she played. It had taken months after his death to remember that she loved it, too.

"Miss Rook?"

Stella started, her hands splaying across the keys. She winced at the dissonant sound as she twisted in her seat. One of the manor's many hired servants stood behind her, wringing her hands.

"There's somebody outside," she said. "He requested to meet with your father."

"I'm not my father, in case you haven't noticed."

"He's in town overseeing a transaction. I've sent a messenger to him. You need to keep your guests busy until he gets here."

She leveled an icy look on her. "You have no right to tell me what I should be doing."

The servant bit her lip and said nothing.

She sighed. "Let him in."

She nodded and vanished through the door. Stella turned back to the piano and resumed playing, her eyes fluttering closed for a few precious seconds while she enjoyed the last moments of alone time. Entertaining her father's guests was not her idea of fun.

"Miss Rook, what a pleasure."

Stella's body locked up at that nasally voice. She didn't take her hands off the keys as she glanced over her shoulder to see Silas Tradow standing in the parlor.

He wasn't alone. The bodyguard from the other night was back, wearing the same dark clothes. It was easier to see him in the better lighting, a fat nose and beady eyes, a pale scar cutting across the bridge of his nose. He kept one large hand wrapped around the hilt of his sword as he fixed Stella with a stare that was both expressionless and wrathful at the same time. On Silas' other side stood a woman who resembled him so closely that they had to be family. Her nose wrinkled as she surveyed the parlor.

"Mister Tradow," Stella managed, forcing a smile.

He gestured to the people with him. "This is Celia, my daughter. And this is our dear friend Tobias."

Celia offered her a tight-lipped smile that Stella returned after a moment. Tobias' expression didn't shift in the slightest.

"Have a seat," Stella said. "My father will be here soon."

Silas swept into the room with a practiced ease, claiming one of the fluffy armchairs in front of the fireplace. Tobias took up a spot against the wall, his eyes never leaving Stella.

But Stella's focus was on Celia as she walked closer to the piano, her critical gaze sweeping over it. The resemblance to her father was uncanny—skin so pale she could have passed for a ghost, a tall and wiry frame, sharp features, and eyes the color of ice. Platinum hair draped over her shoulders in a glossy curtain, a lavender dress hugging her curves before pooling onto the floor. Diamonds glittered at her ears, throat, and wrists.

Her bright red lips puckered as she met Stella's gaze. "Do you play any other instruments?"

Her song slowed. "I'm afraid not. My aunt knew how to play piano so that's what I learned, but I've always been keen on the idea of learning the violin."

Celia's mouth twisted. "What, you can't afford a tutor? I play violin *and* piano, alongside the cello, flute, harp, and clarinet."

The disdain in her voice had Stella narrowing her eyes.

"Blatant displays of wealth are a good way to get mugged in this town," she said sweetly. "You should watch your back before someone puts a knife in it."

Celia blinked at her sharp smile, at the way she eyed the diamond jewelry while her hands slipped further down the keys, seamlessly transitioning into a darker, ominous piece. Silas frowned, but the look of shock on Celia's face was worth it.

Especially when Zoey clamped her hand over her mouth to fight back a fit of laughter from where she stood in the doorway. Even Harvey, who stood behind his sister, smirked.

Tobias eyed them as they settled into seats opposite of Silas. Celia huffed as she flounced to a chair beside her father, shooting a glare at Stella as she continued to play. Her answering smile was saccharine sweet. She disliked dealing with prissy brats. Stella was well aware that most of the city thought of *her* as a brat, but she was happy to be given the opportunity to take that assumption and shove it down their throats. She worked for what she had; she didn't flaunt around her wealth unless it served a specific purpose, and she most certainly didn't brag about all the instruments she played. Nobody even knew she played the piano unless they'd seen it with their own two eyes.

She could only imagine what Jordan Daelik would say if he saw her sitting behind her favorite instrument.

Silas crossed an ankle over his knee as he surveyed Zoey and Harvey. "I met you before," he said to the former, "but I don't recall your name."

"Zoey. And my brother, Harvey."

His brows flicked up as he looked Harvey up and down. If he'd heard anything about Lochridge, then he'd probably been warned to steer clear of him.

"It's a pleasure to meet you both," he said.

Harvey smiled, showing all his teeth. "Likewise."

51

Silas was quick to turn to Stella. "Miss Rook, that is some beautiful playing. You said your aunt taught you?"

"Yes."

"The tutors that taught Celia live in Stokes. If you are interested, I can reach out to them on your behalf. Their skills on the violin are unmatched."

Stella blinked. "It would be hard to learn without an instrument to play. Thank you for the offer, though."

His eyes stayed on her until Zoey cleared her throat.

"So you live in Stokes?" she asked. "With this Workers' Union?"

Silas straightened in his seat, seeming happy with the twist in subject. "Oh, yes. Stephen Trace is a dear friend of mine, and let me tell you, he is an excellent businessman. It's been a pleasure to see him do so well."

Stella paused, her hands featherlight against the keys. "Such a bold tactic to reform Lochridge. I'm surprised it hasn't left those other cities in shambles."

"We don't destroy," Silas said promptly. Stella had a feeling it was recited. "We build up. That is why we're working to form an alliance with Lochridge. This is the biggest town between the Great River and the ocean. Its wealth is unmatched. We don't want to fight for it."

"And yet you're going to," she mused. "Either the Roses or the Ravens are going to meet their end because of your help."

His pale eyes studied her. "Are you worried?"

"About you? Yes. About me?" She smiled. "I know how to handle blood on my hands."

To her surprise, Silas returned her smile. "Then that is something we have in common, Miss Rook." He nodded at her. "I like you. Vicious. Intelligent. You are right to question, but be careful—you don't want to push me away with too many doubts."

She held his stare. "Noted."

A few beats of uncomfortable silence passed. Zoey shot Stella a look, and she was quick to resume her music, banging out the loudest, most cheerful piece she knew. She caught Celia smirking at her, her delicate fingers brushing against her bracelet as if to rub her wealth in her face. Zoey noted Stella's murderous expression and struck up a conversation about life in Stokes that lasted until Marcus walked through the door. Stella had never been so happy to see her father, but unease coiled deep inside her as she watched him greet Silas with a warm handshake like the two of them were old friends. They disappeared into Marcus' office with Tobias and Celia. Harvey muttered something about eavesdropping and went after them, leaving Stella and Zoey alone.

"I don't trust him," Stella said flatly.

"It won't be so bad." Zoey waved a flippant hand. "If he really can help us with the Ravens…"

"Then that would be spectacular. But either he's lying about this army of his and this deal is worthless, or he's telling the truth, in which case he could come after us just as easily. I don't want to suck up to someone who's lying about his intentions, but neither do I want to be hostile to a man who claims to have an army at his disposal."

Zoey smirked. "Have you ever thought of just being *nice?*"

Stella glared at her.

She laughed under her breath. "Why not be excited? This Silas figure has money, and if he's really wanting to turn Lochridge into a booming empire…" She shrugged. "Why not see what it's all about? If we get further into it and don't like what we see, there's nothing stopping us from pulling out."

"He's got money, and money means power."

"Money is just one component of power. Everything else has to do with reputation and ability." Zoey leaned against the piano, but was quick to move away when Stella hissed at her to get off her prized instrument. "Silas doesn't have much in either department. Not here, at least."

Stella brushed her hair over her shoulder. "How certain are you?"

"Very. You shouldn't worry, Stell."

Zoey patted her shoulder before vanishing down the hall after Harvey. Stella slumped against the piano, scrubbing a hand over her face.

Perhaps Zoey and Marcus were right and there was nothing to worry about.

If they were right, there was no harm in confirming that theory, right? Surely they wouldn't mind if Stella did a little snooping around.

A plan in place, Stella allowed her hands to return to the key of her piano, a smile curling over her lips.

CHAPTER
8

The Barter Streets were as busy as ever. Not only did they form the border between the Roses and the Ravens, but the Streets served as the trade center of Lochridge. Jordan hooked his thumbs in his belt as he walked past bars and brothels, restaurants and cafes, tailors and blacksmiths and woodworkers and every kind of store one could think of. Vendors pushed carts of merchandise and waved their products around. Several of them swarmed around Jordan, but one glare from him had them scattering.

He peered through the restaurant windows in search of his family but couldn't find them. They hadn't specified where they were going to eat. He didn't even know if Mateo was with them—his brother had disappeared after the night of the meeting, and Jordan hadn't seen him since.

It wasn't Mateo's fault that his arrival had formed a rift between Lillian and John, but Jordan knew he still hated it when the subject was broached. It had been cruel of the Rooks to bring it up at the meeting, and Jordan knew that was why Mateo had been avoiding the family ever since, but he was determined to track him down and talk about it. Mateo brought a sense of calm to the house. They needed him back.

He walked all the way to the border between the territories. Someone once took red paint to the cobblestones, drawing a definitive line down them. The paint was chipped and faded, now nothing but spots of red clinging between the stones. Jordan stepped over it indifferently.

There was nothing special about the buildings on the Roses' side of the border. Everything in Lochridge carried the same grimy, ramshackle structure, sagging roofs and crumbling facades, the colors washed out from years of rough weather. The smell of salt from the ocean permeated the air. The hairs on the back of his neck rose as he walked through the Roses' portion of the Barter Streets. Most wouldn't dare to attack him in the middle of a crowded street, but a few brave souls would forget the consequences and come after him swinging. Jòrdan's fingers curled a-round his revolvers.

His eyes scanned the area. He only dared a few steps past the border, ready to jump back across if trouble arose, but all he saw were the regular vendors and customers. The Roses didn't have a tattoo to mark their gang affiliation like Jordan and every other Raven did. Jordan thought that was a lapse of judgment on his father's part; his need to force his people to publicly declare their allegiance to him also declared it to their enemies. It was now much harder to get spies into the Rooks' company. John was forced to hire out third parties for his dirty work.

A scuffle of boots behind him had Jordan whirling, his guns flashing in the afternoon light. Whoever it was had already disappeared back into the bustling crowd, nothing more than a nameless face in a sea of people.

Jordan relaxed, sliding his guns back into their holsters.

And then someone tackled him from behind.

Jordan was thrown forward, but his foot stomped against the cobblestones, forcing him upright. He threw his weight back against his attacker, his elbow lashing back in a vicious blow that made contact with somebody's face. A new pair of hands grabbed him by the arm. Jordan used his free hand to draw a revolver. The gun was in his left hand, but he'd practiced enough times to be deadly even without his dominant hand. One final twist had him breaking away, stumbling back across the border as he lifted his weapon.

He was glad to see that he didn't recognize either of the men that now stared him down. If it had been the Rooks he was dealing with, things would be much worse for him, but a few Rose scrubs were nothing. Blood gushed down one's face. Jordan's blow had caught him in the nose. He smirked at them as he leveled both of his guns at their chests.

"I suggest you back up," he said, his voice carrying a lethal edge. The men glared at him, but they took a healthy step back. Jordan didn't lower his weapons. "What do you want?"

"What do *you* want?" the one with the bloody nose demanded, the words slurred. "You were on our territory."

Jordan glanced down to confirm he was behind the remnants of the red line. "No, I'm not."

He snarled. "You were."

"Can you prove it?"

They exchanged a look. "You were over the line, Daelik. Our word is enough."

"Is it?" Jordan crooned. "Do you think anyone will listen to the word of two strangers over that of the Raven heir?"

The other one scowled. "Stay off our turf, Daelik, or there will be consequences."

He merely smirked again as he twirled his revolvers around in a series of smooth turns before dropping them back into their holsters. He didn't want to waste his bullets on ruffians acting as guards.

"Attack me again," he warned, "and you'll learn the true meaning of the word *consequences*."

Jordan turned on his heel with every intention to walk away. But then one of the Roses muttered under their breath, "Dirty heathen."

His vision flashed red, and before he was even fully aware of what he was doing, Jordan had turned, his revolvers appearing in his hands. His hands acted faster than his mind, and he had pulled both triggers before he could stop himself.

The Roses hit the ground. The people around him stared. Jordan blew the smoke off the barrels, holstered his guns, and turned away with a grimace, heading deeper into his territory before anyone could retaliate.

It was stupid to have gone over the border. Getting a quick view of what was happening across the Barter Streets wasn't worth the risk. Jordan's jaw clenched as he headed further south. This entire trip had been pointless; he'd set out with the mission to talk to Mateo, and he had yet to find his half-brother.

The wind tore between the cramped buildings, buffeting Jordan's exposed arms. Lochridge weather was something to behold; some days were warm and sunny, but at least once a week the sunshine was disturbed by massive thunderstorms that threatened to tear the city in half. The dark hue of the clouds over the ocean promised another round of torrential rain. Jordan hated Lochridge weather nearly as much as he hated the Rook family. He hoped a nice gust of wind would blow them right out of town.

He pushed through the door of his house, grateful to be back in the peace of his home. His foot was on the first stair when the peace shattered—John's booming laugh floated out of his office, followed by a nasally chuckle from a voice Jordan recognized.

He was moving in an instant, throwing open the office door to see John, Silas, the bodyguard, and a blonde-haired woman Jordan didn't recognize gathered around the massive desk. They glanced up at his hasty entrance. The woman's pale eyes settled on him. Her brow raised ever-so-slightly, and her lips curved into a smile as her expression shifted into a shark-like hunger that had Jordan freezing in his tracks.

Jordan ripped his gaze away from her and turned to his father. "What's going on?"

"Mister Tradow ran into us in town," he said. "I invited him to talk."

Silas smiled. "I was just coming back from the Rooks' house. They've got a beautiful place, but a few too many flowers, if you ask me."

Jordan couldn't help but note that one of those flowers was in the woman's hand, a plump red rose she held by the stem.

"This is my daughter, Celia," Silas said proudly.

Celia smiled and offered him her hand, her eyes lingering on him far too long to be casual. "My pleasure, Mister Daelik."

Jordan shook it, then glanced at his father. "Usually you don't let new partners into the office right away."

Meaning he *never* did. Silas shouldn't have been invited into the heart of their house, into the office where John kept his most pressing secrets, until after an alliance was secured and John was sure of his intentions. Jordan knew his father well enough to know he was sucking up, trying to make himself look good in front of Silas. He wanted that alliance. And Jordan couldn't lie to himself and pretend that he didn't want it as well, but he just wasn't sure it was worth the risk. John was diving into this without a second thought, not caring about the potential risk of letting a stranger into his home.

John gave him a look that suggested he should keep his mouth shut. "I am making an exception for Mister Tradow because of the unique nature of our agreement."

"What agreement."

They all blinked at his flat words. "The alliance," John growled.

"The potential alliance," Jordan corrected.

"Is somebody worried?" Celia asked, her voice dripping with poisoned honey. "The Rook girl couldn't restrain from expressing her concerns, either."

That surprised him. Stella seemed nervous during the meeting, but it had been enough for her to say it to their faces? He tucked that information away. "I'm not worried." Not if it meant being compared to Stella. "I'm just taking caution. The future of Lochridge depends on an arbitrary decision between our gangs."

Why couldn't his father see that?

"It is not arbitrary," Silas assured him. "In fact, I have a meeting with my friends from Stokes tomorrow night to discuss the situation in more depth. We are treating your city with the utmost care."

Jordan tucked that information away, too.

"We're having an important discussion," John growled, a clear message to stop questioning him in front of Silas and to get out.

Silas picked up on it. "Perhaps we should leave, Mister Daelik. The Rooks were kind enough to show me some of their businesses along the Barter Streets. I gained a lot of information on their inner workings. The tax system they have in place is quite something. Perhaps you would like to show me what your system is like?"

John didn't need to be told twice. He rose from his chair and beckoned the Tradows and the bodyguard—who was introduced as Tobias—to follow him. Jordan pressed himself against the doorway as they passed.

Celia brought up the rear. She slowed as she passed Jordan, one hand trailing down his arm as she smiled at him.

"Don't worry," she murmured, her red lips parting in a smile. "Lochridge might go under, but we'll get to keep a few of our favorite people around." That smile widened. "And I like you most of all."

That might have been the strangest flirt Jordan ever heard—and he'd witnessed more than a few drunk women swaggering up to him and Declan at the local bar. He shook his head. "What is your father doing here?"

"Business," she said. "He's doing business—and don't you let yourself think you can stop him. I see what you and the Rook girl are doing.

You don't trust him. You shouldn't. But the only way to survive this is to trust, because that is the only way he'll see your worth and decide to keep you around." She leaned closer to Jordan. "My father doesn't play games he can't win."

Jordan's expression hardened. Celia gave him a winning smile before sauntering after Silas, the skirts of her dress rustling. Something fell out of her hand—the rose, plucked of all its petals, nothing but a thorny stem lying on the rug.

Jordan's heart thundered as he stared at it. He couldn't decide if Celia had been trying to warn him, seduce him, or threaten him. Perhaps it was some wicked mixture of the three.

He raked a hand through his hair, glancing around to see if anyone else was around to hear Celia's words. The parlor and the kitchen were empty. No one hovered on the stairs. Mateo's bedroom was directly above the office; if his brother had his ear pressed to the floor, like they did as children when they wanted to eavesdrop on John, he might have heard something, but Jordan didn't think he was even home. Which meant there was nobody to confirm Jordan's suspicions, nobody to hear what Celia said and realize there was something about this situation that just wasn't right.

I have a meeting with my friends from Stokes tomorrow night to discuss the situation in more depth.

Jordan's eyes narrowed.

If Silas was there to discuss the situation with trusted friends, then he would reveal his true motives, the real reason he was here in Lochridge. It would be a peek into the mind of the man Jordan's father wanted so desperately to ally with.

It was the smart thing to do. John would be livid if he found out, but Jordan had plenty of practice sneaking in and out of his house in the dead of night—and just as much practice eavesdropping on conversations not meant for his ears.

Jordan turned on his heel and stalked up the stairs. He knew what to do.

CHAPTER 9

The first round of searching turned up nothing. Silas remained in his hotel on the far side of town the entire night. Stella watched until well past high moon, crouched in the shadows, her eyes trained on the darkened window that led to Silas' room. She knew it was his—she'd spent the daylight hours digging for information on where he was staying, and the motorcar parked next to the hotel certainly hadn't come from anyone in Lochridge. There wasn't any movement, no flutter of curtains nor shadow in motion, and nobody had come out the front entrance when Stella finally gave up in the early hours of the morning.

But she was back at it again the following night, her determination doubled. She wore a skin-tight outfit made of black material, her hair braided down her back. As much as she liked wearing white, symbolizing her loyalty to her gang and her family, she had to admit that the Ravens picked the better color. Black was perfect for stealth. Her secret stash of dark garments hid under her bed, ready to be pulled out whenever the situation called for it. And if someone put a gun to her head, she would admit that she liked how she looked; knee-high boots and a tight-fitting tunic, a thick belt low on her hips carrying a pistol and array of knives. It was really a shame that she didn't plan on letting anyone see her.

Night had fallen only a few minutes ago, leaving the faintest glimmer of light still visible on the horizon. Stella tensed as the doors to the hotel swung open and a familiar light-haired man strode onto the street. Her fingers curled around the crumbling bricks that made the ledge of the roof.

Silas was followed by Tobias but not Celia. And judging by the way he expertly turned to the left, heading into White Rose territory, he knew where he was going.

A planned outing. Perfect.

Stella trailed him from the rooftops. Lochridge was narrow and cramped, the roofs a street of their own if you knew how to navigate them. Loose shingles and sagging structures made for a treacherous journey. Stella leaped nimbly from building to building, nothing more than a shadow against the night, her boots silent as she walked.

Silas and Tobias did not exchange a single word. She wondered why they hadn't taken the motorcar—it would have gotten them there a lot faster, but perhaps they aimed for stealth over speed. She glared at the back of Silas' green-and-white suit, but then a flash of movement snagged her attention. Another figure, trailing after the pair. At first she thought it might be Celia, but this figure was taller and broader, and Celia's light hair would stand out more in the dark.

Somebody else, then. Interesting.

Silas turned onto the Barter Streets and disappeared into a raunchy restaurant on the Roses' side. The figure following them halted, surveying the building.

And that's when Stella struck.

She leapt off the low ledge of the building and landed behind the figure. He heard the noise and turned, but she was already in motion, her knives whipping out as she speared for the intruder. He moved with lightning speed, knocking aside her initial blow as he drew a weapon of his own.

Stella scrambled back, disappearing into an alley. The man followed. She dove low, her leg sweeping out and catching his ankle. A worse fighter would have been sent to the ground, but this one regained his balance as he lunged. He wasn't using the gun in his hand—he was here for stealth as well.

So very interesting.

Stella swung her knife again, but the man caught her wrist in his free hand. A knee drove into her stomach. She gasped as she slammed against the wall, and the man laughed.

She recognized that laugh.

Rage coiled through her as the cold barrel of a gun pressed against her neck. Jordan Daelik laughed again, but he stopped as she slid a knife against his ribs.

"Well met, Daelik," she purred. "Might I remind you whose territory we're on?"

They were barely over the border, but they *were* on the Roses' side. Jordan cocked his head to the side as he realized who he'd been fighting. A smile curled over his lips as he looked her over, as he lowered his head towards her.

She felt him smile against her cheek. "I can pull this trigger faster than you can move that knife."

His breath tickled her skin. "Would you like to find out?" she asked sweetly.

He traced the gun down her jaw. "I thought I heard someone on the rooftops. Why were you following me?"

"I wasn't. I was following someone else, and then I became interested in who was tailing them, too." Stella tilted her head back. "What do you want with Silas?"

"What do *you* want with Silas?"

"Are you always going to answer a question with a question?"

"Are you?"

They studied each other in the dark.

"Silas visited my father yesterday," Jordan said. "He seemed interested in checking out our business structure. Does that sound familiar?"

Stella had gone with Marcus and Silas when the latter wanted to check out the Roses' businesses. He'd asked a lot of questions that rubbed her the wrong way, but she'd held her tongue. "You don't trust him."

"I don't trust his boss," he corrected. "Or this Workers' Union." His eyes glittered. "And you don't, either. Celia told me all about the Rook girl who asked some tough questions."

"Celia is a self-entitled brat who likes to brag."

A smile curled over his lips. Stella glared at him.

Jordan huffed a laugh, oblivious to the blade primed to slide between his ribs. "You and I have something in common."

"Besides the all-powerful need to kill each other?"

"We don't trust Silas."

"Bold of you to assume I have the same feelings as you do."

"We stand to lose the same things," Jordan said. "I don't think Silas is as truthful as he claims. I have a feeling that our fathers both took that deal with him because they were afraid the other would get it first. And I think Silas was well aware of that." He paused. "Whichever way it goes ends with half the city dead. I don't like that idea."

"And I don't like the idea of this Union presiding over the remains," Stella added without really meaning to. Shit. Her and Daelik *were* thinking the same thing. "How confident are you?"

"Confident enough to confide in my worst enemy."

Their gazes clashed for another few moments, then Jordan stepped away and holstered his revolver. Stella placed her knife back into its sheath, her eyes never leaving his.

"Another thing we have in common," he said, "is a desire to protect this city and its assets. If this is a trap, there won't be anything left after Silas is done. Our fathers are just too wrapped up in what can be gained to see it."

Stella bit her lip as she studied him. "I came to see if I could confirm his motives. If he's speaking the truth, fine. If not, I'm going to need evidence to convince my father." She sighed. "I can't believe I'm going to say this, but for once, we have a common goal."

His eyes gleamed. "What are you suggesting?"

"A truce." His brows rose, and she amended, "For tonight. We find out what Silas is up to and get him out of town. I don't trust him. You don't either. It's only smart."

She thought of the way they'd exchanged a look after Marcus and John accepted Silas' deal, that shared expression of mute horror. Stella trusted Jordan about as much as she trusted Silas—which was to say not at all—but something she *did* trust in was Jordan's desire to keep his father's empire standing. The empire he stood to inherit one day.

Jordan nodded and extended a hand towards her. "A truce for tonight, little thorn."

She shook it, hating the feeling of his calloused hand against her own. These were the hands that killed Liam and countless Roses. "For tonight, feathers."

It didn't escape her notice how his eyes glinted. She'd killed his men, too. He had reason to hate her.

But she hated him more.

He jerked his chin towards the building. "Silas said he was meeting with friends from Stokes to discuss the situation with Lochridge. If there was ever a time to hear his motives, it would be now." He frowned. "But we need to get inside unnoticed."

It felt strange to be scheming with the Daelik heir. Stella only did this with Zoey and occasionally Harvey. "I think there's a back entrance."

The restaurant in question was Stella's most hated place on her territory. It was a pub at its base, but there were rooms in the back for… *other* activities. The building reeked of incense and cigar smoke. She got a headache every time she walked in. It reminded her too much of the Ravens—bawdy, dirty, and dishonorable.

Stella brushed past Jordan, trying not to show how much having her back exposed to him bothered her. There *was* a back entrance, but it was boarded up, wooden planks criss-crossing over the door.

"There's a window," Jordan remarked.

Indeed, a window on the second floor had been left open. The room beyond was dark. Stella frowned at the opening. The way the ground sloped made it easier to reach, but it would still be a stretch for her. Jordan might be able to jump that high, but Stella had never mastered the art.

"I can't reach that," she said.

Jordan smirked at her before leaning down, his fingers lacing together to form a foothold.

She blinked. "You can't be serious."

He gave her an exasperated look. "I didn't think you were serious about working together, and yet here we are."

"You'll drop me."

"Every word out of your mouth only tempts me further."

She hissed at him. "I feel the need to remind you that we're on my side of the border. One scream, and you are a dead man."

He bared his teeth. "I'll shoot you before you draw in a breath."

Stella mockingly drew in a breath. Jordan had both of his revolvers out in a flash, spinning them by the trigger guards before leveling them at her chest.

"Try me," he snarled.

"You're awfully cocky, thinking you can get away with that." She examined her nails. "I could take you in a fight any day."

"Is that what you did a few minutes ago?"

She dropped her hand, unwilling to give a response. "We have to find Silas before his meeting is over."

Jordan smirked and offered his hands again.

Scowling, Stella stomped over to him and planted her boot into his awaiting hands. She braced her arms on the wall as Jordan rose to his full height, grunting as he lifted Stella high enough for her hands to grip the window ledge.

"As much as I'm enjoying this view," he said, his eyes roaming over the lower half of her body, "could you hurry this up? You aren't as light as you look."

She glared down at him before hauling herself over the edge. One last push from Jordan gave her all the traction she needed to make it up. She drew her gun as she surveyed the empty room, the door that was slightly cracked.

She glanced down to see Jordan backing up several steps. He sprinted for the window, kicking off the wall and launching himself into the air. His fingers gripped the ledge. Stella gritted her teeth as she grabbed him by the wrists and hauled him through the window.

They exchanged a dark look. Stella smoothed out her shirt as she stepped around the massive bed that dominated the room, using the moonlight to navigate. The barrels of Jordan's revolvers flashed as he trailed after her. She felt even more nervous about allowing him to walk behind her with his guns drawn, but aside from starting a fight that would surely get them caught, she had no other choice. She hated Jordan—hated what his mere presence did to her—but she held her tongue. Silas threatened the very foundations of her gang. He was the bigger threat at the moment.

The adjoining hallway was silent when Stella eased open the door. On one end was a doorway; the other disappeared down a flight of stairs. She headed in that direction, her steps nothing but a whisper against the floor. Sometimes business meetings were held in the back rooms downstairs. That had to be where Silas was now.

Perfumed smoke drifted through the hall, causing Stella to wrinkle her nose in disgust. "Do you know who Silas is meeting with?" she asked Jordan in a whisper.

"Just some of his friends from Stokes. I didn't get names."

"His boss?"

"I don't think so."

They eased down the stairs. The main room held tables upon tables of customers. The floor was a plushy red carpet that masked Stella's steps as she skirted around the edge, hiding behind the thick curtain of smoke. She was counting on everyone either being too preoccupied or drunk to notice her and Jordan slipping off together. She could only imagine the rumors that would spread if they were spotted.

There were three rooms in the back. One door was closed tight, light shining through the crack. Voices came from beyond. Jordan pulled Stella into one of the empty rooms, wincing as the door creaked shut behind him. She was already pressing her ear against the wall, listening intently as Silas' nasally voice drifted to her.

"...both have their strengths," he was saying. "They're evenly matched."

"But which is better?" a male voice pressed. "The boss wants a report."

"He'll need to wait a little longer if he wants to make a wise choice. These gangs are too dangerous to experiment with."

Stella froze as she realized he was talking about. She snuck a glance at Jordan but he ignored her.

A woman now interjected. "He's going to want more than that."

"Indeed," Silas said. There was a rustle of paper. "Which is why I'm sending information. The plan will work. In fact, the longer I stay here, the more tensions will rise between the gangs. Lochridge will tear itself apart long before we have to. If we keep this up, the gangs might kill each other and spare us the trouble. Tensions were already high before I got here."

There were a few beats of silence. "They know what they're doing," the woman remarked.

They must be reading whatever papers Silas brought. Papers with sensitive information, no doubt. Stella's mind whirled as she wondered what, exactly, was written on those pages.

Silas would *pay*.

The man grunted. "We'll be back in a week, Tradow. For your sake, I hope this plan works."

Silas' answering laugh was chilling. "Of course it will work. All we need is patience, and we can bring Lochridge to its knees."

CHAPTER 10

It took every bit of self control Jordan possessed to remain hidden in that room, to not burst through the door and confront Silas as he bid farewell to his companions and departed. He made himself wait another three minutes before daring a peek outside.

The room next door was now empty.

"It's clear," he said.

Stella breezed by him, braid swinging. "I believe we're clear on his intentions now."

It was a bad idea to work with her, the girl who hated him and was hated in return. His father would be livid if he found out he hadn't taken the chance to kill her. They'd been alone in a dark alley, an opportunity if there ever was one. But they had a common goal, and he couldn't bring himself to end the tentative truce between them. Silas was the bigger threat at the moment.

Lochridge will tear itself apart long before we have to.

He ran a hand through his hair. "What should we do now?"

"Kill each other?"

"I was referring to Silas."

"Of course." She gave him a condescending smile, but it slipped. "We should tell our fathers. They didn't listen before, but they might now."

He raised a brow. "Oh, yes. They'll love to hear that we worked with the child of their worst enemy to eavesdrop on the businessman they're obsessed with."

"You really call this working together?"

"It's better than shooting each other."

Her lips twitched. "Don't tempt me with a good time."

Jordan crossed his arms, then said, "This will only work if we get both to decline Silas' deal. If your father drops out, mine will jump on the chance, and I imagine it's the same the other way around. We need to convince them to talk to each other."

"Getting them together will be impossible."

"Silas did it."

"Silas dangled something shiny in front of them and got lucky," she said flatly. "What happens if they don't believe us?"

He gave her a lazy smile. "Dear Daddy won't listen to you?"

Her eyes slitted. "Watch your mouth, feathers."

Jordan opened his mouth to say something else, but the curtains that served as a partition between the back rooms and the main dining hall swished. Stella grabbed him by the arm and hauled him into the room, kicking the door shut and wrenching the lock with her free hand. They moved quickly but not quickly enough, for a loud banging sounded on the door.

Stella and Jordan exchanged a wide-eyed look as a man yelled, "I saw you two come back here! These rooms are for business—the ones upstairs are for horsing around. Get out of there!"

Jordan whirled, looking for an exit that wasn't there. He was in the middle of White Rose turf with no escape. Stella rolled her eyes at him. "Get a grip, Daelik," she hissed, unbraiding her hair.

He watched as she undid her braid, her dark curls flowing down her back as she expertly tousled them, one hand undoing the top few buttons of her dark shirt. She stripped off her belt of weapons and tossed it to Jordan before going to the door, where the man threatened to break it down.

"Stay back," she said to Jordan. Then she opened the door.

Jordan couldn't see whoever it was, but he could see Stella as she leaned against the doorframe, only opening the door itself a fraction of an inch. She looked the man up and down. "Can I help you, Martin?"

He stammered. "Oh, Miss Rook. I didn't realize it was you."

"I know which rooms are for what," she snapped. "Whatever you may think, I *am* conducting business back here." She angled her head, her hip jutting out in a pose that was nothing but sensuous. "I'm almost done. He won't want long. Leave us be and make sure there's a clear way out of here in five minutes, or else my father will pay a visit."

"Of course, Miss Rook," Martin blurted. Jordan had the distinct feeling he was soaking in the sight of Stella Rook with her hair mused and her cleavage showing before Stella slammed the door in his face.

She turned to look at Jordan, and he found himself soaking in the sight of her as well.

"Impressive," he said.

"Martin's a fool." She caught him looking. "And you are, too."

"Can't a man look at the beauty in this world?"

She barked a laugh as she snatched her weapons back. "You find me beautiful?"

"I think every man who's ever visited Lochridge has found you attractive, Rook." Jordan hooked his fingers in his belt. "But you already know that."

Stella glared at him as she tied her hair back.

Jordan continued, "You know, if Silas gets his way and annihilates the Roses, I might convince him to cut you a deal if you come work for me. I bet things can get very interesting after hours."

Her amber eyes narrowed. "I sent Martin away, but I can sure as hell call him back if I need to."

His answering smile was crooked. "I'm just letting you know the offer stands, little thorn."

"Big words coming from someone with such a small—"

"Watch it," he snarled.

Stella matched his smile. "Oh, can't take an insult? And here I thought you were tougher than that, feathers."

It was his turn to glare at her. Stella finished knotting her hair at the base of her neck and flung open the door without a word. Jordan trailed after her as she sauntered through the now-empty building. Martin had done his job, it seemed.

The two of them paused at the door.

"Tomorrow at high noon," Jordan said.

She arched a brow. "Are you challenging me to a duel?"

"We'll get our fathers to the meeting place at high noon."

"And how do we do that?" she demanded.

He wrenched open the door. "Figure it out."

Stella let him walk out first. She followed a few minutes after. By then, Jordan had already taken refuge in a nearby alley, watching through slitted eyes as she glanced around—looking for him?—then set off toward her home. Jordan stared after her for a long time before turning on his heel and stalking into the Ravens' territory.

There was rarely an occasion on which Stella had reason to be angry with herself. But she was furious now, fuming as she laid in bed with her hands fisted in the sheets.

She was mad at herself for ever suggesting to work with Jordan Daelik in the first place. Now she had to get her father into the bar across the city at high noon without telling him the real reason.

And she was also angry at Jordan Daelik. For many things.

Dawn light peeked through the gauzy curtains. Stella gave up the ruse of sleep with a sigh. She'd come back before high moon, slipping into her bedroom without trouble, but hadn't slept a wink in the time since. She dressed silently, tugging on an off-white dress that accented her fair skin, combing through her hair and pinning it back with a few practiced movements.

The curtains swirled around her as she pushed open the balcony door, stepping out into the cool morning air. She took a deep breath, finding her solace in the sparkle of the ocean in the distance, in the melody of the songbirds she tried and failed to replicate on the piano.

Her hands gripped the railing. She could do this.

With her mind set, Stella headed downstairs.

The Rook house was a flurry of activity. It wasn't just the immediate family that lived here—beyond Stella and her parents, Harvey and Zoey lived here, alongside a slew of cousins, aunts, uncles, grandparents, and in-laws. It was a big house, but Aunt Melonie just gave birth to twins, and with the family gaining a new member every week, Stella was feeling suffocated in her own home. She pushed through the early-morning ruckus in the kitchen and escaped to Marcus' office.

Her father sat in his usual place behind his desk, pen in hand. His light gray suit was immaculate as always, the gray streaks in his hair looking more pronounced in the light. He was busy; before the gang took up all his time, Marcus was a businessman, dealing in merchandise of all kinds. John Daelik's textile company was still running strong, but Marcus had laid down his own business in favor of overseeing those in his territory, pulling their strings from the safety of his office. The diversity of his operation garnered a lot of money for their family, but it kept him busy. Stella closed the door behind her so quietly that he didn't notice her presence until she scuffed her boot on the ground.

Marcus' head snapped up. "Stella. What's the matter?"

She slid into a chair. "We have a problem."

His brows furrowed. "The issue with the Red Harbor? We've got it under control. This isn't something with Harvey, is it?"

"What issue with the Red Harbor?" Stella demanded, her mission abandoned for the time being.

"Big scuffle there last night. The sailors got into it with some merchants from the Ravens' side of the line. The sheriff had to drag himself out of bed to deal with it." He waved a flippant hand. "I sent some of our people down there this morning to establish connections with the unhappy sailors."

She knew what that meant. Marcus would offer the sailors a deal, giving them whatever they hadn't gotten out of the Ravens in exchange for their loyalty. Preying on their high emotions from the night before to slide his chip into place. Stella leaned back in her seat. "As nice as it is to know I'm the last to hear about this—"

"You're not. I only got the message a few minutes ago, and you're the first I've told."

That warmed her. "We have a bigger problem than that, actually. Silas."

Marcus shuffled the pages on his desk. "I've told you, we've got Silas handled."

"I followed him last night."

He stared at her. "To where?"

"To the Barter Streets where he was meeting with some friends from Stokes. He discussed the situation with Lochridge."

She had his attention now.

Stella smiled. "W—*I* didn't get to hear much of the conversation, but it sounded like he's planning something different than what he's told you and Daelik. I think he wants to get rid of both the gangs. I—"

"Hold on," he said, lifting a hand to silence her. "I never told you to follow Silas."

She blinked. "I didn't realize I needed permission."

"With him? Yes, you do." Marcus shook his head. "We're in a tense situation, Stella. I'm handling it, but I have a very specific plan, and it only works if everyone does their part. Did Silas see you?"

She bristled. "You know better than to ask that."

"This time you got away, but you've been caught before and you can be caught again. What would have happened if he saw you? That would have instantly taken favor away from us."

"That's the point," Stella insisted. "This whole deal with Silas and the Ravens... we're all so focused on *his favor* that we're not seeing the real problem. What do we know about Silas? His intentions? The conversation I overheard last night... It didn't pan out a bright future for anyone involved. If this man has an army big enough to take out an entire gang, then that makes him *dangerous*. Can't you see that?"

Her father didn't even deign to look at her as he rummaged around his desk. "We have nothing to worry about."

"Yes, you do. Back out of the deal."

"I can't, not without Daelik taking it up."

This was her opportunity. "Then talk with Daelik. Convince him it's in both of your best interests to drop the deal and kick Silas out of town. If both of you back out, then Silas has nothing to work on, and you two can console yourself in the fact that the other gained nothing."

"But we gain nothing also."

"Gaining nothing is better than losing everything," she snapped.

Marcus slapped a hand down on the desk. "Stella, enough. You are suggesting that I go to John Daelik"—he snarled the name—"and convince him to drop out of this deal because my daughter had a whim?"

But Daelik's son had a whim as well, she thought. "I am suggesting that you be the bigger man and put an end to this madness before it costs us all dearly."

Anger sparked in Marcus' amber eyes, and Stella knew she had spoken wrong.

"Don't you ever," he growled, "speak to me like that again. Do you understand?"

"But—"

"*Do you understand?*"

Stella froze. No, she didn't understand. How could he be so blind? What about Silas could he not resist? Her father was acting like a madman.

Continuing this argument was an uphill battle, so Stella lowered her head. "I understand."

Marcus relaxed. "Good girl."

The door opened. Stella turned to see her mother hovering in the threshold, her eyes wide as she looked between them. "I thought I heard yelling."

"Nothing that hasn't been resolved," Marcus said smoothly, shooting Stella a glance that warned her to say nothing.

Evelyn nodded distantly. She'd been distracted ever since Melonie's twins were born. Stella rose out of her seat and mustered a smile for her mother. Evelyn returned it and brushed a hand down Stella's back as she passed.

Stella waited until she was in the safety of her room before slumping against the door. No, nothing had been resolved. Her father was brushing aside the problem because he thought he could handle it. Which meant Stella was on her own.

Not entirely.

She glanced up at the clock ticking away on her nightstand. There were a few more hours before she was supposed to bring her father to the meeting place. Marcus wouldn't be coming, but surely she could work a deal in his stead? If she got Daelik to drop the deal, it would be easier to get Marcus to follow suit.

Unless Jordan had as much luck convincing his father. In which case they were screwed.

"Rats," Stella spat, kicking the bed frame.

If her father wouldn't handle this, she would have to take matters into her own hands.

CHAPTER 11

Jordan sat alone at the table, a bottle and a glass resting in front of him. He poured himself a healthy amount of the amber liquid and knocked it back, relishing in how it burned down his throat.

He was still drinking when the door opened and Stella Rook stepped in. Alone.

Her eyes swept across the room, marking the empty chairs around the table where the monthly meetings were held. Then her gaze landed on Jordan. "No luck?"

His only response was a long sip. John hadn't even let him speak once the word *Silas* left his lips. His father didn't want to hear his opinion. End of discussion.

Stella cursed under her breath. "Me neither."

Jordan refilled his glass, the bubbling of liquid the only sound in the room. "What are we going to do?"

She ran a hand over her hair, disrupting the pins holding it away from her face. "Apparently nothing."

"That isn't an option."

Her eyes flicked to him. "You don't order me around."

He put the glass down. "Silas was at my house again today. Talking to my father. Asking about the expenses of his company. I had to drag Pa away just to ask him about meeting Marcus, but I couldn't even get the words out before he shut me down. Our fathers aren't listening to us, which means we're going to have to do this ourselves."

"That might be the whiskey talking."

He studied the bottle in front of him. "Might be. But it's the truth."

Stella sighed and reached for the bottle. Whether it was to take it from him or have a sip of her own, Jordan didn't know, but he held it out of her reach all the same.

"Careful," he snapped. "This stuff is expensive."

"No, it isn't. I have an uncle who drinks it."

He didn't relent. "Well, it's mine."

"You sound like a child."

"I just got through being scolded like one, so I guess that makes me even."

"Daelik," she said, exasperated. "Do you want to get Silas out of town or not? Because if you do, then you need to stop getting drunk and actually be useful for once."

"For once?" he sneered. "How about *you* do something useful instead of trying to degrade me?"

Stella planted her hands on her hips. "I'm not the one with a bottle in my hand."

He placed it back on the table with a petty smile. "Neither am I."

Her eyes—the same color as the whiskey—flashed. "I'm not playing games, Daelik. I came here alone because I thought I could convince John to drop out of the deal, which might make my father think twice about it. But neither of them are here. It's just you and I. If we are really this concerned about Silas, then we need to get him out of this city."

"I'm not playing games, either," Jordan spat. "But do you really expect *this*"—he gestured between Stella and himself—"to work?"

She crossed her arms. "I expect us to at least try."

He barked a laugh. "I thought we didn't order each other around."

"Sober up and we'll try again."

Jordan looked her dead in the eye and knocked back another drink.

Stella narrowed her eyes. "You came here alone, too. And you brought a drink. Meaning you have something on your mind that you want to forget about for a little while. You never expected Marcus to show up—otherwise you wouldn't have gotten yourself drunk." She braced her arms on the table. "You realize what we're dealing with."

"A crazy businessman from a mysterious group wants to take over our town." Jordan lifted his glass in a toast. "And don't forget his creepy daughter."

"You don't like Celia?" Her tone was faintly amused.

"She hung back to talk to me, and that's when I knew for sure Silas' intentions weren't golden." He crossed his ankle over his knee, drumming his fingers on the table. That incident still haunted him. Not what had been said as much as the way Celia said it, the way her pale blue eyes locked with his. It still sent a shiver down his spine. He took another sip of his whiskey to wash the feeling away. "Nobody else was around to see it."

"My family won't listen to me, either," she said, more to herself than to Jordan. "Which means I'm alone."

"I'm here," Jordan drawled.

"You're drunk. And I don't trust you not to kill me."

He gave her a slow smile. "Now why would you be worried about that?"

She gave him a flat look in return. "Last night, when we followed Silas? I was debating if it was proper etiquette to shove a knife in your back." She smiled, showing all of her teeth. "Every. Single. Minute."

"Oh, please. It's not like you could take me."

"Care to place a wager?"

"Sure. We can duel afterwards."

She sniffed. "This is nothing but bold words from a drunk man."

"I could take you in my sleep," Jordan said. "You Roses are weaklings, living out on your farm with your fancy fence and your garden flowers. Do you really think all those roses will protect you if an attack comes?"

"I hear the thorns are rather sharp."

Jordan casually drew one of his revolvers. "I hear my guns are sharper."

She eyed it warily. "Put that away."

"Don't boss me around," he snapped.

"Then stop acting like a child and pull yourself together," she fired back.

Jordan's glass hit the table with a thump as he rose to his feet.

"Insult me again," he snarled, cocking the gun. "I *dare* you."

Stella lifted her chin. "I refuse to stoop to your level. I thought maybe you and I could work something out, but that obviously isn't happening, is it?" A smirk danced across her lips. "You just can't keep yourself in control long enough to do so."

Jordan moved around the table so quick Stella barely had time to blink before his gun was against her head. But before he could pull the trigger, she drew her own weapon and leveled it right between his eyes.

"Don't play games you can't win," she said softly.

The heirs stood face-to-face, neither of their guns wavering as they locked eyes. Jordan's finger tightened on the cool metal trigger of his prized revolver. The whiskey might be muddling his thoughts, but he was damned well aware enough to feel the anger burning through him.

This bitch really thought she could order him around. Jordan had to admit to himself that his anger wasn't entirely directed at Stella; a good portion of it had sprung up at his father's quick dismissal of his concerns. Of his refusal to even let Jordan speak.

"This isn't a game," he hissed.

"But you're treating it like one." Stella tilted her head, her gun remaining firmly in place. "So why don't you stop toying around with me and actually get serious?"

"I am serious."

She arched a brow. "You're pointing a gun at my head with no intention of shooting it, because if you were here to kill me, you would have done so already."

"We're on neutral ground," he growled. The sheriff wouldn't do much if one of them died in their territories, but shots fired on neutral ground would start an investigation. With tensions already running so high in Lochridge, the sheriff poking his nose into his father's business was the last thing Jordan needed.

And from the smile on Stella's face, she knew it.

"Lower your weapon," she said.

With a growl, Jordan retracted his arm. Stella lowered her arm, too. He waited until her shoulders relaxed before he struck, slamming the butt of his gun against her wrist. She cried out as her gun tumbled from her hand, hitting the ground just as he lunged.

Jordan might not be able to kill her, but he could certainly hurt her.

The two heirs went down in a tangle of limbs. Stella spat a curse as Jordan came out on top. Her hand shot out, her nails digging into his face as she tried to claw his eyes out. Jordan batted away her arm with a snarl, pressing his gun against her temple while his other hand went to her throat.

He smirked as she clawed at the hand sealing off her airway. "I'm thinking this was a mistake."

"*You're* the one thinking that?" she wheezed.

His fingers tightened. "You don't get to waltz in here like you own the rutting place and order me around." His lip curled. "You Rooks think you're on top of the world. You walk through this city with your fancy clothes and higher-than-heaven attitude and act like the rest of us don't see right through it."

"It's called dignity." Her voice was weak. "You should try it some-time."

"And you should learn when to keep your rutting mouth shut," he snapped.

Her eyes gleamed. "Big words from someone with a knife in his gut."

Jordan didn't have time to process what that meant before he felt a stab of pain in his abdomen. He looked down to see Stella plunging a tiny blade into his gut. The sight shocked him enough that his hand loosened, allowing Stella to twist under him, throwing him off-balance.

He hit the ground and rolled, coming up on his knees. Stella scrambled after him. He grunted as the Rook heir punched him in the face.

Pain burst across his cheek, but he gritted his teeth and lashed back. His revolver whipped across her face, sending her stumbling back, cursing wildly. He lunged and grabbed a fistful of her hair. She shouted and clawed at his face again. This time, her sharp nails found their target, digging deep enough to draw blood.

Jordan released her and surged to his feet, his steps unsteady. Stella panted as she stood up as well.

"Not so high and mighty now, are we?" he rasped. Stella's hair hung in her eyes, which burned with amber fire. Her shirt was ripped, bruises forming on her throat, blood dripping from the gash the barrel of Jordan's gun had left. Her cheeks flushed red when he looked at her. He smirked as he twirled his gun around. "Looks like I messed up your pretty face."

"I'll rip your throat out," she snarled.

His answering grin was bloody. "I'd love to see you try."

Her eyes narrowed as he lifted his revolver. Stella's pistol was across the room, her knife buried in Jordan's side, leaving her defenseless.

"The sheriff will skin you alive if you do that," she said.

He angled the gun. "Don't worry, little thorn. I have a bullet with your name on it that I'm saving for a special occasion."

Her eyes shifted to the doorway, looking for a way out. Jordan's smile widened.

"Scared?" he crooned.

"Never," she said, but it sounded half-hearted.

Jordan laughed and stepped aside, forming a clear path to the doorway, even going as far as to lower his gun.

"Go ahead," he invited, waving to the doorway. "You're free to go. Run off with your tail between your legs like the coward you are."

She wiped the blood from her face. "One of these days, your comments will catch up to you." Her eyes settled on his. "And I will be waiting."

And with that, she walked out the door.

Jordan waited until her footsteps faded away before holstering his gun. His gaze snagged on the whiskey he'd abandoned on the table. He grabbed the bottle and took a long sip.

It hadn't been wise to bring the whiskey. Attacking Stella Rook on neutral ground hadn't been wise either, but he blamed that on the drink addling his mind.

Jordan let out a hiss of pain as he pulled the knife from his stomach. The thing was tiny, no longer than his pinky finger, the blade so thin it was more of a needle than a dagger. After a moment, he realized it wasn't an actual knife—it was a *hairpin*. Granted, one that had been sharpened enough that a slight scratch was enough to draw blood, but still enough to make Jordan's brows rise. He couldn't remember when in the fight Stella had pulled it out, but even he had to admit it was effective; he didn't think it had caused egregious amounts of damage, but it had been enough to distract him in the moment.

"Well played, Rook," he said aloud, admiring the pin.

Then he cast it aside and gulped down the rest of his drink.

CHAPTER 12

A motorcar was parked outside of Stella's house when she walked up. It was such an unusual sight that she paused for a moment to admire its sleek black exterior, the rubber wheels that were so unlike the wooden wagon wheels she was accustomed to. Last she heard, Harvey had started a bet on how long the car would survive. Not one participant thought it would make it over two weeks.

Her heart drummed against her ribs. The fight with Jordan had left her disheveled, so she snuck in through the back and made it to her room without being spotted. Cleaning herself up was a different story altogether. It took half an hour to fix her hair after Jordan grabbed it, her scalp sore enough to make her wince as she brushed it through. She cleaned up the gash marring her cheek. There wasn't much she could do about the necklace of bruises ringing her throat, but she applied some makeup to lessen their potency.

Stella couldn't help but smile as she slid her hair pins back into her loose braid. She'd pulled one out so smoothly during the fight that she didn't think Jordan had even seen it. That fight had, of course, left her short of one pin and her favorite gun, but she nicked a spare weapon from Harvey's room and strapped it on as she squared her shoulders and marched downstairs.

Marcus was holding court at the head of the dining room table, a wooden monstrosity of stained pine, the edges carved with intricate designs of thorny vines choking people to death. Stella used to trace her fingers along the designs as a child, her mother having told her the people depicted were laughing instead of screaming. Evelyn now sat to Marcus' right. Silas sat on the other end, Celia at his side. Tobias kept a watchful eye from behind him. Several of the other members of Stella's family took up the rest of the table, leaving no room to sit.

So she leaned against the doorway, holding a staring contest with Tobias while she waited for the others to notice her presence.

It wasn't that the others were that oblivious—Stella moved like a cat, her feet silent, her movements agile and precise. Evelyn called it a dancer's grace. She had pushed a young Stella to join the children's ballet class. Stella went to exactly one session before finding the teacher unfavorable. It had been on her way out that she heard someone playing the piano from another room and demanded that Aunt Melonie teach her to play.

"I really would like to learn more about the Red Harbor," Silas said. "I was told it was neutral ground—"

"The Harbor is out of our jurisdiction," Marcus confirmed. "But our people trade there often. Ravens and Roses alike find work as hands down there. It's a lucrative business, but the sheriff has decreed that no one from the feud is to own it. Keeps trade intact, he claims." He shoveled a forkful of Evelyn's famous scalloped potatoes into his mouth. "It's a bunch of bullshit, but we respect the sheriff. He lets us get away with a lot, but we don't want to disrupt him so much that there is cause to find a new one that might be worse."

"The Ravens have a bigger hand in the local law enforcement," Stella added from the doorway. "A new sheriff would likely be in their pocket."

Everyone at the table started, having not seen her. Brows rose as they took in Stella's appearance. Tobias only shook his head.

"Stella," Evelyn said, a warm smile on her face. That was rare. She must like Silas, then, which didn't bode well for Stella's plans. The smile faltered a little as she took in the bruises, but she did well at hiding her surprise. "Join us?"

"She can't," Marcus cut in. "Zoey and Harvey went down to the border. There's a skirmish going down. Four Ravens on our side." He angled his head at her. "I wanted you to oversee, but you weren't here."

"I was busy," Stella said smoothly. "Where?"

"West side of the Barter Streets." His eyes narrowed. "Where were you? You look..."

He didn't dare finish the comment. "You should see the other guy," she said, already kicking off the door.

Silas cleared his throat as she walked out. "So, who owns the Harbor?"

An attempt at conversation—and a dive for information. Stella gritted her teeth and kept walking.

It didn't take long for Stella to track down her cousins. The skirmish was long over, a blood-splattered Harvey nursing his split knuckles while Zoey paced the cobblestone street. A pool of blood formed red lines between the stones.

"What happened?" Stella demanded.

Zoey paused her pacing. "A few Ravens got over the border and stirred up trouble. We got them back over to their side." She cocked her head. "What happened to *you?*"

"Fight gone wrong, but I handled it." She crossed her arms, nodding at the Ravens' territory. "Anyone we know?"

"I didn't recognize them."

Good. That meant it hadn't been Jordan Daelik or any of his cronies. Stella glanced down at Harvey. "They really did a number on you."

He gave her a low, cruel smile. "I'm afraid you look worse than I do, cousin."

A lone civilian ambled past. He caught sight of the three of them and stared, his eyes going wide. Harvey let out a low snarl that had him scrambling for cover.

Stella glared at her cousin. "How many Ravens were there?"

"Three," Zoey answered for him.

Her eyes narrowed. "Father said there were four."

"We only saw three. The other might have skipped out."

Stella turned to scan the street. "What were they doing?"

"They looked like dealers, but they ran off before we could confiscate anything."

Drug dealers. The slimy little rats. They were higher up on the chain of command in Lochridge's black market, and notoriously hard to catch. Stella's hands curled into fists as she turned in a full circle, surveying every inch of the street.

She tried one last question. "Where were they going?"

"They were coming out of that store over there," Harvey snapped, jerking a thumb to a shop behind him. "Are you done with the interrogation? We'll already have to say all this to your old man."

She ignored him as she marched towards the store in question. There was nothing unusual about the quaint little boutique, but dealers often met with potential customers in the most unsuspecting places. A bell rang as she pushed open the door.

A lady behind the counter gave Stella a tight smile, but she ignored her as she scanned the racks of clothing. "We already checked the store," Zoey said, coming up behind her. Indeed, the lady at the counter was giving Zoey and Harvey a wide-eyed look, shrinking back as if she'd already endured one visit from them today.

Stella needed to be on her father's good side. She *had* to if she wanted any shot at covering up what she was doing behind his back. Her insistence on kicking Silas out of town had gotten her in trouble, so now her goal was to get back into Marcus' good graces—and Silas' too. She needed to get close to him, to Celia, for nothing else but to monitor them, to see if they slipped up or misspoke.

The first step of getting back into Marcus' favor would be to do whatever he told her without question—and then going a step beyond.

Which meant she needed to find the fourth dealer.

Stella ignored both her cousins and the lady behind the counter as she marched through the store, shoving aside racks of clothing. A small part of her admired the clothes—ball gowns and dresses of all colors and shapes, the bright fabrics glittering in the light coming through the window—but she shoved that thought down. She had more important things to do.

Though that didn't stop her from making a mental note to return to this boutique later.

She searched the entire storefront, only to find nothing. Zoey gave her a look, her brows raised. Harvey just rolled his eyes.

Stella went to the lady at the counter. "Is there a back entrance to this store?"

She blinked at the blunt question. "There is, but it's hidden. You—"

"Where?"

The lady pursed her lips and led Stella to the nearby wall, pulling aside a rack of dresses to show her the door. "Here," she said, trying the knob and blinking in surprise when it twisted. "It's supposed to be locked."

Stella shoved by her before the words could leave her mouth. The door opened up to a dark alley that ran behind the main street, the passageway narrow and damp. A smile curled over her lips as she took in the man huddled in the corner, counting coins in his hand.

He glanced up and cursed.

"I found him!" Stella shouted, but he was already running. Stella drew a knife and gave chase, her arms brushing the sides of the alley as she ran.

He made a sharp turn, his boots sliding on the slick cobblestones. Stella grabbed the corner of the wall and used it to direct her momentum. She gained another few inches on him, her hair flying behind her as she sprinted after him.

She risked a glance over her shoulder to see no one was there. Where in the bloody hell were Harvey and Zoey?

Light poured in from overhead. The dealer burst out onto a main street. Stella chucked her knife as hard as she could, but she had never been able to throw well while running and her aim was far off. He let out a triumphant shout as he cleared the line of buildings.

Only for it to turn into a scream.

Stella skidded to a halt to see Harvey and Zoey flanking the exit to the alley—the only outlet. Harvey's knife was buried to the hilt in the dealer's shoulder, the coins he'd been holding scattered everywhere.

She grinned. "I knew it."

"You were right," Zoey agreed. Even Harvey begrudgingly muttered an agreement under his breath as he let the man slide off of his knife, sending him to the ground with a spray of blood.

Stella smirked at him as she planted one boot on top of his chest. "Next time," she crooned, "you'll know better than to run." The tip of her boot dug into his injured shoulder. "Strip him of everything he's worth and dump him back on his side of the border."

Marcus seemed pleased with Stella's tale of what happened. He was even happier with the pile of gold she placed on his desk—profits straight out of John Daelik's pocket.

"Good work," he said, counting the coins. He didn't ask what she'd been doing earlier today, for which Stella was grateful. "You just missed Silas. He left a few minutes ago."

She'd heard the rumble of his motorcar on her way in. "My sincerest apologies, Father."

He gave her a rueful smile that told her he picked up on the sarcasm before shooing her out of his office.

She ran into Evelyn in the kitchen, her mother stirring a pot over the stove while sneaking glances at the recipe book propped up on the table. "It smells good," she remarked, snagging an apple from the bowl next to her. "What are you making?"

"Soup." Evelyn dumped some chopped greens into the pot. "And there's bread in the oven." She glanced at her daughter. "What happened?"

Stella's face throbbed. "Nothing I can't handle."

Evelyn pursed her lips but changed the subject. "How did it go with Zoey and Harvey?"

"Fine. We caught a dealer." Stella leaned against the table and took a bite from her apple. "You seem to like Silas."

"He's a nice man. His daughter I could do without, though."

"She's a brat," she muttered.

Evelyn patted her shoulder. "You were raised better than her, Stella. Don't allow yourself to stoop to her level just because she makes you angry. I heard about the incident with the piano the other day."

Stella gave her an innocent look. "What, you mean my plan to *accidentally* let a piano fall on Celia?"

Her mother shook her head. "This is your father's doing," she said, brandishing a wooden spoon in Stella's direction. "He's made you into a monster."

The grin she flashed her only furthered her point.

Evelyn grinned back, one of those rare mother-daughter bonding moments that Stella cherished. Sure, it was because of their mutual wish to dump a piano on somebody, but bonding was bonding, right?

Stella finished her apple. "Do you need some help?"

Evelyn's smile turned softer, as if she, too, recognized this for what it was. "I would love that."

CHAPTER 13

The roar of a crowd greeted him as Jordan pushed his way into the bar. He fought through the throng to get a glimpse of the commotion, cursing under his breath as he realized what was happening.

A brawl had broken out in the center of the bar. Two men were wrestling on top of the broken remains of a table. Jordan didn't know the redhead with the nose that was gushing blood, but he recognized the blond-haired one with the bloody knuckles.

Declan.

A hand fell on his shoulder. "It's me," Mateo said before Jordan could draw his revolvers, his voice raised to be heard over the ruckus. "The other guy started it. I think he might be a Rose." He did a double take as he took in the bruise on Jordan's jaw. "Who marked you up?"

Jordan shrugged. "No one special."

The worst of his injuries were hidden under his shirt. He'd gotten the family doctor to stitch him up, slipping him an extra coin to keep quiet about it. Jordan didn't need his whole family knowing about the fight. A bruise could be explained away easily enough; a stab wound, even if it was small, would garner unwanted questions.

He didn't want his family knowing about his meeting with Stella. Explaining it would mean explaining how they had run into each other in the first place, which would mean admitting to his father that he'd passed on the opportunity to kill her, and also that he'd been eavesdropping on Silas. Jordan didn't think his father would approve of either, so he kept his mouth shut.

His gaze returned to the stage. Declan's tattoo flashed as his fist came into contact with the man's face, sending him sprawling. Both of them were drunk, disastrously so, but Declan had the advantage of being drunk all the time, having long since figured out how to remain functional underneath the haze of alcohol.

"This is his third fight of the night," Mateo said, drawing Jordan's attention. "He's doing good, too."

His usual clothes were messier than usual, his shirt unbuttoned and his dark hair unruly. His gray eyes had a glassy quality to them that had warning bells going off in Jordan's head.

He narrowed his eyes. "Don't tell me you're drunk."

He cocked a brow. "Drinking, not drunk." He waved a hand at an empty seat by the bar. "But my end goal is in sight."

Jordan clenched his jaw. "No more. I need you two, and I already have to wrangle Dec away from this fight."

"But it's just getting to the good part," Mateo protested.

"Pa sent me. We have a job."

His eyes went cold. "Oh."

Jordan fought back a sigh. This was going to be one hell of a night.

He elbowed his way to the front of the crowd just as Declan aimed a drunken kick at his attacker. Jordan winced as he caught a blow to the chin. He really wasn't in any condition to help, but John had insisted that Jordan take him and Mateo despite his protests. He hadn't thought either one would be any count given recent events, but he was disappointed that they'd still fallen short of his expectations.

The redhead punched Declan, who stumbled back. Jordan took advantage of the distance between them and jumped onto the table.

He grabbed Dec's arm. "We've got a job. Let's go."

Declan slid an irksome gaze to him. "Can't you see I'm in the middle of something?"

The redhead tried to slip past Jordan, but he shoved him off the table, sending him sprawling.

"We have better things to do," he said to Declan. "Pa's orders."

He didn't give his cousin time to respond before jumping off the table, dragging Dec with him. Mateo waited by the doorway, brows raising as Jordan marched outside, Declan stumbling along beside him.

More Ravens waited outside. None of them were pleased to have been pulled away from their nightly activities for a job, but Jordan was beyond caring. His mind was too focused on Silas to think much of anything else.

"You seem angry," Declan remarked, taking a swig from a bottle. How he'd even gotten his hands on the drink, Jordan didn't know, but he smashed it on the ground nonetheless.

"Shape up or ship out," he hissed. "I don't know what's gotten into you lately, but Pa's going to be furious if he finds out you're acting like this. Not to mention what Dan will say."

Declan sobered up at the mention of his father. "I don't give a shit what he thinks."

"Well, the rest of us do," Jordan snapped.

He had the good sense to look ashamed. Jordan raked an angry gaze over him before turning to the Ravens.

"We've got an investigation," he said. "A shipment of weaponry went missing from the stockhouse on East Lane. My father put a lockdown on the border until the weapons are recovered. There are six crates of guns and ammunition that need to be found before any of you are allowed to go home." Many of them exchanged glances, their mouths twisting in distaste. Jordan narrowed his eyes. "Do we have a problem with that?"

"It's late," one muttered. "This isn't an emergency. It can wait until morning."

His head jerked up as Jordan grabbed his shirt.

"It is an emergency," he snarled. "If those weapons make it out of our territory, we won't see them again. I don't want Marcus Rook to get guns and ammo for free, and if you have any care of making it through the night with your head intact, then you will get out there and find them." He shoved the Raven back. "Understood?"

He looked down. "Understood."

"Good." Jordan raked a gaze over all of them. "The hell are all of you standing around for? You have your orders—now *move!*"

They burst into action. Jordan's eyes remained on the Raven who'd spoken out as they went down the street. He risked a glance back at the heir before turning to his companion. His voice was too low to hear, but Jordan could see his sneer plain as day as he jerked a thumb at him and made a snide remark.

Jordan's vision flashed red, and before he could restrain himself, his gun was out of its holster.

The Raven dropped before the gunshot could finish echoing over the street. The others paused, eyes wide as they beheld their companion on the ground with a hole in his skull.

Jordan bared his teeth as he lowered his smoking gun. "Does anyone else have a problem?"

They all shook their heads, too scared to speak.

His lip curled. "Then get moving. If those crates aren't recovered by morning, I'll have all your heads."

The Ravens scattered, leaving Jordan alone with Declan and Mateo. He didn't give either of them time to talk before storming off in the opposite direction. They had a lot of ground to cover and not a lot of time to do it, because if they didn't find those crates, John would have *his* head.

"You're pissy," Declan noted, trailing after him.

Jordan's fist clenched. "I've got better things to be doing than wrangling dissenters into place."

He shook his head, his pale gold hair flopping over his brow. "That's part of it, Jordie."

"I also have better things to be doing than controlling my drunken family members."

They both winced. "Sorry," Dec muttered.

He fixed him with an icy stare. "I get that you have shit going on that you don't want to deal with. But I am sick and tired of having to pull you out of bar fights. Your pa already hates your guts, and whether you give a shit what he thinks or not, you still have a duty to this family that requires you to be sober at least some of the time." The words came out a touch harsher than Jordan intended, but they needed to be said all the same. He loved Declan like a brother. He couldn't stand by and watch him waste away. Mateo flinched as Jordan turned to him. "Same goes for you. People say shit about us all the time. You can't just disappear for days because of it."

Both of them looked at the ground. Jordan felt bad enough that he ended his lecture and focused on the street in front of him.

John had said the crates had been missing for two hours at the most. He'd put the border on lockdown the moment he heard about it. There was a chance the weapons were already long gone, but Jordan had a feeling they were still nearby. They turned off the Barter Streets and headed deeper into Raven territory, passing several of John's office buildings. Jordan's hands flexed at his sides as he watched the street.

They walked for half an hour without seeing anyone. A lone wagon rumbled by, which wouldn't have struck Jordan as suspicious until he realized how late into the night it was.

He paused and looked over his shoulder. "Who the hell was driving that?"

Dec tried to stop but ended up stumbling several steps forward before finally bringing himself to a halt. "No clue."

Heavens above, he wasn't worth a shit in this condition. Jordan sighed. "Let's question him."

They jogged after the wagon. The driver noted them coming and Jordan raised a hand to signal him to stop. But he just snapped the reins and kept going, faster this time.

Mateo's eyes narrowed. "I think we found the weapons."

They skidded to a stop, Declan tripping into Mateo. Jordan whipped out a revolver and gave himself the briefest of moments to aim before shooting the driver clean out of his seat. A body hit the cobblestones, and the horses reared up in panic, giving the trio all the time they needed to reach the wagon. Mateo threw back the tarp, revealing six large wooden crates with the Raven symbol stamped on the side. Other merchandise was nestled in between, cigars and playing cards and at least a dozen bottles of Declan's favorite brand of whiskey.

Jordan cocked a brow. "Well, that was easy." He saw Dec reaching for the booze and shot him a look that had him quickly backing away.

It took them a few minutes to track down the scrubs and order them to return to crates back to the stockhouse and to clean the two bodies off the street. Jordan raked a glare over all of them, reminding them of exactly how useless they'd been during the job. By the time they got the crates hauled back to their proper place, Declan was barely coherent and Mateo was trying his hardest to keep him standing upright.

Jordan folded his arms over his chest as he looked at his cousin. "This is pitiful."

He slumped against Jordan for support. "Is there someone else with you, or am I seeing double?"

Mateo scowled. "You're seeing double."

Dec grunted.

Jordan glared as he dragged him down the street. Mateo supported his other side, and the three of them stumbled out of the Barter Streets. Jordan had planned on getting rip-roaring drunk himself after finding the crates, but he supposed that would have to wait until he got home. He'd lock himself in his room with a jar of moonshine and call it a night.

Declan was barely conscious when they shuffled into their house. Jordan winced when he saw the lights were still on.

"Let's get him upstairs," he hissed to Mateo.

They hauled Declan towards the stairs, but a voice from behind them had them freezing.

"What is this?"

Jordan cringed as he turned around. "Uncle Dan."

Declan's father crossed his arms as he surveyed the three of them. Declan had inherited his late mother's blonde hair and wild spirit, but he had Dan's green eyes and muscular body.

"What is this?" Dan demanded again.

Jordan gulped. "Someone attacked Declan."

"Bullshit. He got drunk again, didn't he?"

The silence that followed was answer enough. Dan sneered at his son, who was mercifully unconscious, sparing him from a lecture. Uncle Dan was more uptight than Jordan's father was. He'd been on the receiving end of his lectures enough time to feel sorry for his cousin. Declan didn't act like he cared about what his father thought of him, but he drank enough to suggest that it bothered him on some level.

Dan shook his head in disgust. "He's a disgrace to this family. Get him out of my sight."

It took all of Jordan's willpower to not snap back with a retort. He gritted his teeth and nodded. Dan shot one last glare at Declan before storming into the kitchen.

He sighed. "This is a mess."

Mateo grunted in agreement. "He's going to get himself killed or disowned."

"Stop talking about me like I'm not here," Declan grumbled from between them. Not unconscious, then; he must have been pretending to spare himself from a lecture. "Can we go upstairs?"

"Can you stop getting sucked into every fight you come across?" Mateo snapped.

He narrowed his eyes. Jordan suppressed a groan and dragged him upstairs, Mateo lecturing him the entire way. They dumped him in his bedroom, and Jordan refrained from slamming the door on his way out.

"I've got enough on my plate with Silas without having to wrangle him," he bit out under his breath.

Mateo crossed his arms. "How'd it go with Silas, anyway?"

"He's already visited with Rook, apparently. Both gangs still want the alliance. And he's got a daughter that I really don't like." He glanced at Mateo. "But you would know all that if you'd been here yesterday."

He shrugged. "Didn't feel like hanging around."

"No kidding." He raked a hand through his hair. "Rook shouldn't have started that."

"What's done is done."

"It's not your fault—"

"I know it isn't," he said, more forcefully than Jordan was used to. "But it won't stop everyone from rubbing it in my face, so if you wouldn't mind, I would love it if we didn't talk about it."

Mateo was giving him a look so cold it reminded Jordan of his father. He was quick to change the subject.

"What's your hit off of Silas?" he asked.

He tilted his head. "He's weird. But if he's really offering this alliance..."

"He's offering it to the Roses, too."

"This will go our way. We're a hundred times better than the Roses." He grinned. "Even our name is better. Silas will realize that soon enough, and then we don't have to worry over the feud any longer."

He frowned. "We're taking a huge risk. I don't trust Silas."

"Well, we trust the Roses even less."

Jordan bit his lip. That was true to an extent—they might be at each other's throats, but the Daeliks and the Rooks both cared about keeping Lochridge safe. Or their respective halves of it, at least.

"I'm worried about it," he said. He felt bad not telling Mateo about his fight with Stella, but he couldn't afford anyone to know. Not when it would require explaining so much. Right now, the only thing he had on the Silas front was a bad feeling and a conversation they eavesdropped on.

Lochridge will tear itself apart long before we have to. And before long, we won't have either gang to deal with.

Jordan's throat bobbed.

Mateo clapped him on the shoulder. "Don't be. Pa's a smart man. He'll find a way to spin this to his advantage no matter what way it goes."

Jordan offered his half-brother a faint smile. Mateo might not be his full brother, but he had never thought less of him because of it. It wasn't *his* fault their father had slept around with that barista, nor was he to blame for his birth causing a disruption between John and Lillian that lasted until Lana was born. Mateo evened out their group; Declan was wild and Mateo was level-headed, providing a good balance for Jordan to work with.

"Yeah," he said distantly. "Pa will know what to do."

He left Mateo to look after Declan and retreated to the attic, where he locked the door before pulling a half-empty jar of moonshine out from under the bed.

Stella Rook. He hadn't been able to get the name out of his head. Hadn't been able to get his mind to stop going back to the incident three years ago, when he'd shot Liam Turner and heard Stella's cry of rage echoing across the Red Harbor. That scream—it had been sorrowful, heart-wrenching, carrying every bit of pain that Jordan had inflicted upon Liam before he died.

He sipped the moonshine. He shouldn't feel bad about that incident. It had been his father's orders. Jordan had done it out of loyalty to his family, to his gang.

But he still thought about it. Still reeled every time his mind wandered to Liam or anyone else that he'd interrogated. It had been easier to feel good about it when his every interaction with the Roses was an unpleasant one, but working with Stella last night hadn't exactly been terrible.

Today, however, had been awful enough that he didn't feel so bad about it. His grip around the jar of moonshine tightened.

"Cheers," he said to the empty room, and knocked the entire thing back.

CHAPTER 14

Declan was still asleep at high noon, so Jordan took it upon himself to burst into his room and chuck a glass of cold water in his face. He spluttered awake with a series of curses loud enough to make Lana peek her head out of her bedroom, her eyes wide.

"Dec's grumpy," Jordan said to his sister. He quickly shut the door to Declan's room, even as he cursed Jordan soundly and promised revenge.

"No kidding," she said, tucking a book under her arms as she came to watch the show. "Did he get in another fight?"

"Naturally." He winced as there was a thump from Dec's room, followed by the rattling of the doorknob. "Get out of here before that monster figures out how to work the door."

The door swung open. Declan—shirtless, bruised, hungover, and sopping wet—glared at them. "I heard that."

"Good. Your ears still work." Jordan shoved him. "You're lucky I waited until your father was gone before I got you up. You look like shit."

He had the good sense to wince as he raised a hand to probe a nasty bruise along his jaw. "It was worth it."

"Was it?" he demanded. "We needed you last night, but you couldn't even walk in a straight line. You're turning into the Harvey Rook of our family."

Declan's jaw clenched. He hated Harvey with a fury; to be compared to him was the lowest of insults, but Jordan thought he deserved it. He and Mateo were tired of hauling him back home, avoiding Dan, and cleaning him up so he was presentable the next morning. Declan was his closest friend besides Mateo. He would risk his life to save him, but Declan needed to take on at least *some* responsibility.

"Get dressed," Jordan said. "I'll get you some coffee."

Declan grumbled and kicked the door shut. Jordan got a glimpse of his bare back before the door closed, and as always, he was taken aback by the pale scars criss-crossing over his shoulder blades, so faint it was hard to tell if they were there. No matter how many times he and Mateo had asked, Declan had never revealed where they came from. The door slammed before he could get a good look, and Jordan exchanged a glance with Lana before filing down the narrow stairwell to the kitchen.

Lana slid into a chair around the kitchen table. "What are you going to do?"

"About Declan?"

"He's going to get himself killed," she said matter-of-factly.

He chuckled as he slapped a coffee percolator onto the stove. "What's going to happen is he'll get himself in one too many fights, then *Dan* will kill him." He dumped water and coffee grounds into the percolator and set it to boil. Most everyone had gone out for lunch, leaving the kitchen—and the rest of the house—blessedly empty. "We need to get him off the drinks."

"Good luck with that."

Jordan glanced at his sister. Her thirteenth birthday was in a week.

He turned back to the stove. "Has Pa talked to you recently?"

"About what?"

He shrugged. "I don't know. The Ravens? The feud?" He glanced at her again. "You joining the gang?"

Lana blinked. "He wants me to?"

"No, I—" Jordan raked a hand through his hair. "I was helping out when I was younger than you. I'm surprised Pa hasn't roped you in already. Don't get me wrong, I'm happy for it. You don't need to be exposed to that. Not now and not ever." He leaned against the counter. "I was just wondering if he's tried to talk you into it at all."

She shook her head, one hand coming to rub her left wrist, which hadn't yet been adorned with a raven tattoo. "No, he hasn't."

"You tell him no if he does," he said harshly. "I'm not letting my little sister get pulled into the feud."

Lana scowled. "It's not your decision to make. What if I want to join the Ravens?"

Jordan moved so fast that Lana barely had time to blink before he was leaning over her. "Listen to me," he hissed. "You do not want to join the Ravens. Not unless you want to learn how to kill people, how to cut them up to get information out of them, how to hate half of the people in the city." He grabbed her shoulder. "Everyone in this family accepts the feud with open arms. I sure do. But you are innocent, Lana-bug. I don't want to see that change. Pa can't force you to do anything. I think Ma would leave him and take you with her before allowing that to happen. But if you agree to join, if you get that tattoo on your wrist, there is no going back."

Lana stared at him, her gray eyes, the same as their father's, stretched wide. Jordan felt bad for scaring her, but if that is what it took to keep her out of the feud, then he was more than willing.

Especially with Silas in town.

"Do you understand?" he asked quietly.

She nodded, trembling as she scooped up her book and darted out of the room, refusing to look at Jordan.

"You didn't have to be so harsh," Declan said from the doorway.

Jordan ignored him as he checked on the coffee, his thoughts swirling. Lana would probably avoid him for the rest of the day. He didn't blame her. He'd even take a lecture from both his parents if it meant she would refuse John when the time came.

He handed Declan a cup of coffee and made one for himself. "Are you feeling better?"

Declan grunted as he claimed the seat Lana abandoned. "Do I look like I'm feeling better?"

No, he did not. He'd dried off and put a shirt on, but his wet hair still hung in his eyes, which were bloodshot and tired. Jordan hid his frown behind his mug. "You are going to have to handle this. Dan was livid last night. When you two are at it, it causes tension in the house, and when there's tension here, Pa takes it out on everyone but those who deserve it."

Declan winced. John took out his anger in the worst of places, yelling at Lana or Lillian over matters with the Rooks and slaughtering Roses whenever there was trouble at home. It was his way of dealing with problems and Jordan doubted they'd ever be able to shake him from it.

"Get it under control," he said, sipping his drink. "Mateo and I are tired of dealing with the backlash. We've got enough on our plate with Silas to have to worry about you."

Declan relented with a faint nod. "This thing with Silas. Mateo mentioned it last night." He cocked his head to the side. "Do you really think he's capable of taking out one of the gangs?"

"He wants to. I don't know if he has the ability to, but it's not wise to underestimate him."

He snorted. "He's a fool, Jordan. A fool with a bunch of money and not enough sense to keep it hidden." He raised his mug. "Mark my words, he'll be mugged by the end of the week—if he hasn't been already."

Jordan's jaw clenched. "You only saw him one time. The meeting the other day... He was different. Colder. More confident." *Crueler*, his mind whispered. And that was just the meeting in his father's office—nevermind the conversation he eavesdropped on with Stella. *That* was enough to make Jordan's stomach do an unpleasant flip every time he thought about it. "I never had a great feeling about him, but it got worse." He shivered. "And don't even get me started on Celia. That girl is *cold*."

Declan raised his brows. "Who's Celia?"

"Silas' daughter. She's about our age."

"Is she pretty?"

Jordan bared his teeth. "*Declan.*"

"Sorry, sorry." He raised his hands in mock surrender. "You can't blame a guy for asking. I might get lucky."

Jordan studied the bruises on his face. "With the way you're looking right now, I severely doubt it."

He picked up a spoon and studied his reflection in it, unable to hide his slight wince. Jordan shook his head. The bruises would take time to fade. They spread from his jaw up his cheekbone on the left side, a smear of blue and purple. His eye was swollen. There was a scratch over his brow that would probably leave a scar. Jordan knew it hurt something fierce, but it was his own damn fault for getting into a bar fight in the first place.

How Declan lived his life jumping into every fight he came across was beyond Jordan. Make no mistake; John Daelik's son had been in plenty of fights himself. He didn't become Lochridge's sharpshooter without cause, and the faint scars on his knuckles didn't come from nowhere. But *living* for a fight? Starting them without cause? That was Harvey Rook behavior, and Jordan would not stand to see his favorite cousin reduced to the role of the family psychopath.

"Get it under control," he said again, then walked out.

CHAPTER 15

Lana wasn't in her bedroom when Jordan stopped by the next day to make amends. The fact that Lillian or John hadn't cornered him yet meant she had kept their conversation to herself, but she was avoiding Jordan like the plague. He checked all of her usual haunts, but she was nowhere to be found, probably curled up somewhere with a romance novel.

Sighing, Jordan vowed to talk to his sister later and headed out the door.

It was just past high noon, still a while before nightfall, but Jordan headed down to the beach early with his sketchbook tucked under his arm. He was determined to make the most of his secret place by the ocean before night fell and made it too dark to see. He walked by the Red Harbor, heading down the slope to the wall of rocks beyond it. The rocks seemed to cut off this section of the beach from the ocean, but Jordan expertly slipped between them, picking his way through the hidden pathway to the tiny stretch of beach on the other side. There wasn't much to see. It was high tide, leaving only a sliver of sand to walk on, but it was hidden, and quiet save for the crash of the ocean against the shore and the occasional caw of a raven in the distance. It was peaceful, his sanctuary among a city of bloodshed and chaos. Perfect for sketching.

Jordan nestled against his favorite rock. It was shaped just right to form a seat, his back at a nice angle and his legs propped up, the sketchbook in his lap and a pencil in his hand. He flipped to his newest work of art. It was a portrait of his family. He'd done several before, but they had been years ago, leaving Lana as a young child, and he thought it was time for an updated version. He lowered his pencil to the page to shade in the side of Declan's face.

Jordan had always possessed an artistic streak. It drove his father crazy, who believed his heir should be more focused on how to fight than how to draw. As a result, Jordan was a skilled warrior and Lochridge's best sharpshooter, but that hadn't stopped his passion for sketching, which his mother had quietly nurtured behind his father's back. Drawings lined the walls of Jordan's room, papers pinned to the wall that were filled with sketches of everything from birds in flight to the sunset over the ocean to portraits of his sister to a realistic drawing of a raven that he was rather proud of. John hadn't been up to Jordan's room in so long that he didn't think his father even knew about them.

The wind picked up the salt-tinged air and blew it in Jordan's face, rustling the pages of his sketchbook. He didn't pay it any mind, too focused on his work. This was his time, his passion. The one place where his father and the feud couldn't reach him.

It wasn't that Jordan was against the feud. Marcus Rook was an asshole, plain and simple. He'd screwed over Jordan's father so many times that he'd lost count, and the Rook family as a whole consisted of pretentious, self-absorbed brats that snubbed their noses at the southern half of the city. Harvey was the most violent person Jordan knew, Zoey was known for breaking the heart of every man she came across, and Stella…

Stella was a different story altogether.

Jordan had never been against the idea of the feud. The Rooks had wronged his family too many times, and he was more than happy to get his revenge. But that hadn't stopped a part of him from reeling at the bloodshed, from feeling sick over the sheer amount of violence the feud had caused. He never understood why John and Marcus had thought it was a good idea to involve outsiders in their spat, why they had formed entire gangs and carved out sections of the city to call home, why they had involved their entire families in it.

He never understood why his father made him do some of the things he did. Why he had to interrogate Roses and enforce codes and do so much dirty work. It was for that reason he didn't want Lana anywhere near the gang—he didn't want to see his sister stripped of her innocence, worn down by brutality like Jordan himself had over the years. He might not have the courage to bring his doubts before his father, but that wasn't going to stop him from protecting Lana with everything he had.

Jordan sketched until the sun dipped below the horizon, the rocks casting deep shadows over him. He squinted at the page as he used the dying light to hurriedly finish off the picture. When he was done, he leaned back and admired his work.

He glanced up at the darkened sky, the stars just visible. Now it was time to get to work.

No one looked his way as he slipped onto the street, his dark clothes helping him to blend in amongst the shadows. The neutral territory where Silas stayed was on the northern end of the city, only accessible by going through White Rose territory. Jordan made it over the border without being seen by the guards on duty. He smirked as he wound his way through the streets.

He wasn't as familiar with Rose territory as he was his own, but he'd walked through these streets enough to know where he was going, to know how to slip past patrols and prying eyes. Even so, he let out a sigh of relief as he crossed onto neutral ground. His body ached all over from his fight with Stella, and he hadn't exactly felt like brawling with some Rose guards for being on their turf.

Silas' hotel came into view. It wasn't anything fancy, a simple three-story building with a crumbling facade, but it was the nicest place to stay on neutral ground. Jordan crouched in the shadows, watching the door, but his eyes involuntarily slipped up to the rooftops on the far side of the street. Stella Rook had been up there last time. He couldn't count on her just giving up; she trusted Silas just about as much as he did, which wasn't much at all. The last thing he wanted was to run into her, so he drew deeper into the shadows, monitoring the rooftops as much as the hotel.

He hid there for hours. He was just about to stand up and stretch his aching legs when the front door swung open and Silas strode out. Once again he was trailed by Tobias but not Celia. Jordan wasn't particularly upset about that; the girl unnerved him. Well, the whole trio did, but Celia most of all.

Jordan pushed off the wall and followed on silent feet, this time taking care to remain out of sight from anyone that might be lurking on the rooftops. A few times he thought he heard a noise up there, perhaps the scuff of a boot against the shingles, but he couldn't see anything. He hoped it was just his overactive imagination as Silas stepped over neutral ground and back into Rose territory.

Going back was dangerous, but Jordan didn't have a choice. After the last conversation he was privy to, there was a sinking feeling in his gut that told him Silas was nothing but bad news. He had to find something, anything that stood as evidence to convince his father that Silas' intentions weren't good.

Even if it made his skin crawl to be on White Rose ground.

Silas didn't take the same path as last time, this time aiming for the western end of the Barter Streets. The buildings pressed in around them, creating deep pools of shadows that Jordan took advantage of. His eyes narrowed as Silas slowed in front of a bar. It was a lot nicer than the last one, clean and neat and a fine representation of what establishments on Rose territory typically looked like. Silas nodded at Tobias, who held open the door as the two of them slipped inside.

Jordan waited until he was sure they wouldn't come back out before approaching the bar. It was late enough that the Barter Streets were mostly empty, but he still came at it from the back to avoid any passersby.

There was a back door, but when Jordan tried the handle, he found it was locked. Grumbling under his breath, he dug through his pockets. He ended up pulling out the hairpin Stella Rook had stabbed him with—which he had kept after all, hoping to one day repay the favor. As it turned out, a pin sharpened to such a fine point it was as good as a knife made for an excellent lock pick, and Jordan had the door unlocked within a minute. He smiled to himself as he threw it open.

But his smile slipped as a voice rang out from behind him.

"Funny to see you here, feathers."

Jordan whirled, dropping the pin in favor of his revolvers. Stella Rook angled her head at him. She wore her usual smirk, but there was something colder about it, an ice in her eyes that he hadn't seen since the months after Liam's death. It was enough to make him stop short, his fingers hovering over the triggers.

Stella eyed the guns. "Go ahead, Daelik. Shoot."

He narrowed his eyes. "I didn't realize you had a death wish."

"I don't." She tossed her hair over her shoulder. "But the fact you

102

haven't shot me already tells me you're too much of a coward to do so. And I don't like having cowards on my territory." Her gaze snapped to the left. "Get him out of here."

Jordan didn't have time to react before a figure bolted from the shadows and slammed into him. A grunt slipped out of him as his back hit the wall. He managed to keep a grip on his revolvers, but in reality, they were no use to him. His presence had already summoned the Rook heir and whatever heathens she'd brought along with her; firing a gun would bring every Rose close enough to hear it. And this close to the border, that would be a *lot* of people that weren't on Jordan's side.

He twisted, breaking away from the grips of the two Roses that had come at him. He reeled in his shock when he realized they weren't the only two; Stella was now surrounded by a small army of Roses.

Her smirk seemed more genuine this time. "I had a feeling you would try something, so I brought reinforcements."

Jordan's eyes narrowed as Zoey and Harvey appeared on either side of her, the former aiming a gun at his face, the latter flashing a wicked smile that had his stomach churning.

She had known. The bitch had *known* he would stake out Silas' hotel again—and she'd guessed that Silas would return to the Barter Streets, cutting through White Rose territory to get there and providing a perfect opportunity for her to catch Jordan on the wrong side of the border. Jordan gritted his teeth as he surveyed his options. His cover was blown, that was for sure. It wouldn't matter if he shot now. But he was outnumbered and outgunned, and with Harvey Rook giving him a hungry look that suggested he was ready for blood, Jordan didn't feel too confident about his chances in a fight.

It was time to change tactics.

Jordan gave Stella a lazy smile as he holstered his guns. "We aren't far from the border, Rook. I would *love* for you to guess how many people I've got waiting on the other side, ready to pounce the moment there's a gunshot."

"Good thing they won't hear one," Harvey drawled, drawing his knife.

But Stella stuck her arm out, stopping Harvey mid-stride. "What is your business here, Daelik?"

He raised a brow. "I think you already know, little thorn."

"I am going to give you five seconds to get your ass over that border," she snapped, eyes narrowing at the nickname. "The only reason I'm not killing you now is because I have better things to be doing."

He didn't miss the way her gaze shifted behind him as she said that. Stella was here for the same reason he was—to get information from Silas. Picking a fight, no matter how one-sided it was, would mean alerting Silas of their presence, blowing the entire mission for them both.

Stella might not want Jordan to get any information, but she didn't want to lose her shot at figuring out Silas too. He hated that, but right now, it was the only thing going in his favor.

"That's a shame," he crooned, hooking a finger in his belt. "I was looking forward to another fight."

If Stella was still hurting from their last encounter, she didn't show it. In the dark, Jordan could just make out the bruises marring her neck, the gash on her cheek.

Her eyes narrowed. "I would be careful with what I say if I were you."

"It's a good thing you aren't me, then."

The corner of her lips curled upwards. "Indeed." Jordan tensed as she signaled to her men. "Get him out of my sight before he can cause any trouble," she ordered.

His answering smile was wicked as he stepped toward Raven territory. "I'm trouble aplenty, little thorn. But you don't control me. If you want me to leave, all you have to do is ask nicely."

Harvey snorted. Zoey narrowed her eyes. Stella only lifted her chin. "Get off my territory."

Jordan sucked on a tooth. "That's not nice."

"Allow me to rephrase, then. Get off my territory, or I'll pump you full of lead."

Oh, she really wanted him gone. His smile widened. "You're mean, Rook."

Her eyes narrowed to slits. "Please?"

Jordan grinned. "There you go."

The Roses fell back as he tucked his hands into his pockets and sauntered by them, Stella glaring daggers at him the entire time. It was an effort to keep up a nonchalant presence when his heart was pounding against his ribs so violently he was surprised the others couldn't hear it. Jordan was knee-deep in shit right now, trapped on the wrong side of the border with half the Roses surrounding him, no help in sight. The only thing going for him was the presence of the person he trusted even less than the Rooks. If it weren't for Stella's desire to eavesdrop on whatever conversation Silas was having right now, Jordan would have been a dead man five minutes ago.

The other Roses didn't seem happy about letting Jordan go. Harvey looked downright pissed. But Stella's eyes were still on the building, and Jordan had the distinct feeling that she hadn't told them about her true purpose here.

And maybe it was that realization that had him leaning close to the Rook heir as he passed by.

"For someone who was so keen on getting our fathers to work together," he murmured in her ear, "you sure are hellbent on making sure I'm in the dark on this situation." He smirked. "You knew before you came that I would be here—and you knew exactly why."

Stella met his gaze. "If you hadn't attacked me, we might be having a different conversation right now."

The conversation was so quiet that only the two of them could hear it. Jordan lowered his head. "Maybe so. But the fact remains that if you keep this up, I'll be forced to do the same."

"That would put us at a stalemate, Daelik." She smiled. "At least this way, one of us is getting what we want."

Jordan huffed a laugh. "If this was turned around, and I found you on Raven territory... I wouldn't hesitate to kill you. You're a coward, Stella Rook."

She leaned closer. "And you're a filthy degenerate, Jordan Daelik. Good luck getting back into Rose territory. I know to expect you now."

She pushed him away. Jordan smirked down at her before backing away, trying to uphold his confidence, ready to pull his guns in a moment's notice. None of the Roses dared to go against Stella's orders by attacking him. Harvey seemed to be the only one inclined to do so, but Zoey kept a firm hand on his shoulder, a silent reminder to fall in line.

Jordan didn't dare put his back to them until he was sure they were out of sight. Then he turned on his heel and ran across the border, not stopping until he was well within the confines of his territory. Anger swirled through him, hot and vicious, furious that he'd once again allowed *Stella rutting Rook* to get the upper hand.

He glared over his shoulder as if he could still see Stella smirking after him.

Two can play this game, Rook, he thought. *And I intend to win.*

CHAPTER 16

Stella Rook wasn't afraid of showing her distaste towards something, no matter who it offended, which is why she didn't hesitate to wrinkle her nose as she walked into the restaurant. She liked to think that her side of Lochridge was nicer than its southern half; the Rooks were certainly more proper than the Daeliks most of the time. *Most of the time* being any circumstance when her cousins were not involved.

But the sad truth was that Lochridge as a whole was a bloody, filthy, crime-ridden city. Perhaps some establishments in Rose territory were a touch nicer than their Raven counterparts, but the grand majority of businesses were just as seedy as the last. This restaurant was no exception. It was the same place where Silas had gone the first night Stella followed him, and it hadn't improved in the days since. The dim lighting made it hard to see, several couples taking advantage of the shadows that gathered in the corners, perhaps thinking that Stella couldn't see them as they kissed each other with a tad too much passion to be casual. The place reeked of whiskey and cheap perfume. Normally Stella wouldn't have dared to step foot into such a dirty place, but she had the unfortunate luck of having business here today. She could only pray that she could get this wrapped up quickly, for the foul air was putting her into a foul mood, and she couldn't do anything if she couldn't hold herself together.

So she squared her shoulders and marched inside.

It was fairly busy for this time of day. Her eyes scanned the crowd, picking out Harvey's familiar dark hair. Her cousin lounged on a bench in the corner, a glass of red wine dangling from his fingers and women hanging off him. His hair was tousled, his shirt one button away from being undone, and there was a soft, wicked grin on his face that had his entourage leaning closer with lustful expressions.

The sight was enough to make Stella's stomach flip. She didn't enjoy seeing *any* man parading himself in front of a flock of women, much less one that shared her blood.

Stella stood there awkwardly, her tongue stuck in her mouth as she tried to find a way to break up Harvey's party without infuriating him. Perhaps the real problem she had with this restaurant was the fact that it served as Harvey's favorite haunt. Thankfully, the girl sitting in his lap noticed her presence and nudged Harvey's shoulder.

His amber eyes narrowed, his easy demeanor vanishing. "What are you doing here, cousin?"

The words were laced with danger. Stella crossed her arms. "I need you."

"You *need* me." Harvey drew out the words, quirking one brow. "I never thought I'd hear those words out of your mouth."

She gritted her teeth. "I'm suspecting more trouble at the border tonight. I want you to oversee a patrol to make sure none of the Daeliks pull anything."

What she wanted was for Harvey's presence to scare off Jordan. Last night's little spat had wasted precious time; by the time Stella got rid of Jordan and then convinced the Roses she brought along that the threat was over and they could leave, Silas had already wrapped up his meeting. The only information Stella had gotten was a vague mention of Stephen Trace, Silas' boss, which wasn't anything new.

Stella intended to find out more tonight, but she couldn't do it if Jordan Daelik was there, too. After their last two encounters, she didn't foresee it going well. But since the Ravens had to travel through White Rose territory to reach the neutral ground where Silas was, that meant she had a chance at stopping Jordan long before he got close.

Harvey made a low noise in the back of his throat. "Are you really trying to drag me out of here?"

He gestured to his admirers. The brunette snuggled up next to him pouted and said, "It looks like it's going to rain tonight. You should stay here."

"And you should stay out of our conversation," Stella said coldly. The girl's mouth fell open, but she was already turning back to Harvey. "I need you."

"Like you needed me last night," he pointed out. "I did you a favor already, cousin. That Daelik rat came over the border and you didn't even let me fight him. I'm not doing it again."

"Tonight you can fight him," Stella offered. "If you run across him."

He raised both brows. "You must be desperate if you're willing to bargain."

"Harvey, please."

He gasped. "Another word I'd never thought I would hear from you. Are we sure this is the real Stella Rook?"

The women giggled. Harvey flashed a lopsided grin, then cocked his head to the side.

"How'd you know Daelik would be there, anyway?" he asked. "What is he up to?"

"I heard a rumor he was planning to scope out our side of the Barter Streets," she lied smoothly. "There was a skirmish there the other day, and our border patrol claimed they saw him. I want to make sure he doesn't get his way."

As she spoke, her gaze wandered to the far side of the room, where curtains sectioned off the back rooms—the same rooms where she and Jordan had eavesdropped on Silas. She wasn't entirely sure of why she hadn't told her family about it. After her failed attempts to bring it before Marcus—first her suspicions after their first encounter with Silas, then her plea for him to meet with John Daelik—she didn't think revealing her meeting with Jordan would go over well. Marcus trusted Silas. If Stella told him that she had worked with *Jordan Daelik* of all the rats in this city, Marcus would throw a fit.

With good reason, too. Jordan was a killer. Stella's stomach did another flip as she thought of Liam, of everything that Jordan did to him. Of the fight the two heirs had just the other day.

She couldn't let him get the upper hand on this, couldn't let him know more about this situation than her. She had to stay ahead of him. And if that meant employing Harvey's services, then so be it.

Stella rose to her full height, looking down her nose at Harvey. "I realize this isn't your cup of tea, *cousin*, but allow me to remind you that you are walking a thin line with my father. If you have any interest in stopping your situation from getting worse, then I suggest you get up, shake off your pride, and do as you're told." She smirked at the girls, all staring at her. "It would be quite the shame to see you stripped of your title. I doubt the ladies will find you as attractive if you aren't a leading member of the White Roses."

His eyes narrowed in a way that she knew meant trouble. Stella lifted her chin, refusing to show a hint of weakness as she held his gaze.

Let him decide if it was worth it to toy with her.

In the end, Harvey must have decided it wasn't, because he removed the arm that was around the brunette's shoulders and rose to his feet. "My apologies, ladies, but duty calls." He gave them a lazy smile as he buttoned up his shirt. "I'll catch you tomorrow night."

A few of them pouted. The rest gave him little waves and wandered off to find someone else to feed off of like the little bloodsuckers they were.

Stella couldn't help but glance at her cousin as he drained his drink and fell into step beside her. "What are you even doing here? Those girls aren't your type."

He frowned. "And what is my type?"

"Dark-haired and unwilling to go out with you." Her mouth twisted. "You like chasing after the people that *don't* want you, not bloodsuckers who throw themselves on anyone and everyone."

He chuckled. "Hard-to-get is a fun quality, I must admit."

"You're sick."

Harvey just laughed again.

The border came into view. Stella slowed.

"I want you to stay here," she ordered, pointing to exactly where she wanted Harvey situated. She thought it was the most likely place for Silas to come through, meaning it also would be where Jordan would come. "All I care about are the Ravens. Anyone else is free to pass."

"And if they don't show?" Harvey asked, crossing his arms.

It was disappointing to think that she went to all that trouble to drag Harvey here only for Jordan to not show up. She picked at her nails, unbothered. "If that happens, then we'll be doing this again tomorrow night."

Harvey scowled. "You can't make me."

"I can and I will. Now get into position."

She sauntered off. Harvey let out a cry of outrage behind her. "Where are you going? You're not just going to assign me here then skip off."

Stella grinned at him. "As much as I would *love* to hang around, unfortunately I have more important things to be doing."

"You said I was leading a patrol!"

"Did I?"

"Stella—"

She waved at him. "I'll see you in the morning, Harv."

Harvey shouted a slew of filthy words that Stella chose to ignore as she flounced away, her steps as light as the breeze.

With that out of the way, it was time to get down to business. Her first stop was to a little dress shop on the far end of the Barter Streets. The shop was closed for the night but Stella had swiped a key and stowed her night clothes behind the counter. She changed as fast as she could in the dark and made a quick escape, her black outfit rendering her as just another shadow in the night.

The hotel was quiet when she approached. She made it to her usual place on the rooftop across the street and settled down. Silas had made his rounds again today, stopping by Rook Manor for a few moments to chat before going to do the same with the Ravens. Stella had no idea if he was still there or not, but the dark windows suggested he wasn't here.

She stayed for an hour, her heedful eyes scanning for movement below, watching for both Silas and the Ravens. At one point a pedestrian wearing a dark shirt strolled by. It took Stella several moments of debating whether or not to attack him before she finally determined he didn't look like a Raven and allowed him to go on his way. Still, she remained tense long after he was out of view, her muscles tight and shoulders taunt, ready to pounce at a moment's notice.

Thunder rumbled in the distance. The hairs on the back of her neck stood on end as she watched lightning dance over the ocean, the storm coming in hard and fast. It felt ominous, eerie. Stella suppressed a shiver. It felt like someone was watching her. She tried to shake the feeling, but a soft noise, no more than the scuff of a boot behind her, had her whirling, her suspicions confirmed as she took in the dark figure towering behind her.

A dark figure with a gun in his hand.

Stella flung herself to the side as a gunshot rang through the air, perfectly timed with another crack of lightning. She nearly threw herself right off the edge of the roof but stopped just in time. Her hair whipped around her face as she lunged to her feet, thunder shaking the ground beneath her.

The rain began to fall as she faced her attacker with slitted eyes.

"Next time," she growled, "you'd better not miss, feathers."

CHAPTER 17

The rain lashed against her face as Jordan stared down at her. "You shouldn't be here, Rook."

"I shouldn't be here?" She barked a laugh. "The only way to *get* here is through Rose territory! This land is as good as ours!"

Jordan titled his head, water running down the bridge of his nose. "For all you know, I went the long way round outside city limits."

"But you didn't."

A crooked smile. "Prove it."

A bolt of lightning streaked across the sky, lighting up Stella's surroundings. She got a split-second view of Jordan's face—his expression cold, his eyes slitted against the rain. "You're never going to make it back over the border," she said, her voice infused with more confidence than she felt. Harvey and all the other Roses she'd stationed at the border should have stopped him on his way through. They'd been given a singular task and still failed spectacularly. She was going to wring their necks the moment she made it back—assuming she made it out alive. "You won't make it far."

"It's a good thing I have no intention of going to the border right now," Jordan drawled. "I'm here for Silas."

"What a coincidence," she deadpanned.

"If both of us are here, then neither of us are going to get what we want. I'm not leaving, which means if you want any hope of stopping Silas, then you need to get the hell out of my way and let me figure out what he's up to."

She put a hand on her hip. "You're a fool if you think I'm going to let you keep all the information to yourself."

He had the nerve to look offended. "I never said I would!"

Stella arched a brow.

Jordan rolled his eyes. "Why do you have to be so pissy all the time?"

"And why do you have to be such an idiot?" she seethed. "Get out of here!"

He clicked his tongue as he spun his gun around. "You can't make me."

Her eyes narrowed as his sing-song tone. "This is my turf, Daelik. You have no right—"

"You're a real bitch, you know that? Strutting through this city like you own the damn place. That first night we trailed Silas, you and I had a moment. We connected. For once, we were heading for the same goal. It didn't last, not that I thought it would, but it was there for long enough that I think both of us realize how serious this situation is." He stepped forward, driving Stella back to the edge of the roof. One more inch, and she'd be over the edge, but Jordan seemed oblivious as he continued his rant. "I want to kill you, Rook. I really, *really* do. And I know for a fact that you share the sentiment."

"You deserve to die."

"Probably true." His lips quirked to the side. "Nevertheless, both of us are unfortunately alive. I want Silas gone. And if you do, too, then you'll be a good girl and step out of the way."

Stella rose to her full height. "Excuse me?"

He shrugged, his eyes lighting in amusement.

Stella was used to insults being thrown at her, and she'd long mastered the art of taking them without batting an eye. But Jordan had a way of throwing all her careful practices out the window. And his *tone*—

Stella gritted her teeth. "I have no intention of letting you waltz in and out of White Rose territory any time you please. It is *my* turf, and you will do well to respect it." This time, she took a step forward, putting her face-to-face with the Raven heir. "You're right that we both want Silas gone. But you're an arrogant bastard with an ego as big as the ocean and a violent streak I hope gets you killed one day. I refuse to bow down to someone who tried to kill me two days ago."

"To be fair," he mused, "you tried to kill me as well."

"Why do you have to be such an annoyance?" she snapped, the words coming out before she could stop them.

Jordan's eyes lost their amusement. "Darling, I want you to realize something. The only reason—and I mean the *only* reason—I haven't killed you already is because in this moment, I know that you have the same intentions that I do. As much as you piss me off, I cannot justify killing a woman in cold blood when she is only here for the same mission I am, which is to protect this city from whatever threat Silas poses." He bared his teeth. "I'm more than an annoyance. I'm a *threat*. And if you don't get that through your pretty little head, then I'm going to put a bullet through it instead."

Stella barked a laugh. "When you put it like that, it almost sounds like we're working together." She leaned close. "You and I don't have the same mission. You're wanting your father to have the upper hand, while I want mine to be ahead. Our intentions might be similar, but they aren't the same, because they're only going to work against each other. Silas can send your Ravens to hell, for all I care. My only concern is keeping my gang—and my *city*—free from harm."

That was a partial truth. As much as Stella disliked the Ravens, she didn't want to see them all dead. They had families—they were husbands and wives and mothers and fathers and sons and daughters. Stella didn't give a rat's ass what happened to the Daelik family, but she also didn't want half the city dead in the street.

She hadn't dared to voice that aloud. Marcus certainly wanted all the Ravens dead, and he would likely frown upon Stella for thinking otherwise.

"I don't want to work with you," Jordan said flatly. "I want you to get out of my way."

"Good luck with that," she crooned.

"Rook, I swear to the heavens—"

"You'll never make it back to your territory alive. I've got half the Roses guarding the border, my cousin Harvey among them." She grinned at the slight twinge of fear that entered Jordan's eyes at the mention of Harvey's name. "I bet you'd *love* to fight him on your way back. If you leave now, I will tell the border patrol to stand down and allow you safe passage."

He snorted. "I got here fine on my own. Your little patrol missed me completely."

Her eyebrow twitched. "I don't think your luck is good enough to do it again."

A slow grin spread across his face. "Why, you would be surprised with the amount of luck I have. Here I am, standing before Lochridge's most coveted woman, and not only is she not actively trying to kill me, but she's actually stuck around long enough to have a conversation with me." He winked. "I'm beginning to think you like me, little thorn. Perhaps we can take this to my place—"

That was her breaking point.

Stella moved so quickly that Jordan didn't have time to react before she was on him, taking him by surprise and knocking him off-balance. His gun went off, the shot ringing in Stella's ears, but it missed her by a wide margin as the two heirs hit the roof, the rain making the shingles treacherously slick. Jordan fired again. She felt the heat on her face, but it only fueled her rage as she clawed her way to the top of the fight and punched him square in the jaw.

"*Never*," she snarled, "make a comment like that again." She hit him again, her hand throbbing in pain from the poor form of her first blow. "You don't get to kill the man I loved and then make these smartass comments about taking me to bed. *You don't get to!*"

Stella was grateful for the rain, the water streaking down her face hiding the tears that spilled over. She missed Liam—missed his laugh, his smile, the way his warm hazel eyes twinkled whenever he looked at her. She missed him, and Jordan had been the one to take him away.

"Damn the feud," she whispered. "Damn Silas, damn everything else. I will murder you in your sleep if you say something like that again."

Jordan swiped his tongue over his busted lip, tasting the blood and rain coating his mouth. "You're cute when you're angry. You remind me of a dog that's gone feral. It's fun to watch."

Stella let out a shout and tried to punch him again, but Jordan caught her arm and bucked his hips, sending her face-first towards the ground. She threw out her hands to stop herself, but by then Jordan had already pushed her off and was rising to his feet.

"You really need to get those anger issues under control," he spat, swiping a hand over his bloody mouth. Lightning lit up his features, showcasing the ire in his eyes with frightening intensity. "It's not smart to take a swing at every person who ticks you off."

The most frustrating part of that statement was that he was absolutely correct, and that only made Stella want to hit him more. She drew her weapon, but Jordan moved fast, grabbing her wrist and pointing the gun away just as she fired. The bullets shattered shingles behind him. Lightning flashed again, so bright that it blinded Stella for a second, the thunder so loud it reverberated in her bones.

Loose strands of her hair stuck to her face as she snarled at Jordan. She was about to throw a barbed insult at him, but movement on the ground caught her attention.

It was three people, huddled together in the rain, making a run for the front door of the hotel. Stella couldn't see their faces, but she recognized Silas' thin and lanky form, Tobias' towering figure, Celia's slender shape.

She whipped her gaze back to Jordan, but it was too late—he'd seen what she was staring at. He released her wrist as he took the three of them in. "Look what the storm washed up."

They dashed into the hotel, all three of them dripping wet. Thunder roared, drawing a small shriek out of Celia, who elbowed her way past Silas to get inside. Jordan's lips twitched in amusement; Stella couldn't hide her own smirk.

Jordan caught her expression with a sly smile. "At least we have one thing in common."

"And what would that be?" she asked icily.

"A mutual hatred for that brat."

Stella pursed her lips as she edged to the side, trying to angle up a better shot. "I don't hate her."

Jordan moved with her, matching her every step with one of his own. "Is that so?"

"I despise her. There's a difference."

"I see."

Her lip curled. "Don't mock me, feathers."

He gave her an innocent look. "But it's fun when you get riled up so easily."

Another flash of movement caught their attention. The curtains that blocked Silas' window were flung open—and a certain dark-skinned bodyguard stared right at them.

Jordan let out a curse. "Tobias sees us."

From this distance, with the rain falling in sheets and both of them wearing dark clothes, Stella doubted he could get much of a visual—but apparently he could see enough to realize that two people holding guns were on the rooftop across the street.

Shit. It hadn't been Stella's plan to be seen by anyone the Tradows associated themselves with. But between their raised voices and attempts to attack each other, Stella realized she and Jordan had made quite the ruckus, especially considering they were on neutral ground where things were typically calmer. She exchanged a look with Jordan as Tobias continued to stare at them.

"I don't think he recognizes us," Jordan said in a low voice.

"But he definitely sees us," she murmured back.

He cocked his gun. "I can line up a shot."

"And kill him?"

"It might drive Silas back to Stokes."

"It might piss him off if you murder his bodyguard."

He sucked on a tooth. "I don't have to *murder* him…"

"Jordan Daelik—"

"I must be in trouble if you're using my full name." His mouth curved into a smile as he spun his gun around. "But it's a good thing that you aren't the boss of me."

And with that, he lifted his gun and fired.

CHAPTER 18

The window shattered. Tobias flung himself back as glass shards rained down. Jordan thought he heard a distant scream and prayed it was Celia.

By the time Tobias made it back to his feet, Jordan was already sliding down the drainpipe and hitting the street at a run. He heard Stella whisper a curse as she fled after him.

"How dense are you?" she whisper-shouted. The words were barely audible in the heavy rain. "Now you've put a target on your back!"

He glanced at her. "And why would you be upset about that?"

It was a genuine question. Stella's jaw clenched. "Because I don't want this *thing* with Silas to get any worse. There's a balance between the gangs that needs to be upheld, because otherwise we all descend into chaos. Silas putting a target on you will disrupt the balance."

Jordan halted, his boots sliding across the wet cobblestones. "That's why you don't want Silas here? Because of the balance?"

"There's a lot of reasons," she said, crossing her arms. "But yes, that would be one of them."

Jordan angled his head at her. "And that's why you haven't killed me, even though you've had the chance. You're afraid of what my father would resort to if his son dies at your hand."

Her eyes sparked. "And you aren't?"

That was a good question. Of course he was afraid of the wrath of Marcus Rook, but Jordan wondered what Stella would think if she found out that John didn't care what happened to him. As long as the dirty work got done, his father was content to let his entire family rot.

"I think you and I are a lot more alike than most people give us credit for," Jordan said finally.

Why was he saying these things? Nothing had changed between him and Stella—they'd done this dance since they were kids. They'd had a thousand opportunities to kill the other but never acted, yet they still hated each other enough to claim they wanted to. Jordan had never questioned it before, but now...

He narrowed his eyes at the Rook heir, her amber eyes full of malice, her dark hair plastered to her face.

Silas was a problem. He thought back to that first day he followed him, when he and Stella had put their strife aside for long enough to work together. That hadn't been all bad. And they had been on White Rose territory at the time, which meant Stella knew the ins and outs of every building there. She had knowledge that Jordan could only hope to obtain.

What if...?

No—that was an insane idea. It would never work.

Still, that little voice in the back of his mind liked to talk.

Stella flipped her rain-soaked braid over her shoulder. "You're mad if you think that." She turned on her heel and stalked away. "Good luck getting back onto your territory. I hope Harvey kills you to save me the trouble."

"Perhaps I'm insane," he called after her. "Or maybe you're antsy because you realize it's true."

Stella's only response was to give him a vulgar gesture as she stormed away.

Jordan laughed to himself, trying to dispel the tension running through him. What a strange situation this was. His father would slaughter him if he found out.

But hopefully he'd never figure it out. That was Jordan's plan, anyway. He could handle this himself. Getting Silas Tradow out of town couldn't be hard, however difficult it seemed at the moment.

Jordan realized with a jolt that he was still staring after Stella. He shook his head, his mind turning to the situation at hand—getting across the border without being spotted. This was the far side of Rose territory; he could get over the main border by going through the Red Harbor, but that still left the rather daunting task of *getting* to the Harbor without being spotted.

He was turning toward the border when he heard a voice shouting behind him. It was hard to hear what was being said over the storm raging around him, but he didn't have to make out the words to know that whoever it was, they were angry. Jordan dove for cover as two figures appeared at the end of the street, water sloshing at their feet as they marched in his direction.

"They can't run forever," the taller one growled. Jordan didn't recognize the voice—it was deep, raspy. "They're around here somewhere. I can feel it."

"Unless you can see them," the other snapped, "then your *feeling* is useless."

That nasally voice... Jordan reared in surprise. It was Silas, swaddled underneath a thick raincoat. It was only then that he was able to place the other man—Tobias, whom Jordan had just heard speak for the first time. The two came to a halt just in front of Jordan, sheltering themselves from the rain underneath the same awning Jordan hid under. He pressed himself into the shadows, his hands slipping down to cradle his revolvers.

"This is madness," Silas muttered, more to himself than to Tobias. "We can't just let some rat shoot out our window and get away."

"This city is like a maze," Tobias grunted. "We'll never find them."

"Well, maybe you should try harder! Why didn't you go after them instead of sitting around like a fat target!"

Jordan was now close enough to see Tobias' eye twitch. "I was trying to see who it was."

"And did you?"

"No." He winced. "It was a man and a woman, both wearing black. From the Raven clan, probably."

"This far from their territory?"

Tobias shrugged. "Perhaps."

Water dripped from the brim of Silas' hat. "Do you think it was the heir?"

Jordan went still.

But Tobias just shook his head. "Doubtful. He's supposed to be a sharpshooter, and if he was aiming for me, he missed by at least a foot."

"The wind could have thrown it off."

Another shake of the head. "I don't think so."

Jordan bristled. He hit right where he intended to, thank you very much. He'd aimed for a vase sitting next to the window and hit it dead on. His intention hadn't been to kill or even harm Tobias; it was to scare him and the Tradows out of town. But judging by the thin line Silas' mouth formed, it appeared his plan had backfired.

"I won't forget this," he said. "We're going to hunt down the culprit and make them pay."

"This city is full of criminals. It could have easily been anyone."

"Then we kill them all," Silas said angrily. "That's practically the plan as it is!" He fisted his hands, twisting to survey the rain-soaked street. "I'm going to find them."

"You mean you're going to send *me* to find them," Tobias said dryly.

Silas barely spared him a glance. "Exactly. And I want you to get to work immediately. Whoever it was, they have a head start. But I have a feeling they'll be back, and that's when we'll strike." His lips curved into a hateful little smile that had Jordan's breath catching in his throat. "This city will be in ruins, but I intend to start with the rat that thinks they can cross me and get away with it."

And with that, he flipped up the collar of his jacket and stalked away, leaving Tobias to trail after him wordlessly.

Declan threw himself onto the couch. "I've been thinking."

Jordan looked up from his sketchbook. "I know that's hard for you to do, but you don't have to brag about it."

Lana giggled from where she was cuddled up next to him, watching him draw. He'd planned to make amends with her but hadn't found the right opportunity yet. He thought she'd been avoiding him until a few minutes ago when she curled up on the couch and rested her head against his shoulder, giving his hand a light squeeze that told him all was well. It had warmed Jordan's heart enough that he'd gotten halfway through his newest sketch in record time.

"You're an assh—"

"Language," Jordan and Mateo said in unison, giving pointed looks to where Lana sat. His half brother lounged in the armchair across the room. His girl Jasmin snuggled in his lap, the two of them looking all for the world like the star-crossed lovers Lana's romance novels were always talking about. Declan glared at everyone in the room.

Jordan laughed as he raised his hands, his pencil dangling from his fingers. "Go ahead."

"I don't want to say it now," he muttered.

"Tell us!" Jasmin said. She was a beautiful girl with raven-black hair that framed her face in soft curls, her deep blue eyes—the color of the ocean rather than the cold ice of Silas' eyes—glimmering with amusement. "We're dying to hear."

"You can all bite my ankle." Declan shook his head. "I was just going to say that there's a new bar on Etcher Street. One of those fancier ones that serve food, too. I thought about all of us going down there tonight." He paused. "Not you, Lanabug."

Lana pouted. "You're no fun."

"Ouch." He turned to Mateo. "What do you say?"

"I was going to study tonight..."

"You study every day. Let's have some fun tonight."

His dark hair shined in the light as he angled his head. "Are you going to get into a fight?"

"No promises, but I'll try not to," Declan said brightly.

Mateo rolled his eyes. "Why not?"

"I'll be there," Jasmin said.

Dec let out a cheer and turned to Jordan. "Well?"

He winced. "I've got somewhere to be tonight."

"Again? You've been busy every night."

"Because there's stuff that needs to be taken care of." Jordan resumed his sketching. "It's my job to make sure things don't get out of hand."

"You need to relax, cousin. Have some fun. A drink or two."

Jordan clenched his jaw. "I'm fine, thanks."

That was a lie. Last night had been a hectic whirlwind. He'd barely made it over the border with his head intact, having been spotted by the guards Stella had stationed there. His father had already gotten two reports this morning that the Roses had increased the number of people on their border patrol, meaning it would be near-impossible for Jordan to get back over there again.

And it hadn't helped that he spent the entire night pacing his room in an attempt to sort his emotions. His footsteps had been loud enough that

Uncle Dan banged on the door in the middle of the night and demanded that he quiet down. That hadn't been a fun conversation, and it certainly hadn't improved Jordan's mindset any.

Even now, he chewed on his lip as Declan and Mateo debated what would be appropriate to wear to the bar tonight. Silas' words from last night still weighed on his mind, haunting his steps. He was glad the Tradows hadn't paid a visit today; he wasn't sure if Silas still considered him as a suspect for the broken window, but he didn't feel like being subtly interrogated. Nor did he feel like interacting with a man who stated that he planned to kill an entire city of people only a few hours ago.

Jordan gripped his pencil so hard it nearly snapped. He wished his father had been there to hear what Silas said. Then he wouldn't be questioning Jordan's distrust towards the man.

But unfortunately for him, there only seemed to be one other person in the entire city of Lochridge that shared his view.

And she hated his guts.

You and I are a lot more alike than most people give us credit for.

Dec and Mateo were still talking, Jasmin watching the exchange with an amused smile. Lana looked like she was about to fall asleep on the couch, so Jordan extracted himself out from under her.

"You're leaving?" Dec asked, breaking from his conversation long enough to raise a brow at Jordan. "Is our company not good enough for you?"

Jordan tucked his sketchbook under his arm. "Excuse me if your ugly face is too much to bear."

"You poor thing," he crooned.

He ignored him as he walked upstairs, mind reeling.

That first night we trailed Silas, you and I had a moment. We connected. For once, we were heading for the same goal. It didn't last, not that I thought it would, but it was there for long enough that I think both of us realize how serious this situation is.

When you put it like that, it almost sounds like we're working together.

Jordan hadn't really thought about those words as he said them, but now he realized their meaning. He halted in his bedroom doorway, his jaw clenched as he stared into the distance.

He didn't trust Stella. He didn't trust Silas.

My only concern is keeping my gang—and my city—free from harm.

Stella at least wanted the city safe. Silas seemed keen on destroying it.

The only reason—and I mean the only reason—that I haven't killed you already is because in this moment, I know that you have the same intentions that I do.

But did he trust the Rook heir more than this stranger?

He gripped the doorway so hard the wood groaned underneath his hand. Neither option was appealing, but he knew what he needed to do.

With his mind made up, Jordan tossed his sketchbook on the bed, strapped on his revolvers, and headed back downstairs.

Dec and Mateo glanced up as he reentered the room. "Well, look who's back," Declan drawled. "You must have looked into the mirror and realized my face isn't the ugliest one in this house."

Jordan leaned against the couch. "Forget the bar. Let's stir up some trouble."

Declan's green eyes gleamed. "I'm listening."

CHAPTER 19

The scents of gunsmoke and fresh rain made for a beautiful combination in Stella's opinion, even if she didn't particularly like the circumstances. The clouds had cleared, leaving the Barter Streets soaking wet as shots rang out. She dove for cover behind the corner of a building. A second later, Zoey and Harvey joined her, the former panting for breath, the latter grinning like a fiend. Blood dripped from a gash on his forehead, only adding to the image.

"What do they want?" Zoey spat, risking a look around the corner. The Ravens had mustered together an impressive group to attack the border in retaliation to the extra guards Stella had stationed there. She'd finally gotten Marcus' approval to secure the border even further. It was a lot of work to keep guards there as it was, and finding extra men willing to do border duty was a task, but Stella had done it, and the number of Ravens that slipped over every day had dwindled down to nothing.

Until the Ravens ambushed the border patrol.

She leaned past Zoey to get a look of the battle, but a bullet hit the brick directly over her head, and she jerked back. Jordan Daelik's laugh reached them over the cacophony of gunshots and shouts. She raised her gun with every intention to shoot him, but Zoey grabbed her hand.

"He's taunting you," she said. "If he wanted to hit you, he would have."

Harvey cracked his knuckles. "I'll take care of it."

The girls didn't have time to stop him before he was dashed out onto the street. Stella hissed. "Does he think he's bulletproof?"

126

"Apparently so," Zoey muttered. "Come on."

They charged. People moved aside when they saw Harvey coming, giving them a clear path to follow.

Stella's eyes sought out Jordan in the fray. She finally caught sight of him, wearing his usual dark shirt with the sleeves ripped out, his revolvers gleaming in his hands. His expression shifted when he saw her, going from cocky to dead serious in a second. It was unusual enough that her foot slipped and she fumbled for the next step. By the time she regained her balance, Harvey had made it to Jordan and tackled the Raven heir to the ground.

"Shit," Stella and Zoey said at the same time.

They dove for Harvey, but Declan Thatcher made it there first, delivering a swift kick to Harvey's side that had him hissing in pain. His head snapped up, locking in on its new target. Stella felt a little sorry for Thatcher as he bristled under the weight of her cousin's gaze.

Zoey got there first. She punched Thatcher, positioning herself between him and Harvey, who returned his focus back to Jordan. Blood dripped down Thatcher's nose as he snarled at Zoey. She pulled her gun, but Mateo Daelik appeared out of nowhere and knocked her arm aside. Suddenly the fight was going in their direction, and Zoey yelped as Declan got in a blow in retaliation for the punch she gave him.

Harvey's head snapped up at his sister's cry of pain. But Jordan used the distraction to pull Harvey's favorite knife out of its sheath. Stella froze as he stabbed Harvey right in the gut.

"*No!*"

Zoey flung herself towards her brother, the fight all but forgotten. Jordan scrambled back, Harvey's knife still in his hand, disgust on his face as he stared down at him. Harvey was going absolutely feral on the ground, attempting to fight past Zoey to get to Jordan, presumably to get his knife back and kill the Raven heir with it.

Jordan sneered. "That'll teach you White Rats. It doesn't matter how many guards you put on the border; you'll never be able to keep us out."

He spat on Harvey and raised a hand. The other Ravens halted. Another signal from Jordan had them retreating over the border, looking rather confused.

Stella frowned. That was it? She realized with a jolt that John was nowhere in sight; whatever the purpose of this expedition was, Jordan had been the one behind it.

Her eyes narrowed as Jordan smirked at her. "What is this?"

"A lesson, little thorn." He ambled towards her, still well within White Rose territory, enough of his Ravens behind him that she didn't dare lift a finger against him—even as he grabbed her by the arm and yanked her forward.

"Let go of me," she snapped.

Jordan hauled her closer. "I thought we didn't take orders from each other," he whispered in her ear.

She pried his fingers off and backed away. Jordan just laughed and tossed Harvey's knife on the ground before sauntering away, his Ravens going with him.

Zoey gaped from where she knelt next to Harvey, applying pressure to his wound. "What the hell was that about?"

"I don't know," Stella replied, rubbing her arm. "But I don't like it."

"I'm going to kill him," Harvey wheezed.

She glared down at him. "You haven't even been stitched up yet, and you're planning murder?"

"The best time to plot revenge is when you're still bleeding."

Stella shook her head in disgust. "Get a wagon over here," she ordered her men, standing around awkwardly after the Ravens' abrupt exit. "The rest of you, secure the border."

Several of them exchanged a look. Stella read their expressions with narrowed eyes.

"Do we have a problem with that?" she growled.

One brave soul dared step forward. "Are we really going to let them get away?"

"They attacked us," another chimed. "We shouldn't let them retreat—we should go after them!"

This was met with a murmur of agreement from the other Roses, the one who spoke first sweeping a pointed look over the bodies scattered across the border, Ravens and Roses alike. It was small for a border skirmish—especially considering both heirs *and* Harvey had been involved—but enough of Stella's people were down to make the others nervous.

She gave them a haughty look. "Did you not hear my orders? I told you to secure the border, not to chase down Raven grunts intent on making trouble."

"They're right," Harvey rasped, attempting to reach around Zoey to retrieve his knife. "We should kill them for starting this."

Zoey ordered him to be quiet, but the damage was already done. The Roses' confidence soared, and the first one squared his shoulders as he faced Stella.

"The Ravens shouldn't be able to get away with a stunt like that," he said. "We need—"

Stella's blood turned to ice. "You shouldn't be able to get away with such blatant disrespect, and yet here we are."

He flinched at the bitter words. "They're getting away—"

"They're getting away because I want them to. Chasing them into their territory where they have reinforcements waiting is not a wise plan. I am the heir to the White Roses, in case you've forgotten, which means that I call the shots when my father is not here." Her amber eyes blazed. "Unless you want me to put your head on a pole as a warning to others, I would suggest that you stop questioning my authority and secure the damn border."

He froze, his mouth open but no reply coming out. Stella raked an icy look over him.

And finally, he lowered his head.

"We'll secure the border," he muttered.

"Louder."

"We'll secure the border," he bit out, louder this time.

Stella raised her chin. "Good. And when you're done with that, you can scrub the blood off the street." Her lip curled at the bodies. "I don't want Raven filth stinking up our side of the city."

She turned, giving Harvey one last glare before stalking away.

The doctor ended up having to sedate Harvey before even being able to look at the wound. Stella knew for a fact that he would be raving mad when he woke up, so she took care to make sure most of her family had some errand to run, leaving the house empty for when the monster awoke. Once her task was done, she trudged upstairs to change out of her bloody, filthy clothes.

She tugged off her shirt with a sigh. She had a feeling that today's skirmish had something to do with her and Jordan's *encounter* last night. That was the only way to describe it—it had been part sneak attack, part argument, part conversation. Worst of all, Stella hadn't been able to get *any* of it out of her head.

Her jaw worked as she wriggled out of her trousers. One knee had ripped during the fight; Zoey would appreciate the style, but Stella had no use for them anymore. She threw on a dressing gown and padded across the hall to deliver them to her cousin, folding them up as she went. But the crinkle of paper had her pausing, frowning at the garment as she dug through the pockets, producing a square of paper that was folded in on itself.

Stella blinked. She hadn't put that there.

Zoey was keeping vigil over Harvey, so her room was empty. Stella dropped off the clothes and went back to her room, locking the door behind her as she unfolded the paper.

> *The rocks on the shore just south of the Red Harbor.*
> *Meet me there tomorrow morning. Nine o'clock.*
> *The border will be clear for you.*
> *Come alone.*

She blinked. Rubbed her eyes. Frowned at the page. Read the neat cursive script three times before the meaning finally settled in.

Someone wanted to meet her?

Stella sat on the end of her bed, pondering over the note. She was fairly sure she knew the location it mentioned, an outcropping of rocks just past the south end of the Harbor. An odd meeting place, but out of the way enough that they wouldn't be seen. But it was *south* of the Harbor—Raven territory. And if they were promising the border would be clear...

A Raven sent this. No doubt slipped it into her pocket during the fight. She tried to recall who she had run past, who she had bumped into during the fray. Jordan Daelik was the first that came to mind, Declan Thatcher a close second. She'd been up close and personal with both of them, and they were high enough in the Raven hierarchy that they could clear the border as promised. Stella couldn't fathom what Thatcher would want with her, so that left Jordan.

Her mind wandered to the look Jordan had given her earlier. She thought it had been weird—what if it signaled something deeper?

Her fingers toyed with the corner of the page. This was most likely a trap. Walking into Raven territory? With orders to come alone? It screamed of a setup. But Stella couldn't deny that she was interested in what this was all about.

She shook her head. "This is madness," she said aloud. It didn't matter if it was Daelik or Thatcher or any other Raven; meeting up with them was insane. Her father would have a stroke if he found out Stella had walked willingly into what had to be a trap.

Stella fiddled with the note, biting her lip. It was madness, and yet...

She was curious.

CHAPTER 20

In the end, it was her curiosity that won out, and at a quarter until nine the following morning, Stella Rook found herself walking towards Raven territory.

The note promised the border would be clear, but it hadn't specified which part would be open, and Stella wasn't foolish enough to think the entire Raven border would be left unguarded for her. Since the meeting place was near the Harbor, that's where she crossed over, her brows rising as she realized that the area was indeed free of guards.

"Impressive," she said to herself.

She'd spent the entire night pondering on who she was meeting with. The feminine curve to the handwriting made it hard to guess. Jordan Daelik was still the prime suspect, as she didn't really know who else it could be, but why? Of course, this was likely to be a trap, but if Jordan had called her here to actually *talk*, then what could it be about? They'd already come to a standstill on the Silas situation, and anything beyond that didn't seem right in her head.

It felt strange walking through Raven territory in broad daylight. Stella wasn't wearing her night clothes, which would have helped her blend in. Instead, her white blouse was glaringly bright in the sunlight, a corset bearing stitching in the shape of roses layered on top. A pair of loose-fitting trousers, a thick leather belt, and her favorite boots completed the look. She'd tied her hair back at the base of her neck, one strand playing across her cheek as she hopped over the fence that marked the edge of the street and walked down the slope to the beach.

Waves crashed against the shore. Sometimes on warm, calm days, children would swim and hang out on the beach. But the ocean was a wicked, violent thing, beating against the sand and rocks with the ferocity of a caged beast. Today was no different. The water rolled, angry and vicious, daring Stella to get closer so it might pull her under. She stopped a few feet short of it and swept an assessing gaze over the shore. There was a clear stretch of beach directly beside the Harbor, but it faded into a mess of jagged rocks and broken shore. Her eyes settled on what she could only assume was the aforementioned group of rocks. It was like someone had hurled a bunch of boulders against each other and left the remains to sit on the beach, their sharp edges looking about as inviting as a loaded gun pointed at one's head. Stella picked her way over to them, her boots sliding on the sand, all too mindful of the street just up the hill and the people that could pass through at any given time.

The rocks glared down at her. Stella couldn't see any sign of life, just dull gray stone that had seen its share of foul weather. Somewhere in the distance, a bell tolled, signaling the change in the hour.

It was nine o'clock, and no sign of anyone. Stella huffed as she turned her gaze to the street. "You're late, feathers."

"Perhaps I was early."

She yelped and whipped around. Jordan Daelik materialized out of nowhere and leaned against the tallest rock, grinning at Stella. She fumbled for her gun, but he raised both of his hands, showing his lack of weapons.

"I just want to talk," he said. "Look."

He unbuckled his belt, taking off his two prized revolvers and laying them on top of a short, flat boulder. He pulled a knife out of his boot and laid it next to the guns, even going as far as to pull a tiny pocket knife from his trousers and toss it on the pile.

"No weapons," he said, raising his hands once more. "And nobody but the two of us. I just want to talk."

Stella wrapped both hands around the handle of her gun. "My apologies if I don't believe you."

Jordan winced. "I swear to the heavens, Rook, nobody else knows about this. I cleared the border for you and picked a time where I knew the street would be quiet. We won't be interrupted. I know we aren't friendly with each other, but I have to discuss something with you." At her skeptical expression, he added, "It's about Silas."

At least her hunch had been right. Stella studied him from head to toe, looking for any hidden weapons. When she didn't see any, she lowered her gun, gingerly placing it next to Jordan's. Next came her knife, then the tiny blade from her boot.

"How did you get the note into my pocket?" she asked.

"Slipped it in during the skirmish yesterday." Jordan raised both brows as she stepped away from the rock. "The pins too."

She scowled. "Seriously?"

"You *stabbed* me with one of those."

She had, hadn't she? Stella couldn't help but smirk as she pulled out the pins holding her hair back. They clinked against the assortment of weapons and she dropped them on top of the rock and faced Jordan again. "Happy?"

"Not at all," he said, turning away. "Come with me."

Stella blinked as he vanished. She edged forward, eyes widening as she realized there was a gap in the rocks, barely big enough to squeeze through, positioned just right so that one couldn't see the opening until they were right on top of it. She sucked in a breath and shuffled through.

The passageway opened up to a narrow stretch of beach. It was high tide, only giving a few feet of sand to walk on, smaller boulders scattered throughout. Jordan plopped down on the largest of them. He must have been hiding in here when Stella approached—that's why she couldn't see him.

"This is... an amazing place to hide," she said, awed. "I never would have guessed there was a way through the rocks."

"It's not good if you're afraid of tight places," Jordan admitted. "But it's nice. I think I'm the only one who knows about it."

She arched a brow. "You *think*?"

"I've never told anyone about it, and I've never seen anyone else here besides you, but I don't know *for sure*." He shrugged. "We should be fine as long as we don't make a lot of noise."

The wind blew a strand of dark hair into Stella's face. She brushed it aside as she studied Jordan. "No whiskey this time, I see."

He winced, no doubt recalling their last planned meeting, which had ended in the hairpin situation. "I'm all sober."

Stella folded her arms over her chest. Jordan seemed perfectly at ease, sprawled out as he was, but her mind refused to allow her to relax. Jordan noticed her tension with raised brows.

"Relax, Rook," he drawled. "I'm not here to kill you."

"Sounds like something a killer would say."

"I'm not—"

"A killer?" she asked, arching a brow. "Because we both know that's dead wrong." At his smirk, she rolled her eyes. "That wasn't supposed to be a joke. What do you want, anyway?"

"I want Silas gone," he said simply.

She angled her head. "Funny. It's almost as if we've talked about this before."

He sat up. "We have. And it went badly. But I'm hoping this time can be different."

Stella stared at him for a moment. He seemed genuine. And so far, no trap had been sprung, so she gingerly took a seat on the boulder opposite him.

"Five minutes," she said. "And only because I'm wondering what's gotten into you."

Jordan wasn't deterred. "The other night, when you and I got into that fight—"

"When you snuck up on me and tried to kill me."

"When we *fought*," he said, giving her a look, "and I shot out the window—"

"Which I *told* you was a bad idea."

"Rook," he said, exasperated. "Let me talk?"

Stella raised her hands in mock surrender and motioned for him to keep going.

"After you went on your way," Jordan said, "I saw Silas and Tobias, trying to follow us. Silas kept talking about finding the person behind it and killing them. And no," he added, seeing her expression, "I'm not worried about them coming after me. I'm worried about them coming after everyone. Silas basically said he wants to kill the entire city. Not just one gang—he said the entire city would be in ruins. That doesn't affect just one of us. We're talking hundreds of people whose lives are being put on the line."

"Since when are you so concerned with the greater good?"

Jordan scowled. "I don't give a shit about that. I just want to keep the city safe. And I know you do as well."

Stella snorted. "Of course we do. It's Lochridge. We both want it."

"Right," Jordan said, standing up. Stella watched warily as he paced the small stretch of beach. "The Ravens want it. The Roses want it. And now Silas and his boss want it, too. But they're taking advantage of us, of the feud. They're preying on the conflict between our fathers to slide their chip into place. My father is so concerned with looking better than Marcus that he hasn't even stopped to consider if this is what he really wants or needs." He whirled to look at Stella. "I mean, just look at us! We've both been trying to see what Silas is up to, but because we keep butting heads, we aren't getting anywhere." He raked a hand through his hair, blowing out a deep breath. "This is going to sound crazy. And I mean absolutely insane. But we had that one night—that first time we both followed Silas to that pub on your territory and listened in on his conversation. We got somewhere that night. We got information, we knew his motives. The plan to get our fathers together didn't work, but why should that mean that *we* can't work together?"

Jordan faced her, his expression as earnest as she'd ever seen it. "I don't like you, Stella. I know you hate my guts. But if you had heard the same conversation I was privy to two nights ago, then you would know that there's no doubt Silas is bad news—not just for either gang, but for the entire city. I don't know how long we have to stop him, but I know that us trying to do it individually is only working against us."

Stella tilted her chin. "You had that speech planned, didn't you?"

Jordan blinked, then scowled. "I might have practiced it beforehand, yes. But everything I said is true, isn't it?"

She pressed her lips together. "I won't deny it."

"Trust me," he said. "If there was anyone else I could go to, I would. Most of my family believes in what Silas is selling, and the rest would be too scared to go against my father. As much as I hate to say this, you're the only person I have that distrusts Silas and isn't afraid to act on it."

"So you're suggesting that we work together," she said, crossing her legs.

"Yes."

"For how long?"

"Until Silas is gone." Jordan's hands curled into fists. "Until I—until *we*—are sure his boss is no longer interested in Lochridge. Or at least until we can convince our fathers that Silas isn't golden."

Stella sucked on her tooth. "What happens if people find out?"

He raised a brow. "Is that a yes?"

"I'm withholding my decision for the moment," she said primly.

Jordan shrugged. "I don't think anyone will find out as long as we take precautions. We could set up meetings, follow Silas at night, see where he goes and who he talks to. If we're working together, then we would both be able to cover the entire city, rather than me being stuck on this side and you having to stay on Rose territory. It would benefit us both."

"It would," Stella agreed, rising to her feet. "Only if we could set aside our differences long enough to do it." She smoothed her hair. "Unfortunately, I don't think we'll be able."

"I'm willing to do it," Jordan said, watching her walk towards the entrance to the secret beach. "Are you telling me that you can't put it aside for long enough to ensure Lochridge's safety?"

Stella's glare was so cold it could have made water freeze. "You aren't the one who had their lover killed."

Jordan flinched. "Rook—"

"If you think I'm going to work with you," she hissed, "then you really are an idiot. I'm the one who found their lover bleeding out on the Harbor. That would have been bad enough, but since then, all you have done is rub it in my face like you're rutting *proud* of it." She bared her teeth. "Liam was the love of my life, and you damn well knew it. Perhaps it makes me a weak person that I can't put it aside, but until I feel that you wouldn't do it all over again just for fun, I can't just forget it." She turned away, fighting back tears. "You're right about Silas. Maybe we can work something out where we both get the information we need. But an alliance is not on the table."

She marched towards the rocks, but Jordan's voice came from behind her, so quiet she nearly missed it.

"I didn't know he was your lover," he said.

Stella froze.

"My father has me interrogate Roses all the time," he continued. "I'm good at it, but I don't enjoy it. Liam... I remember him. I remember everything I did to him. Pa told me he was high up within your gang and that he had information on your family. I tried to get that information out of him but he wouldn't break, so I was told to bring him to the Harbor and put him down."

Stella glanced over her shoulder to see Jordan standing awkwardly on the beach, wringing his hands.

"I didn't know until afterwards that he was with you," he said softly. "It wouldn't have changed things if I knew, but it made me less willing to interrogate people afterwards. It made me break up with the girl I was with at the time because I was afraid of retaliation." He held her gaze. "I'm sorry for killing him, Stella. I really am. And I'm sorry for all the times I taunted you with it. I would take it back if I could, but since I can't, I promise you that I won't mention him again." He dropped his gaze. "I'm sorry."

Stella felt like she'd been punched in the gut. This wasn't the Jordan Daelik she knew—this was someone unfamiliar, far too genuine and kind to be the heir to the Ravens. She was oh-so-tempted to believe that it was all an act, but the look in his eye, the softness of his voice…

He meant it. As much as she didn't want to believe it, Stella knew he was speaking the truth.

It took her a minute to find her voice, to shape her mouth to form words.

"I…" She swallowed. "That's good to know."

Jordan dipped his head. "I mean it."

Stella hugged herself, not knowing what to do with herself now. "You said you eavesdropped on Silas?"

Jordan nodded. "And let me tell you, it wasn't pretty."

CHAPTER 21

The two heirs stayed on the beach for an hour. Jordan recited the conversation he heard between Silas and Tobias. Stella listened with narrowed eyes, her jaw working as she mulled over it.

"None of this is good," she murmured.

"It isn't," he agreed.

Jordan couldn't decide if the note had been a good idea or not. He had never learned how to read; John skipped the finer parts of his education in favor of teaching him the ways of the gang. Lana had been taught by Lillian, and Mateo had taught himself over the years, and Jordan had long debated over who to ask to write the note before eventually deciding on his sister. He trusted her not to ask questions, and although she'd been rather confused by it, she wrote it without telling anyone.

He glanced at Stella. The tension was thick enough to cut with a knife. Both of them were still unarmed, but he had no doubt they could draw blood with their bare hands if push came to shove. Jordan meant every word he said, and while they'd come to a shaky truce, he didn't know how long it would hold. Stella had sobered up after Liam came into the conversation, and it felt weird speaking with the Rook heir when she was acting so much milder than usual.

"So," he said. "Are we really working together?"

She glanced at him. "Are we?"

"I suppose. As long as we can put the feud aside and not kill each other in the process."

Her eyes narrowed. "It sounds like you're regretting this."

His smile was wicked. "Actually, no. Usually I have to deal with my ugly-ass family on missions, but now I get to work with the woman all of Lochridge swoons over. The male counterparts of your family must feel extremely lucky."

Stella clicked her tongue. "*I* am certainly regretting this."

Jordan winked at her. She glared in response.

Why was it so fun to get under her skin?

Stella perched on a rock opposite Jordan and crossed her legs. "Has Silas been to your house recently?"

"I haven't seen him in person, but I know he's been checking out businesses along our side of the Barter Streets. Going in, asking questions, buying trinkets." He shook his head. "He's doing research."

Her face remained impassive. "He's not doing anything illegal, but he's getting all of his pieces into place. We have to find out what he's up to."

The word *illegal* rang a bell in Jordan's head. "We don't have to prove what he's doing to our fathers. If we just find *anything* he's doing wrong, we can bring it to the sheriff."

Stella tilted her head. "He's just going to think that we're trying to get back at the other. If I go, he'll assume it's because Silas announced he's going to ally with the Ravens."

"Not if we both go."

"That's asking for trouble."

"The sheriff can be reasoned with for the right amount of money. We'll come to him together to get Silas out of town and pay for his silence. Nobody else has to know. Even if he spilled the secret, it wouldn't take much to pass it off as drunken ramblings."

"That could work," she murmured. "But if this Trace fellow is really so focused on Lochridge, it wouldn't stop it forever."

That was true. Being kicked out of town wouldn't stop Trace from sending somebody else to do his negotiating. Jordan drummed his fingers on the leather cover of his sketchbook. "It's a start."

She nodded. "First we need to catch him doing something the sheriff wouldn't approve of."

Jordan's brown eyes gleamed. "I sense a stakeout coming on."

The two heirs briefly returned to their homes to dispel suspicion before meeting up outside of Silas' hotel just as night fell over the city. Jordan didn't mention that he had to come through White Rose territory to get here; Stella didn't ask. She once again wore all black—both of them now armed—and Jordan found himself sweeping an appreciative gaze over the outfit as they took refuge on the rooftops. It wasn't the same one Stella used to spy on Silas the first go around—they'd moved a few houses down to stay out of sight if Tobias tried to spy on them again.

Jordan made himself as comfortable as he could on the cracked roof. "You look good in black," he said. "Almost makes me think you're a Raven."

She glared at him over her shoulder. Jordan wore black as well, his sleeveless shirt showing off the tattoo on his wrist. There wasn't a strict dress code for the gangs, but Jordan knew his father would frown if he wore white. Stella almost always wore a low-cut blouse in some shade of ivory or eggshell. Jordan supposed she had her own stash of dark clothes for when she had reason to spy on someone.

Like tonight.

"You should try white some time," Stella said wryly. "See if it makes you a Rose."

He snorted. "Oh, please. I work too hard to wear white—it would get stained too easily."

"Hard to hide all the blood on your hands when you wipe them on a white shirt," she quipped.

He put a hand over his heart. "Low blow, little thorn. I'm stung."

Sarcasm dripped off his voice. Stella turned her gaze back to the street.

Jordan's voice lowered a level. "Am I making you mad, little thorn?"

She glared at the boarded-up window. They had done a little poking around and discovered that after the incident, Silas had changed rooms, opting instead for one on the top floor. "Stop calling me that."

His grin was a flash in the dark. "I'm having fun. We should do this more often."

Her hands curled into fists. "Insult each other in the dead of night when we're supposed to be keeping quiet and watching for our target?"

"You say that like it's a bad thing."

Stella faced him once more, the moonlight making her fair skin turn deathly pale. "This *is* a bad thing, feathers. There is somebody in our town we are so worried about that you risked your life by coming to *me* for help." Her lip curled. "You've killed people before. People that were close to me."

"I said I was sorry." It sounded childish to his own ears. "Might I remind you that *you* have killed people I know, too. Wasn't it my cousin just last month?"

"A cousin you weren't close to because he was from out of town. Besides, Harvey was the one who killed him."

"But you're the one who tracked him down."

She huffed a breath. "He should have known better than to wander onto our side of the border. You could have at least warned him. It's your family's fault this feud ever started."

Jordan snorted. "My father wasn't the one who served up poisoned wine at dinner."

"No, but John was the one to first gather a gang and ransack Marcus' business. That caused the incident with the wine."

"Marcus slandered him in public."

"John accused him of cheating on his taxes."

"Marcus was the one who screwed their friendship to begin with by lying to him about the business deal they were both after."

"According to *your* side of the story."

Jordan snorted again. "That's your best argument?"

"I don't see the need to defend my family's every action," Stella said coolly.

"I imagine you say that a lot in connection to your cousin," he mused.

"Harvey?" Stella rolled her eyes. "That would be one person I *wouldn't* mind you killing, Daelik."

Interesting. Jordan knew Stella wasn't particularly fond of Harvey, but this was more extreme than he thought. "Why don't you do it yourself?" he asked. "You're perfectly capable."

Her eyes narrowed to slits. "What's that supposed to mean?"

Jordan tucked a hand behind his head. "It can mean whatever you want it to, little thorn. I was just suggesting that you are well aware of what it takes to murder another human being."

Those eyes narrowed further. "Don't call me that again."

He smiled, showing all of his teeth. "Little. Thorn."

Stella lunged.

She was quick, Jordan had to admit. He rolled out of the way, drawing his revolvers as he came up on his knees at the edge of the roof. Stella paused as she took in the guns, her hand flitting down to touch her own.

"I thought we agreed not to kill each other," he spat.

Her mouth was set in a sneer. "Did we?"

Jordan cocked his revolvers, loading a bullet in each of their chambers. "We had an agreement."

"But we said nothing about hurting one another."

He snarled. "Don't play with me, Rook. You're not the only one who is nervous about this arrangement. Don't make me shoot you because I'm frightened of what you might do."

"You? Frightened? And here I thought the tough act meant you weren't afraid of anything."

His fingers tightened on the triggers. Oh, how badly he wanted to put an end to this here and now. One of these days, he would put a bullet through her chest.

But movement on the ground below had Jordan pausing. "Silas," he hissed, lowering his weapons. Stella glanced down to see Silas Tradow walking down the street, the door to the hotel swinging shut behind him. Tobias wasn't with him as usual—Jordan could only assume the bodyguard was off figuring out who shot at them the other night.

"What is he doing?" Stella murmured.

"I don't know," Jordan said, "but we're going to find out."

He put his revolvers away. They'd agreed to put the feud aside. It wasn't working, but he had to at least try.

For now.

CHAPTER 22

Silas walked like a man with a purpose. Jordan's eyes narrowed as he entered Rose turf, he and Stella following from the rooftops. He snuck a glance at her as they left neutral ground, but she didn't as much as look at him, a storm brewing beneath her expression.

Jordan expected Silas to veer off onto the Barter Streets as he usually did, but to his surprise, Silas walked right over the border and into the heart of Raven territory. The guards on both sides were familiar enough with the situation that they didn't stop him. Jordan and Stella were forced to go around the long way to avoid being seen together.

"This is new," Stella murmured. She fell back, letting Jordan take the lead in the area he was more familiar with. They caught up to Silas just as he turned a sharp left, heading towards the ocean.

"Aren't you glad we're working together?" he asked. "You would never have been able to get this far into my land otherwise."

She glared at him in the dark. "What about all that bravado you had a few days ago when you were going on about how you wouldn't hesitate to kill me if you ever caught me on your territory?"

His smile widened. "You're too pretty to kill, little thorn."

She looked very much like she wanted to snap back a reply, but she stopped herself as Silas made another turn, coming onto a street that was empty save for the lone person waiting at the end. He perked up when he saw Silas approach.

"Mister Tradow, I presume," he said, offering a hand.

Silas shook it. "Indeed. A pleasure to meet you."

The man tucked his hands into his pockets. Jordan caught a flash of a tattoo peeking out from under his sleeve. A Raven, though he didn't recognize the face.

"I was told you wanted information on Lochridge," he said.

"Just one part of it," Silas corrected. "The Red Harbor."

Jordan and Stella swapped a look as the man frowned. "What do you want to know about the Harbor?"

"Everything. The history, who owns it, who works it. *Everything.*"

If the man found that to be an odd request, he didn't show it. "Well, it's one of the few parts of Lochridge considered to be neutral ground. The gangs tried to fight for it in the past, but the sheriff—"

"Yes, yes, I know that part," Silas interrupted. "Tell me the rest."

He arched a brow. "You said you wanted to know everything."

Silas clenched his jaw. "I did indeed, but let's keep moving regardless. Who owns the Harbor?"

"Timothy Evans. A lazy bloke, if you ask me. He just hides out in his office all day and reaps the profits off the Harbor." He spat on the ground. "Not the way it should be, but what can I do about it?"

Silas' eyes gleamed. "A lot more than you know. Where could one find Mister Evans?"

"Like I just said, his office. It's that little shack on the far end of the Harbor." He cocked his head. "What do you want with Evans?"

That was a question Jordan wanted to know the answer to, but before Silas could answer, shouts echoed towards them. Stella and Jordan pulled back as dark figures appeared at the end of the street.

"Hey!" one shouted.

Silas' head jerked up. He took off before Jordan could read his expression, the Raven already fleeing in the other direction. The others gave chase, and Jordan's breath caught in his throat as he realized who they were.

"Shit," he spat.

Stella stiffened. "Is that—"

"Raven patrol." He scrambled back. "We have to get out of here."

He slipped off the roof before Stella had a chance to respond. She let out a low hiss and ran after him. Behind them, the shouts of the patrol grew louder as they fanned out to find their suspects.

Jordan couldn't be mad at them—they were doing exactly as they were told. The way Silas and the other were standing in the alleyway, the patrol leader had likely flagged them as drug dealers and sent the hounds in. As much as it annoyed him, he was kind of proud that they'd actually done their job.

But the fact remained that Jordan could not, under any circumstances, be seen together with Stella Rook, which is why he grabbed her arm and hauled her down a side street.

The buildings closed in as the street narrowed. Jordan tore down it, all but dragging Stella along with him as they fought to stay ahead of the patrol. Stella let out another little hiss that had him gritting his teeth, but he ignored her as he squeezed between two stores, taking advantage of the tiny alleyway beyond.

"What the hell was that?" Stella snapped.

"A patrol." The alley was too narrow for Jordan's broad shoulders, forcing him to turn sideways and shuffle down it awkwardly. "We couldn't be seen."

"We wouldn't have been seen if we had just stayed on the roof."

"I've started ordering the patrols to check the rooftops when there's suspicious activity." His mouth quirked to the side. "You know, since a certain somebody likes to hang out up there and wreak havoc from above."

Stella planted a hand on her hip. "You're the rutting heir," she said tartly. "You couldn't have just gone down there and told them to get lost?"

His back slid along the rough brick wall as he sat down. "I didn't want Pa to hear about it and ask questions." He patted the ground next to him. "Have a seat, little thorn. We need to wait out this patrol."

Her nose wrinkled. "It's dirty."

"Are you too good to sit on the ground?"

Her mouth tightened, and she sat down next to Jordan with a huff. He could still hear the patrol, the shouts growing distant with each passing second but still close enough to have him on edge. The general population didn't realize that there were crevices and alleyways nestled between every building in Lochridge; if a person wanted to disappear, they damn well could. Jordan made sure his patrols were aware of these crevices, but given that he had only recently discovered this one for himself, he thought they would skip right over it.

Stella was doing her best to avoid eye contact, so Jordan fished around his pockets until he found a cigar. He dug out a match and lit it before Stella realized what he was doing.

"Can you not do that here?" she hissed. "It reeks."

Jordan blew a mouthful of smoke right at her. "You Rooks really can't stand to be around us uncivilized folks, can you?"

Her lip curled. "You're disgusting."

He didn't deign to respond to that comment, instead taking a long draw from his cigar before saying, "I don't like that Silas is poking around the Harbor."

Stella jumped on the change in conversation. "It doesn't make sense. What would he want with Evans?"

"No clue."

Their eyes met.

"I don't have a good feeling about this," he admitted. "Evans is a money-hungry shark, and Silas is someone with money."

She pursed her lips. "You think Silas is going to bribe Evans."

It wasn't a question, but Jordan nodded all the same. "It's the most reasonable explanation I see, but I just don't know *what* Silas wants out of him."

"That is the question," she agreed. "The good thing is, Silas bounces around between our houses daily. Between the two of us, we should be able to keep tabs on him."

Jordan rolled his cigar between his fingers. "And now we'll be able to communicate and see what he's been up to on the opposite turf."

"As much as I hate to say it," Stella bit out, "I think this alliance was for the best."

Jordan chuckled under his breath. "You don't have to sound so enthused."

"I'm the farthest thing from it."

He laughed again and stood up. "I don't hear the patrol anymore. I think we're in the clear."

He offered Stella a hand up, but she ignored it as she rose to her feet. He didn't understand how she could make the act of *standing* look so graceful, but somehow she pulled it off.

"Do you want to try again tomorrow night?" he asked. "We can meet at the beach."

Stella's mouth twisted. "That's probably for the best." She gave Jordan a slight nod as she turned north. "I'll see you then, feathers."

The words didn't seem to have quite the bite as they usually did. "See you then, little thorn," he called after her.

The late nights going after Silas had taken their toll on Jordan's sleep. He wasn't shocked to be woken up at high noon the following day, but he was surprised to see that Declan was the one standing over him when he forced his eyes open.

"Rise and shine, Jordie," he said. "We've got company."

Jordan groaned into his pillow. Dec shrugged and walked out, letting the door swing shut behind him. After a few minutes of trying to go back to sleep, Jordan sighed, kicked off the blanket, and sat up.

It took him a while to wake up, to throw on some clothes and drag a comb through his hair, to deem himself presentable enough to go downstairs. He had given little thought to the company Declan mentioned, but he wasn't entirely surprised to see Silas and Celia sitting at the kitchen table with the rest of his family, enjoying a hearty lunch that Lillian and Lana had prepared.

Celia perked up as he walked in. "There he is! We were getting worried."

Jordan forced a smile. "Late night. My apologies."

John gave him a warning look as he slipped into the unoccupied chair between Declan and Mateo. The two of them exchanged a look as Celia smiled at Jordan from across the table.

Oh, he really didn't feel good about this.

He tuned out most of the conversation in favor of the food. He'd skipped supper last night to meet with Stella, and he didn't care that both Silas and his parents were giving him disapproving looks as he scarfed down his meal and went back for seconds. The small talk bored him and Celia unnerved him, so he was ready to get as far away from this house as possible.

Celia pushed back from the table. "You'll have to excuse me. Where might I find the ladies' room?"

Lillian pointed her down the hall. Celia slid out of her chair, the skirts of her turquoise dress swishing as she vanished through the doorway. With her gone, Jordan could finally relax, shoveling down the rest of his meal and making a break for it.

"What is up with you?" Mateo hissed, trailing him out. Jordan glared as he and Declan followed him down the hallway. "You're acting weird."

Of course he was. Yesterday had been a whirlwind. An alliance with Stella Rook? Following Silas? Listening in on his conversation about Evans? Jordan wanted someone to rant to, but he didn't know how Dec and Mateo would react, so instead he said, "It's nothing."

The two exchanged a look. "Sure," Declan said, drawing out the word. "*Nothing.*"

"Nothing that concerns you," Jordan corrected.

Mateo scowled. "We're only trying to help you. Pa isn't happy."

"Pa can get over it," he snapped, storming down the hall.

Mateo swapped another look with Declan before trailing after him, his expression worried. Normally Jordan would have been grateful for his brother's concern, but he wasn't in the mood for it right now. He had a lot of things to do and not a lot of time to do them, which meant he had to find an excuse to get out of this house that wouldn't upset his father.

He let out a sigh. "Everything is fine," he said. "I've just got a lot on my mind." His voice lowered. "And I hate being around Celia."

Dec let out a light laugh. "Can't blame you for that."

Jordan turned towards the stairs, but a flash of movement caught his eye. The door to his father's office was cracked open. It was enough to make Jordan pause. John *never* left his door open, especially when he wasn't in the room. Most of the household was in the dining room, so who could be in the office?

Declan followed his gaze and cocked a brow. "Someone's in there."

"Who would be stupid enough to go in there without permission?" Mateo asked under his breath. "The last time we tried it, we got our asses handed to us."

The trio exchanged a look and lunged for the door. Mateo got there first and threw it open, stopping so suddenly that Jordan crashed into him, Declan slamming into his back and nearly sending the three of them tumbling to the floor. Jordan regained his footing and swept a gaze across the room, his brows rising as he realized who the culprit was.

"This isn't the washroom, Miss Tradow," he drawled.

Celia Tradow looked over her shoulder at them. She stood in front of the bookshelf, a stack of John's ledgers pulled from their places, the most current one open in Celia's hand. A slight blush rose to her cheeks as she faced him fully, but her eyes were as cold as ever.

"Indeed it isn't," she ground out.

Jordan leaned against the doorway as Declan and Mateo fanned out, blocking the exit. "I would ask you what you are doing in here," he said, "but it's quite obvious, isn't it?" He jerked his chin towards the ledgers. "Snooping through somebody's finances is quite the dirty move for someone of your prestige."

"I'm not snooping," Celia said primly.

Declan arched a brow. "It sure looks that way, sweetheart."

"Asking to use the washroom, then sneaking into somebody's office?" Mateo shook his head. "Maybe it's different in Stokes, but that's considered rude here."

Celia's nose wrinkled as she turned back to the bookshelf.

"I wasn't snooping," she said again, returning the ledgers to their rightful places. "I was looking for the washroom and thought this was the right door."

Declan snorted. "And the ledger magically appeared in your hand?"

"I thought they were pretty," she retorted. "So I came in for a closer look."

Jordan gave a pointed look to the book in Celia's hand, with a worn leather cover on the brink of falling apart, the pages filled with John's awful handwriting, brimming with smudged ink and bent corners.

"I'm sure," he said dryly.

"It's the truth."

"I might be tempted to believe it had my mother not pointed you in the opposite direction." He kicked off the doorway. "Get out, Celia. You have no business here."

Her chin jutted up as he gestured to the hallway. Mateo and Declan stepped out of the way as she flounced through, her turquoise dress brushing Jordan's legs. She halted right in front of him, leaning in far too close to be casual.

"Tell me, then," she purred. "Where *is* the washroom?"

Jordan gave her saccharine-sweet smile. "The door at the end of the hall."

She followed his gaze. "That's the front door. It leads outside."

"Is it? Silly me."

Declan choked on a laugh behind him. Celia's eyes slitted.

"I'd watch it, Daelik," she said. The friendliness seeped out of her voice. "You're walking a fine line."

"It's a good thing that's my specialty," he crooned, already turning away.

He stalked away, leaving Celia standing in the hallway, her glare burning a hole in the back of his shirt as he dashed up the stairs and out of sight.

CHAPTER 23

"She was snooping through Pa's office! Had her nose buried in his ledgers! Who knows how much information she gathered while she was there, but does Pa care? *Of course not.* No, he thinks Celia is a little angel who can't do wrong because her daddy is some big-shot from Stokes. If I'd been the one snooping through his office, I would've gotten my ass whipped for it." Jordan stopped short, staring at her. "What?"

Of all the things Stella Rook planned to do today, sitting on a hidden beach listening to Jordan Daelik rant about his father had not been one of them. But here she was, leaning against a rock while she watched Jordan pace back and forth, his boots leaving deep prints in the sand.

"Nothing," she said innocently. "Please, carry on."

Jordan raked a hand through his hair, the sandy-brown locks standing on end as he resumed his pacing. "It isn't right. If I didn't know better, I'd say the Tradows had cast a spell on this whole town, making everyone do their evil bidding."

"The spell must have missed us."

He kicked the sand. "Apparently."

Her eyes skipped to the rock she leaned against. A leather-bound book rested on it. Jordan had been writing furiously in it when she arrived. He'd been quick to snap it shut and tell her about Silas' visit, but she couldn't help her interest. She was quite fond of the idea of the Daelik heir keeping a diary where he ranted about everything with the same energy he was complaining about Celia with now. Her curiosity had her reaching out with a discreet hand, gently pulling the book towards her.

"Don't touch that," Jordan said, jabbing a finger at her.

Stella gave him an innocent look. "I was just moving it out of the way so I could sit."

She slid it a few inches to the left and made a show of sitting down, crossing one leg over the other. Jordan scowled at her. "I've already had one woman trying to pull that trick on me today. Don't feed me bullshit, Rook."

She shrugged. "Can't blame a girl for being curious." She wiggled her fingers at the book. "I bet there are big secrets in there. One look inside and I'd have enough information to bring the Raven gang to its knees."

Jordan snatched it up. "Not exactly."

Stella leaned back and gave him an assessing look. They'd arrived early to the beach, each trying to get there before the other, ending with both of them present at an hour until nightfall. They couldn't be seen together, so they'd waited until darkness fell over Lochridge before making their way to Silas' hotel. Stella had time to kill and a curious mind, so she fixed Jordan with an appraising look and said, "Your father seems like a genuine piece of work."

He let out a humorless laugh. "That's putting it mildly."

"Is he always like this, or is it just because of Silas?"

"You mean, was he always a piece of work? Absolutely. Silas just made it worse." He sat down opposite Stella. "Marcus ain't no piece of cake, either."

She searched for the words. "He's a bit intense at times."

Jordan arched a brow.

"He's very intense a lot of the time," Stella amended. She didn't dare say it to Jordan, but deep down, she'd feared Marcus when she was a little girl. Something about the way he walked and talked and carried himself, the way he spoke down to her, the way she heard him ranting about John Daelik into the late hours of the night. That fear had stuck with her even years later, she supposed. "There's a certain way he wants things done, and he doesn't take no for an answer."

"Sounds rude," Jordan remarked.

"He's a respectable man," she sniped. Just because Marcus intimidated her didn't mean she wouldn't rush to defend him; he was her father, after all. "Marcus is better than your father any day."

He leaned back. "Both of our fathers have their problems, but I'm not here to argue over which one is better." He huffed a laugh. "I just came to complain."

Stella realized how childish her words sounded and blushed.

"You know what?" she said, laughing under her breath. "This conversation sounds a lot like the one we had at Carmilla Park."

Jordan propped himself up, his eyes going wide. "Rutting hell, you're right."

That had been thirteen years ago, when the two of them were seven years old. Lochridge used to have a little park on the east side, not far from Stella's house. Back then, the gangs were no more than a handful of men paid off by their fathers, and Evelyn and Lillian—who had been fast friends long before the feud started and were still friends despite it—had tried to set up playdates between Stella and Jordan. The two of them had overheard their fathers complain about the other side enough to be wary, so nervous around each other that the "playdates" often ended with them ignoring each other as they ran around Carmilla Park.

It hadn't been until their last playdate that they finally got along when Jordan, mad at his father for grounding him, told Stella about his predicament. The two had spent an hour complaining about their families until John showed up, having caught on to the playdate scheme, and drug Lillian and Jordan away. Stella never forgot the look of disgust on his face—the look that made her realize her father had been right about the Daeliks all along.

Lillian and Evelyn were forbidden from seeing each other after that. There were no more playdates. A year later, Carmilla Park was torn down and a shopping district put in its place.

Jordan chuckled. "I can't believe I still remember that."

"Me neither." Stella shook her head. "Our mothers would at least approve of this."

His lips twitched. "A grown-up playdate."

She smirked. "Just like old times."

They grinned at each other. But Stella's smile slipped and she looked away, heat rising on her cheeks. Jordan's jaw clenched as he averted his gaze.

They might be working together, but that made them allies, not friends. Stella couldn't let her guard down; Jordan might have kept true to his word so far, but she trusted him about as far as she could throw him. When everything was said and done, they would go right back to their old dynamic.

Tension filled the air, thick enough to cut with a knife. Stella squinted at the sky. "I think it's dark enough now."

"Right," Jordan said distractedly. "We should go."

He stood up. Stella joined him, feeling rather awkward as she allowed him to go first, slipping out of the hidden beach and onto the darkened streets beyond.

They took up their usual positions on the roof, though Stella took care to sit a few inches further away, putting as much distance between her and the Daelik heir as she could. If he noticed he didn't let on, his jaw working as he fiddled with the book in his hands. He'd taken it with him, not trusting Stella to not ditch him and go back for it if he left it at the beach.

Which, in all fairness, had been her plan.

She wondered what was in it. Notes? Journal entries? It had to be something personal—the way he was writing in it when she walked up suggested nothing less. But what?

"You can quit staring," he drawled.

She realized she had been sizing up the book instead of looking at the hotel. "I wasn't staring," she said.

He gave her a dry look. "You're not getting it."

She propped her chin up. "What's in it?"

His arm curled around the book. "None of your business, Rook."

"Feisty," she purred. "Must be important, then."

He rolled his eyes at her. "It is important to no one but me, but I'd rather not have people looking through it." He waved a hand at her. "You're my worst enemy."

She barked a laugh. "It's so believable when you say it like that."

"You are my enemy. It's just on hold for the moment."

Stella flipped her braid over her shoulder. "It's because of my irresistible charm. You've fallen into my trap, lured by my beauty, and there is no escape."

Jordan leaned closer. "Is that so? And here I thought you didn't like people making comments about your looks."

"I don't like people making comments about taking me to bed," she corrected, "but if my looks get me what I want, then I'll talk about them all day."

He clicked his tongue. "A look into the mind of Stella Rook. Just as vain as I thought."

She pushed him, not hard enough to knock him down, but enough that he felt it. He shoved her right back. She was about to get him again when movement caught her eye.

Her jaw went slack. "Is that..?"

"Celia?" Jordan finished, eyes narrowing.

It was her. Only she wasn't dripping in finery as she usually was, bright gowns and enough jewelry to fund a bank—tonight she wore a black, tight-fitting outfit that mimicked Stella's. It was so out of place that Stella had to blink several times to make sure it was her. But that shock of white-blonde hair was not to be mistaken.

"What is she doing?" Stella asked.

"I don't know," Jordan answered, voice low, "but I intend to find out. Let's go."

CHAPTER 24

Celia took the same path her father had days ago when Stella first followed him, breezing past the usual midnight crowds in the Barter Streets. Everybody was too busy to notice her walk past. Or maybe they noticed and didn't care. People in Lochridge knew better than to look too hard at anybody wearing something like that.

Stella expected her to enter the same pub from last time, but Celia walked right past, her stride never wavering.

Jordan made a low noise in his throat. "Where is she going?"

"Bloody hell," Stella gasped. She'd forgotten the Daelik heir was behind her. She turned to see him smirking at her, folding his muscled arms over his chest.

Shame burned at her cheeks as she remembered what happened a few minutes ago. She was letting her guard down again—something that she couldn't do, no matter how fun it felt to joke around with Jordan. Under that cocky front, he seemed... *Fun.* Likeable. Not the man she was used to. But it was messing with her head, and Stella didn't know what to think.

Celia wasn't affiliated with either gang—yet—so she casually strolled the border in between, one foot on each side. There were *supposed* to be guards on Stella's side of the border who were *supposed* to stop anyone wearing black, but nobody raised a hand against Celia. As Stella edged closer, she could see why. Celia wore a bandolier of small curved knives, the leather straps criss-crossing over her chest.

"She's armed," Stella noted aloud.

She and Jordan followed Celia out of the Barter Streets. Stella realized she was heading for the Red Harbor. That tickled something in the back of her mind, but she shoved the feeling aside as the line of buildings ended.

They couldn't stay hidden above the street anymore, but Celia was already disappearing into the Harbor. Tall lamps illuminated the docks, rendering the ships as nothing but ghostly silhouettes against the night sky. Water lapped in the distance. Sailors and deckhands bustled to and fro, getting ready to set sail come morning. It would be easy to lose someone in such organized chaos.

Jordan hissed. "We can't be seen in there together."

Of course not. "I'll start on my side of the border, you go on yours." The Harbor itself was neutral ground, each half nestled against the gang borders. "Search for Celia. If you don't find her, we'll meet in the middle."

Jordan slid off the roof. Stella gave him a minute head start before shimmying down the drainpipe. Celia was nowhere in sight, lost among the ruckus of the Harbor, but she was here somewhere. A girl like that would turn heads when she walked through.

Stella herself drew some attention as she sauntered through. She didn't know if it was her status or her general appearance or this outfit in particular, but some sailors stared openly as she brushed past them. Jordan had been doing that all night. Even when he was drunk at their first meeting, slumped in his chair with a glass of whiskey in his hand, his eyes had taken their fill.

Stella fought her way through the throng, hissing as someone stepped on her foot and didn't apologize. She searched for the culprit but saw a flash of light hair instead.

Her eyes narrowed.

Stella shoved past a group of sailors to get to Celia, but she was already turning away, her knives glinting in the lamplight as she headed back towards the Ravens' side of the Harbor. Stella prayed to the heavens that Jordan would be there to intercept her. Celia seemed ignorant to Stella's presence as she kept walking, hips swishing as she waltzed past a sailor who let out a low whistle.

Celia's head whipped to the side. "Who was that?"

Stella threw herself behind a stack of crates as the sailor stepped forward. "Sorry, ma'am, you just—"

Metal flashed through the air, and Stella reined in a gasp as the sailor stumbled back, the hilt of a knife protruding from his throat. Blood seeped down the front of his shirt. The Harbor took on an eerie calm as he teetered one step back before collapsing.

Another image of another body on the Harbor flashed through Stella's mind. The sailor had dark hair and skin, but her mind blurred the lines between past and present, giving him golden hair and warm hazel eyes.

Stella choked on the image of Liam and did her best to lock it up in that chest in the back of her mind, throwing the key into the ocean before his memory could consume her.

Celia whirled. "Does anyone else want to whistle at me?" she demanded of the assembled crowd. When nobody answered, she drew another knife and flipped it in her hands. "Then get lost."

They scattered. Celia's platinum hair gleamed as she watched them go, her red lips curling into a hateful smile. Stella remained where she was. She'd assumed the prissy Celia had no training in self-defense, but it appeared she had been wrong.

"Fancy to meet you here, Tradow."

Celia whirled as Jordan stepped into view. His hands rested on the handles of his guns, his brown gaze surveying Celia. She hissed at him. "What are you doing here?"

He cocked a brow. "What am *I* doing here? You're the one who just killed one of my men."

Stella's gaze dropped to the sailor. A Raven tattoo was just visible underneath the sleeve of his shirt.

Celia, to her credit, didn't appear fazed. "He should have known better than to objectify me."

"This is Lochridge. Everyone whistles when they see something they like."

Her glossy hair slipped over her shoulder as she bent down to pull the knife out of the sailor's throat. "I wanted to see what the night life was like," she said, wiping the bloody blade on his shirt.

"And are you pleased?"

"Not at all."

Jordan shrugged. "It's what you get for coming to a place of business for *night life*. If you wanted a good time, you should have gone to the Barter Streets." He offered her his arm. "Perhaps I could take you there."

"I don't need an escort," she snapped.

Jordan's easy grin didn't waver. "Oh, I think you do. Otherwise I might be tempted to report this little incident to the sheriff or my father. The former would lock you up. The latter would have you killed in response."

She rolled her eyes, unbothered. "John wouldn't risk his deal with my father."

"You'd be surprised with the things he'll do to people who kill his own. To people who snoop through his office." Jordan's grin turned sharper as Celia's expression tightened. "What *I* will do to those people if provoked."

"Neither of you would risk it," she said simply.

Stella's fingers curled around the edge of the crate. Jordan's eyes flickered to her for the briefest moment, eyebrow raising slightly as he took in her hiding place. Celia's back was to her. She could line up a shot if she wanted—maybe even take out Celia *and* Jordan if she fired quickly enough—but Stella forced her hands to remain still.

Jordan didn't give her away as he returned to his conversation. "That's quite the getup," he remarked, nodding to Celia's clothes. "Mind if I ask?"

"I do, actually." She sheathed her blade. "What I do with my nights is none of your business."

"Since you killed one of my men, I daresay it is."

Celia slitted her eyes. "It won't happen again."

"I find that hard to believe, Miss Tradow." He winked. "Or can I call you Celia?"

Stella resisted the urge to roll her eyes.

Celia crossed her arms. "If I answer your questions, will you allow me to leave *without* an escort?"

"Depends on how good I find your answers." He tilted his head. "What are you really doing out here?"

"My father told me to check out the night life—everywhere. He wants to get a grasp of what Lochridge is like. How safe it is for a woman." She patted her knives. "Which is why I came prepared."

"And you came to the Red Harbor?"

"I was interested. I've heard the owner is a piece of work. What's his deal?"

It finally occurred to Stella what she'd been trying to remember. Silas asked that Raven about the Red Harbor—who owned it, specifically. He'd asked her father the same question a few days prior. Just like he'd been asking about the other businesses in Lochridge.

Her eyes narrowed. Something was going on.

Jordan was wise enough to not answer her question. "What does your father want with Lochridge?"

She blinked at him innocently. "To form an alliance with it."

"What kind of alliance?"

"Are you hoping for a hand up in the deal, Daelik?" she asked. "Because I have sway with my father. I can put in a good word for you—but I won't be so willing if you keep asking me silly questions."

A skillful deflection of the question. Jordan's gaze shot to Stella for another moment before he sighed. "Fine, get out of here. I won't report it, but if this happens again—"

Celia waved a flippant hand. "I know, I know. You'll have my head. Message received." She flashed a smile. "It was nice seeing you, Daelik."

He grunted a response. Celia sauntered away, her long hair swinging with every step, leaving the dead sailor's body behind.

Stella caught Jordan's gaze again before vanishing into the crowd. No one dared to whistle at *her*. In the distance she heard Jordan ordering the sailors to carry the body away. Stella felt a twinge of pain. She'd never killed someone so quickly. She'd endured dozens of people whistling at her or eyeing her from a distance, but they always got a warning before she pulled the trigger. Celia's fast response told her everything she needed to know about her intentions.

She returned to the rooftop. Jordan clambered up a few minutes later, cursing under his breath as he plopped down next to Stella.

He dragged a hand through his hair. "She was helpful."

"You caught her over the dead body of one of your people. Being *helpful* was the last thing on her mind. She just wanted to get out of there."

"Seems like you have experience."

"Perhaps," she said vaguely.

A smile tugged at the corners of his lips. "At least you don't get your panties in a bunch every time a man looks at you the wrong way."

Her smile was savage. "Whistle at me and find out."

Jordan let out an obnoxiously loud wolf whistle that made Stella grateful for the shadows concealing her burning cheeks.

"Dirty rat," she hissed.

He dropped a wink in her direction. "I said the people of Lochridge whistle at the things they like. Why should you be any different?"

Her laugh was disbelieving. "You like me?"

"I like the way you look. There's a difference."

Stella shook her head. "You're annoying."

"Only to you, little thorn."

She didn't even have the heart to correct the nickname.

She stretched out her legs. "What are we going to do? Celia didn't give us anything to work on."

"Then we'll have to find something else," he said. The streetlamps casted the softest of glows across his face, illuminating the set of his jaw as he stared out into the distance. "Silas is bound to slip at some point. We will be ready and waiting for that moment to happen."

They exchanged a look in the dark.

"You didn't sell me out back there," Stella said. "You saw me hiding behind the crates and could have ratted me out."

"But I didn't."

"But you didn't," she agreed.

Jordan tilted his head. "It would have been counterproductive to rat on you, Rook. It would look suspicious if both heirs were there, and I needed to talk with Celia when she thought we were alone."

"So it had nothing to do with your feelings about my appearance."

"Not at all. You're pretty to look at, little thorn, but you are off limits."

Stella rolled her eyes. Was she delusional, or did this feel nice? The easy banter was one thing, but with Jordan Daelik? She rubbed a hand over her head, wondering if she'd hit it at some point during the night.

Jordan was a killer. He'd been the one to murder Liam and leave him to die, sprawled out on the wooden planks of the Red Harbor. Stella hadn't made it in time to save him. No one had. There was still a stain on the planks, a dark spot his blood had made that hadn't quite washed away, prompting Stella to avoid that area of the docks entirely. She'd been in such a rage afterwards that she marched into the Ravens' territory and shot every Raven within sight until her father tracked her down and put an end to her heartbroken rampage. She couldn't even recall how the situation had been smoothed over; the next few days were nothing but a blur in her mind.

Jordan was a killer. But so was she, and she didn't know what that made them.

The thought of Liam had Stella jumping to her feet. "I should go."

Jordan smirked as he joined her. "Ah, yes, you have an image to maintain. It's important to get that beauty sleep."

She gave him a simpering smile. "One of these days, your comments will catch up to you."

"But not today," he said.

She rolled her eyes. "I'll see you tomorrow, birdbrain."

"I can't tomorrow. Next day?"

Stella thought through her schedule. Her family had a meeting with the merchants from the Barter Streets, followed by a family dinner Evelyn had insisted upon. "I don't think so."

"The day after that, then."

"That works," she said. "I'll meet you at the same place by the beach at nightfall."

"I'll see you then," Jordan said.

Stella watched him slide down the drainpipe and disappear into the night.

"I'll see you then," she echoed.

CHAPTER 25

It was well into the night when Stella let herself onto the Rook property. The intricate iron fence that surrounded the grounds had one main entrance, but there was a hidden gate in the back, the latch and hinges disguised among the design of flowers and vines and birds. Stella stole across the darkened grounds. There were still lights on within the house, meaning people were up—meaning Stella had to take the hard way in.

She darted through the massive maze that served as the rose garden and approached the trellis that climbed up the house, wisteria dripping off of it. She was lithe enough to scamper up it without trouble, swinging her legs over the railing of her balcony, a sigh of relief escaping her as her feet touched down on the other side. It was simple work to pick the lock on the balcony doors and let herself into her room.

But she froze as she realized she wasn't alone.

Zoey's amber eyes swept over her cousin. "What are you doing?"

"What are *you* doing?" Stella demanded.

Zoey hefted up her arms in answer. They were laden with clothes. Stella's wardrobe was flung wide open, dresses and skirts and blouses scattered all over her bed and vanity.

"You're going through my clothes?" Stella asked incredulously.

"I have a date," she said, "and you have the best clothes." She eyed Stella's dark attire. "Don't tell me you wore *that* to whatever man you were out to see tonight."

Of course her cousin thought Stella had snuck out in search of a date.

She relaxed. "I was trailing a Raven I found suspicious earlier. No other man involved."

Zoey clicked her tongue. "Trailing Ravens is a job for a scrub, not the heir. Let someone else do it. Better yet, let Harvey do it so he can blow off some steam."

"Harvey would beat the guy into a pulp."

"Exactly. A perfect way for him to get his anger out."

Stella cleared room for her to sit on the bed and began unlacing her boots. "How is he?"

"The wound is healing, but his attitude is not." She held up a shimmering blue dress and spun around to let Stella see it. "Does this look good on me?"

"A new man?"

"You know it. His name's Matthew."

"Too formal for a first date. And who is this Matthew?"

Zoey exchanged the dress for a shorter one. "I met him in the bar last night and he asked me out. I hadn't had a chance to tell you. This one?"

"Doesn't match your color." Stella unhooked her belt. "Have you tried talking to Harvey?"

"Of course I have. He doesn't listen to me anymore." Her voice dipped into a snarky drawl. *"I'm not a child, Zo. I can handle myself. Stop letting Stella boss us around."*

Her impression of Harvey was spot-on. Stella sniggered as Zoey held up another dress. "That one," she said, eyeing the dusty-pink piece. "That one is perfect."

Zoey examined it in the mirror. "You think so?"

"Of course. I haven't worn it in years. You can have it."

She grinned. "This is why I raid your closet, Stell. You have the best clothes, the best taste, and the best sense of generosity."

Stella snorted. "Don't let any of the Ravens hear you say that."

"Naturally."

Zoey folded up the dress in her hands and sauntered out of Stella's bedroom. Stella called after her, "You're going to clean up this mess, right?"

"Maybe," she called back, "or maybe I'll postpone it until you do."

And then she was gone, back across the hall to her own room. Stella shook her head and started to clean up her room.

Morning came with a bright spear of light right into Jordan's eyes. He groaned and sat up, wincing as he realized he'd fallen asleep at his desk, his cheek bearing a red line where the edge of his sketchbook had dug into it all night. It took him a minute to wipe the sleep out of his eyes, to stretch his arms overhead, to figure out what his name was and what was so important about today.

Right. Lana's birthday.

His little sister was turning thirteen. He'd barely talked to her since his warning about joining the Ravens, too busy with everything to find the time, so he had made sure his day was clear in order to make amends. He'd even turned down the offer to meet Stella tonight. As fun as it was to rile her up—and as nice as it was to share some easy banter with her despite their violent past—he needed to fix things with his sister today. She was officially a teenager now. He wanted to make sure he was on her good side.

Jordan padded downstairs. Declan nursed a hangover with a cup of coffee; Mateo silently glared at him from across the table. Jasmin sat at Mateo's side, bathing in the sunlight coming in through the window. They'd been going steady for a year now, and Jordan was thrilled for them. He liked Jasmin. While she bore no tattoo on her wrist, the West family was one of the key investors in John's textile company, meaning Jasmin had the Daelik family's favor without officially being a member of their gang.

Jordan offered Jasmin a smile as he slid into a chair between her and Declan. "Are you here for Lana's birthday?" he asked.

Her usual soft smile graced her lips. Jasmin was every bit as gentle as she was beautiful. Mateo loved that about her. "I'm on my way to the boutique, but I brought her a present. You'll wish her a happy birthday for me, won't you?"

"Of course," he said, taking the wrapped package from her. She worked as a seamstress at a boutique in the Barter Streets. One day she hoped to put her university credit to the test and open a shop of her own. "Do you want some coffee?"

"Mateo already offered."

Mateo seemed pleased with the pleasant flow of conversation. Jordan decided he didn't want to know what his hungover cousin had said to piss his half-brother off; the biggest fight Jordan and Mateo ever had was when Jordan made a snide comment about Jasmin that had Mateo rushing to defend her honor. In his defense, he'd been very, very drunk at the time, but that hadn't stopped Mateo from pounding him into the floor. And that had been before he even started courting her officially.

Jasmin hung around for a few more minutes before glancing at the clock and declaring she had to go. Mateo walked her out, all smiles and gentle kisses to her cheek, but when he returned, his angry gaze fixed on Declan.

"You've got a filthy sense of humor," he hissed.

Declan lifted his head. "All I said was that Jasmin's sister was pretty. That's not—"

"You asked if you could date her," Mateo snarled.

Jordan cleared his throat. "Can we not do this right now? Lana will be awake any minute."

His voice carried enough warning to make them shut up. The three of them had gotten into plenty of shenanigans over the years, but Jordan remained the leader of the group. He allowed for no mercy when it came to his sister. Dec and Mateo understood and averted their gazes.

Lana, unsurprisingly, was awake well before either of her parents were, bounding down the stairs in her pajamas, a wide smile cracking across her face. "It's my birthday!" she said.

"It sure is," Jordan said, wrapping an arm around her shoulders. He pressed a wrapped parcel in her hands. "This is from Jasmin. You'll get your other presents later."

She ripped it open with the ferocity of a rabid dog, her grin widening as she unfolded a dress of royal blue. It was obvious Jasmin had put a lot of effort into it; the full skirts had been stitched by hand, the bodice detailed with intricate designs of swirls and flowers. Lana rushed upstairs without another word. When she came back down, she wore the blue dress, a matching ribbon holding her hair back.

Mateo chuckled. "I'll tell Jas you like it."

The day passed in a flurry of excitement. The Daelik house was decked out with streamers and garland. Songs were sung and instruments

167

were played. Lana ate cake for breakfast and opened presents afterwards, squealing in delight at each one. Jordan had gotten her a box of chocolates—her favorite—and a framed drawing he'd done of a princess and a knight, having taken inspiration from the fairytale romances she was so fond of. That night the family took a carriage to Lana's favorite restaurant. A hefty tip on John's part had the owners clearing out the entire back of the restaurant to give the Daeliks a sense of privacy. Lana grinned from her position at the head of the table. She still wore the blue dress, and the rest of the family had dressed up for the occasion. Jordan wore a suit, a dark jacket buttoned over a black undershirt, though he'd left the tie behind to make it a tad more casual.

Three courses were served before the waitresses brought apple pie topped with caramel and cream. Lana's eyes widened as a waitress dropped off a huge portion—double the size of Jordan's—at her side of the table with a knowing smile. Jordan saw his father slip the waitress an extra coin for her effort, which he took as a good sign until he saw Lillian narrowing her eyes. Right. John had cheated on her once before with a barista. Mateo, the product of that affair, now sat to Jordan's right. Jordan wondered how often Lillian saw John being nice to another woman and feared for their relationship.

John set down his fork without trying his pie. "Lana," he said, "you are now a young woman. I know today has been a nice day for you, and I hate to ruin it by talking business at the table, but I have something I would like to ask you."

Every muscle in Jordan's body locked up. *No. Not today.*

John smiled at his young daughter as she squirmed in her seat. "Lana, I would like for you to take your proper place as the second-in-line to my legacy. I want you to join the Ravens."

CHAPTER 26

"*No!*"

The word exploded out of Jordan. The waitresses stopped to stare. John gaped at him. Lana stared, her face impassive. Lillian was the only one who seemed to appreciate Jordan's outburst.

John glared at him from across the table. "Jordan, if you have something you would like to discuss with me, then you can do so in private. Please don't make a scene."

"Don't make a scene?" he echoed. "You're the one making her birthday about you! She had no place in the gang."

"I want to give my daughter the chance to become a member of our family legacy," John countered.

"You want to make her a part of the feud."

"It's not your decision, Jordan," Lana muttered, but it seemed half-hearted.

Jordan bared his teeth. "I've done everything you've asked for years," he hissed at John. "I've taken part in the feud. I've enjoyed it, even. When you have a demand, I have been the perfect son. When I had problems about Silas, you told me to move on, *and I did.*" A blatant lie, but he didn't know that. "Don't drag Lana into this. It's not her fight."

Uncle Dan gave him a disapproving frown. "Stella Rook was fighting her father's battles long before she was Lana's age."

"Is Stella Rook really the role model you want for Lana?" Jordan snapped.

"She is a bitch," Declan agreed under his breath, earning a heated

169

glare from his father.

"This isn't your place," John said. "This is a decision between Lana and I."

Jordan squared his shoulders. "Lana will do whatever you ask her to because she's scared of disappointing you. You should have more sense than to allow a thirteen-year-old girl to participate in the feud!"

"Don't tell me how to—"

"*She will be killed.*"

Those four words rang across the restaurant, drawing a gasp from Lillian. They were cruel words, but true ones, and Jordan gritted his teeth as he stared down his father. As he shot a pleading look at Lana, silently begging her to not take part, just as he asked her. She shouldn't have to deal with this.

John was the first to recover from the outburst. "You're going to scare her," he chastised.

"Better scared and innocent than brave and corrupted."

"You think I would corrupt my daughter?"

"I think this feud has corrupted the entirety of two families, and while I am not arguing that it shouldn't take place, I am asking you to leave Lana out of it. This isn't her fight. She doesn't have to be involved at all."

"The Roses will involve her eventually," Dan said.

Mateo crossed his arms. "No reason to speed up the process."

Jordan snapped his fingers. "Exactly! The Rooks seem content to leave her alone, but the moment you parade her around as a Raven, a target will be placed on her back. Do you really want Stella Rook hunting her down? Or worse, Harvey?"

John's jaw clenched. "This is not your decision."

Jordan felt his chest hollow out. No. He couldn't do this. Lana was the only one out of them that hadn't had to see bloodshed from a young age, that hadn't been exposed to the feud, that had remained innocent and pure this entire time. She didn't deserve this.

Across the table, Lana stared at her brother, her eyes wide.

"Jordan is being overprotective," John said to her. "We won't throw you into battle with Harvey Rook your first day on the job. I promise that you won't be in any danger."

Don't make a promise you can't keep, Jordan thought, but he kept quiet, holding his sister's gaze.

Lana looked at him.

Then she gave the tiniest shake of her head.

Don't do this, Lanabug.

She turned to John. "I want to join."

There was a rattle of dishes as Jordan shot to his feet, slamming his napkin down. Lillian flinched at the sudden movement, and Dan hissed his name. "Don't do this. You're going to ruin Lana's birthday."

"Better than ruining her life," Jordan snapped, stalking out of the restaurant.

"You're in a mood."

Two days later, Jordan sprawled out across the sand of his hidden beach, a cigar clenched between his teeth, glaring at the last traces of daylight on the horizon. Stella planted her hands on her hips as she glared down at him. "Get up."

"You don't order me around."

"I do if I have a reason to. I don't know what's wrong with you, but this is pitiful, Daelik."

Jordan glared at her from the corner of his eye. "Leave me alone."

She let out an exasperated sigh. "I thought we were trailing Silas tonight."

"Plans have changed. I'm going to stay right here and wish I'd brought moonshine while *you* either go home or follow Silas—I don't care either way, as long as you leave me alone."

Her eyes narrowed. "I heard a rumor that the Daelik heir wasn't spending time with his family. Care to elaborate?"

Damn her and her people watching for gossip about the Ravens. "I have my reasons."

"I'm sure you do, but if you expect me to leave here without you, I need to hear them."

Jordan propped himself up, his elbows digging into the sand. "Fine. My thirteen-year-old sister just got roped into my father's gang despite my warnings." He took a long draw from his cigar. "Reason enough?"

Stella frowned. "Lana?"

"Get her name off of your lips," he snarled.

She gave him a look. "I'm not going to hunt down your sister, feathers. I don't harm children." She leaned against a nearby rock. "I still remember the time when your family kidnapped me and held me hostage until Father paid the ransom. I wouldn't do that to Lana."

Jordan vividly remembered that instance, when Stella had her hands tied to a chair in the living room while he, Declan, and Mateo gawked at her from the doorway. They'd stuck their tongues out at her before running away, sniggering under their breath. They couldn't have been much younger than Lana, and the thought of the Rooks doing something like that to his sister had Jordan's insides twisting.

"She's too young for the gang," he said.

"I joined the Roses when I was younger than she was," Stella said.

"And look how well you turned out."

Her eyes flashed. "Watch it."

"Lana doesn't need to be part of the feud," he said. "It's not her fight. Every other member of my family enjoys being part of the gang, and I'm no exception, but that's never been what Lana has dreamed about. She likes to curl up with a romance novel and leave the world behind."

He hadn't talked to his family since Lana's birthday dinner. He'd booked himself a hotel room and locked the door with a jar of shine he'd nipped from Declan. The meeting with Stella had forced him to sober up, but he had no intentions of going home anytime soon.

He wondered if Lana had already received her tattoo.

Stella sighed, a gusty breath of air that drew him from his thoughts. "That is a shame," she said. "My mother convinced my father long ago to never hurt Lana because she had no involvement other than the unluckiness to be John's daughter. But now that she's joined, that case is moot."

Jordan's jaw clenched. "If somebody hurts my sister, I will rip their throat out."

"Duly noted." She kicked off the rock. "Now get up. You need a distraction."

He gave her a slow look. "I already told you, I'm not going anywhere."

Stella looked about five seconds away from wringing his throat. "Now is not the time to be stubborn, Daelik."

"Leave me alone."

"I will not."

He blew a mouthful of smoke at her. "I'm not in the mood."

"Well, that makes two of us." Before he could react, Stella plucked the cigar from his fingers, dropped it on the ground, and crushed it beneath her boot, extinguishing it in the sand. Jordan let out a cry of outrage, but it was too late.

He shot to his feet. "What was that for?"

She leveled a haughty look on him. "Are you telling me that you'd really rather stay here, wallowing in your own self-pity and pouring your health down the drain by puffing on such a foul, reeking object as that? We have work to do, birdbrain, and I will not stand by and watch my only ally degrade himself like this."

Jordan huffed. "I take one night off and you throw a fit?"

Her eyes flashed. "You show up barely sober, your shirt untucked, your boots unbuckled, and your hair uncombed. I can't smell you over the reek of that cigar, but I doubt you've bathed in the last couple of days. And that attitude of yours has seen better days, too. This isn't taking the night off; this is being reckless and neglecting basic hygiene and expecting me to do all the work instead of pulling yourself together long enough to help." Her nose wrinkled. "I guess I should have expected as much from a Raven."

His blood boiled, but she was already turning away, muttering under her breath as she stalked off. The disdain in her voice seared through him. He dropped his gaze, wincing as he realized she'd been right. He looked like a mess.

His mouth twisted. It never ceased to bother him that his gang had such a bad association. How could John ever hope to win Silas' favor when his people were known for spending their nights in pubs and gambling halls? Jordan fought back a sigh as he stooped down to buckle his boots. He stuffed his shirt into his belt, straightened his revolvers, and ran a hand through his hair in hopes that it wouldn't look quite so dismal, and it was with a wrathful determination that he stormed past the rocks to catch up to Stella.

He didn't have to go far. The Rose heir smirked at him from where she stood just past the entrance, her arms crossed.

"I knew you'd cave," she said.

Jordan glared at her. "Let's just get this over with."

Her smirk widened, but she said no more as she led the way to their usual spot by Silas' hotel. They sat in silence as they watched shadows move back and forth behind the curtains. The street remained quiet.

"Is that true, what you said?" Jordan asked, breaking the silence. "That Evelyn convinced Marcus to leave Lana alone?"

"She has a soft spot for children. She always wanted to have another child after me but was never able. The fact that she and Lillian were friends for so long probably contributed as well." Stella stretched out her leg. "My father might be tempted to take Lana hostage as a bargaining chip, but I don't think he would actually hurt her. It's Harvey you need to look out for."

"Your cousin needs to be put in an asylum."

"I'm a fan of military school myself, but that works too."

He shot her a surprised look. "Really?"

A small grin played on her lips. "I even requested an application from that school in Westhaven. The next time he screws up, I'm shipping him off."

Jordan's laugh bounced off the buildings. Stella hissed at him to be quiet.

"I always knew you didn't like Harvey," he said, "but I didn't realize how deep it went."

"I spend most of my time keeping him in check. If it was up to him, he'd march into your house and slaughter everyone he found. I'm more keen on the political side of it. Back your opponent into a corner until they have no choice but to surrender."

He clicked his tongue. "You're revealing dangerous secrets, Rook. What would your father say?"

"No worse than what *your* father would say for skipping out on your family for days."

His mood took a nosedive. "He shouldn't involve Lana."

"You're right. He shouldn't. But what are you going to do about it?"

Jordan's silence was answer enough.

He had no rutting clue.

He searched his pockets for another cigar but came up empty. Stella had gone back to watching the hotel, leaving him free to look at her. Her expression took him by surprise—placid, thoughtful, almost calm. *Unguarded.* It surprised Jordan so much that his next words slipped out of his mouth.

"Do you—" He clamped his lips together, but Stella had already turned to him, brows raised, so he forged on. "Do you ever wish the feud didn't happen?"

There. He said it. The words hung in the air between them, and Stella's brow furrowed.

"Of course I do," she said. "Who doesn't?"

The answer surprised him, too. "Why?"

"What do you mean, why? Who in their right mind wouldn't want to take back twenty years of strife and bloodshed?" Her gaze turned distant. "Just because I participate doesn't mean I enjoy it."

He studied Stella, an idea forming in his head. He glanced down. Silas' room window was dark. The Tradows didn't appear to have anywhere to be tonight.

Better to be scared and innocent than brave and corrupted.

He turned back to Stella. "Would you be opposed to scaring a little girl for the greater good?"

Of all the things Stella planned to do tonight, being let into the Daelik house by its own heir was not one of them.

Jordan seemed to sneak out often, because he knew just how to bypass the guards stationed around his home. He moved with a practiced ease, helping Stella up the drainpipe on the side, sneaking over the roof, and slipping through the window into the attic.

It was too dark for Stella to get a good visual, but she thought she saw the outline of a bed as Jordan cracked the door open. This was a guest bedroom, probably.

"It's clear," Jordan hissed. "Third door on the left. Remember the plan."

The plan was simple enough. Stella arranged her hair on either side of her face as she went to the right door and braced her hand on the handle. Jordan gave her a light nod. She set her features into a cool mask as she opened the door, letting it swing open on silent hinges. She could just make out a girl sleeping in the bed, her figure outlined by the dim moonlight. Her breathing was soft and even.

Stella hated to disrupt her, but as Jordan said, this was for the greater good.

So she drew her knife and flung herself on the bed.

Her hand slapped over Lana's mouth before she could scream. The girl's eyes widened as she pressed her knife—the dull side so as to not hurt her—against her throat.

"It's nice to meet you, Lana Daelik," she crooned. "My name is Stella Rook."

Lana's eyes widened further.

She traced the knife along her throat. "A little birdie told me that you joined the Ravens. Congratulations. Do you have your tattoo yet?"

She shook her head frantically, pressing as far back into the bed as she could to get away from the blade.

Stella flashed her a smile. "Ah, what a shame. No tattoo means it isn't too late to back out." Her fingers dug into her cheeks. "I look forward to meeting you on the street, Lana. You and I will have lots of fun together. My cousin Harvey wants to meet you, too." Lana let out a low moan, and Stella dug in the knife. Not enough to hurt, but enough for her to feel the pressure. "Careful, feathers. I don't want to hurt you." Her smile was wicked. "Yet."

A tear streaked down the girl's cheek, and Stella decided she'd scared her enough. "I'm going to let you go this time, but you have been warned. If you mess with the White Roses, there will be retaliation. You will not like the consequences, Daelik. This is your only warning. If you scream when I let go, I will not hesitate to kill you."

Then she was gone, darting back through the door and snapping it shut behind her. She threw herself up the stairs. Jordan tugged her into the attic a split second before Lana's door opened and the tear-streaked girl teetered out, looking around for her attacker. Stella and Jordan watched through a crack in the door as she gaped around before flinging herself downstairs, no doubt to find her parents.

"What did you do?" Jordan breathed.

"I frightened her." Stella examined her nails. "No permanent damage. A few nightmares, perhaps, but nothing she won't recover from."

Jordan shook his head, a smile tugging on his lips. "You should get out of here. Lana is about to raise hell when she wakes my parents." His smile slipped. "Thanks, Rook. I know it's not really your place to help with my family affairs, but I appreciate it."

"Putting terror into the hearts of young Ravens was part of the oath I took when I was born."

He rolled his eyes. "I mean it, little thorn. You aren't as bad as I thought."

Stella studied him in the dark, the boy who wanted nothing more than to protect his little sister. "You're not so bad either, Daelik."

CHAPTER 27

It took an hour to calm Lana down enough for her to explain who she'd seen. John sent out patrols to comb the streets for Stella, but Jordan had given her careful instructions on where to go. With her grace and stealth, they'd be chasing a wraith in the dark.

Jordan made his own escape shortly after Stella. As expected, Mateo came to his hotel room before dawn to tell him of Lana's attack—and to tell him that Lana was no longer willing to join the gang.

Mission accomplished.

It was hard to feign ignorance, to not come to Stella's defense when the rest of his family cursed her for what she had done. Lana still trembled when Jordan entered the house, Lillian rubbing her back while coaxing sips of tea into her. She took one look at him and flung herself into her brother's arms.

"I'm sorry I didn't listen to you," she sobbed. "I thought I was going to die. Stella Rook had a knife to my throat and I thought—"

He shushed her, brushing a hand over her hair. "It's alright, Lanabug. There's no way she's going to get back in here." His gaze flickered up to his father, the portrayal of a son concerned with his family's well-being. "Right?"

John rubbed his temples. "Right."

There was no apology from his father. Jordan hadn't expected one. The entire family pretended the incident at Lana's birthday dinner never happened, that Jordan hadn't skipped out on the family for two days— even though he'd been right. He silently gloated for the rest of the day.

But his mood was dashed when a messenger handed him a sealed envelope that afternoon, no name or return address to be found.

Jordan ripped it open, staring at the swirling cursive inside without understanding a damn thing it said. So he waited until his parents left Lana alone for a minute, then snuck up beside his sister and dropped the note in her lap.

"Read this for me, please," he whispered.

Her brows scrunched as she whispered the words.

S and C are at my house. They have a meeting with their friends tonight. I thought we could join them.

—LT

"What does that mean?" she asked, handing it back.

S for Silas. C for Celia. And LT for little thorn.

A smile played on Jordan's lips as he cast the letter into the fire.

"Just some business I have to take care of." He ruffled her hair. "Get some rest, Lanabug."

He met Stella on the same rooftop. She wore her usual black, the tight material hugging every dip and curve, her long braid snaking down her back. She glanced at him. "Given that the Ravens have been combing the streets for me all day, I'm assuming it worked."

He gave her a crooked grin. "Like a charm."

"Good. I really didn't want to come into confrontation with her."

"Thank you again for doing that," Jordan said softly. "For doing it, *and* for not taking advantage of it."

Her face softened. "If I had a little sister, I wouldn't want her involved, either." She smirked. "But now you owe me one, Daelik."

"Name your price." She opened her mouth, and Jordan quickly amended, "A reasonable price, that is."

Stella had the nerve to look crestfallen.

Silas appeared about twenty minutes later. Jordan was grateful to stretch his aching legs as he followed Stella across the rooftops. She moved with a grace that Jordan could never hope to master, leaping from rooftop to rooftop with barely a sound. It wasn't a wonder he hadn't been able to catch her until now; she was so quiet that sometimes he mistook her for another shadow.

Silas led them to the same pub as before. He entered through the front; Jordan and Stella climbed through the window in the back and crept downstairs. The pub was quieter than it had been last time, but the same meeting room in the back was occupied, leaving Stella and Jordan to take the one to the left.

A man was speaking, not the same one from last time, though his accent was similar.

"That could work. How attached are the gangs to it?"

"Jordan," Stella hissed. "Give me your book."

His hands curled protectively around his sketchbook. He'd brought it with him in case he had time to kill. "No way in hell."

Stella muttered a curse and ripped it out of his hands. He tried to protest, but she flipped to the back of the book—a blank page—and grabbed the pencil from him.

"A fair amount of people from both sides are employed there," Silas said from the other room. Stella jotted something down, and Jordan realized she was recording the conversation. A smart move, but he was still nervous at seeing his sketchbook in the hands of the White Rose heir. "They rely on it as neutral ground, a trade center of sorts. Celia went down there a few nights ago to scope it out and ran into the Daelik heir."

The man made a low noise. "We heard about that. Rumor has it one of Daelik's men fell at her hand."

Silas coughed. "I know she acted before it was time, but it will not happen again."

"It better not. The boss was unhappy."

"It won't happen again," Silas reassured him.

Stella scribbled furiously on the page as the first man spoke again. "We can have the Red Harbor occupied by the end of the week. There's a ship about to leave from Vance; we can chock it full of our men and an offer from the boss to buy out the Harbor. Do you know what the owner is like?"

There was a rustle of paper. "Timothy Evans. Stays in his office and almost never shows his face, just stays holed up and collects his profits. The right amount of money would sway him. But remember—we've got to be subtle. If Daelik or Rook catches wind that I am behind the change of ownership in the Harbor, then the entire plan will go downhill."

Jordan exchanged a look with Stella. They weren't the people Silas was referring to, but a Daelik and a Rook certainly knew about their plan.

"Subtle. Got it." The man hummed to himself. "Do they know who Ritton is?"

"I've kept my business in Stokes as vague as possible. As far as I know, they don't know who Ritton is. I don't think he's ever done business in Lochridge."

"I think you're right, but I'll talk with him to make sure."

"You can have the Harbor by the end of the week?"

"Consider it done. The boss won't mind having such an important trading post no matter which way the dominoes fall."

Silas sighed. "I'm still having trouble deciding which gang I should pick. They're evenly matched."

The man hummed to himself. "There's got to be a weakness you can exploit."

"The Rook-Daelik feud has been going on for two decades," he argued. "I need to keep the best from both gangs for ourselves while eliminating everyone else. Marcus Rook and John Daelik both need to go—their history would complicate things. Most of their families as well."

"What about the heirs?"

Jordan and Stella swapped another glance.

"Oh, they're something else," Silas said. "They'd both be useful. The Rook girl is intelligent, but she doesn't get along with Celia very well."

"And the Daelik boy?"

"Celia wants to keep him around. Told me that ever since they first met. And they say he's good with the guns—the best sharpshooter in the city."

Stella let out a little hiss at being dismissed simply because Celia didn't like her. Jordan smirked at her and motioned for her to keep writing.

"You'll figure it out," the man said. "I know you, Tradow. You get the job done." There was a thump, objects being shifted around, papers rustling and the scuff of boots on the floor. "I think the twins are coming down next week to check in. The boss will probably want an answer by then."

"I'll see what I can do."

"Alright. I'll make sure this all gets back to Stokes. You take care in the meantime."

Stella lowered the pencil as the door opened and shut, two pairs of footsteps fading down the hallway. Jordan glanced up at her once he was sure they were gone. "Well?"

Stella slumped against the wall. "He's going to take over the Red Harbor." She raked a hand through her hair, pulling curls out of her braid. "This is bad."

He tapped his book. "We have a written record of their conversation. Do you think they'll go for it?"

"Our fathers? Heavens, no. If they didn't even give us the time of day to express our concerns, they won't listen to a record we jotted down. They'll just think we made it up, if they even sit down to read it in the first place."

"So this whole meeting was for nothing," Jordan muttered.

Stella angled her head. "Not exactly. *We* know what they're up to now. We know Silas is planning on taking over the Red Harbor, but he's afraid of us finding out because he knows it would look bad on him." Stella flipped through her notes. "*We've got to be subtle. If Daelik or Rook catches wind that I am behind the change of ownership in the Harbor, then the entire plan will go downhill.*"

His eyes gleamed. "So let's make it go downhill."

Stella caught onto his train of thought. "If we can prove that Silas is behind the coming takeover of the Harbor..."

"Then our fathers will finally realize what he's up to and kick him to the curb," he finished. "Brilliant. You're smarter than you look, little thorn."

She rolled her eyes. "You know a lot about not looking smart."

He clutched his chest. "Oh, what an insult."

"You were drunk during that first meeting we had, and look how it ended. If that isn't a lapse of judgment, then I don't know what is."

"Unlike most people, I am perfectly capable of making rational decisions while intoxicated."

"So working with your enemy is rational."

"An enemy of my enemy is my friend," he countered.

She raised a brow. "So we're friends now?"

"I don't know. Are we?"

Stella opened her mouth to answer, but footsteps from outside had them pausing. The sound faded—just someone walking past—but

Stella's features were etched in worry. "We should get out of here."

A part of him screamed at her to answer the question, but on the outside Jordan just swallowed. "Right. Let's go."

CHAPTER 28

The wind whipped her hair into her face as Stella and her family made their way to the Barter Streets. Marcus had left his office in favor of checking in with his businesses in person. Stella was glad; it was high time her father focused on his gang again.

The Rook family garnered more than a few stares as they made their way downtown. Evelyn had opted to stay behind to help Aunt Melonie with her newborns, leaving Stella, Marcus, Zoey, and Harvey as the lone representatives. Harvey grinned at anyone that dared to look too long, his hand drifting to the hunting knife looped through his belt.

"It's a nice day," Zoey remarked, a bland attempt at conversation. Stella peered up at the cloud-ridden sky and couldn't think of a proper response, so they lapsed into silence once more.

Marcus went through the businesses of the Barter Streets one by one. Stella couldn't help but glance towards the southern end, where several Raven guards watched her carefully. She flashed them a smile before tossing her mass of hair over her shoulder and flouncing after her father.

By the time they made it to the end, raindrops had started to sprinkle the ground. "What a nice day," Stella muttered to Zoey, her tone mocking.

Zoey pinched her. "A little drizzle never hurt anyone. At least it's not storming."

"Don't jinx it," Harvey warned.

"*Rook!*"

He rolled his eyes. "Too late."

The four of them turned to see a different kind of storm watching them from the border. John Daelik's light brown hair whipped in the wind, the gusts so harsh they threatened to rip his black suit right off his body. His eyes were the same color as the clouds above. Stella didn't recognize everyone that he was with, but she picked out a few of his close advisors and friends, and her eyes widened when she saw who stood to John's right.

Silas raised a brow as he surveyed the assembled gangs. Tobias was behind him, his ever-present shadow. Celia stood to his side, wearing a green dress that matched his suit, her jewelry emerald-themed today. "How pleasant to see you here, Mister Rook."

John didn't seem to hear him speak. "What are you doing out here?"

Marcus made a show of surveying the red line that marked the border. "What am I doing on my own territory with my own family? My, what a predicament."

Stella smirked, but it slipped as another figure emerged from the back of the crowd.

Jordan's eyes snapped to Stella's face. She kept her expression impassive as she returned his stare.

John narrowed his eyes on Marcus. "Your daughter attacked mine in the night."

Oh. *Oh.*

"What are you talking about?" Marcus demanded.

John stabbed a finger at her. "Your bitch of a daughter attacked Lana the other night."

"Watch who you're calling a bitch," Stella snarled.

He sneered. "My apologies."

Her blood heated at his tone. "I did not attack your daughter."

"She saw you with her own two eyes."

"I did not *attack* her." A half-truth still counted as a truth, didn't it? "I have no interest in harming Lana, nor does anyone else in my family. You'd better watch your tongue before you fling accusations again."

"We won't tolerate attacks against my little sister," Jordan said.

The words didn't have near the bite they usually did. This felt strange—arguing with Jordan on a public street like they always did, but this time feeling no ill intentions towards him. Knowing that he fully believed her on this subject. Knowing that *he* was the true culprit here.

"I won't tolerate being falsely accused," she shot back.

John stepped forward. "Listen here, Rook—"

Harvey whipped out a gun. "Get back on your rutting side of the border."

John looked down at the foot he had on the line, his toes on the Rose side. Then he looked Harvey dead in the eye as he stepped over.

"What are you going to do about it?" he asked softly. Harvey made to step forward, but Zoey grabbed his arm. The Ravens had them outgunned, and judging by John's smirk, he was well aware.

Stella didn't miss Jordan's jaw clenching. This wasn't like John—he usually stayed firmly on his territory. Stella had a feeling he was showing off in front of Silas. Indeed, Silas' pale blue eyes widened in appreciation of the spectacle before him.

She narrowed her eyes. If John wanted to play, they would play.

Stella drew her gun and marched up to the Daelik patriarch. His brows shot up as she pointed her gun at his face and snarled, "Get back over the border or I'll make you eat a bullet."

Jordan stepped forward, drawing both revolvers. The other Ravens dared closer, but none came over the border as Harvey ambled forward with a wicked grin.

John just smiled. "Do it. I dare you."

Stella met his gaze.

And pulled the trigger.

Every person present flinched as the gunshot echoed through the streets—including John Daelik, who jolted at the blast of heat the barrel pushed into his face. His eyes darted to the gun Stella had moved just a few inches over, firing into the blank space next to his head.

"The next one," she said softly, cocking the gun and returning it to its original position, "goes through your skull."

He held her gaze for a long, long moment. A raven cawed in the distance, the only sound.

Then he took a step back.

"You're weak," he said. "You can't even pull a trigger when you have someone at gunpoint."

"Don't tempt me with a good time."

John just smiled. "The next time you have me at gunpoint, Stella Rook, you'd better pull the rutting trigger."

And with that, he turned on his heel and stalked away.

Silas hung back long enough to give Marcus and Stella an approving look before trailing after him. And then they were gone, disappearing into Raven territory without a backwards glance.

"That was impressive."

Jordan turned to see Celia walking up to him. He'd fallen behind to allow his father to storm ahead. Silas had already caught up to him, the two locked in a deep conversation. Giving Silas a tour of their territory wasn't on his list of fun things to do today, but his attempt to slip away unnoticed was botched when he heard John address the Rooks.

Rats, it had felt weird trying to be mean with Stella again. The two of them had crossed a line at some point, but Jordan wasn't really sure where the line was or what it meant, only that it made it hard to look her in the eye with their families standing right there.

"What was impressive?" he asked, finally replying to Celia. "Us or the Rooks?"

"Both. The way your families can become so angry after just seeing each other."

"There's a lot of bad blood between Pa and Marcus Rook, and they've passed it down to the rest of us."

Celia pursed her lips. "That Rook girl is something else."

He looked at her sharply. "What does that mean?"

"She pointed a gun at your father's face and you didn't even flinch. She's all bark and no bite, hmm?"

His shoulders relaxed. "Yeah. A lot of bravado masking a weak soul." He tilted his head. "You've got a hidden side to you, as well."

She gave him an innocent look. "I do?"

They hadn't talked since the incident at the Harbor. Jordan hadn't *wanted* to talk to her. Every time she looked at him, something primal in him screamed to run, to get away from that ice-cold gaze.

"I never told my father about the Harbor," he said. "He heard about it and dismissed it as a rumor. Didn't think it was possible for you to have killed one of his men."

She lifted a shoulder in a shrug, her pale hair spilling across her arm. "What a shame."

"I suppose you aren't going to tell me what you were really doing at the Harbor so late at night?"

"What were *you* doing at the Harbor so late at night?" she fired back.

"Following you."

Celia barked a laugh. "You're funny, Mister Daelik."

Jordan flashed her a cocky smile. "Do you really think we ran into each other by mistake?"

Her eyes narrowed, taking in his expression, realizing he was serious. "You really were following me."

"I was." He leaned in close. "I don't trust you. Or your father, for that matter." He caressed her cheek, a lover's touch to anyone that was watching. "Watch your back, Celia Tradow. You never know what's lurking in the shadows."

Celia's red-painted lips parted into a smile. "Likewise, Jordan Daelik."

He smiled. "I'll see you around."

Celia leaned out of his touch. He turned away, a triumphant smile tugging on his lips.

CHAPTER 29

The cobblestones were rough underfoot as Stella sprinted down the Barter Streets, ignoring Zoey's warning, telling her to come back before she got herself killed. A crowd had formed on the docks of the Red Harbor. Stella recognized her father's dark hair and shoved her way towards him.

She got halfway there before she saw it. Saw him.

The body sprawled out on the wooden planks. Blood seeped from the hole in his chest, dripping through the cracks in the planks to the ocean raging below. The life was bleeding out of those eyes, face tilted to the sky without seeing it. The red rose he'd tucked in his shirt pocket now laid on the ground next to him, the petals crushed and trampled underfoot. He was pale underneath the bruises marring his face. Unmoving. Still.

Dead.

Liam was dead.

Stella didn't know when she started crying, only that her cheeks were wet when Zoey finally caught up to her, wrapping an arm around her cousin and trying to pull her away. She fought out of her grip, dropping to her knees beside Liam. She pressed two fingers to his neck. There was no pulse. She hadn't expected one.

A scream tore out of her throat. It echoed across the Harbor, wild and wicked and full of rage. Stella trembled as she lifted her head to look at her father. "Who?" she rasped.

Marcus started but did not answer.

Her voice rose to a shriek. "Who?!"

He swallowed. Regained his composure as he stared his heartbroken daughter in the eye.

"Jordan Daelik," he said.

Beside Marcus, Harvey angled his head, his eyes slitted. But Stella's vision blurred as her rage focused on that name, her anger directing itself at those four syllables.

"How," she gritted out, the word guttural.

Marcus started saying something about how he didn't know, the Ravens had gotten ahold of classified information, they shouldn't have known Liam was connected to the Rooks—

His voice faded out as Stella's fingers curled around Liam's stiff hand. Ever so gently, she brushed a hand over his face, closing his eyes, those warm hazel irises never to see the sky again.

No more smiles.

No more stolen kisses.

No more sitting side-by-side at the piano.

And worst of all, no more goodbyes.

"Where is he?" she choked out.

Everyone blinked. "Who?" Zoey asked.

"Jordan Daelik. Was he caught?"

"No—"

"Is he at his house?"

"I don't know—"

"Tell me where he is," she snarled.

Marcus stepped forward. "You can't get revenge. Not tonight. You need to grieve."

She bared her teeth. "I need to put him in the ground so Liam can have justice."

His face paled. "Stella."

She ignored him as she stood up, her eyes on Liam's face. He looked peaceful. If it weren't for the blood soaking the front of his shirt, the bruises on his face and neck, she would have thought he was sleeping.

She turned to Harvey. "Give me a gun."

He cocked a brow, but drew a revolver and dropped it into her awaiting hand. "Stella," Marcus tried again, but she was already brushing by him, her eyes scanning the assembled crowd for anyone with a Raven tattoo.

"Don't follow me," she snapped as she stepped over the border and onto the Raven's territory, the gun a comforting weight in her hand.

Stella jolted awake with a gasp, her blood-soaked dreams still flashing before her eyes. Not dreams—memories. Memories of Liam as she last saw him alive, walking through her mother's rose garden with his hands tucked in his pockets. Then later that night, his corpse on the Red Harbor.

I'll make it up to you later. Deal?

Deal.

She kicked off the blankets, dragging a hand through her tangled hair. She did her best to take the memory of Liam and condense it down into a small ball before shoving it into the chest in the back of her mind, twisting the key in the lock with savage ferocity. Thinking of him made her fingers tremble and vision blur. She couldn't afford to let thoughts of him overtake her mind when she was working with his killer.

Jordan Daelik. Every time she heard that name, she heard her father rasping it, felt the rush of anger that had overtaken her the night Liam died.

Stella laid back down, her breathing uneven, but sleep did not visit her again that night.

She was late to their meeting.

It took her a while to collect her thoughts and gather up the courage to face Jordan. It wasn't that she was scared of him—she was wary of what memories his presence would unlock, what feelings would rush up. She needed him. Jordan was the only way to get access to the Ravens' side of the deal. He gave her free passage onto the Ravens' territory when they were following Silas, an open link to whatever Silas was doing with the Daeliks, insider knowledge that Stella could only hope to gain one day. She needed him, and he needed her. She couldn't kill him.

Not yet.

The anger was good. She'd been getting too close to him lately, had let her guard down too many times in his presence. As much as it hurt, the memory of Liam was a good reminder of why she should be wary around Jordan.

Stella clenched her fists and blew out a breath between her gritted teeth, and it was only once she had regained her composure did she start walking again.

When she slipped between the rocks and entered Jordan's private beach, she was surprised to see him with his book in his lap, a candle dripping wax onto a nearby rock. His pencil flew over the page, using the candlelight to see by, his eyes narrowed in concentration. She wondered, not for the first time, what he was writing.

Jordan slapped the book shut before she could get a good look. "Ready?"

She nodded. "Let's go."

The route to the hotel was as familiar as the back of her hand. Jordan climbed up to the roof first, then turned and offered Stella a hand up. She ignored him and climbed up herself, unwilling to accept his touch.

They took up their usual positions on the roof, Jordan with his legs dangling over the edge, Stella kneeling low with one hand braced on the ground. Silas' window was dark. She wasn't expecting anyone to come out tonight, but she hoped all the same. The distraction would be welcome.

Silas emerged before the heirs could exchange a word. Stella pushed off the roof and all but sprinted after him, leaving Jordan to trail behind.

Silas was alone this time, and he was taking his sweet time strolling through Rose territory. Stella was all too aware of Jordan's presence behind her, his soft intakes of breath right before he jumped across a gap, his muttered curse when his foot slipped. She honestly didn't care if he fell or not.

"Lana is doing better," Jordan said quietly, breaking the silence. "She's stopped shaking like a leaf."

"Good."

He chuckled. "You put the fear of God into her, little thorn. Don't make a habit of scaring kids, please."

"Fine."

"And that face-off down at the border was something else. Celia cornered me afterwards. There's something off about her. She wants something out of me, but I'm not sure what her motives are."

"Interesting."

He angled his head to the side, his brown eyes narrowing. "Lots of one-word answers tonight. Are you feeling alright?"

"Yes."

"That was on purpose, wasn't it?"

Stella pressed her lips together. "Just be quiet."

"Aha! She said more than one word at a time!"

Her head whipped towards him. "Shut up, birdbrain. I don't feel like talking."

"Well, I do feel like talking," he countered, "and I also want to find out what is the matter with you. It's going to be a hell of a night if you continue to be sour throughout it."

She only glared at Silas' back as he entered his usual pub.

Jordan let out a sigh. "You're going to make me guess, then. Was it the border skirmish?"

Stella descended in silence, unwilling to give a response.

"Silas? Celia?"

Nothing.

Jordan chewed his lip. "Your family? Your father? Harvey?" He angled his head. "Did something happen to someone?"

Stella eyed the window she and Jordan usually went through. It was closed tonight. "You could say that."

"Tell me," he pressed.

"Why should I?" she said blandly. "You'll just taunt me with it."

Understanding dawned in his eyes, but a gunshot sounded before he could respond. For a brief, wild second, Stella thought it was Jordan shooting at her, until she spotted the figures running towards them.

Bloody hell.

"Run," she snapped, not waiting around to see if Jordan obeyed. She sprinted as fast as her legs would take her, bullets flying past her as she ran deeper into the heart of Rose turf.

She didn't dare look over her shoulder, not when she was being chased by her own people. Whether it was the guards at the border or a different patrol, she didn't know, but she did know that she had just been spotted wearing the enemy's color in an area known to shoot anyone wearing black on sight.

A huff of breath told her Jordan was still on her heels. "What do we do?" he hissed through gritted teeth.

Stella turned a sharp corner. A bullet pinged off the bricks overhead. "If I knew, we wouldn't be in this situation."

She risked a glance at him to see him openly glaring at her.

"I said I wouldn't speak of Liam any more," he growled. "And I've kept my word. Why are you upset about it now?"

Stella glared back. "Just because you don't talk about it doesn't mean it didn't *happen*." Her hands trembled. "It doesn't stop me from thinking about him, from remembering what happened to him. My childhood friend. The man I gave my heart to. *You killed him*."

"Rook—"

"*Now is not the time.*"

They rounded another corner. Stella was going so fast that she nearly slipped, but Jordan grabbed her arm and roughly hauled her upright.

"I apologized," he hissed.

"You still killed him," she snarled, ripping her arm away as tears threatened to stream down her cheeks. She *never* lost composure like this, but the dream of Liam in the early hours of the morning had wrecked her. "You hunted him down." She choked on the memory of Liam's pale face, his body cold and eyes glassy with death. She had never cried as hard as that day. "You hunted him down and beat him and shot him and *left him to die!*"

The Roses had gained some ground. The conversation took Stella's mind away from the fight, and she made a wrong turn by accident, putting them at a dead end.

"Shit," she breathed.

But Jordan was already pulling his revolvers. "Do I have your permission?"

Stella hated to do it. She really, really hated it, and she hated Jordan even more. But the only other option was risk getting caught with Jordan *rutting* Daelik while wearing his color, so she gave him the barest of nods.

The Roses rounded the corner, and Jordan opened fire.

"The incident with Liam happened three years ago," he shouted over the gunfire.

"I loved him!" she screamed.

The Roses fell back, Jordan twisted to face her as he reloaded his revolvers. "Would it help if I said sorry?" He paused. "Again?"

She gritted her teeth. "I don't need your pleasantries."

"Then what do you need?"

The question took her aback. When she didn't answer, Jordan sighed, cocked both guns in unison, and marched out of the alleyway. There were three short shots, and when he returned, his expression was murderous.

"I only killed him because my father told me to," he said, stepping over the bodies of her Roses. "I didn't hunt him down for sport, Stella. It's part of the feud, just like everyone else that I've killed, everyone that *you* have killed." He gestured at the carnage around him. "This is nothing. You've got blood on your hands just as surely as I do, Stella Rook."

Yes, she had blood on her hands. But Stella hadn't really participated in the feud before Liam died. She'd gone to the meetings and exchanged insults with the Daeliks and carried out tasks for her father, but mostly she stayed away. She hadn't been one to get her hands dirty.

Then Jordan killed Liam, and everything changed.

Her teeth gritted. "But you *did* hunt him!"

"And I'm sorry!" he exploded. "Whatever it takes for you to get over this, let me do it. I don't like thinking about it anymore than you do."

"I highly doubt that. If you were really sorry, you wouldn't have rubbed it in my face all those times." Her mouth twisted. "If your father ordered you to kill someone else, would you do it?"

"Stella—"

"Would you do it?" she demanded.

He hesitated. "I—" His face flushed. "Probably."

"Then save your apology," she snapped.

Jordan scrambled after her. "But if Liam Turner showed up again and my father ordered me to kill him," he said hurriedly, "I wouldn't do it. That was before I knew you, before I considered you as…"

"As what?"

"As a friend."

Stella reeled back.

"We aren't friends," she ground out.

"Why not?"

"We hate each other," she said, glaring at the corpses on the ground.

"Why, because of the feud?" His eyes blazed. "I thought we both wished it never happened."

"But it did."

Jordan dared a step closer. "Give me a reason why we can't be friends."

"Because of the feud. Our families. They wouldn't allow it in a million years."

"Our rutting families don't dictate our relationship," he said, his face bleak.

"We are working together to bring Silas down. What happens when this is all over? Do you expect us to just go out for tea?"

He snarled. "I expect us to realize there might be something beyond this stupid fight. It's our parents who hate each other, not us."

Anger seeped through her. "In what rutting world do I not hate you?"

Jordan studied her. "I was hoping this one." He scratched the back of his neck. "We make a good team, you and I. This feud doesn't have to last forever. Our fathers will die, we will inherit the gangs, and then we can make our own damn decisions. We can end this for good. I've been thinking about it. The reason we hate each other is that we've killed people that belong to the other's group. Without our fathers' friendship falling apart, without the feud… we might have been friends. Marcus and John were friends at one point. Evelyn and Lillian were. Why can't we give it a try?" He lifted his gaze to look at her. "You helped me with my sister. You're helping me with Silas. Who am I to say that you are a bad person?"

Stella clenched her jaw, even as her fingers shook. What he was suggesting…

"I hate you because you killed Liam," she choked out, but it was half-hearted.

Jordan looked crestfallen. "For the last time, I'm sorry, Stella. If I could take it back, I would." He raked a hand through his hair. "I would take a lot of things back."

Stella studied him, the realization slapping her in the face. "You don't want your sister joining the Ravens because you regret ever doing so."

Jordan looked away, and that's how she knew she was right. Her eyes widened.

"Jordan," she breathed.

He huffed a laugh. "Don't you have regrets?"

"Of course I do."

"Then you know what it feels like."

A quiet, pensive silence filled the air. Stella angrily wiped at her cheeks, knowing they were red and blotchy. She was a beautiful woman, but she was an ugly crier.

Jordan said quietly, "I've been thinking about our fathers. They're so wrapped up in their feud that they can't see another danger staring them in the eye. Pa won't even listen to me. He thinks he's got it all figured out, but he is being blinded by hate. Twenty years of conflict, and for what?" He wrung his hands. "I'd rather put myself at risk by proposing a friendship than to blind myself with envy and hate. I don't want to become the next John Daelik. And I don't think you want to become the next Marcus Rook."

"No," she breathed, her voice so quiet it was nearly lost in the night. "I don't."

He glanced at her. "Then let's not make the same mistakes they did." He stuck out his hand. "I would like to be your friend, Stella Rook."

Stella stared at him, at the hand he offered. At the promise that came with it.

She wanted to hate him. The bodies of her own Roses were dead at his feet and the worst feeling she could conjure up was a dull sadness that seeped through her bones.

Stella stared at Jordan and wondered if she had lost her head. This was betrayal of the worst kind, and she couldn't even bring herself to feel bad about it as she took his hand.

"Same to you, Jordan Daelik," she whispered.

He gave her hand a light squeeze before he released it. Stella dropped her gaze, pressing her hands against her legs to keep them from shaking.

It was an insane idea. But Stella couldn't help but feel at peace with it.

CHAPTER 30

Stella and Jordan lapsed into silence after their conversation, and it was while she was helping him sneak back into his territory did Jordan spot a hotel by the Barter Streets and was struck with a brilliant plan. Silas' hotel room was left unattended most hours of the day, and he thought they might be able to glean some answers from it. Surely there would be something lying around—records or correspondence of some sort that would show what he planned to do. Jordan proposed this idea to Stella in the early minutes after high moon.

The Rook heir didn't quite meet his gaze. "He's coming for lunch at my house at high noon. If you could get into the room without being seen, I can keep him distracted."

And that was how Jordan found himself loitering outside the hotel as rain pelted him from above.

He kept to the shadows as Silas, Celia, and the broad-shouldered Tobias walked past. Celia wore a flowing blue dress that brought out the color of her eyes. Silas' usual striped suit was immaculate. Jordan drew back as they passed by. He waited a full three minutes to make sure they weren't coming back before slipping into the lobby.

The clerk read a book behind the desk. She glanced up as Jordan tossed a small pouch in her lap.

She frowned as she sorted through it, gold coins clinking from within. "This will cover your stay for a few nights. May I get you a room?"

"I was hoping it would cover you giving me a spare key to whatever room belongs to the three people that just walked out of here." Her brows rose, and Jordan clarified, "And for you to keep quiet about it."

The clerk weighed the pouch in her hand before tossing him the key.

It didn't take long for Jordan to track down the right door. Silas had acquired a three-room suite for his group after Jordan's stunt with the window scared them out of their old one. Jordan slipped into the small living area that served as a connection between the bedrooms, locking the door behind him. He had to be quick.

He started with a rudimentary search of the living room, but he found nothing other than a discarded bracelet that obviously belonged to Celia. He entered the first bedroom. It was bare save for a bag in the corner that held clothes and weapons. Tobias' room, if he had to guess. The bodyguard hadn't even bothered to unpack.

In the next room he found a wardrobe full of dresses and skirts, an entire case of jewelry placed on top of it, hair products beside that. After some digging, Jordan found the black outfit he'd seen Celia in at the Harbor, her bandolier of knives hidden underneath. He found some stationery in her luggage but all of it was blank.

That left one last room. Jordan entered Silas' room with watchful eyes. He spotted the window that he and Stella watched from the top of the neighboring building. The curtains were closed. Jordan moved quickly, shifting through Silas' collection of striped suits and funny hats. The man had an unwise amount of gold stashed in various places throughout his luggage. Jordan couldn't help himself from swiping a pouch of it to replenish the money he'd given the clerk.

He looked through drawers and suitcases and closets but found nothing of interest. The rooms were frighteningly bare—the only people who went to such great lengths from keeping personal information out of their rooms were those with something to hide.

Jordan clenched his jaw and turned for the door.

Wait.

Something brown peeked out from behind the lamp on the nightstand. He moved it aside to find a small, leather-bound notebook. Jordan eased it open. A ledger.

Perfect.

He recognized the numbers, but he couldn't make sense of the words written next to them, so he tucked it into his pocket. After one last glance around to make sure he hadn't missed anything, Jordan rushed downstairs, tossing the clerk another coin along with the key to ensure her silence. She gave him a pretty smile as he vanished through the doors.

Stella wasn't fond of huge dinners with family and guests. Things in her family had a tendency of getting out of control very quickly when they were all gathered together. Shoving them all at one table so they were forced to look at each other only added fuel to the fire, and having guests over was just embarrassing.

Marcus opened the door to let Silas and Celia in while Tobias took up a position outside. The Tradows smiled at the Rooks, but Stella did not return it.

Jordan would be in their hotel room right now, searching for clues.

And she had agreed to be friends with him.

"Miss Rook," Silas said to Stella. "After our discussion the other day, I have something for you." He handed her a sleek black box. "Here you are."

The gesture raised warning bells in her mind, but she forced a smile as she slid it open. She blinked in surprise.

"A violin," she murmured, lifting the instrument out of its cushioned box. The oiled wood gleamed. She couldn't help herself from plucking a string, the single note filling the room, filling that part of her soul that yearned for music. She glanced at Silas. "Thank you."

He smiled. "I had it imported from Stokes. The card in the box has the address of the best tutor I know. Now that you have an instrument to play, you should learn how."

It was a beautiful instrument and a surprisingly thoughtful gift. Stella caught Celia rolling her eyes behind her father's back. She smiled at Silas and said thank-you again before carrying the violin up to her room.

After carefully placing it in its box and leaving it on her bed, she returned downstairs, gracefully taking her usual seat to her father's left. Marcus sat at the head of the table, Silas on the opposite side. Evelyn sat to Marcus' right, Celia at the same position to Silas. The rest of the long table was filled in with Stella's family.

They'd dressed up for the occasion, too. Stella herself wore a flowy dress with billowing sleeves that she'd always been fond of. With her hair done up and the ring of bruises around her neck fading, she thought she looked rather pretty. It was a shame that the only people who would see her would be her family and the one man in this city she *wasn't* trying to impress.

The table itself was laden with a feast fit for a king. Dishes of roasted chicken, scalloped potatoes, and thick soups surrounded a centerpiece of red roses. Dessert consisted of lemon bread and candied orange slices and apple tarts drizzled in honey. Stella pulled her plate towards her, plastering a smile on her face whenever Silas glanced at her from his end of the table.

This was going to be torture.

"I must thank you for the invitation," he said to Marcus. "I've learned a lot about the Lochridge customs in my time here, but I daresay the food is the best of all."

Marcus let out a hearty laugh. "I would have to agree with you there. There's nothing better than a homemade feast, Lochridge style."

Celia picked at her chicken. "I prefer the food from Stokes. It isn't as greasy."

Stella resisted the urge to leap across the table and shove Celia's face into the bowl of creamed corn. Instead she turned to Silas. "What are the customs in Stokes like? I imagine the Workers' Union has some unique traditions."

He had told his companion at their meeting that he was keeping his information concerning Stokes as vague as possible. If that was his plan, then Stella was determined to make him talk about his hometown as much as possible. Eventually he would slip up and give her something to work on.

He chewed thoughtfully. "Stokes is not as pleasure-oriented as this town is. We are focused on hard work and integrity. We work from dawn till dusk and sleep soundly at night, no matter what our job may be."

A vague answer if there ever was one. Stella flashed a smile. "What line of work are you in?"

"Business management. I help manage for Stephen Trace—that's my boss, the leader of the Union. I keep track of his expenses and employees and so on and so forth."

"And now you're his representative?"

"I volunteered for the job. I visited Lochridge once before on a trip with friends and enjoyed its atmosphere."

Interesting. "Are you good friends with Mister Trace?"

Silas laughed. "I wouldn't be in charge of so many of his affairs if I wasn't. He trusts me, and I trust him in return. We've been friends for a long time."

Stella smiled and took a bite of her chicken.

"I've been doing research on the Union," Harvey said, earning a surprised look from nearly everyone at the table. He sat two chairs down from Stella, Zoey wedged between them. "I've heard nothing but good things. Seems to be an effective group."

Zoey and Stella exchanged a look.

Silas' blue eyes fixed on Harvey. "You and I agree on that, Mister Rook. The Union gets a bad reputation because of its unusual tactics, but it is effective."

Harvey nodded his agreement, to Stella's horror. The only people that would think the Union was a good thing would be someone who benefited from it like Silas obviously did. Stella eyed Silas' gold watch and wondered if Harvey was just sucking up to gain favor with the Workers' Union representative, either to help the Roses get the alliance or for his own benefit.

Zoey's eyes flashed as she stared at her brother, but she said nothing. Stella wished she would speak out, wished that anybody at this table would so that she would know she wasn't the only one who protested.

The only one besides Jordan Daelik, at least.

She didn't quite know what had possessed her to befriend him. His words were true, yes. What he'd said about them turning into their fathers had rang a bell in Stella's mind, had made her realize she didn't mind the veiled banter with Jordan as much as she had in the past.

Still, she couldn't get Liam's face out of her head, couldn't help but feel that this was the ultimate betrayal. Working with Liam's murderer? She was crazy. And worst of all, it undid everything Stella had worked so hard to achieve these last three years, upending her grand plans to avenge his death. She was no better than Jordan was, and that made her insides twist.

But if Jordan had only been acting on his father's orders when he killed Liam—she believed his words were true—then the majority of her reason to be angry at him was moot. It was John she should have a problem with; ever since Stella and Jordan had started working together, he hadn't jeered over Liam's death, hadn't rubbed it in her face. It was like talking to an entirely different person.

But it was *Jordan Daelik.* Just because she found little reason to hate him didn't mean the rest of her family would feel the same way. Stella would be killed if her secret was found out. Marcus would disown her and let Zoey or Harvey take her place as the Rook heir. Zoey was older but Harvey was male, and Stella knew her father had always wanted a son. The thought of her crazed, violent cousin becoming the leader of the White Roses made her stomach churn. The streets would run red.

Stella was in too deep to turn back now, so the only thing she could do was keep her mouth shut and pray for the best.

CHAPTER 31

Stella waited for twenty minutes before Jordan slipped through the rocks, his book tucked under his arm. His eyes widened in surprise. "You're early."

She was sprawled out on Jordan's usual rock, the top button of her blouse undone. "I had to get out of there. Silas extended his stay."

Night had fallen, and Evelyn, ever the proper hostess, invited Silas, Celia, and Tobias to stay in the guest bedrooms just down the hall from Stella's. She gritted her teeth every time she thought about it. A raven perched on the edge of a rock, rustling its wings, but one glare from Stella had it shooting back into the sky.

Jordan tossed something in her lap. A small book, not the same one she'd seen Jordan writing in. She picked it up between two fingers. "What is this?"

"A ledger I found in Silas' hotel room. It was the only thing worth taking. He keeps his secrets well."

Stella flipped through it quickly—a bit *too* quickly, for her finger caught the corner of a page, slicing it open. A single drop of blood hit the paper before she drew her hand back.

She cursed, sucking on her finger.

Jordan frowned at where the blood splattered on the margin at the top of the page. "You stained it."

She scowled. "We'll have to take the page out if we plan on returning this to Silas' room."

He nodded and carefully tore out the page. After a moment, he ripped off the top margin, separating the stain from the written words. Stella opened her mouth to ask what he was doing, then closed it as he picked up a pencil and lowered it to the page, his brown eyes narrowed in concentration. She caught herself studying his face and averted her gaze.

"There," he said, sitting back.

She studied his handiwork. The red drop of blood had been transformed into the petals of a small rose. A delicate stem was sketched underneath. The drawing was simple, yet there was a quiet elegance to it that Stella found herself drawn to.

"You're very talented," she remarked, thinking of the book he was constantly working in. She assumed all this time he was writing in it, but perhaps he used it for something else. "Do you draw often?"

He shrugged, ripping the page further so the rose was isolated on a small square of paper. "I sketch a lot." A wry smile. "My father hates it. He says it's not masculine."

Stella remembered his face when he was drawing the rose. Eyes narrowed in concentration, mouth quirked ever-so-slightly to the side. It had been a quiet, peaceful expression, not the arrogant smirk she was used to.

It was... *nice.*

"I don't think we should worry too much about what our fathers say," she said at last. "Their opinions aren't worth much outside of business and bloodshed, and even then it's questionable."

A smile curled over his lips, and her heart fluttered in response, something that both horrified and excited her.

"Here, you can have it," Jordan said, holding out the sketch. "Since it's your blood and all."

She took it from him. Their fingers brushed together. She jerked back, wondering if she imagined the way Jordan's eyes lingered on her outstretched hand.

Stella shoved the drawing into her pocket and used her other hand to *carefully* flip through the ledger, using the candle she brought along as a light source. It was about half-full, a neat list of expenses. She didn't recognize all the shorthand Silas used, but the amounts of money alone were enough for her to frown.

"He is blowing a lot of money," Jordan said, peering over her shoulder.

Stella shook her head. "He mentioned during the dinner today that his job in Stokes is to manage his boss' expenses. This could be Silas' expenses, or it could be Trace's."

Jordan studied. "Then why so many dates from last week? He's been in Lochridge for days now. He shouldn't have anything to record."

"Unless he's buying stuff for his boss."

"But where would he keep it?" he asked. "I've been in his room. Nothing seemed out of place. I didn't recognize any of the merchandise he could have bought from the Barter Streets."

She sucked on her teeth. "It might not have been from the Barter Streets. Black market dealers operate in every part of the city. Or he might have paid someone to hold whatever he bought until he's ready to leave or can have someone from Stokes take it back home." She studied the ledger once more. "Victory is a brand of whiskey, right? He's made multiple purchases of that."

"I've never seen him drunk," Jordan murmured.

Stella couldn't resist. "Maybe *you* were too drunk at the time to notice."

His eyes narrowed to slits. "My point was, nobody can buy that much Victory and drink it all without somebody noticing. He's stashing it somewhere."

"But where?"

Jordan drummed his fingers on his leg. "I think we're going to need more than just a ledger."

He was right. A list of expenses wasn't enough. "But you've checked his hotel room and found nothing. Where else can we look? It's not like we can travel all the way to Stokes and search his home."

"I don't know," he admitted. "We need to find out why he's bleeding gold with nothing to show for it."

Silence fell between them. Stella's jaw worked as she glanced at Jordan. He sat with his legs dangling over the edge of the rock, the wind playing with his light brown hair.

"I feel like a storm is coming," she said at last.

He glanced at her. "How so?"

"I just have this bad feeling. Like something is about to happen."

He snorted. "Whenever I get that feeling, Declan just tells me I have indigestion."

Stella choked on a laugh. "Your cousin is something else."

"He really is," Jordan agreed. "Always got a bottle in his hand and a snide remark on his tongue." He smirked. "Victory actually happens to be his favorite brand of whiskey."

Stella leaned back against the rock, eyes trained on the ocean. "Why does he drink so much, anyway?"

He shrugged. "I don't know, to be honest with you. He clams up every time I mention it." His voice lowered. "His father isn't exactly cream of the crop, though. Dec's got scars on his back that I know didn't come from a fight. He goes out of his way to disrespect Dan, and there's a lot of bad blood between them." He stretched back next to Stella. "Something happened between them, I think. Something I don't really want any part of."

"And what about Half-Daelik?"

"He hates that nickname."

She rolled her eyes. "Mateo, then."

Another shrug. "Mateo is the product of an affair trying like hell to be someone respectable. He studies. Wants to go to a university. He's courting a girl and treating her better than our father treated my mother."

"Do you know who his mother is?"

"A barista from the west side. I never met her; she dropped Mateo off on our doorstep when he was born, accepted Pa's payment to keep quiet about it, and skipped town. No one's heard from her since." Jordan glanced at her. "What about your family?"

It was Stella's turn to shrug. "Zoey's nice. We talk about clothes and boys, which seems to be her entire life. She got her heart broken when she was sixteen and hasn't had a serious relationship since."

"And her brother?"

Stella laughed. "The psychopath, you mean?"

"Your word, not mine."

She chuckled. "Sometimes he's alright. But we have to tip-toe around him because anything could set him off. Zoey's really the only one who can keep him in check, and that's only part of the time." She glanced at Jordan. "In all seriousness, though, if you ever pick a target in the Rook family to kill, it better not be Zoey. Killing her will snap the only leash we've got on Harvey."

He winced. "Noted."

They lapsed into silence. Stella snuck a glance at Jordan. He caught her looking and quirked a brow.

"This is weird," she blurted out of desperation to fill the silence.

"What, talking about our dysfunctional families in front of the heir of the family that they've had grief with for years?" Jordan laughed. "Yeah, a little."

Stella elbowed him. "It's just strange being so open with someone that you've hated for your entire twenty years of living."

His expression softened, turning thoughtful. "That's true."

She risked a glance at him in the dark, his eyes thoughtful, his face lacking the arrogant smirk she was used to. It was different. A good kind of different.

But before she could continue the conversation, a voice reached them.

A nasally voice that was all too familiar.

Jordan's brow creased. "That's Silas."

Stella shot to her feet. "He's supposed to be at my house tonight."

The two exchanged a look and rushed out of their hiding place. Sure enough, Silas Tradow strolled down the street, the wind carrying his voice to them. Tobias and Celia were with him, the latter wearing her black getup. There was a black briefcase in Silas' hand that swung back and forth with every step.

Stella and Jordan swapped a dark look before trailing after them.

The trio walked with a brisk pace, their steps more urgent than before. Stella didn't wait to see if Jordan followed before launching towards the street, her dark clothes hiding her frame, nothing more than another shadow in the dark. A huff of breath told her Jordan was following, but her eyes remained pinned on the Tradows as they entered the Red Harbor.

They disappeared among the bustle of the Harbor within seconds. Stella's boots hit the cobblestones, footsteps behind her telling her that Jordan was still close.

"I wonder what's in that briefcase," she murmured.

"Only one way to find out."

Jordan cast a quick glance around to make sure the coast was clear before darting behind a stack of crates. Stella followed him, her face flushing as they pressed close to remain hidden from both Silas and the

JAYDEN THOMPSON

sailors. It felt very much like when she was a child, her and Zoey and Harvey ducking behind furniture while they spied on Marcus.

Only this wasn't a game, and if they were caught, there would be consequences. The White Rose and Raven heirs, alone together? Oh, how people would talk. She gritted her teeth and forced herself to focus as they trailed the Tradows as deep into the Harbor as they dared go.

Jordan clenched his jaw. "Where are they going?"

That was a good question. Stella watched Silas look around, his pale gaze settling on a sailor with a Raven tattoo a few feet away. A cheerful smile crossed his face as he approached, the perfect businessman. The two had a conversation, Celia and Tobias watching from a safe distance away. Stella couldn't hear what was being said, but she definitely could see when Silas opened his briefcase, removed a paper and pen, and had the sailor sign it. The deal was finished with a shake of their hands, and then Silas strode away with a bounce in his step.

She caught Jordan's gaze and raised both brows. He responded with a tiny shake of his head.

What was Silas doing?

The two heirs watched him make his way through the Harbor, shaking hands and giving out warm smiles. He didn't open his briefcase for every interaction he had, but when he did, there was a signature passed on, and his partner looked more than pleased.

It wasn't until Stella recognized the next sailor that she realized something.

"Gang members," she breathed in Jordan's ear.

He stilled. "You're right."

Whatever Silas was doing, he was going after the gangs. Stella eyed the raven tattoo on the last sailor he spoke with, the familiar faces the previous ones had. Not just Jordan's gang, but hers too.

"You went to his hotel room," she murmured. "You didn't see anything like this?"

"No, and I searched everything. Whatever he's having them sign, it was somewhere else."

They watched him move on to his next victim, Celia trailing after them.

"We have to figure out what that is," Jordan said.

Her mind whirled. "It couldn't have come from his hotel room. He's

209

staying at my house tonight, and he didn't have that briefcase with him."

Jordan blinked. "He didn't come from your house. He came from the other direction. And Celia has those clothes—they must have snuck back to the hotel room at some point."

He was right. Stella cast a look in the direction they came from, the direction of his hotel.

"How much time do you think we have?" she asked.

"At this pace?" Jordan considered. "He's about halfway through the Harbor. We've got a few minutes, at least." He glanced at her. "What are you thinking?"

Stella faced him, her eyes gleaming. "Are you up for a little break-in?"

CHAPTER 32

Jordan had watched the hotel for so many nights in a row that he'd memorized every crack and crevice in its front facade. He skidded to a halt outside of the door, but Stella caught his hand before he could open it.

"We can't both go in there," she hissed.

Right. Jordan swept an assessing look over her. She was wearing all black—the Ravens' color. It would look suspicious if she walked into a hotel on neutral ground wearing the enemy gang's color.

"I'll go and let you in through the window," he said.

Stella nodded and vanished into the night. Jordan fought for his composure as he pushed open the doors.

The red-headed clerk glanced up as he walked in, then did a double-take. "M—Mister Daelik, how may I assist you?"

She remembered him. Jordan drew up an easy smile and leaned against the counter, his tone conversational. "That man I checked in on from room thirty-two. He's still there?"

Her eyes shifted back and forth. "Yes, but—"

Jordan dropped a handful of coins on the counter. "I'll be needing a spare key."

She paled. "I can't do that."

"Let me rephrase." He had a revolver out in a flash. He didn't point it at her, but the presence of the gun alone was enough to make the clerk gulp. "Give me the spare key for room thirty-two or you will have quite the mess to clean up."

Two minutes later, Jordan twisted the key in the lock, and the door to room thirty-two swung open.

He went straight for the window and flung it open. Stella grunted as she clambered inside. Jordan offered her a steady hand and tugged her into the room.

Her nose wrinkled as she sauntered to the bed, her amber eyes taking in everything. Jordan lit a lantern as they began their search. They cleared Silas' room first, then Celia's, then Tobias', then the living room in the middle. When nothing came up, Jordan went back to the first room and searched the bags again.

"Nothing," he muttered, throwing aside a handful of coins that had fallen to the bottom.

"This is a lot of money," Stella remarked. "But no jewels. Where does Celia keep her valuables?"

Jordan peered under the bed. "There's a vault in the lobby."

"So she put all her jewelry in the vault downstairs? Seems impractical."

He looked up at her. "Where else could it be?"

She paced the room. "Is this the same room as last time?"

"Yes."

Stella stopped pacing, her eyes going to the painting on the wall. It was just a simple mural of the ocean at sunset, a pop of color against the dull tan wall, but what if...

Jordan came to the same conclusion as she yanked the painting off the wall, revealing a hole behind it.

He cursed, his voice awed. "He carved a bloody hole in the wall."

"A secret vault." It was chocked full of rolled-up papers and diamond-encrusted jewelry and pouches bursting with money. Stella pulled a page out and scanned it. "It's a contract." She let out a curse of her own. "A contract to join the Workers' Union."

Alarm shot through him. "Who signed it?"

"It's blank."

Jordan pulled out another bundle of papers and examined them. The words made no sense to him, but he could tell they were the same document. "Silas is looking to recruit." Another smaller bundle was pulled out of the hole. Jordan swore, his voice low and filthy. "And these *are* signed."

Panic sharpened Stella's eyes. "By who?"

He thumbed through them. "I don't know. I can't read. But there's twenty in total. Deckhands at the Harbor, if I had to guess." He glanced up at her. "Silas is sweetening the deal for the Harbor by making a bunch of employees quit at once, joining the Union instead. If the owner thinks it's going under, he has more incentive to sell."

"Subtle," Stella noted.

"Right. He doesn't want any of this tracing back to him."

Stella scanned the contracts with a sigh of frustration. "These contracts had to have been made by Silas' boss, but without proof Silas himself has a hand in this, I don't think it will be enough to prove it to our fathers."

"If we tell them and then the Harbor gets a new owner, that should be proof enough."

"I'd prefer them to come to their senses *before* the Harbor is bought out by a man who doesn't even live in Lochridge."

Jordan whipped out a pencil and notepad and handed them to Stella. She scribbled down the names of the men on the contracts, then he rolled them up and returned them to their secret vault. The painting was returned, the lantern extinguished, and the ledger Jordan stole the last time he was here was put back in its proper place. Stella and Jordan turned to the doorway, but footsteps in the hall had them freezing.

"That—" Stella started, but Jordan grabbed her by the arm and hauled her into the closet. And not a moment too soon—the door opened, and Silas walked in, dropping his briefcase into the armchair.

"That went better than expected," he said.

Tobias walked in and went straight for his room. Celia closed the door behind her, playing with her curtain of white-blonde hair. "It did. Rook and Daelik must not be running their gangs well if their people are so eager to switch sides."

Jordan had a sliver of a view, but his focus was not on the conversation in front of him. It was on Stella, the two of them crammed into the tight closet, so close that he could feel her breath on his neck. He was acutely aware of every place their bodies touched, of her heart pounding in time with his, of the hand he still had on her arm.

Light filtered through the crack, just enough for Jordan to see her throat bob.

Silas let out a chuckle. "Indeed." He glanced at the clock. "Speaking of, we'd better head back. I don't want them to wonder where we've been."

Celia sneered. "The Rook girl will be the one to ask the question. I guarantee it."

"She is a problem," he murmured.

Stella stiffened as Celia tossed her hair over her shoulder. "I don't like her attitude. You should let me take care of her."

"Killing the Rook heir will look mighty suspicious, don't you think?"

"Then we blame it on the bloody Ravens! She's got a whole line of enemies that would love to take the fall."

Stella's teeth flashed in the dark. Jordan squeezed her arm in silent warning.

"Now is not the time for action," Silas said, voice firm. "All Stella Rook has right now is a theory. The same can be said of the Raven heir— he doesn't trust us either. Our first step will be to gain their trust, and *then* we can see about further action." He gave her a sharp look. "I don't want things with Stella to escalate."

Celia leaned a hip against the table. "What's the stick up her ass, anyway?"

"I've talked to her father a bit." Silas moved out of Jordan's view. "Her lover was killed by the Daeliks a few years back. She wasn't very involved with the gang before that, but the incident pushed her to really step up as the heir." His voice faded, suggesting he'd turned his back to them. "He says he's sorry for what happened, but he's glad that it did. Stella Rook is a name that Lochridge won't forget anytime soon."

Jordan wasn't sure Stella was breathing. Through the crack, he saw Celia's eyes gleam. "I can make them forget."

"No, you won't," Silas said sharply, moving back into view. "We need to be more subtle than that. Hold off on any action concerning Stella Rook, and that is an order." He paused. "Daelik, too. I don't know what's going on there, but—"

Jordan was surprised to see a softer expression enter Celia's eyes. "I like him. He's got potential."

"He's not better than Rook."

"Difference is, he's good to look at."

Silas straightened. "Don't tell me your fascination with the Daelik boy stems from your attraction to him."

Celia twirled a lock of hair around her finger. "I want to keep him around."

Not a confession, but close enough to make Jordan see red. Silas sighed. "Celia, we have to remain level-headed and unblinded. Don't let your feelings get in the way, or I will be forced to handle things."

Celia didn't seem too happy with the prospect. She pouted as she stalked to her room, presumably to change. Silas watched after her with narrowed eyes before picking up the briefcase and heading towards the painting on the wall. Jordan held his breath as Silas removed the painting, opening up the secret safe and placing the briefcase inside. If he noticed anything amiss, it didn't show. Just as he put the painting back, Celia returned, her black attire replaced with a dark blue dress. Jordan raised his brows as he watched her tuck a knife into a hidden pocket.

Silas called for Tobias, and the three of them exited the room. Jordan didn't dare to breathe until he heard their footsteps fade away, and even then, he waited another minute before easing open the closet door.

Stella tumbled out, her cheeks bright red. The two heirs exchanged a look, and without another word they lunged for the window to make their escape.

It wasn't until they were well down the street with the hotel out of sight did they dare talk again. "I'm tempted just to plan an assassination on Silas and call it done," Stella muttered.

She couldn't hide the slight tremor in her voice. Jordan had seen the change in her eyes at the mention of Liam, so he was careful not to broach the subject. He doubted Stella wanted to talk to anyone about it, much less *him*.

Jordan pulled a spare bullet from his belt and twirled it between his fingers. "Me too, but Stokes is a big town. Trace could send someone else to take his place." He made a face. "Though I will not stop you from killing Celia if you so wish."

She bared her teeth. "That bitch is plotting my murder!"

He raised a brow. "Do you expect me to do something about it?"

She leveled a glare so cold on him that a chill went down Jordan's spine.

"I don't want you to do anything," she said, her voice carrying a lethal edge. "I am going to rip her rutting throat out and toss her into the ocean.

She's been a priss since the moment we met, and if she thinks she can try to kill me…"

Stella finished by drawing a line over her throat. Jordan chuckled under his breath. "Whenever you plan to take on Celia, please let me know. I would pay to watch that fight."

A half-hearted smile broke through her angry expression. "A duel at high noon would be interesting, wouldn't it?"

Jordan grinned as he leaned against a lamppost. "That would be amazing."

Stella shared his grin for a second, but it faded. "We've got to figure out what to do," she said, folding her arms over her chest. "This is getting out of hand. He's vying for the Harbor, yes, but he's also going after the very members of our gangs. I don't want rats from Stokes sticking their hands into my city."

Jordan paused, gripping the bullet between two fingers. "Stokes."

"What about it?"

"That's where Silas is from, right? Where this Trace figure is from. Where the entire Union started." He looked at Stella, hit with a sudden realization. "We don't have to prove what he's doing in Lochridge. All we have to do is tell our fathers about what happened in Stokes and all the other towns under the Union. If their situation was anything like ours…"

Stella came to a stop. "Those towns didn't have the situation with the gangs, but they might have still faced a hostile takeover. Or at least something bad enough to make our families think twice before throwing their hat in with Silas."

"Exactly," Jordan breathed.

She grinned. "Feathers, that's genius."

"But how do we get information on Stokes?" he mused.

"My father's heard of the Union before. He didn't have details, but he heard it from someone in this city. Stokes is close enough there has to be someone who's visited recently or has family there."

"So all we have to do is figure out who that is."

"Without Silas finding out," Stella added.

A grin curled over Jordan's lips. "Looks like we have our work cut out for us, little thorn."

CHAPTER 33

The next morning did not go as planned.

Stella wanted to slip out first thing and search for a connection to Stokes, but her careful planning was thwarted when Harvey banged on her door at dawn and told her they had a job. She didn't feel like facing her father, so she allowed Harvey to give her the details, and an hour later, she found herself standing on the outskirts of Lochridge.

"This is a waste of time," she muttered. The Western Road stretched out before them, picking up at the end of the Barter Streets and cutting all the way to Westhaven. It was the busiest road leading in and out of Lochridge, and Marcus had gotten a tip that the Ravens had a shipment of contraband coming in with intentions to sell on the black market. Stella didn't know why he couldn't have sent some low-level scrubs to intercept the wagon instead of the heir and her cousins, but she knew better than to question her father.

Even if her insides were boiling after what she heard the night before.

"It's not a waste of time," Zoey said.

She and Harvey sprawled out in a grassy spot next to the road. Stella didn't dare sit next to them; there was far too much dust being kicked up by the carriages passing through, and she didn't want her clothes dirty. "It could be hours before he comes."

"Or it could be minutes. We just need to stay alert."

Stella glared at the road. "This is not a job for the heir of the White Roses."

"You're impatient today," Harvey remarked. He had his knife in his hand and was using the tip to squash a line of red ants passing through, killing them one by one. "Why?"

"I have better things to do than to sit on the dirtiest side of Lochridge, watching for a man that might not arrive until nightfall."

Zoey perked up. "Maybe not that long. Look."

Stella followed her gaze to see a wagon drawn by two horses coming towards them. The wagon was covered with a tarp, but its driver was in plain view, his shoulder-length brown hair tied at the base of his neck.

"He matches the description," she murmured.

Harvey stood up, the ants forgotten. "He sees us."

Indeed. The man snapped the reins, and the horses picked up speed, going from a steady canter to a run.

"Shit," Zoey said.

The wagon was coming in too fast for them to stop. Stella pulled her gun, intending to shoot the driver off of his seat, but then Harvey ran past her. A shout rose in her throat as he launched himself at the speeding wagon, grabbing the side of it just as it shot past.

Stella's mouth dried out. "He's mad."

"We already knew that," Zoey said, grabbing her arm. "Come on!"

They sprinted after Harvey. Stella let out a hiss as the wheels kicked a cloud of dust right at her, but she became distracted as she realized Harvey had made it over the edge and was now inside the wagon. He grabbed the driver by the neck and shoved him off. He screamed as he fell, hitting the ground with a thump right in front of Stella and Zoey, who skidded to a stop.

He peered up at them, panting through clenched teeth. "What is the meaning of this? I—"

Stella planted a boot on his chest. "State your business here."

"I'm just delivering a shipment of goods," he groaned.

"To who?" Zoey demanded.

"Man named John Daelik." He spat out a mouthful of blood. "What is the purpose of this?"

"What are you delivering?"

His eyes shifted between the two of them. "Textiles."

"Textiles," Stella repeated slowly. "To John Daelik."

"Yes."

She pulled out her gun. "So you're telling me that you're delivering textiles to the man who owns the biggest textile company on this side of the Great River? Seems a little suspicious, don't you think?"

He stammered. "I don't—"

Harvey rode up on the wagon, grinning like a devil. "I think he's lying, cousin. Care to look?"

Zoey smirked as she flounced over to the wagon and flipped the tarp back. "Would you look at that."

Harvey jumped over the seat and picked his way through the wagon. "That's a lot of booze you're transporting."

"Guns and ammunition, too," Zoey said, picking up a small pistol between two fingers. "This beauty has been banned in the East for over three years. What's a chap like you doing delivering it to the head of the biggest gang in Lochridge?"

The man's face paled. Stella cocked her gun. "I don't see any textiles in that wagon, and unless you were completely blind to the contents of your delivery, that means you were lying to my face. And do you know what I do with people who lie to me?"

His throat bobbed. "No, miss. I don't."

She sneered. "I kill them."

She fired, and the man jerked once before falling still. She picked her way over the body, holstering her gun as she joined Zoey next to the wagon. It was laden with boxes of guns and heavy ammunition, bottles wrapped in burlap nestled in between. Stella pried open a sack and was met with money and playing cards—counterfeit coins, if she had to guess, and the cards were no doubt rigged so that they could be read from the back.

"Every bit of this is illegal," she said. "The fake coins aside, I guarantee he didn't have a permit to transport the weapons or the liquor."

Harvey hopped off the wagon, dust kicking up on Stella as his boots hit the ground. She hissed at him, but he just asked, "Do we take it to the sheriff or keep the spoils for ourselves?"

Her father hadn't specified what he wanted done with the goods. "If we take it to the sheriff, then we have to explain what happened to the driver. No, we'll keep what we need." An idea formed in her head, and a grin spread across her face. "Actually, set aside the weapons." She pointed to the pistol Zoey had picked up earlier. Oh, the Ravens were going to hate this. "I have an idea."

"That was highly unnecessary."

Stella looked up from where she laid across the rocks with her feet propped up. Jordan stood in the entrance to the beach, his arms crossed.

"What?" she asked innocently.

He scowled. "Don't play dumb."

She propped herself up on one elbow. "I have no idea what you're talking about, feathers. Please, do elaborate."

He came to stand right in front of her. "Somehow, a shipment of merchandise addressed to my father went missing, only for the sheriff to get an anonymous message that contraband was being stashed at our most prominent business on the Barter Streets. And when we told him the claims were bullshit and he checked for himself, guess what he found?"

Stella made a show of tapping her chin. "He found the contents of the shipment your father ordered, which also happened to be highly illegal contraband?"

Jordan narrowed his eyes to slits. "I know you're behind it, Rook."

"Of course I'm behind it," she said with a laugh. "Father had me intercept the shipment, and I thought we'd have some fun with it." She tucked her hands behind her head. "In all fairness, we actually helped you. The goods made it all the way to your territory without trouble."

Jordan's expression cracked. "You're a bitch."

Laughter traced the words. Stella grinned as she sat up. "I take that as a compliment."

He sat down next to her. "My father is pissed."

"I would expect no less."

He glanced at her. "Did you have any luck finding information on Stokes?"

Stella huffed. "No, that stunt today took all my time. What about you?"

"Not much better. Everyone I've talked to so far has never even visited Stokes. It's a big town, but it's not prominent in anything. The people seem to keep to themselves."

"There has to be a reason for that," Stella murmured. "I bet the Workers' Union had a hand in it."

"Oh, definitely. We just have to prove it." Jordan stretched out his legs. "Those contracts are worrying me. What exactly did they say?"

Stella tilted her head as she remembered something Jordan said last night. "You can't read?"

"Most of Lochridge is illiterate. I don't see how that's a surprise."

"You've sent me a note before."

He glanced at her. "I had my sister write it. Ma taught her how to read, and she's always got her nose buried in a book. I've had her read off all the notes you've sent me, too."

Stella tilted her head. "You're the son of a businessman. I thought your father was prepping you to take over his empire once he passed. That's going to prove difficult if you can't read."

He shrugged. "If it was up to my father, he would live forever and keep me as his heir for just as long. All he cares about is cementing *his* legacy while he's still around to enjoy it—what happens after he dies is meaningless to him."

"Harsh," she said, frowning.

He laughed under his breath. "You're telling me. Out of my entire family, only my parents, Lana, and Mateo know how to read well."

"They taught Mateo?"

"Mateo taught himself. He wants to be a lawyer—says he wants to go to the university in Morisville and study law. He's been gathering up the courage to ask Pa for the money for a year now."

Stella couldn't help but show her surprise. "That's... Good for him. It would be quite the accomplishment."

"It really would," Jordan agreed. "I'm rooting for him, but I doubt Pa will fork over enough for him to go. He's been saving up his own money, but it won't be enough." A sadness filled his eyes. "Mateo's the best of us. If anyone deserves to get out of this town and be a big-shot lawyer somewhere, it's him."

Stella picked at the hem of her shirt. "I used to want to go to that university," she admitted quietly. "Years ago. I planned on going to Morisville and studying—" She broke off with a laugh. "I wanted to study fashion design."

Jordan choked. "You're kidding."

"I am not." Stella grinned at the memory. "I had it all planned out, too. Go to the university in Morisville, then move to Richter City and become a famous designer. The last thing I wanted to do was stay in Lochridge my entire life."

Oh, how vividly she could remember those days. While Lochridge possessed an abundance of interesting things to do, Stella had always turned her nose at how filthy and uncivilized it was, how dirty and grimy and ugly it stayed. Richter City was her plan of escape, her shining castle among a wasteland. Her *dream*. To turn her love of clothes into something that could support her—something that could get her away from the violence and bloodshed and filth of her childhood home.

"So what changed?" Jordan asked.

A wave of sadness crashed into her. "A lot of things. The feud picked up steam. The gang was growing every day. Father wanted me to stay home and help. I refused at first, but after everything with Liam…" She dropped her head. "It got me invested in the feud. After that, I never looked back."

Liam was supposed to have come to Richter City with her. Her plans had died with him. She snuck a glance at Jordan's face to find his expression stricken.

"I'm sorry," he whispered.

She looked away. "Some things just aren't meant to be. No need to apologize."

A beat of silence passed between them.

Jordan cleared his throat. "Mateo's girl is a designer. She wants to own a boutique one day."

It was a weak attempt at livening up the conversation again. Stella gave him a smile that she didn't feel. "Good for her."

"Yeah," he said listlessly.

They lapsed into awkward silence. Stella fiddled with her hands before shooting to her feet.

"It's dark," she said. "We'd better get to the hotel."

"Right." Jordan stood up as well. "Let's get moving."

Stella let him go first, then silently trailed after him, trying to focus on the task at hand rather than the problems of the past.

CHAPTER 34

The violin mocked her.

It sat in its box on the end of her bed, silently jeering at her. Stella hadn't played it yet; while poking around her half of Lochridge for anyone that might have a connection to Stokes—a search that had turned up nothing—she'd swung by a music shop and purchased a beginner's guide for playing the violin, complete with three basic songs to learn. Her fingers itched to pick up the instrument, to leaf through the guide and start playing, but a small part of her didn't want to acknowledge the thoughtful gift Silas had purchased for her. It felt too much like letting her guard down. And after hearing the conversation between Celia and her father last week, letting her guard down was the last thing Stella wanted to do.

So she shoved the violin into her closet, content to forget about it for the time being.

Rook Manor was quiet. Stella had avoided her father for days, not trusting herself to keep a civil head around him after what she'd heard Silas say the other night. The fact that Marcus had discussed Liam with him was enough to irk her; him saying he was *glad* it happened because it got Stella involved in the gang was enough to make her see red.

It was the truth. Liam's death had pushed her to be more active in the gang, to seek revenge against the Ravens rather than letting Marcus and the others do the dirty work, to forge a name for herself as the heir to the White Roses. The incident three years ago had changed her, for better or for worse, but Stella wanted to wring Marcus' throat for discussing it with a man he hardly knew.

She pulled out her dark clothes from underneath her bed and dressed. Something fell out of the pocket and fluttered to the ground. She drew in a sharp breath. It was the drawing Jordan had made, crafting a rose from the drop of blood.

They hadn't spoken in nearly a week, their nightly outings dwindling in light of feud violence. Harvey had led a small team of Roses into Raven turf in retaliation for another round of accusations John had thrown their way. Stella hadn't seen the carnage for herself, but she heard the blood-bath was so violent that the leader of the Raven border patrol had vomited all over himself before fleeing the scene. Both sides of the border had ramped up their patrols, leaving it nearly impossible for Jordan to sneak across Rose territory to join Stella by the hotel. She'd taken advantage of the situation to catch up on some much-needed rest, utilizing her daylight hours to search for information.

But her search had come up empty. There was nothing—not a rumor or a whisper about Stokes. It was like people didn't even remember the city existed. Every lead Stella chased brought her to a dead end, and her frustration was growing by the hour. Her only consolation was that Jordan might have found something—after a near week of silence, she'd finally slipped a note past the guards telling him to meet her at high moon. Surely he had more luck.

Stella twirled the paper between her fingers. The smart thing to do would be to throw it away. She couldn't afford to have any evidence of what she now did with her nights. The chances of her family realizing Jordan had drawn it were slim, but if they found it, there would be quest-ions. Zoey would certainly pry, and Stella wasn't a good enough artist to pass it off as her own.

But the part of her that loved music and harmony, the part that noticed the small details in the tiny work of art... It screamed at her to keep it. To save it.

Her gaze landed on her vanity, at the jewelry box kept there. She crossed the room in three steps and tore it open, hunting through brace-lets and earrings and necklaces until she pulled out a locket. The necklace was made of gold, an oval-shaped locket with an intricate design on it that gleamed in the candlelight. She flipped it open. On the inside was a portrait of her family, taken when she was much younger. There was no remorse as Stella ripped it out and replaced it with the rose drawing, trimming the edges of the paper to make it fit.

It was beautiful. A simple drawing in a golden locket, the spot of red a bright contrast to the cream-colored paper.

Stella's fingers curled over the locket as she slipped the thin chain around her neck.

She finished dressing, double-checking to make sure her gun was secure at her side before blowing out the candles and climbing down the trellis outside. She was halfway to the secret gate when a flash of movement caught her eye. Cursing under her breath, she threw herself behind the nearest rosebush, her braid tangling among the thorns and flowers.

The figure came fully into view, a woman wearing all black, her platinum hair cascading over her shoulders.

Stella's eyes narrowed as Celia Tradow sauntered to the secret gate.

How she had found out it was there, Stella didn't know. It was hidden. Marcus had shown it to Stella when she was just a child; nobody aside from them, Zoey, and Harvey knew about it. How had Celia discovered it? More importantly, what was she doing here?

Marcus had insisted the Tradows enjoy the hospitality of the Rook family for another night, despite them having stayed only a few days ago, meaning they were here until morning. As much as she disliked them, Stella had been keen on the idea of keeping them out of the streets, so she'd quietly pledged her support, careful not to appear too pleased with the idea. Secretly, she had been glad of her mission in town, if only to get out of the house and away from Celia's sneers. But now Celia was sneaking off the property in the middle of the night, her knives gleaming where they were strapped over her chest. She was up to something, and Stella was determined to figure out what it was.

She stole across the ground, slipping through the gate as quietly as possible while picking flower petals out of her hair. Celia was far ahead, not taking near the caution Stella was. Perhaps she wasn't afraid of getting caught. Or maybe she was just more confident in her abilities to sneak by people. Either way, Stella was able to trail her easily, moving like a wraith in the shadows.

Celia entered the city proper and took a right, heading down the Barter Streets towards the Red Harbor. Stella took to the rooftops, watching Celia from the safety of above. Her stride never wavered as she strode through the streets, her hair white in the moonlight.

Stella expected her to go all the way to the Red Harbor, so she was surprised when Celia veered off, disappearing into an alley. The shadows ate her up, concealing her from view. Stella gritted her teeth. Her eyes searched the street, but she'd lost her.

"Rats," she muttered.

And that's when a knife flew out of the dark.

The blade whisked by her head, nearly catching her cheek. Stella scrambled back. Her gun was in her hand in an instant, eyes narrowed as she retreated further back.

"I know someone is there," Celia crooned from below. Stella still couldn't see her. "Someone is on the roof, thinking they are oh-so-clever. Why don't you come down so we can have a talk?"

She didn't know who it was. Stella found solace in that fact as she drew a knife of her own.

"Show yourself," Celia demanded.

Stella would do no such thing. She had to get out of here, had to find Jordan and tell him Celia was up to something. She chucked her knife across the street. It clattered to the ground, drawing Celia's attention as she launched herself across the rooftops.

Below her, Celia let out a wicked scream. A blade caught Stella's arm, making her slip. She felt herself falling, but she lashed out with her hand, catching the drainpipe on the edge of the building and lowering herself to the ground. But by the time she made it there, Celia was already on her, a whirlwind of shadows and steel.

Stella lashed out with a vicious kick. Celia returned it with a punch to the ribs that had her breath whooshing out of her. She clamped her lips shut, refusing to let any noise pass. If Celia found out who she was, this entire game was over. Silas would know that Stella was onto them, and he could spin that information to use it to his advantage. There was no way in hell she would give him that chance.

She kicked Celia again, driving her back out onto the street and into the moonlight. There she paused, chest heaving, her blonde hair swirling around her face like a ghostly halo. She drew two knives, holding them by their tips, her delicate fingers curled around the blades. "Show yourself," she snarled.

Never. Stella retreated, eyeing the narrow exit to the alleyway behind her. If she could just reach it…

"*Show yourself!*" Celia screamed, but Stella was already in motion.

She lunged for the exit, but Celia sent a knife hurtling her way. Stella grunted as a sharp pain flashed through her shoulder. She glanced down to find the hilt of a knife buried in her back, the tip poking through. The sight was enough to make her sick, but she kept running, ripping the knife out and dropping it behind her.

Stella sprinted, faster than she had ever ran before. She heard Celia giving chase, but she had been confused by Stella's exit. The passageway she took was hard to see in the dark. This was one time that Stella's extensive knowledge of Lochridge held an advantage over the Tradows.

She stumbled, her head swimming, the edges of her vision going dark. She had to make it to the beach. *Now.*

At long last, the cropping of rocks by the beach came into view. Stella fell against the rocks, gasping for breath. It took everything she had to remain standing, to lift her head and croak, "Feathers."

There was a flash of movement, then Jordan was there, his arms holding her up. A delirious part of her mind noted his smell, the scent of gunsmoke and seasalt, and leaned into him.

"What happened?" he asked, brown eyes wide.

"Knife," Stella managed. Jordan wrapped an arm around her, his other hand pressed against her shoulder as he guided her to the ground. She didn't fight him. It felt good to lie down, to have his arms wrapped protectively around her. She was too weak to fight the tide of emotion that washed through her. "I was stabbed."

It was so, so cold. Her eyes felt heavy, and she let them close.

"Stabbed?" Jordan asked. "By who?"

When she didn't answer, he grabbed her face with both hands and demanded, "Who did this to you?"

It was the pure intensity in his voice that had her drawing up enough strength to choke out, "Celia," before darkness claimed her.

CHAPTER 35

Her breathing was the only sound in the room, the gentle rise and fall of her chest the sole thing Jordan cared about.

After she came to the beach, her face pale and her clothes soaked with blood, Jordan's entire world screeched to a halt. Then she'd collapsed in his arms. She needed help. Jordan hadn't known where to take her, where would be safe for the both of them, so he ended up carrying her to his house. It was late enough that everyone was asleep, no one to witness him sneaking her into his room and stitching up her shoulder.

But now the morning light leaked through the window, and Jordan had to wrestle with the fact that Stella Rook was unconscious on his bed.

Jordan brought the chair from his desk over to the side of the bed, and that's where he now sat, watching her through tired eyes. He'd taken off her bloodstained shirt, a sloppy bandage plastered over her shoulder and another cut on her arm. A quilt now covered her up to her neck, but Jordan could make out the shape of the golden locket she wore. He'd been too hurried to remove it like he probably should have done. Now he wondered where it came from. It had been tucked under her shirt; had she always worn a locket, or was it new?

Heavens above, he shouldn't be acting like this. What did he care about the Rose heir's choice in jewelry? But he couldn't get his eyes off of it, try as he might.

The last few days had been torture. Not a whisper of information about Stokes, and without being able to go through Rose territory to get to Silas, he'd been driving himself out of his mind. He missed having someone to talk to, someone else who saw the dark thundercloud hanging overhead and was willing to do something about it. Declan and Mateo had picked up on his mood and drug him to the Broken Bottle four nights in a row in hopes that the booze would drive his raging thoughts out of his head.

It hadn't helped.

His gaze drifted to the bandage peeking out from under the quilt. He would kill Celia. There was no doubt in his mind that it had been her knives to do this damage. She would pay. Slowly.

Stella's eyelids fluttered, and Jordan braced himself as she let out a breathy sigh before opening her eyes to reveal those bright amber irises. She blinked once, twice. Then she looked at him.

And the world stopped spinning as their gazes clashed.

Jordan drew in a breath. "I didn't know where else to take you."

She blinked again. "Where are we?"

"My bedroom."

Surprise flared in her eyes, and her gaze slid past him to study the room. Jordan tensed as her whiskey-colored eyes drank in the pictures on the walls, all of the sketches he'd done over the years and pinned up for display. Suddenly her presence felt too intimate. Too personal.

He loved it and hated it at the same time.

Stella's throat worked as she looked at him again. "How—?"

"You collapsed and I brought you back here to stitch you up." A wry smile. "I've had a lot of practice." How many times had he stitched Declan up after a fight? "It's morning now."

"Celia and Silas were staying at my house," she murmured. "I saw Celia sneaking out and followed her, but she realized she had a tail."

"Does she know it was you?"

"I don't think so."

"Good," he growled.

Stella sighed. "I couldn't find anything about a connection to Stokes."

"I didn't, either." Jordan shook his head. "But that's not important. How are you feeling?"

Her eyes flashed at the sudden change in topic. "I'm fine, but I need to get out of here before your family finds me."

"The door is locked, and nobody comes up here much, anyway. You're safe for the time being."

She studied his face before averting her gaze, her hands coming up to undo her messy braid. Jordan tracked every movement as she unwove her hair. Each pin she pulled out sent another chocolate-colored curl cascading down to frame her face, to rest against her shoulders.

He made a show of leaning back as the pins flashed in her hands. "Keep those away from me. They're dangerous."

Stella made a low noise as she dropped them onto the nightstand. Her eyes flickered up to see his gaze still pinned to her.

"Why?" she asked quietly. "You could have walked away, the Rook heir dead and no blood on your hands."

He leaned closer. "Why did you come to me in the first place? The Roses' territory was a stone's throw away. There would have been plenty of men to help you, but you came to me."

Her expression remained hard. Jordan moved from his seat, coming to sit next to her on the bed.

"I saved you," he said softly, "because that is what friends do. You trusted me enough to come to me when you were injured, and I made sure to hold up to that trust."

I saved you because I care about you.

The unspoken words hung in the air between them. Stella sat up, her hand clenched in the blanket to hold it up.

"I do trust you," she breathed. "And that is crazy to say. My entire family hates your guts. I've wanted you dead for what you did to Liam. You hated me until just a few days ago. And yet…"

"Yet?" he pressed.

Her eyes dipped down. "I don't want to be your enemy, Jordan Daelik."

The confession was so quiet that Jordan almost missed it. He grinned, and a full smile bloomed over her lips. And she looked so damn beautiful in that moment that Jordan couldn't resist curling his fingers around a lock of Stella's hair. Couldn't resist leaning in close enough to catch a scent of the luscious floral perfume she wore.

"I don't want to be your enemy either, Stella Rook," he murmured, and then he kissed her.

It was like the world came to a pause, the very air around them holding its breath as Jordan's lips met hers. She melted against him, giving no hesitation as her arms wrapped around his neck. His hands slid into her hair, the silky strands weaving through his fingers. It was like magic. Warmth spread through him, lighting his blood on fire, sending sparks through his body, grounding him and making him dizzy all at once.

This. This is what he needed. What he wanted. What he unconsciously hoped for.

He pulled back to look Stella in the eye. She smiled at him, a genuine expression, not the smirk he was used to, and that alone sent his heart thumping.

Beautiful yet dangerous. Stunning yet lethal. Bewitching in every regard. He loved her and hated her all at once, and he didn't know what kind of person that made him. His heart was on a knife's edge and he wanted to feel it bleed.

So he angled his mouth over Stella's once more and let the fire raging in his blood consume him.

Stella fell back against the pillows, pulling Jordan with her. He couldn't get enough, couldn't pull back out of fear that the world could come to an end if they stopped. It felt like his heart was exploding, what little space remained between them thrumming with raw potential. Jordan couldn't get close enough. He wanted more—hell, he *needed* more—

There was a knock on the door, and Jordan ripped away, his eyes wide with panic. Stella tensed as the doorknob rattled but stayed shut—it was locked. Jordan hurtled for the door as Declan drawled from the other side, "You locked us out, Jordie? Really?"

"What do you want?" Jordan demanded. He pressed a hand against the door, making sure it remained closed.

"We're going to get food," Mateo said. Shit. His brother was out there, too. "Dec is very hungover and very pissy and I would like some help controlling him."

"Don't make this about me," Dec snapped.

"I don't—" Jordan swallowed. "I can't."

"Oh, please, you coward. You always come." Declan rattled the doorknob again. "Why don't you open the door? Have you finally realized your ugly face is too much for us to bear?"

He really was in a mood. Jordan hated to leave Mateo to fend for himself, but what other choice did he have? He glanced back at Stella, panicked. She mimed throwing up, and Jordan all but shouted, "I'm sick!"

Declan grunted, but Mateo asked, "What's wrong?"

Stella patted her stomach. "Stomach hurts," Jordan supplied.

He had the distinct feeling Declan was rolling his eyes on the other side of the door.

"Just go without me," Jordan said, impressing himself with the sickly waver he was able to put in his voice.

Declan sighed dramatically, then two pairs of footsteps thudded down the stairs. Mateo paused long enough to tell Jordan to feel better. Then they were gone, and Stella slumped against the pillow as Jordan groaned and leaned against the door. Their gazes met from across the room. Jordan felt a smile tugging at the corners of his lips.

"*Nobody comes up here much*, huh?" she said, rubbing her injured shoulder.

He fought back a wince as he returned to her side. "At least the door was locked."

She made a strangled noise in the back of her throat as Jordan reclaimed his seat on the edge of the bed. He leaned in to finish what they started, but she pulled away, eyes downcast.

Jordan hesitated. "What's the matter?"

"I need to get out of here," she muttered.

"I sent them away. They won't be back if they know what's good for them."

Stella gave him a tiny shrug, wincing at the movement.

His jaw clenched. "That's not what this is about. What's the matter, little thorn?"

She looked up, facing him fully, those damning eyes boring into his with an intensity that made him blink.

"There is no way this can work," she whispered. "Not in a million years. You and I..." She closed her eyes. "I trust you, Jordan, but my family does not. And your family doesn't trust me. If someone finds out, the two of us are dead."

"Stella," he murmured. But he felt a crack in his heart, a fissure in the fleeting fairytale that sprang up the moment their lips met.

Her eyes opened. "If what happened less than a minute ago is any indication, then this is doomed from the start. We are setting ourselves up for failure."

The words were true. He knew that deep down. But that didn't stop disappointment from flooding him, didn't stop him from leaning in to brush one last kiss against her cheek.

"We'll find a way," he whispered. "Not today. Not tomorrow. Perhaps not even this year. But eventually we will become the leaders of the gangs, and then there is nothing anybody can say to either of us."

"That's a long time away."

"I'm willing to wait."

A rueful smile curled over her lips. They both knew good and well that by the time they got there, things would have changed too much. The chances of one of them being dead by that time were astronomical.

This is doomed from the start.

Jordan pulled away, running a hand through his hair as he stood up. "You're right," he said. "You need to get out of here."

She stood up, grimacing as she rotated her shoulder. "Thank you."

"No problem, Rook."

Stella came closer to the wall, her eyes narrowed as she studied the drawings that hung there. "You're a talented artist. The book you're always working in… It's a sketchbook, right?"

He nodded as he dug through his wardrobe, tossing Stella one of his shirts to wear. Hers had been ripped and stained with blood, so he'd thrown it into the fireplace downstairs and watched until it was nothing but ashes. "I like it. It clears my head."

She huffed a laugh as she tugged on the shirt. "I know what you mean. I play music to ease my mind."

His brows shot up. "You play an instrument?"

"The piano."

Jordan shook his head in disbelief. "I can't imagine the rough-and-tumble Stella Rook sitting behind a piano."

"Well, until recently I couldn't imagine Lochridge's sharpshooter taking the time to draw." She did the last button, rolling up the sleeves and tucking the hem into her waistband to fit her slender frame. He'd purposely picked a white dress shirt, and from a distance, he thought it would easily pass as one of her usual blouses. "I'm great at it, by the way. I'm going to learn the violin next."

He tried to imagine it, Stella sitting behind a piano, relaxed enough to actually play, but was unable to conjure up the image. He opened his window, frowning at the ever-lightening sky. "Can you stay out of sight of the guards or do you need me to distract them?"

She tossed him a haughty look. "Of course I can stay out of sight. I'm not Marcus Rook's daughter for nothing."

She placed a hand on the window, judging the narrow walkway beyond. Jordan had a feeling it would be nothing for her; the way she leapt across the rooftops suggested she was a natural. But she paused in the opening, glancing back at him once.

"Thank you again," she said.

He forced a smile. "You're welcome."

"Same time tomorrow?"

He shook his head. "No, you're injured. I'll go alone tomorrow so you can catch some rest. The next night, though."

She nodded, her gaze not quite meeting his. "I'll see you then."

"Yeah."

Stella swung herself out of the open window. Jordan watched her walk across the roof and shimmy down the drainpipe, making sure she was safely out of sight before latching his window shut. Having her gone did little to ease the feeling in his stomach. It felt as if he'd been punched in the gut.

Jordan stared out the window and realized he missed her already.

CHAPTER 36

Stella was in so much trouble.

Not with her family—Celia and Silas were still in their bedrooms when Stella slipped through the backdoor. Nobody gave her a second glance as she rushed upstairs, though Zoey noted the men's shirt she wore with a teasing smirk. Her cousin wisely kept her mouth shut, and Stella made it to her room without trouble.

She shucked off her clothes, unable to resist the realization that Jordan's shirt smelled of gunpowder as she balled it up and shoved it to the back of her wardrobe. With that out of the way, she dressed quickly, pulling on a light, flowy dress with sleeves that covered her wounds and a pair of sandals. She drug a comb through her hair and spritzed on an unhealthy amount of perfume. Once she was presentable, she gracefully made her way downstairs, trying to keep up the semblance that she was perfectly fine.

But she was not fine. Bloody hell, she was a far cry from it. Celia's attack had been enough to send her mind reeling, but collapsing into Jordan's arms, waking up in his room, his lips on hers…

She shuddered, running a hand down the skirt of her dress. She was in trouble. No doubt about it.

In that moment, Stella had wanted nothing more than to kiss him again. But they were sworn enemies—or their fathers were, at least. A relationship between them would never last. Agreeing to let her and Jordan be friends was one step in the wrong direction; kissing him was a full-blown leap.

A slimy, dark feeling wormed its way into her heart. Forget upsetting her father; being with Jordan was a betrayal of Liam on every level. She didn't know how she had ended up like this, how she had caught feelings for the one person she swore to hate. But how could she loathe him when the feeling in her stomach felt like love? How could she justify putting a bullet in his chest when all she wanted to do was kiss him again?

Stella's mind was a rabid beast, her thoughts as angry as the ocean during a thunderstorm. She didn't understand where she had gone wrong to end up here, but more than that, she couldn't help but wonder why she didn't feel bad about it.

By the time she made it downstairs, freshened up and feeling somewhat relaxed, Silas' group was in the dining room, Evelyn and an army of servants bringing out breakfast. Celia held court at the end of the table, presiding over an argument between Harvey and Zoey. Stella swept in before it could get heated. Celia's pale blue eyes surveyed her from across the table, and Stella had a feeling she suspected something was off.

So Stella served the first strike.

"Did you sleep well?" she crooned, her smile saccharine sweet as she slid into a chair next to Celia.

Her eyes widened for the briefest second before she returned Stella's smile. "Like a baby. Yourself?"

"Oh, I didn't sleep well at all." Stella feigned a yawn. "I heard noise downstairs in the middle of the night. All the tension with the Ravens has me worried about assassins and such, so I got up and looked around. I thought I saw someone wearing dark clothes walking across the property, but they were gone between one blink and the next, so I convinced myself I was just dreaming, but now I'm not so sure."

She took complete satisfaction at the flicker of worry across Celia's face. "I'm sure it was just a dream," she said, and Stella knew she was worried because of how nice her tone was—trying to resolve the problem before Stella could push the subject any further.

Across the table, Zoey gave Stella a wry look. She knew she hadn't been in the house last night; Stella's answering glare warned her to keep her mouth shut.

"I'm hoping it was just a dream," Stella said, responding to Celia, "but you can never be too careful." She flashed a sharp smile. "Can you?"

Her icy eyes narrowed. "No, you can't."

Stella heard the front door banging open, and a moment later, one of Stella's cousins collapsed against the table, panting for breath.

She frowned. "Oliver? What's wrong?"

"Ravens," he wheezed. "Trading at the Harbor. Old man Daelik is there."

"What?"

Stella winced as Marcus entered the room, amber eyes blazing with wrathful fire. "The Harbor, you said?"

Oliver managed a nod. His face was flushed—he must have ran all the way from the Harbor. One look from Marcus had every Rose at the table jumping to their feet, weapons clinking. Silas stood up, too. "Perhaps I can be of help."

Stella gritted her teeth. "We wouldn't want to bother you with such a trivial matter."

"Nonsense. I would love to witness a confrontation. Come along, Celia."

Rats. Stella suppressed a groan.

The group clambered onto horses and carriages and took off, making it to the Harbor in record time. Sure enough, Stella spotted John Daelik's tall frame where he stood with a group of sailors, deep into a conversation. But her throat constricted as she made out the person next to him, his sandy hair ruffled by the wind.

Jordan.

"Damn it," Stella whispered. Zoey, thinking she was referring to the group of Ravens behind the Daeliks, nodded her agreement.

Marcus stormed across the docks. The sailors saw him coming and scattered, unwilling to be caught in the crossfire of a skirmish. The Harbor was neutral ground, but that didn't mean blood wasn't shed here. It was called the Red Harbor for a reason, after all. Even the ravens took flight, opting to circle the sky where they could watch the confrontation from above. Stella's breathing tightened as Marcus halted right on top of the stain on the planks, the place where Liam's blood had seeped into the wood.

Jordan caught Stella's gaze. His face betrayed nothing, but Stella still remembered the press of his lips against hers, his hands sliding into her hair, the look in his eyes as he stared at her like his life depended on it.

"What are you doing here?" John demanded.

Marcus sneered. "I could ask you the same thing."

"I have business in the Harbor that doesn't concern you."

"You're paying off the sailors, just like you were before Mister Tradow arrived."

"And you weren't?"

"You never proved it."

"I didn't have to," John snapped. "You all but admitted it."

Marcus barked out a cruel laugh. "Is that so? Unlike you, I have actual proof that you have been paying off sailors. I have a meeting with the sheriff about it next week."

Something like surprise flickered in John's gaze. Stella found Jordan again, not entirely by will, his brown eyes narrowed as he surveyed her father. His gaze slid to her once more, and she felt her heart flutter in response.

One kiss. *One kiss* and she was a wreck.

Stella tuned out the conversation as John accused Marcus of bluffing, as Marcus' eyes glinted with anger, as Jordan slowly drew his revolvers, as Harvey snapped a warning that had everyone tensing.

But she snapped back to attention when Declan Thatcher unslung his rifle and pointed it at Harvey's face.

"Watch your mouth," he snarled.

Harvey grinned in feral delight. A cold sense of dread slithered down Stella's spine as her cousin reached for a weapon—not his gun, but for the hunting knife at his side.

Zoey muttered a low warning, but Harvey was already in motion, diving low to avoid the blast of Declan's rifle. Someone screamed as the gunshot rang across the Harbor, narrowly missing the other Roses. By the time Declan loaded another bullet, Harvey was on him, knocking the gun out of his hands and tackling him to the ground, his knife gleaming like quicksilver.

Jordan let out a shout and leapt to his cousin's side, slamming into Harvey before the knife could find its mark. Stella couldn't just stand there. She dove for Harvey, catching his arm and dragging it back. She met Jordan's gaze once more, her own panic reflected in his eyes.

Zoey appeared at Stella's side, hissing something in Harvey's ear. He snarled in response. She tried to pull him back but he twisted in her grasp, sending both Zoey and Stella stumbling back. Jordan lashed out and knocked the knife away, but that didn't stop Harvey's fist from connecting with Declan's face a moment later.

The Red Harbor descended into a cacophony of shouting. Stella was vaguely aware of John and Marcus screaming at each other as she and Zoey tried and failed to pull Harvey off of Declan, Jordan and Half-Daelik doing the same from the other side. Harvey tired of their nagging and lashed back with his elbow, catching Stella right in her injured shoulder. She fell back with a grunt. Jordan's eyes widened as he realized what had happened, and Stella froze as a bitter anger entered his eyes.

"Enough," he growled, and with that word he gave up every sense of trying to remain civil.

Jordan's boot slammed into Harvey's face. Blood gushed from his nose as he turned his eyes, livid and gleaming with anger, onto Jordan, locking in on his next target.

No.

Declan groaned as Harvey threw himself at Jordan, the two going down in a tangle of limbs and snarls. Harvey aimed a punch at his head, but Jordan twisted at the last second, using his momentum to send Harvey sprawling. Stella wasn't sure she was breathing as Jordan clawed his way to the top of the fight. His fist smashed into Harvey's jaw, sending his head rocking back.

The look in Harvey's eyes wasn't just mad. He was livid. Furious. Thrumming with anger.

It was a look that could kill, and Jordan was on the receiving end of it.

Jordan drew back his bloody fist to deliver another blow. Harvey bucked, throwing him off-balance. Stella's shout caught in her throat as Jordan was thrown to the ground, Harvey reclaiming his position on top, cocking his arm back...

"*Enough!*"

Everyone froze at the nasally voice that cut through the chaos. For the first time, Stella found herself thankful for Silas' presence as he stepped between the Roses and the Ravens, Celia next to him, Tobias a raging thunderstorm behind them. Stella didn't miss the gleam of his curved blade as he drew it.

"This is no way to live," Silas said, eyeing Jordan and Harvey. "Come on, get up. Celia and I are tired of watching this."

Harvey sneered at Jordan before licking the blood off his knuckles. Then he was gone, stumbling back to Zoey's side. Marcus flashed him a disapproving look.

Celia flitted to Jordan's side, clicking her tongue as she helped him to his feet. Anger pounded through Stella at the sight—especially as she looked right over Declan, still sprawled on the ground. Jordan gave her a tight smile and helped Declan to his feet. Mateo rushed to their aid. The three of them glared at Harvey, Declan's forest-green eyes glinting with barely concealed anger, Mateo's stormy-gray ones narrowed in the most wrathful expression Stella had ever seen from him. Half-Daelik carried the levelest head out of the entire Daelik clan, but Stella couldn't blame his temper for finally coming to the surface when Harvey was involved. Her cousin merely smirked and licked his knuckles clean.

It took a lot of effort for Stella to keep her breakfast down.

This was all wrong. Stella didn't want to fight the Ravens—and she sure as hell didn't want the Tradows acting as peacemakers. Silas now looked between them, the snarling John and Marcus, the smiling Harvey, the fuming Declan, the shell-shocked Stella, the eerily quiet Jordan. His pale blue eyes narrowed as he surveyed the Roses and the Ravens in turn.

"This has been most interesting," he said. "All it takes is an accusation to have you at each other's throats." He tilted his head, his pale hair slipping over his brow. "Interesting," he said again, and something about the way the word rolled off his tongue had the hairs on the back of Stella's neck standing on end.

But then he clapped his hands. "I will not stand for anymore brawls. I am here to dispel tension, not cause it. If either of you are still interested in an alliance with the Workers' Union, then you will learn to remain civil around your enemies." He flashed them a smile. "I assure you, it is a very useful skill."

A skill he practiced, it seemed. John shot one final glare in Marcus' direction before signaling to his family. "Let's go. I don't feel like being around Rook scum any longer."

Marcus bared his teeth, but it went ignored as the Daeliks turned away. Jordan shot Stella one last look before shaking off Celia's hand and limping after his family.

Harvey spat on the ground before stalking away. Zoey trailed after him, and the rest of the Roses took their cue to leave. Stella, however, remained rooted to the spot, her eyes on Silas, watching to see which group he would follow.

But Silas tilted his head to the side, deep in thought for a few seconds. Then he turned and walked up the Barter Streets, straddling the line between the gangs. Celia shot Stella a cold look before following, Tobias as silent as ever as he followed.

Stella narrowed her eyes. He was planning something.

She just didn't know what.

CHAPTER 37

An invitation arrived at Jordan's house the following day.

"*The Tradow family warmly welcomes you to attend a peace gala at the Saltare in two days' time.*" John's eyes flicked up from the invitation as he read the rest of the details. "Is this a joke?"

The entire family was crammed in the living room, watching him read off the invitation. Jordan didn't think it was fake; he thought he recognized Silas' handwriting from the ledger he stole a while back.

"A peace gala," Mateo mused.

"Sounds like bullshit to me," Declan muttered.

He was bruised from his fight with Harvey. Jordan himself wasn't in great condition; the thought of attending a *gala* when his face was covered in bruises and what he was fairly sure was a broken rib was laughable. But John just frowned and said, "The Saltare is in Rose territory."

"They're probably invited," Jordan said. "After Silas' little speech and the fact it's a *peace* gala"—the word was mocking—"I would assume the Rooks got an invite as well."

John grunted under his breath and retreated to his office, still studying the invitation.

The crowd in the living room slowly broke up. Jordan escaped through the front door, hoping a walk would clear his head. A *party*. Either Silas was stupid or he was playing them somehow—and Silas was smarter than he appeared to be.

Jordan fingered his revolvers as he ambled towards the Red Harbor. The skirmish yesterday had broken up quickly, but all he could think about was the look he exchanged with Stella in the heat of battle. Jordan's body ached in all the places where Harvey's fists had found their targets, but it was his chest that ached the most.

She wouldn't get out of his head. Try as he might, he couldn't force her out. He was supposed to be the heir to the Ravens, but what kind of heir got intimate with their greatest enemy? He had taken her to his bedroom and stitched up her wounds, and the kiss—

Oh, the kiss. He was in so much trouble.

"Jordan!"

He turned to see Celia coming after him, her platinum hair swaying in the breeze. She smiled at him, perhaps the first genuine expression he'd ever seen from her.

"Are you alright?" she asked, coming to a halt.

Jordan paused too, sweeping a gaze over Celia's dark green dress before asking, his tone flat, "What do you want?"

She blinked innocently. "I just wanted to see if you were alright after the fight yesterday."

"I'm fine. What do you really want?"

She tilted her head. "I didn't realize how thick the tension was between your families. I've seen some members of your gangs get into fights, of course, and I've heard the stories." She twirled a lock of hair around her finger. "Is it true that your father beheaded a Rose that tried to assassinate him?"

"That was a rumor the Rooks started to get the sheriff on our trail," Jordan lied. John *had* actually beheaded someone before—but the sheriff hadn't been able to prove it, so it was passed off as a rumor. Jordan flashed Celia a sharp smile that was more of a grimace. "They say the real beheader is out there somewhere, waiting to take on the next person who crosses them."

Let Celia unwrap the layers of meaning in that warning.

She examined her diamond-encrusted bracelet. "I've never seen someone beheaded before." Her eyes flashed up to him. "Seems like an interesting way to die."

His eyes narrowed. "What do you want, Celia?"

She dropped her hands, smirking at him, a twin expression to her father's supercilious smile. "I want a lot of things, and I am very close to getting them." She angled her head. "I'll see you at the gala, Jordan."

The way she said his name sent a shiver down his spine. Jordan tensed, but Celia was already walking away, the skirts of her emerald dress swishing with the movement.

Jordan curled his fingers around the butt of his gun as he watched her walk away.

The Daeliks weren't the only ones to receive an invitation. Stella recognized Silas' handwriting on the note her father unfolded, the golden ink gleaming on the creamy paper. The gala would be held at the Saltare, an event hall on White Rose turf, starting at five o'clock in the evening. There would be music and wine and food and dancing. The note said the Rooks were welcome to invite anyone they wanted. Marcus and Evelyn rushed off to prepare the invites—Marcus had intentions to pack the Saltare full of members of his gang to tip the scale in their favor—leaving Stella to pass the invitation off to another family member before retreating behind her piano.

The violin was still upstairs, calling her name. Stella hadn't dared touch it yet.

The note was eventually passed around the entire house. Zoey was the last to get her hands on it. She took one look at the line that called for formal attire and dragged Stella into town with intentions to purchase a new dress.

"We have plenty of dresses at home," Stella muttered.

Zoey kept a firm grip on her arm as she led her into the Barter Streets. "There is no such thing."

Stella sighed. If her cousin was going to drag her into this, she might as well enjoy it. As much as she wanted to keep her mind sharp, she probably needed the distraction.

"Do you remember that place we were at a while back, looking for that drug dealer?" she asked. "They had some nice dresses. Ball gowns, and a lot of them."

Zoey's amber eyes gleamed. It didn't take long for them to find the shop—the Pins and Needles Boutique—but when they entered, the lady behind the counter blanched and refused to make eye contact with them.

The last time they'd been in here, they'd been chasing after a drug dealer that was later stabbed in the back alleyway. Stella gave her a clipped smile and ushered Zoey deeper into the shop.

Zoey hummed to herself as she went straight for a rack of ball gowns in various shades of white. "The bad thing about always having to wear white," she said, "is that a white ball gown looks an awful lot like a wedding dress."

Stella grunted her agreement. "Father didn't say we had to wear white. It's a party. We should do something different."

She arched a brow. "Your parents would disapprove."

"As long as we aren't wearing black, I don't see the problem."

"Still."

Stella fingered the gauzy fabric of a sapphire gown. "What do you think about Silas?"

"What do you mean?"

"I mean, he's planning on killing off one of the gangs, and yet he's playing peacemaker."

Zoey held a white gown to her chest and examined her reflection in the mirror. "The reason for the gala is to get a feel for each of the gangs and how they interact in a tense situation." She glanced at Stella. "It's smart, in my opinion."

Stella inspected a different dress, the silk smooth in her hand. "But don't you think there's something… *off* about this? Silas acts strange to me. And don't even get me started on Celia."

"Now I agree with you on that." Zoey hung the dress back up and moved on to another. "Did you see her lusting after Jordan Daelik yesterday? She was flaunting around for attention. As pretty as she is, she sure is desperate." She selected another garment. "All in all, I hope she and Daelik become a thing. They deserve each other."

Stella bit her lip. "But then Celia's favor would rest with the Ravens, and Silas seems to go along with his daughter quite a lot."

"Well, maybe they'll get together, then Daelik will break her fragile little heart. Everybody wins that way."

Stella's jaw clenched but she turned away before she said something unwise. The idea of Jordan and Celia being together rubbed her the wrong way. Her eye caught a flash of silver, and a smile curled over her lips.

"Oh, Zoey," she sang, sauntering across the store. "I have something for you."

She held it up with a flourish. Zoey's eyes widened as she grinned. "You know me too well, cousin."

She grabbed the dress from Stella and rushed over to hold it up in the mirror. Stella leaned against the wall. "You can't *not* try it on."

It only took a minute for Zoey to track down the dressing room and change. When she emerged, her tunic, trousers, and boots had been replaced by a slim gown of pure silver that glimmered like liquid metal. It hugged her every curve, a slit cutting its way up her leg.

Stella clicked her tongue. "I've got a pair of shoes that will go with it. And that diamond necklace Richie gave you before you dumped him will be perfect."

"And a bracelet, too," Zoey murmured, twisting this way and that while she examined her reflection. "It's not white, but I think it'll pass inspection." She turned to her cousin with a grin. "Now it's time to find you something."

"I already have plenty of dresses."

"But nothing this fancy." She grabbed her arm, not bothering to take off her silver gown before dragging Stella to the nearest rack of clothes. "It's time to go hunting."

An hour later, a pile of dresses of various shades of white and silver lay on the table in the dressing room. Stella frowned as she examined the newest dress Zoey ordered her to try on, a cream-colored monstrosity that made her look like a bride. The others had at least been pretty, potential outfits for the day she married, but this was an explosion of ruffles and tulle and beads.

"It itches," she muttered, tugging at it. "And it doesn't suit my form."

Zoey sighed dramatically. "It's the last dress here that even remotely resembles white. You've got to pick one."

Stella ignored her as she ducked back into the dressing room. She was grateful to change back into her usual blouse, today paired with sandals and her golden locket, which she kept hidden beneath her shirt. The shopkeeper had come by long ago to oversee the two of them, Zoey's dress already purchased. Stella gave the lady a grim smile as she observed the pile of clothes.

Zoey gave a disappointed sigh as she saw Stella in her normal clothes.

"You're a bore, cousin. Can't you pick out *one* dress?"

She drifted off to look at the other racks on the far side of the store, the side that she and Zoey had avoided because of all the bright colors. "I'm not a bore," she muttered.

Zoey arched a brow. "And you're going to prove that to me by picking one of these?"

"Precisely."

There were dresses in all shades of emerald and sapphire and lavender. Stella studied each one with a critical eye, running her hands over the fabric. Zoey, for once, remained quiet, her silver dress in a bag that dangled from her fingertips as she watched.

Stella let her gaze drift across the store. A flash of color caught her eye. She moved towards it, a gasp escaping her as she saw the full dress, hanging off a mannequin in the store window. She'd completely missed it on her way in.

It was perfect.

Zoey let out a low whistle as she followed Stella's gaze. "That'll certainly draw some attention."

"My parents would kill me," Stella breathed.

"All the more reason to do it." She nudged her. "Get it. It will look great on you."

Stella grinned and turned to the shopkeeper. "How much for the dress in the window?"

CHAPTER 38

The Saltare was a palace among the grimy cobblestone streets. Made of white stone and marble floors, it was a grand sight with its giant pillars and crystal chandeliers and sweeping staircases leading to the balcony overlooking the dance floor. The building itself took up an entire city block. The main room was massive, wide windows lending a view of the ocean in the distance. A string quartet held court in one corner of the room, a buffet laden with food and wine on the other side, tables and chairs draped in dark purple cloth dotting the space.

The Roses were already present when Jordan's family entered. He searched for Stella in the crowd but landed on Marcus and Evelyn instead, the former wearing a white suit, the latter decked out in an ivory gown with pearls. Zoey Rook wore a dress of pure silver that suited her frame, her chin-length hair held back by matching pins. Beside Jordan, Declan blatantly surveyed the women in the crowd.

Jordan thumped him on the head. "Stop drooling and keep your hands to yourself."

"And be on your best behavior," Mateo chimed in from Jordan's other side. "We all remember what happened the last time you wore a suit."

The last time the Daelik family attended a formal event such as this, Declan had gotten into a fistfight with another guest, the brawl destroying several tables, bottles of wine, and both of their suits.

Declan muttered something under his breath and stalked to the bar.

Jordan spotted Celia and Silas at a table next to the string quartet. The

Daeliks took their seats on the left side of the dance floor. The Rooks had taken up the right, their tables packed. Jordan noticed the table holding the immediate family had one empty spot. Stella still hadn't arrived yet.

His heart skipped a beat, and he cursed himself in his mind. He shouldn't be excited to see her. He had to get those thoughts out of his head.

Silas himself had escorted the Daeliks through the Roses' territory. It had taken Marcus' blessing for them to pass through without trouble. That hadn't stopped some passersby from glaring at their carriage on their way to the Saltare, a fact that had infuriated his father.

Jordan took his seat, tugging at the collar of his suit. He didn't enjoy dressing up; he'd been forced to leave his revolvers at home, and although there was a knife tucked in his boot, he missed the comforting weight of his prized guns at his sides.

The band struck up a lively tune. Several couples flocked to the dance floor, and Jordan was pleased to see there were Roses and Ravens alike—they weren't proud enough to avoid each other entirely, but each group kept their distance. Mateo offered his arm to Jasmin, who'd agreed to come with them on the sole condition that she didn't have to wear black. Her lilac gown—one of her own creations—swished around her ankles as Mateo pulled her onto the dance floor.

Jordan leaned over in his seat to pinch Lana on the arm. "Care to dance, Lanabug?"

She wore the royal blue dress Jasmin had gotten her for her birthday. She grinned and took Jordan's arm. "I would *love* to."

Jordan and Lana stuck to the far corner of the dance floor. They could both dance well—a result of the lessons Lillian insisted they take—but their last concern was formality. This was just a brother and a sister having a good time at a gala. Lana grinned like a fiend as Jordan spun her a-round as fast as he could, the skirts of her dress fanning out in a sea of deep blue.

Mateo and Jasmin slid over. "What were you just telling Dec about keeping your hands to yourself?" he teased.

Jordan shot him a filthy gesture that probably had his mother choking on her wine. "I couldn't resist a dance with the prettiest girl here."

Lana beamed.

The song ended, switching to a slower one. Jordan led Lana off the dance floor, earning a rare smile from John as they reclaimed their seats. But Jordan's smile didn't last long. A gasp rang out across the room, and he twisted in his seat, frowning as a newcomer entered the hall.

His mouth dried out as he realized who it was.

Those amber eyes were as bright as he'd ever seen them as she sauntered into the room. Her footsteps carried an air of importance, shoulders squared and head high as she moved with that dancer's grace, fully aware that she outshone every woman present.

Because she wasn't wearing white or silver like the rest of her family. Stella Rook wore red.

A full-length scarlet gown brushed the floor as Stella breezed to her family's table. It hugged her chest, accenting every curve before flowing to the ground in a series of sheer, voluminous skirts that shimmered with every movement. She didn't walk in it; she floated, the full skirts swishing and glittering, like the petals of a rose had been dipped in starlight and sewn together. Her hair was swept back with golden combs, a few loose curls escaping to rest on her bare shoulders. A single red rose was woven into the updo.

She looked regal. Elegant. Flawless.

Perfect.

She looked at him, just once, her whiskey gaze meeting his own. The corner of her red-painted lips curled into a sensual smile. It vanished as quickly as it came, leaving Jordan to wonder if he'd imagined it as Stella slid into a chair.

Lana sucked in a sharp breath and hid behind Jordan as Stella raked a disdainful look over the crowd. "Damn," Declan muttered on the other side of him.

Stella's parents gaped at her. Only Zoey seemed unsurprised, hiding her grin behind her wine glass. Stella flashed them all a sunny smile as she once again met Jordan's gaze across the room.

"Bloody hell," Jordan breathed.

The next hour passed traitorously slow. Jordan tried his best to ignore Stella, going as far to turn his chair so his back faced the Rook table. He used Lana as an excuse, his sister nervous around the Rose heir after their last encounter. Silas flitted between the tables, greeting each guest with a warm handshake. His usual green-and-white suit and hat had been replaced by one of black and white. Celia walked behind him in a dress that matched her eyes, the pale blue material making her look as if she was encased in ice. She smiled at Jordan but he pretended he didn't see it. Once Silas finished his rounds, he went up to the string quartet. They stopped playing as he stepped onto their platform.

Silas clapped his hands together, effortlessly drawing the room's attention. "I pray that you all are enjoying yourselves."

There was a murmur of agreement. A tense as things were between the Roses and the Ravens, each group was skilled at ignoring the other. The food and wine was enough to keep everyone distracted. Jordan raised his glass in a toast.

"I would like to thank you all for coming," he said. "In my hometown of Stokes, it is a tradition for groups or individuals that have a disagreement to host a party to resolve tensions. The bigger the disagreement, the bigger the party."

Jordan's mouth twitched as he took in the luxury of the Saltare. This was a big party, indeed.

Silas continued, "I have always been fond of the idea of enemies joining hands with intentions of peace." He smiled. "So if it is agreeable to both parties, in the prospect of peace between the Ravens and the White Roses, I would like to propose a dance between Jordan Daelik and Stella Rook."

Declan spat out his wine. The entire Daelik family choked. Jordan himself froze. Across the room, Stella caught his gaze, her eyes narrowed.

Jordan felt his heart stop. It was easy enough to pretend to hate her when they were on opposite sides of the room, but a dance? Forced to be so close to her? When she was wearing that dress? Half the city was here to witness Jordan losing his mind.

Silas looked between the two of them expectantly. Jordan sighed and rose from his chair, straightening the lapels of his suit. "Let's get this over with."

Stella rose gracefully from her seat, her crimson dress glittering even as her mouth twisted with distaste. "A quick song, please."

Silas gestured to the band as he stepped down from the platform. The quartet quickly settled into position. Jordan walked onto the dance floor, so shiny that the lights reflected off the polished wood. Stella met him in the middle. Her gaze was fixed on his face, her expression betraying nothing.

There was no way he could pull this off.

The band started up. Music swept through the room, rich and lively and powerful. Jordan awkwardly stepped forward, resting one hand on her hip, the other taking her own. She placed a hand on his shoulder and then they were off, spinning around in a slow dance. Neither of them smiled. Jordan avoided her gaze, his eyes set firmly in the distance as he led her through the dance, every muscle in his body locked tight.

You don't want to be here, he reminded himself as he spun her around. *You hate her.*

But when she faced him again, he couldn't help himself.

"That's quite the dress," he said. "Your parents must have been thrilled."

Her smile was venomous. "They didn't know what I was wearing until I walked in."

Jordan choked a little. "Will you get in trouble?"

To the unknowing eye, it would appear as if the two heirs were exchanging their usual barbed insults. Stella tilted her head to the side. "Perhaps. My father would rather scold me for the color of my attire than address the problem about to smack him in the face."

"Well, I certainly appreciate the gesture. You look..." *Devastating.* "Good."

A small smile played across her lips, but she quickly masked it. "I wore it just for you, feathers."

"Oh?"

"Of course. Who else would appreciate me wearing the most expensive dress the boutique had to offer?"

Jordan smirked. "I think every man here is appreciating this, little thorn."

Stella spun around again, the scarlet dress fanning out, the soft material swishing against Jordan's legs. "Is that so?"

"Mm-hm."

"Well," Stella crooned, "not all of them have had the pleasure of me waking up in their bedroom."

It took more self-control that Jordan cared to admit to keep his face neutral. "That was an entirely different situation and we both know it."

Did he imagine it, or did the hand she had on his shoulder seem to tighten, her fingers digging into the material of his jacket?

"It wasn't... all that different," Stella murmured.

The music kept playing. It was a lively tune that Jordan was rather fond of. Stella glanced towards the string quartet, and for the briefest moment, he saw her expression soften, her eyes fluttering close as her head tilted back.

Enjoying the music, he realized. She had told him she played piano. He wondered if that was the expression she had when she played—soft, vulnerable, letting the music sweep her away to another word.

Jordan and Stella continued dancing, each avoiding the other's gaze. Jordan was all too aware of the assembled crowd, of his family and Stella's, every eye focused on the two heirs. Their gazes were abrasive, grinding against Jordan's skin and leaving it raw. But that was nothing compared to the weight of Stella's gaze, her bright eyes staring at him with enough heat to set something on fire.

And that was all it took to remind him that the last time they'd been alone together, his lips had been on hers.

Those lips now curled into a half-smile that had Jordan's heart pounding.

"We need to arrange another meeting," Stella murmured, her voice lower than before. She didn't quite meet his gaze—instead she looked across the room, where Silas and Celia watched them through slitted eyes, the latter's hand curled around her wine glass as she stared them down. Jordan grimaced for the benefit of the onlookers as he turned back to Stella.

"We have a meeting," he reminded her. "Tomorrow."

They were supposed to meet last night, but with the gala coming up, Jordan had sent word to cancel. He wasn't proud to admit he'd chickened out—the idea of seeing her again so soon had made him nervous. Stella had returned the note with a request to meet the night after the ball to recommence their scheming.

Stella stiffened at the reminder. "Right."

The corners of his lips pulled up into a wicked smile. "Were you hoping for another meeting a bit sooner, little thorn?"

Her eyes flashed up to him. "Were you?"

A breathless inquiry. Jordan's blood was molten metal running through his veins, a white-hot fire pouring through him. He wanted nothing more than to kiss Stella again, to pull out those golden combs and let her hair cascade down her back, to not have to pretend to be her enemy when she destroyed him with every look. Jordan always considered himself to be the type of person who didn't get wrapped up in meaningless crushes, but he had fallen so hard his bones ached.

"I think that would be dangerous, little thorn." His voice lowered. "Imagine the trouble we would get in if we were to meet at that spot by the beach tonight at high moon."

She went utterly still. "I could only imagine."

The music hit a crescendo. Jordan spun around, pulling Stella with him.

"You would bring some blankets," he mused, "and I would bring a bottle of wine, and we'd be there until morning. That's quite the fantasy, isn't it?"

"Quite," Stella managed.

Was he really doing this? This wasn't the plan. The *plan* had been to avoid Stella entirely for the night—but that had been uprooted when Silas told them to dance. It had been an order disguised as a request. Silas was marking their every move to see which side would cave first. As much as they hated each other, Marcus and John would have tied their children together to dance if it meant getting Silas' approval.

The song ended. Jordan halted, his hand still resting on Stella's hip. It was that moment, that brief second of silence, that they stared at each other without their masks.

Then a polite smattering of applause interrupted the moment, and Jordan and Stella were quick to step away from each other.

Their eyes met once more as they prepared to walk to their respective sides of the dance floor.

And Jordan murmured, "I'll meet you at high moon, little thorn."

CHAPTER 39

Stella was distracted for the rest of the night. It was enough for Zoey to notice and wave a hand in front of her cousin's face. She dredged up some excuse about not feeling well that satisfied her family, but she could only hope it was enough to account for the heat that rose in her cheeks every time she glanced at the Ravens' side of the room.

I'll meet you a high moon, little thorn.

She gripped her glass so hard she was surprised it didn't shatter.

The next few hours were torture. There was food and wine. Lots of dancing. She watched as Jordan pulled his little sister onto the dance floor, both of them grinning. The sight was sweet enough to even make Evelyn smile, watching the pair with misty eyes. But the mood was dashed when Celia floated over and booted Lana out of the way in order to dance with Jordan. He was ramrod straight throughout the entire dance, ice-cold compared to the relaxed man that danced with his sister only a moment before, and the last note of the song hadn't even finished playing before he was walking away. Celia gaped after him, her ice-colored dress glittering under the massive chandelier. Stella smirked as she flounced away.

Stella had never been so happy for a gala to end. The Ravens left out early. Harvey had vanished long ago, his eyes on a dark-headed girl in the crowd. Marcus insisted on staying a few minutes after to thank Silas profusely. Stella could only bear a few minutes of his ass-kissing before she excused herself, escaping outside to the awaiting carriage. Harvey stumbled inside a minute later, his shirt untucked and hair mused, giving

Stella a lazy smile before slumping in the corner of the carriage and promptly falling asleep.

Her parents didn't lecture her on the way home like she expected—Marcus seemed in uncharacteristically good spirits, and although he did make a comment about the color of Stella's dress, Evelyn quickly cut in and said that she looked beautiful, and that was the end of the conversation.

It was a pleasant evening, all in all. Stella's dress had passed inspection. Harvey didn't get into a fistfight. The gala had gone without incident. The food had been good. And although she'd only taken part in one dance, it was perhaps the most interesting dance of her life.

Because that dance came with a promise.

High moon.

It was roughly ten o'clock when the Rook family returned to their manor. Everyone was tired from the gala, so it didn't take long before people began peeling off towards their bedrooms. Zoey hadn't even come home, having gone away in the arms of another man halfway through the gala. Stella waited until her parents and Harvey had retreated to their rooms before darting upstairs to hers.

She was really going to do this.

Stella paused to look at her reflection in the mirror, soaking in the sight of her in the red gown before slipping it off. The dress had cost her a small fortune—twice the amount of Zoey's dress, which hadn't been cheap—but it had been worth every second. She left her hair in place as she tugged on her black outfit, boots and leather and weaponry replacing her finery.

Ten thirty.

Stella paced her room. Her eyes landed on the golden locket—she'd taken it off for the gala, but now she slipped it on, the metal cold against her flushed skin.

Eleven o'clock.

She dug a satchel out from under her bed and shoved two quilts into it.

Eleven thirty.

Stella Rook was normally a woman of composure and grace.

But right now, she was a mess.

She climbed down from her balcony and stole across the darkened grounds. It was something she had done a thousand times, but this time, it felt different. She never had to sneak out to see Liam. He'd been accepted by her family. Marcus never had a problem with him, and Evelyn adored him. He had been free to come and go as he pleased.

But Jordan?

That was another story altogether.

There was nobody present when she slipped between the rocks. This brought a slight frown to her face—she was a few minutes early by her rough estimation, but Jordan was almost always here first. She told herself it didn't matter as she spread one blanket over the sand and took a seat on it, watching the moonlight glimmer over the ocean.

The time ticked by. Stella's fingers drummed against her thigh, her foot jiggling with anticipation.

Imagine the trouble we would get in if we were to meet at that spot by the beach tonight at high moon.

Maybe he'd reconsidered. They would get into trouble if someone found out.

Or maybe it had been a trick all along.

Stella toyed with the locket. She'd been so sure... So positive...

She shook her head. He would show. He had to.

But did she even want him to show? No matter how hard she tried, she couldn't get that voice out of her mind, the one that whispered of traitors and betrayals. Liam—

His face came to her mind, unbidden. Stella shoved it into that chest in the back of her mind, twisting the key so hard it snapped.

Jordan Daelik was many things. He was her enemy, her rival. He was a trickster and a manipulator and a murderer.

But so was she, and if they were both corrupted, they might as well do it together.

That kiss in his bedroom, it had lit her world on fire. Not just the kiss but the fact that Jordan saved her. He brought her to his house and stitched up her wounds. It was dangerous in so many ways, but he'd done it. For her.

He had to show up tonight.

But where was he?

Stella closed her eyes and sighed. The time continued its endless parade. She didn't have a watch, but she suspected it was well past high moon at this point, and Jordan still wasn't here.

She stood up, reaching for the end of the blanket to fold it up, but a noise behind her had her whirling, drawing a gun in one hand and a knife in the other.

Jordan froze, lifting his hands in surrender, a bottle of wine dangling from his fingers. "I come in peace."

The breath rushed out of Stella. "You came."

"Of course I came. I'm late because Declan roped me into a conversation about—" He shook his head. "It doesn't matter. I was caught up, but I'm here now." He held up the bottle. "And I brought the wine."

"I brought the blankets," Stella said awkwardly, nudging the quilt with her foot.

The moonlight glimmered in Jordan's eyes as he looked her up and down. "You didn't wear the dress?" He sounded vaguely disappointed.

Stella snorted. "Do you expect me to be stealthy while wearing the brightest outfit on this side of the ocean?"

"I suppose not."

Jordan took a seat on the quilt, and Stella gingerly sat next to him. He still wore his suit from the gala, but now his revolvers were strapped to his hips, as if he couldn't bear to part with them for more than a few hours at a time. Now that she thought about it, the gala was the first time she'd seen Jordan without his guns in years.

He cracked open the wine and took a swig before handing it off to Stella. Her sip was smaller and more precise. She'd had plenty to drink at the gala; the last thing she needed was to be intoxicated.

She handed the bottle back to Jordan. Their fingers brushed together, sending lightning bolts racing down her spine. Their gazes met once again, and the realization of what they planned to do out here slammed into Stella.

Jordan licked his lips. "So."

Stella shifted uncomfortably.

"We're out here," he said, "alone. In the dark. Just like we said."

She smirked. "Are you nervous?"

He jumped. "Me? Nervous? No, I'm— Are you nervous?"

She couldn't hold his gaze anymore. She dropped her head, a lock of hair hanging in her eyes. "Of course I'm nervous," she said softly. "If our parents find out about everything we've done, the reasons won't matter to them. We'll be disowned before we can explain."

"And?" Jordan pushed.

"And," she said, "I've decided that I don't care." She looked up at him. "What I said last time was true. I don't want to be your enemy, Jordan. And if you don't want to be mine, then I see no reason for us to continue the feud of our fathers. That is their war to wage, not ours."

His jaw clenched. "That might be true, but so was the other thing you said. If our families find out, we're dead. We have to hide it from them."

"There's no way we can hide forever."

"We've done well this far. Who says we can't keep it up?"

"Logic." Stella played with her locket once more. "Eventually, we will slip up. Someone will find out, and this entire dance will come to a very bloody end." She looked at him, fully looked at him, his brown eyes dark in the night. "We've already agreed that this is doomed from the start, but that doesn't mean the start has to be bad."

During their conversation, Jordan had leaned closer to her. Their breath mingled as they stared at each other. He was close enough that Stella could take in that familiar scent of seasalt and gunpowder. It intoxicated her, as potent as any drink and just as addicting.

They shouldn't be doing this. She shouldn't *want* this. That voice wormed its way into her mind once more, whispering hideous things about what would happen if her family discovered the truth. But the fear was half the thrill, and Stella leaned deeper into Jordan's scent.

Gunsmoke and seasalt. She realized she loved it.

"Jordan?" she whispered.

"Yes?"

"Kiss me."

And he did.

He crashed into her. She leaned against him, falling deeper into his embrace, that voice falling silent as her blood pounded in her ears. His hands cupped her face as he drew closer, his lips finding hers. She pressed into him, pulling him close, her mind going numb.

Jordan pulled away an inch, his lips grazing her cheek as he whispered, "We are in so much trouble."

"Only if we get caught," she breathed.

He kissed her again. His hands slid into her hair. The golden combs she'd so carefully arranged before the gala were tugged free without a second thought and discarded. The rose in her hair came next, tossed onto the beach, the red petals appearing black against the sand. Her dark hair cascaded over her shoulders. Jordan ran his fingers through it, smirking in pleasure as her breath hitched.

Stella wanted the moment to last forever, but she was forced to pull back to gasp down a few breaths of precious air. His gaze softened as he looked at her. He pulled her to his chest, and she could feel his heart pounding, the beat as crazy and erratic as her own.

"We'll make this work," he swore, his voice low and guttural. "I promise."

All sense of logic and rationality left her mind, and Stella believed him.

Her hands slipped down to her belt, pulling off her weapons and setting them aside. Jordan tilted his head and did the same, relieving himself of his prized revolvers without even batting an eye. Unarmed, their cheeks flushed and their eyes bright, the two heirs faced each other. And when Jordan lowered his mouth to Stella's again, she did not resist.

CHAPTER 40

The sky lightened with traces of red and orange. It wouldn't be long before the sun peeked over the horizon, the ocean stretching out to close the distance between the beach and the sky.

Jordan's eyes were half-closed, his breathing soft. His arms were wrapped around Stella under the quilt. She'd had the foresight to bring two blankets—one of which they laid on, the other draped over them, shielding them from the cool morning breeze.

Stella shifted. When he glanced down, he found her eyes, the amber stark in the morning light, studying him.

They stared at each other for a few breathless seconds.

"Do you regret it?" Jordan breathed. He kept his voice low, as if afraid to disturb the quiet stillness of the morning.

"No," Stella said, her voice just as soft. "Do you?"

"No," he whispered.

She smiled, a soft expression that Jordan was not used to seeing from her. He tugged her closer, pressing a kiss to the hollow of her throat while his hand came up to play with her hair.

He loved that hair. The rich curls were like silk as he ran his hand through them. Stella carried a distinctively floral scent. She smelled of roses, of course—she lived in a house surrounded by them—but there was something else, too, deeper notes of jasmine and lilac. He breathed in her scent as he rested his chin against the crook of her shoulder.

A glitter of gold caught his eye. It was the golden combs from Stella's hair, the ones he'd tossed aside last night without a second thought. The rose was a few inches away, its crimson petals half-buried in the sand.

Jordan picked it up and twirled it between his fingers. "I've always liked the red ones better than the white." His artistic eyes always looked for the color, for the pretty things. White was pretty, but it didn't match the aesthetic of a red rose.

Stella eyed it. "You haven't heard my mother's story."

"There's a story?"

She nodded. "She heard a story when she was a kid and it made her like white roses over any other. I've heard it a thousand times."

He pulled her closer, dropping the rose and returning his hand to her hair. "Tell it to me," he invited.

She rolled over to face him, eyes twinkling. "I doubt it's your kind of story, feathers."

"Try me."

A gentle smile appeared on her face, and it was the softest Jordan had ever seen Stella look. It warmed him to see her opening up, letting herself be vulnerable in front of him. He didn't realize how much he craved Stella's trust until she gave it to him.

"Once upon a time," Stella started, voice soft, "in a land far, far away—"

"A fairytale?" Jordan asked, arching a brow. "That's the grand story?"

She pinched him. "I said it wasn't your kind of story, but you *insisted.*"

He held up his hands in surrender. "Carry on."

Stella scowled, but it faded as she picked up her story. "Once upon a time, there lived a princess of unimaginable beauty. She was coming of age, and the king decided it was time for her to marry, but there were no princes or lords in the land that suited her. To please his daughter, the king held a competition to find the best man in all the kingdom. He designed a series of trials to test the bravery, strength, intelligence, and kindness in each man. The winner would receive the princess' hand in marriage.

"The trials went on for months. There was everything from archery to dragon-slaying to tests of knowledge. By the last trial, only ten men remained in the competition."

Stella closed her eyes. "'For the last trial,' the king declared, 'you shall all go out into the kingdom and bring back a gift for the princess. Whoever brings the gift that pleases her the most shall win the competition.'

"And so the men set out and scoured the kingdom for the best gift. Most came from wealthy families and spent vast amounts of gold on jewels and dresses for the princess. But one contestant, a young knight, realized the princess lived in a gilded castle and had all the jewels and dresses she could ever want. After much thought, he decided to create something unique—the most beautiful flower the world had ever seen, a blooming plant that would capture the princess' heart.

"The young knight rode to the farthest corner of the kingdom and enlisted the help of an ancient witch, the only person he thought capable of creating such a gift. The witch saw the knight's heart was true and agreed to help him. She took a length of white silk and cut it into pieces no bigger than her hand, then sewed the pieces together into the shape of a flower. With a touch of magic, the silk formed petals of purest white, and the flower took root in the ground, the most beautiful plant to have ever graced the earth.

"The young knight was overjoyed. 'I shall call it a rose,' he said, and he dug up the flower and carried it back to the castle."

Here she paused, eyes flickering to Jordan, but he was fully intrigued. "Keep going," he urged softly.

She obliged him. "When he arrived, weary from weeks of travel, he saw the other contestants and their gifts of jewels and dresses and perfumes. The princess saw the young knight from afar, the white rose in his hand, and was overcome by the flower's delicate beauty.

"'For you, my princess,' the knight said, bowing low as he handed it to her. 'It is called a rose. It is the most beautiful flower in all the kingdom, for there is no other like it. Its beauty is unique, just as you are.'

"The princess took the rose in her hands and wept at its beauty. 'It is the most beautiful gift,' she cried. 'And I declare you the winner!'"

Stella's voice lowered. "The other competitors stood by and watched as the young knight gave the princess the rose. Their hearts were hardened as she picked the knight over them, after they had poured out their life savings in securing the most expensive gifts they could find. Jealousy overtook them, and they picked up their swords and killed the young knight in their rage. The princess screamed and dropped the rose. It landed on the body of the young knight and soon became stained with his blood. Thorns broke out along its stem and the rose took root in the ground. A great rosebush shot up and overtook the land, trapping the young knight's killers in its thorny grasp."

Jordan went still.

"The princess wept as she beheld the blooming roses," Stella continued, "all shades of red, not one white rose to be found. The knight's perfect gift was lost to the world. In its place bloomed darkness, born of spite and nurtured by bloodshed. The princess fled into the castle and locked herself in the highest tower, vowing to never marry unless a man could bring her something even more beautiful than the young knight's white rose. As the stories go, she remains up there to this day, locked in a castle overtaken by red roses, her tears watering the flowers below."

Her voice fell silent, the only sound the gentle splash of waves against the sand. Jordan's gaze fell on the rose, its red petals stark against the white sand.

Like bloodstains on a white rose.

Jordan shivered. "That's a beautiful story." Beautiful, yet haunting.

"It is," Stella agreed, pressing against him. "I first heard it when I was four years old. From then on, whenever I saw a red rose, all I saw was the knight's blood." Her eyes went distant. "I hate the color red."

"Why?"

"It's the color of violence." She tilted her head back to look at him. "Think about it. Red is everywhere. It's the way we bleed, the way we see when we're angry, the way the fires of hell burn. Nothing good has ever come out of that color." She shuddered. "And Lochridge is bathed in it."

Jordan considered that. And then—

"Next time I'll bring you a white rose."

She huffed a laugh. "You'd better not. It's just a reminder of the feud."

"I guess," he murmured. "Would a pink one work?"

Stella arched a brow. "You're not going to quit, are you?"

He gave her a lazy grin. "Anything for you, little thorn."

Stella sighed, her fingers twining with his. The breeze caught a stray lock of her hair, making it dance across her face. Jordan tucked it behind her ear, each movement gentle and unsure. He was new to this—whatever *this* was. Jordan Daelik and Stella Rook... Those were names to be used to depict opposite sides of a war. They shouldn't be used in reference to gentle kisses and calm mornings and fairytales told at the break of dawn.

Jordan loved the idea of their names being used together for something other than bloodshed, but that was a revelation he would have to keep to himself. If anyone else found out...

We've already agreed that this is doomed from the start, but that doesn't mean the start has to be bad.

Jordan swallowed. "What do we do now?"

"We go home. Clean up." She glanced at him. "Forget this ever happened."

His throat tightened. "We have a meeting tonight."

"That's when we remember again."

Jordan closed his eyes and leaned his forehead against hers. "We need to follow Silas again tonight. As much fun as this was, he is the priority."

Stella grumbled under her breath. "I suppose we will. I'll meet you at the hotel again?"

"Sounds like a date."

They smirked at each other.

"Only we would make a date of spying on someone," Stella said.

"Silas *was* the one who brought us together, so it only seems fitting."

She snorted.

"It's true, isn't it? Without him coming to Lochridge and posing a threat, we would have never found a reason to work together. And without working together..." His hand trailed down her back. "This never would have happened."

"You make Silas sound like a saint when you put it like that."

"He's the farthest thing from it." He paused. "Actually, Celia is the farthest thing from it. I'm growing tired of her trying to woo me."

Stella arched a brow. "Is the big, bad Raven tiring of all the attention? I would have thought a woman trying to seduce you would have stroked your ego."

Jordan shivered. "Usually, but Celia makes me nervous. I can't ever tell if she's trying to flirt with me or threaten me."

"It might be both."

"I'm not interested either way."

Stella chuckled as she sat up, her hair spilling over her bare shoulders. Jordan drank in the sight before she tugged her shirt on. She smirked at his disappointment but kept dressing. With a sigh, Jordan pulled on his clothes, too. It was dawn; if they strayed for much longer, they would risk running into family members while trying to sneak back into their houses, and that would make for unnecessary questions.

Especially considering that Jordan was still wearing his suit from last night.

He looped his gun belt around his waist, the weapons clinking together. He frowned at the horizon for long enough that Stella asked, "Is something wrong?"

"I just have a bad feeling about everything," he said, tying the straps around his thighs that kept his revolvers from swinging around when he walked. "It sounds silly, but…" He shook his head. "The sky is red."

Stella frowned at the sky, marking its color with narrowed eyes. "So it is."

"There's an old tale sailors use. *Red sky at night, sailor's delight. Red sky in morning, sailor's warning.* A red sky in the morning predicts bad weather at sea. At night it means good weather is on the way." He glanced at her. "You aren't the only one who's wary of that color."

Her lips formed a thin line. Though she said nothing, Jordan heard her voice echoing through his head.

It's the way we bleed.

He gave his head a shake to clear the thought. "I'd better get going. I'll see you tonight?"

She nodded. "We've got a criminal to catch."

Jordan hesitated, his hand still holding Stella's. He didn't want to leave this. Ever.

But he forced himself to press one last kiss to her lips and walk away.

CHAPTER 41

Jordan was a storm of emotions and pent-up energy when he stumbled through the front door a few minutes later. He wasn't expecting anyone to be awake at this hour, so shock shot through his body as Declan drawled from the kitchen, "Did you have a good night?"

His cousin leaned in the doorway, sipping his coffee, his green eyes glinting with amusement as he took in Jordan—disheveled, tired, and still in his gala finery. Declan looked surprisingly relaxed for someone who had no doubt spent the entire night in the bottom of a bottle. The sleeves of his loose-fitting shirt were rolled up to his forearms, his eyes were clear, and he'd even combed his hair. Jordan glared at him with every ounce of anger his distracted, sleep-deprived mind could muster before heading for the stairs.

Declan followed him.

"Did you have a rough ride?" he crooned. "You look like complete and utter shit, cousin."

Jordan reached the door to his room in record time. "Go to hell, Dec."

He put a foot in the way before Jordan could slam the door. "Anyone I know?"

Declan knew who Stella was, but he didn't *know* her, not in the ways that mattered. Jordan convinced himself it wasn't a lie as he said, "No."

Declan relented and let Jordan close the door. He stripped off his suit, tossing it carelessly onto his desk before tugging on his usual attire. He swore he could still catch a hint of Stella's perfume on his skin. As much as he wanted to hold on to the scent forever, he made himself troop downstairs to take a long, scalding hot shower.

It helped. A little.

By the time he returned to the kitchen, his sandy hair plastered to his forehead, Mateo had joined Dec at the table, the two holding a hushed conversation over their coffee. A conversation about Jordan, apparently, because they fell silent as he entered the room.

"I know you're talking about me," he muttered, pouring himself a steaming mug.

They swapped a look. "I think everyone is talking about you," Mateo said, a bit apologetically. "Not after what happened last night."

Jordan nearly dropped the mug. "What happened?"

They couldn't know. There was no way they could know—

Declan sipped his coffee. "Celia Tradow showed up here last night."

Jordan relaxed. They didn't know. But—

"What was Celia doing here?" he demanded.

They exchanged another look, one that put Jordan on edge. Mateo cleared his throat. "She demanded to see you. We told her to go away because it was well past high moon at that point, but she insisted, so we went upstairs to find you, but you were already gone."

"She wasn't pleased," Declan added.

Jordan's fingers curled around the handle of his mug. "Why did she want to see me?" *What in the heavens could have prompted her to visit me in the early hours of the morning?*

Mateo shrugged. "I don't know. She was still wearing her dress from the gala. It didn't seem like the two of you had made arrangements, so we told her to go away." He winced. "Nicely, of course. Pa was insistent we didn't insult her, but I think the fact you weren't here was insult enough."

"It isn't like I'm married to her. She shouldn't be insulted if I don't come to her every beck and call."

"We know that. You know that. Even the Rooks know that. But Celia's got this idea that you fancy her or something."

Jordan stifled a groan. He didn't like Celia, not in the way she seemed to like him. She paled in comparison to Stella—literally. Celia's white-blonde hair and pale complexion was nothing compared to Stella's rich brown curls and the golden hue of her skin. Celia was pretty like ice, cold and sharp and piercing, but Stella was pretty like the sun, radiant and enthralling but deadly if you stared too long.

"If she comes here again," Jordan said, "tell her I'm not interested."

Declan's expression was pained. "We did. I know we're trying to impress her father, but Celia's not your type. I don't think anyone in Lochridge would want her for more than a few hours."

Jordan let out a soft grunt of amusement and was happy to let the conversation drop.

The trio skipped out to find breakfast on the Barter Streets before John could wake up and pester Jordan with questions about where he'd been last night. Jordan stayed out long after, finding excuses to stay away. He even continued his search for a connection to Stokes, a mission that had been derailed after Celia and Stella's fight, but by evening, he ran out of leads to chase and was forced to face the music.

John glowered at him from the other side of his desk as Jordan entered his office.

"I've been requesting to see you all day," he growled.

Jordan gulped as he slid into the chair directly opposite his father. "I've been busy."

"Busy avoiding me." He laced his hands behind his head. "Where were you last night?"

"At a bar." Lie. "With a woman." Truth. "Doing things." Bullshit answer.

John's eyes narrowed. "Celia Tradow is desperate to see you."

"I'm not interested."

"I'm well aware of that, but the fact remains that Celia possesses the most valuable connection to Silas. I need you on her good side, Jordan. She had a lot of sway with her father. For whatever reason, she seems to be infatuated with you, so you are going to use that to establish a connection with her."

Jordan choked. "The girl's a brat."

John leveled a sharp look on him. "And you are a loyal member of the Ravens, which means you follow orders."

His fingers curled around the arms of his chair. "I didn't realize this was an order."

"Don't test me, Jordan."

His voice carried enough of an edge to make Jordan clamp his mouth shut.

John nodded. "Good. There's another matter we need to discuss as well."

"What?"

"My men found a Rose snooping around a store on Fifth Street. He had an entire sack of gold he'd nipped from businesses along the Streets. Intentions are unknown and he refuses to talk, so I want you to get information out of him." John ran a hand over the stubble on his chin. "He might be behind the weapons that went missing two days ago."

Jordan went still. "Another shipment went missing?"

"Yes, and we're no closer to figuring out the culprit than we were the first time—which is why I need you to take care of it."

He deflated, his good mood dissipating like smoke in the wind. "Today?"

"Right now. You know where to find him."

Of course he did. The warehouse on Dawson Avenue.

John's expression suggested he wasn't in the mood for arguing. Jordan knew better than to push his father on this subject; he had before, and it had turned nasty in more ways than one.

So he bit his tongue, nodded, and rose from his chair.

"Good luck," John called after him.

It took everything he had not to blow up on his father then and there. But he forced his mouth to remain shut as he stalked out of the room.

The Rose had light hair and blue eyes, a younger man with stubble on his jaw. Aside from a scratch on his forehead and a tiredness in his eyes, he looked no worse for wear.

It was Jordan's job to change that.

The Rose's eyes widened as the Raven heir stepped into the room, his guns at his hips and his sleeves rolled up. Jordan didn't have to introduce himself. He merely stepped towards the chair the Rose was tied to, his brown eyes studying him head from toe.

There was a long moment of silence.

Then,

"What do you want with me?"

The voice had a surprising amount of confidence behind it. Jordan angled his head. "I want to know what you were doing on my turf in the dead of night."

He jutted his chin out. "None of your business."

Jordan shrugged as he cracked his knuckles. "If you want to do this the hard way…"

The Rose paled as he circled the chair. "I'm not giving you any information."

"You don't have to *give* me anything." Jordan's hand shot out, grabbing the Rose by his hair and wrenching his head back, forcing him to look at Jordan where he stood behind him. "I intend to take it."

The remaining color drained from his face. Jordan saw the shift in his eyes—the giving up.

He smiled. "The longer you hold out, the more fun I have, so why don't you save yourself the trouble? What were you doing in Raven territory?"

"I—"

"Tell me!"

"I didn't mean any harm—"

"That isn't an answer."

The Rose let out a low whimper. "Money. I needed the money."

"Money." Jordan's tone was flat. "Did the Rooks tell you to take it?"

"No," he rushed to say. "No—my gambling debts. I have to get them paid off before old Rook finds out. The boss don't like it when his people have debts to the other gang." He spoke so fast he tripped over the words. "He would have sent his nephew to skin me alive if he knew about it."

His grip on his hair tightened. "You're sure?"

"I swear!" the Rose cried, his eyes going wide as Jordan drew his revolver in warning. "I swear! Rook had nothing to do with this!" He struggled against the ropes holding him down. "Please let me go!"

Jordan studied him for a long moment.

Then he let his revolver drop back in its holster.

"If I ever see you on my territory again," he breathed, "I will rip you apart piece by piece and feed you to the ravens. The only reason I'm even letting you go is because I know Rook will punish you for getting caught."

He yanked his head further back, demanding his attention. "Do I make myself clear?"

"Yes," he moaned.

Jordan released him. "Good."

His knees threatened to give out in relief as he stalked through the door. The intimidation tactics didn't always work—sometimes the presence of the Raven heir and the knowledge of his reputation was enough to make some spill their secrets, but at times it had to go further. Jordan hated it when things got bloody; when he had to use fists and knives and bullets to make a man talk. He loathed it, in fact, but not having to do it today...

His steps were a little lighter, his breathing a little easier as he ordered the guards out front to return the Rose to his territory and to increase tonight's border patrol to make sure there were no further incidents. They rushed off without a hitch, scared of the same reputation that made Roses shake in their boots, knowing good and well the Ravens who failed to keep the border secure to begin with would likely be executed.

Jordan's mouth twisted as he stepped outside. One day he'd be in charge of the gang, and he'd never have to do dirty work like this again. That's what his father did—sat behind his desk and sent Jordan out to get blood on his hands. Jordan didn't care to be like his father in a lot of ways, but not having to visit this warehouse ever again certainly appealed to him.

He raked a hand through his hair as he debated what to do with the rest of his day. The search for information about Stokes had turned up nothing, meaning his time was free. Maybe he'd grab his sketchbook and head out to his spot by the beach—

The beach. Jordan felt his face heat as the memory of last night crashed into him. He'd blocked it out of his mind before facing his father, unwilling to let his expression betray him, but now there was no one around to witness Jordan Daelik, heir to the Raven gang, blushing at the thought of Stella Rook.

Bloody hell, he already missed her. Missed the feel of her lips, the scent of her perfume, the glint in her eyes. She was stunning, dangerously so, a lethal blade hiding underneath a beautiful exterior.

And she was driving Jordan insane. *In a good way*, he thought. Or hoped, at least.

CHAPTER 42

The cobblestone streets were silent as Stella slipped onto the roof across from Silas' hotel. Jordan was already there, waiting for her with a sly smile that had her heart racing. His head tilted as he took her in. "Afraid to be seen with me?"

With the memory of Celia's attack so close, Stella had modified her outfit. Her original black shirt was ruined, so she replaced it with a similar one with a hood to conceal her features. A cloth mask covered the lower half of her face, her hair braided and tucked out of sight. If there was a chance of running into the Tradows again, she didn't want to be recognized.

Stella brushed away her disguise and accepted Jordan's kiss on the cheek. "Aren't you?"

His mouth tightened. "Perhaps."

"Is something wrong?"

"Wrong?" he echoed. "Hell yes."

Something *was* wrong—she could tell by the set of his jaw, the look in his eye. "What is it?"

"My father."

"You'll have to be more specific," she said dryly.

He looked down. "I don't really want to talk about it."

She scooted closer to him. "Does it have to do with Silas?"

"Part of it." He huffed. "Pa wants me to be nice to Celia."

Stella choked. "Celia? As in *the* Celia?"

"As in Celia Tradow, Silas' daughter, an entitled brat and all around priss?" Jordan let out a humorless laugh. "That's the one."

"What are you going to do?"

Jordan smirked. "First," he said, running a hand down her leg, "I am going to enjoy the sight of you in black. Second, you and I are going to come up with a scheme to get the Tradows out of town for good." He paused, considering. "If Celia keeps coming after me, I might get Dec and Mateo to help me scare her off."

Stella cocked a brow. "You, Thatcher, and Half-Daelik? You're asking for trouble." The trio was well known for their antics, especially when they were younger. Stella hadn't heard of anything noteworthy they'd done recently. Everyone thought they had finally grown out of it, but she had a feeling there was still a mischievous streak hiding down deep.

"They don't like it when you call them that," Jordan said, his expression pained.

"Get used to it, birdbrain."

He laughed softly and angled his mouth over hers. Stella melted. The kiss was brief—they had a mission tonight—but it was enough to make her feel like she was floating on air. They settled down on the roof, sitting closer together than they ever had before, Jordan's arm draped over her shoulders.

She could stay here all night. She planned to, until Silas walked out of the hotel. Celia and Tobias were behind him, the former in her all-black getup, the latter a brooding shadow.

Jordan and Stella exchanged a look. "We've got trouble," he murmured.

Stella narrowed her eyes. "They're heading for the ocean. Come on."

She launched into motion, tugging up her hood and mask as she jumped to the next building. Celia and Silas held a hushed conversation on the ground. Stella prayed it would be enough to distract them as she and Jordan trailed them from the rooftops. Once, Tobias glanced up, sending Stella's heart rate skyrocketing as she fell back into the shadows. If Jordan hadn't been there to steady her, she would have fallen.

The trio appeared to be headed for the Red Harbor, but they stopped a street short, ducking into a narrow alley. Stella crouched low as she noticed two other men were already there, long coats obscuring their tall frames, their raven-black hair blending into the night. Twins, she realized.

"We've made an offer on the Red Harbor," the one on the left said.

"Ritton will arrive in person tomorrow."

"Good," Silas murmured.

"How soon will you own it?" Celia asked.

"It's a matter of days, sweetheart. One talk with the owner revealed that he's been looking to sell for some time, but without the Rooks or Daeliks able to buy it out, there's nobody wealthy enough to take up his asking price." The man on the right sniffed. "The boss wants to ensure it will make a profit even if the rest of the plan doesn't go well."

Silas waved a flippant hand. "Even if the town goes under, we can make a profit off the Harbor. Ships will still dock in Lochridge, and it won't be hard to set up a mercantile and a restaurant to accommodate the sailors."

Stella and Jordan exchanged a look of muted horror. Silas was still planning to buy out the Harbor, and they had made no progress on convincing their fathers the docks were in danger.

The left one looked Silas up and down. "And what about the gangs? Have you gotten any closer?"

"We're looking to establish connections with both," Celia said. "The Ravens are more promising at the moment, but I'm worried about the heir. He's expressed concerns before. But I think I can sway him."

"It's still undecided," Silas said smoothly, shooting his daughter a look. "Stirring up tension while remaining the peacemaker is a hard task. But I think I've done it. Both sides are right on the edge; now it's just a matter of seeing who falls first."

"And then?" he pressed.

"Then we decide. Use one gang to eradicate the other, leaving us with only half the city to conquer. That will prove much easier once we have the Red Harbor in our hands. Both sides put a lot of weight on the Harbor, and if it starts refusing them..."

Stella's fingers dug into the crumbling rooftop as the twins nodded. "The boss is getting impatient. He thought you would have made more progress by now. I like the plan, but you have to speed it up."

"Once it goes down, it'll go fast. I'll have Lochridge cleared by the end of the week, and then we can focus on the next steps."

The end of the week.

Stella felt like she was going to be sick.

Silas and his partners were still talking, but Stella scrambled back, her breath coming too quick. Jordan put a hand on her shoulder.

"This is messed up," he whispered. "We were right. He doesn't want an alliance." His face paled. "He wants an extermination."

Stella looked up at him. "We can't let him have this city."

"But how the hell do we stop him?"

That was the question, wasn't it? The two of them watched the Tradows bid their friends farewell and go back the way they came. The twins watched after them for a long moment before heading the other way.

Stella rubbed her temples and started pacing the rooftop. "What do we know so far?"

Jordan played with his revolver, spinning it around in his hand. "Silas wants to side with one gang. Once he makes that decision, he's going to use both his army and the gang's resources to take out the other. He's purposely stirring up tension between them with the *alliance*, making it so we're at each other's throats."

"Then he's sweeping in and playing peacemaker," Stella continued, still pacing, "so both sides have reason to trust him. With this alliance in the balance, everyone is willing to give him all the information he needs to plan his takeover."

"Which starts with the Red Harbor," Jordan picked up. "Whichever way this goes, his boss will have the Harbor under his belt."

"So that when he makes his decision, no matter how bloody things get, he'll have one source of income when it's all said and done."

Jordan caught his revolver. "Because he's not planning an alliance with either gang. He's using the tension to get one to kill the other, then he's going to turn on that one."

Stella came to a halt. "This is bad."

"It really is." Jordan's face was grim. "It means that Silas won't show his true colors until it's too late. And nothing we've discovered is solid enough to convince anyone."

"We still have to look into Stokes."

"I reached out to every contact I know that might have a connection, and it turned up nothing." He shook his head. "It's not right. You're telling me that *nobody* on my half of Lochridge has ever visited the city?"

She bit her lip. "I didn't think of it like that."

"There has to be something," Jordan said, rising to his feet. "Someone who knows what the hell is going on here."

She resumed her pacing. "Celia knows. If your father wants you to suck up to her, perhaps—"

"I'm not kissing ass to get information."

She arched a brow. "It might be our only chance."

"I am *not*—"

"Alright, alright!" She held up her hands in mock surrender. "No need to get snippy."

"I'm not snippy," Jordan grumbled.

Stella tilted her head. "Are you alright?"

Jordan started, taken aback by the question. "Why wouldn't I be?"

"You seem off."

"I'm fine."

His voice was too high, and his gaze didn't quite meet hers. Stella frowned and said, "Tell me what's going on."

He blinked, stared into the distance, and then said, his voice distracted, "This is a strange question, but has your gang been stealing weapons from us?"

It was Stella's turn to blink. "How many weapons?"

"Entire crates are disappearing from our stockhouses."

She frowned. "As far as I'm aware, our weapons-stealing operations aren't that evolved. The most we take is the guns off of whatever scrubs we catch over the border." She cocked her head. "But who would steal weapons from you if not us?"

He chewed his lip. "That's what we're trying to figure out. We caught one of them but couldn't get any information out of him. It didn't seem like the Roses were behind it, but…"

"I don't think it's us. Perhaps that gang from the southwest corner?" She couldn't recall the name, but there was a miniscule group that ran around the slum districts. "I don't know, Jordan."

He shook his head. "We'll figure it out."

Silence reigned for a moment, making Stella twitch. Were a few missing weapons really upsetting him so much?

"My father might have some contacts," Stella said at last. "I'll reach out, see if I can get a reply."

Jordan nodded. Whatever was bothering him tonight had him acting stranger than usual, his eyes distant even as he looked at her. "Tomorrow night?"

The words were bleak. They were running out of time and they both knew it.

"Tomorrow night," Stella agreed.

CHAPTER 43

The parlor was quiet when Stella slipped into her usual place behind the piano. Voices echoed through the open door, Harvey and Zoey arguing over something that Stella hadn't deigned to figure out. She'd taken one step into the kitchen before deciding that the piano was a better place for her.

A soft sigh escaped her as she slid a hand over the keys. She didn't play as much as she used to, but lately she had been trying to get back into it. Music was her passion, her escape, and heavens knew she needed something to distract her these days.

She hadn't played but three notes when she heard the front door slam. Zoey burst into the parlor, looking about as mad as Stella had ever seen her. Her fingers froze on the keys. "What's wrong?"

"My brother," she spat. "I tried to talk to him like you've been asking."

Stella slowly pushed back from the piano. *That's* what they had been arguing about? "And?"

"*And*, did you hear that door slam five seconds ago? He's furious."

Stella folded her hands in her lap. "Let him be mad. I'm glad you finally talked to him."

"Tried," Zoey corrected. "I tried to talk to him. And it didn't work."

She winced. "It's the thought that counts?"

Zoey blew out a breath and plopped down next to Stella. "I'm worried about him," she admitted. "Yes, I know he brings all of this on himself, but I'm scared to death he's going to get himself killed." She scratched the back of her neck. "I hate that I'm always the one standing up for the psychopath, but he's my brother. If I don't have his back, no one will."

Stella squeezed her hand. "You're doing good."

She fiddled with her bracelets. "Harvey told me otherwise."

"Harvey is a violent, egocentric asshole who gets a thrill out of starting fights. I don't think you have anything to worry about."

A light laugh escaped her, but there was a sadness in her eyes that made Stella's heart wrench.

"Hey," she said, nudging her. "I can't let you mope around like this. How about we hit the Barter Streets?"

Zoey arched a brow at the window, the daylight fading into darkness. "Now? You never want to go out this late."

"Well, tonight's different." Stella jumped up and pulled Zoey with her. "We can eat at the Lascer, and afterwards we'll shop at the boutique across the street."

She smirked. "I see what this is. You're just using this as an excuse to go shopping."

Stella's answering grin was wicked. "I didn't realize I needed one."

Zoey rolled her eyes and allowed Stella to pull her out the door. Zoey was still dressed up from a date she had earlier in the evening, wearing a deep purple dress so short it barely went past her hips and so much jewelry it jangled with every movement. It was a stark contrast to Stella's off-the-shoulder white blouse and tight-fitting pants that were such a dark brown they nearly matched her hair. Leather boots with golden buckles reached up to her knees, matching the gold jewelry adorning her wrists and ears and the locket around her neck. With her lips painted red, a brush of rouge across her cheeks, and her hair left to spill over her shoulders in soft brown curls, Stella thought she made for a fine sight as she linked arms with Zoey and marched into town.

Their intended destination was crowded when they arrived, but the owner of the restaurant saw the Rook heir waiting in line and rushed to amend the situation. The girls were seated in the very front, a narrow window lending them a view of the street. Zoey watched the foot traffic while Stella studied her menu, and when she glanced up, she saw her cousin deep in thought.

"Are you alright?" she asked, setting the menu down. "Is this just about Harvey?"

Zoey shrugged. "Orion and I broke up today."

"Who?"

"Orion? The guy I've been dating?"

Stella narrowed her eyes. "For how long?"

Her cheeks flushed. "Four days?"

Stella groaned as a waiter brought two glasses of wine. "You can't expect me to remember the name of every man you've kissed. That list would be longer than the Western Road."

Zoey sipped her drink. "Well, I thought it was going well, and then I found out he's married and had to call it off."

"How thoughtful of you."

"I don't like your attitude," she said, giving her a cross look as she made a show of studying her menu.

Stella examined her reflection in the window. "I don't like how you jump on every good-looking guy that crosses your path, and yet, here we are."

The menu slapped down on the table. "Excuse me?"

She gave her a flat look. "Come on, Zo. Don't play dumb. Ever since Kieran broke it off with you—"

"Don't say his name," she hissed.

Stella raised both brows. "This is exactly my point. You got your heart broken, and instead of letting yourself grieve properly, you ran towards the next guy with open arms. And that's what you've been doing for the last four years."

Zoey picked at the polished wood table. "There's nothing wrong with having fun."

"Depends on the fun." Stella swirled her wine. "We've talked a lot about Harvey's behavior, but we've never addressed yours. What you're doing isn't healthy. You've gone through more men in the past week than I have in my entire lifetime."

Zoey's eyes flashed. "Maybe the reason for that is because I haven't been stuck up on my dead lover for three years!"

The words slapped Stella in the face. She flinched, and Zoey's lips puckered, her regret clear in her eyes. But Stella was already pushing away from the table, her vision flashing red.

"Stella, wait!"

Stella stormed past flabbergasted customers that were quick to scramble out of her path. Zoey caught up to her as she made it to the street, and she pressed her hands to her sides to keep herself from hitting her cousin.

"Stell, I'm sorry," she panted. "I didn't mean it like that."

"Then how did you mean it?" she demanded. "I didn't realize there was anything wrong with grieving a loss like that."

Zoey raised her hands in surrender. "All I meant is that we both lost someone close to us. My reaction was to have fun instead of settling down, and your reaction was to pucker up and isolate yourself."

"Because there's a difference between a breakup and a funeral, Zoey."

She flinched. "I'm sorry. I didn't mean to sound so callous."

Stella glanced back at the restaurant, but her appetite was gone. "Come on," she sighed. "Let's just head to the boutique."

Zoey didn't respond, so Stella muttered a curse under her breath and crossed the street, her insides churning. Thankfully, she didn't have to dwell on her thoughts for long; a shout drew her attention, and she twisted towards the sound.

Zoey's eyes narrowed. "It's coming from the border."

Stella was already in motion. "Let's go."

The two fought their way through the crowd of people trying to get away from the commotion. A gunshot rang out, and the people panicked, nearly knocking the girls over in their haste to get away. Stella let out a growl of frustration and shoved past the throng. The border came into view, and her breath hitched as she realized who was behind the commotion.

Zoey broke past the line of people and stumbled to Stella's side, only to pull up short with a curse. "Is that—"

"Harvey," Stella growled.

At least half a dozen Raven guards were dead, their bodies piled up on the line that marked the border. On top of the heap stood Harvey Rook, his hair hanging in his eyes. He was drenched in blood; the crimson staining his shirt was so dark that had Stella not seen what color it was before he left the house earlier, she would have never guessed the fabric was originally white. His knife dangled from his fingers. Aside from a small cut on his jaw, he looked unharmed, his eyes blazing with unholy fire as he faced off against the remainder of the border patrol desperately trying to keep him from advancing into their territory.

Stella swallowed the bile that rose in her throat as she marched towards him.

"The hell is going on here?" she demanded, her voice carrying. The Barter Streets had completely emptied in a matter of seconds, leaving Stella and her cousins alone with the Ravens. She swept a look over them, marking their unfamiliar faces, the tattoos on their wrists. Harvey slowly ripped his gaze away from them to look down at Stella, and she nearly blanched at the look in his eyes.

Cold. Deadly. Void of any warmth.

It was like looking into the barrel of a loaded gun.

"They crossed the border," he snarled. "I'm dealing with it."

"We didn't cross," the leader of the surviving Ravens snapped. "You jumped over here and—"

He didn't have time to finish his sentence. Harvey hopped down from the piles of corpses, putting himself directly in front of the Raven as his knife flashed. The move was so fast that Stella didn't see the cut until blood spurted from his neck and the Raven collapsed, his end so quick that he didn't even have time to draw a final breath.

The others scrambled back. Rage poured through Stella, and she drew her gun.

"Enough!" she shouted. "Harvey, stop this!"

Harvey looked at her over his shoulder.

"Make me," was all he said.

And Stella's vision went red.

"This is the last straw," she said, her voice quiet but lethal. "You have screwed around one too many times, cousin. Whatever happened to being a loyal member of the gang? To following orders? You are throwing everything my father has told you out the window, and for what? To see a few Raven scoundrels dead on the street?"

The Ravens were using the opportunity to slip away unnoticed. The moment Stella stopped talking, Harvey's gaze swung back to the Ravens, who bolted the moment his wild eyes settled on them. Stella shouted a curse as her cousin lunged, his knife raised and a look in his eye that made her insides churn. She tried to go after him but Zoey grabbed her arm.

"Don't," she said quietly. "If you try to get him when he's like this, you won't come back out."

Stella ripped her arm away. "I can't just let him go on a rampage!"

"You can't stop him, either."

She cursed again, each word filthier than the last. "He can't get away with this!"

Zoey shouted her name, but she was already chasing after Harvey. Her gun was still in her hand. She was confident in her abilities to put a bullet through her cousin's head, but she just couldn't bring herself to do it. Zoey would never forgive her. Marcus would have her thrown from the gang faster than she could blink if she killed the Roses' top enforcer. She could try to just disable him, but that would only make things worse; Harvey didn't respond kindly to those who injured him, and Stella didn't want to be on the receiving end of his wrath.

That left one option—standing helplessly to the side as she watched Harvey catch up to the Ravens.

It wasn't right. Stella wasn't one to shy away from violence, but seeing Harvey gut the Ravens made her sick. This whole thing made her want to puke. What was the point? This was unnecessary violence, unneeded bloodshed. And for what? Because Harvey was pissed off?

He finished off the last one and turned to Stella, eyes glinting.

"I don't appreciate the interruption," he growled. "We're supposed to present a unified front, but you telling me off in front of the bloody Ravens isn't helping anything!"

Stella blinked several times before finding her voice. "*I'm* the one not presenting a unified front? You're the idiot who keeps going against orders!"

"Because you're making me look weak!" He raked his icy gaze over Zoey, too. "I am not a child. I don't need a babysitter."

Zoey crossed her arms. "Until you stop *acting* like a child, we will continue to watch over you." She flung a hand at the corpses on the ground. "Stunts like this are exactly why we've gained no ground with the feud. Every time we get somewhere, you undo all of our progress with shit like this!"

Harvey's eyes blazed, and his blood-slicked fingers gripped his knife even harder. "They were trying to cross the border."

"Did they cross?" Stella asked.

"They were trying—"

"They were *trying*. Which means they hadn't actually stepped foot over the border yet, right?"

She was met with a sullen silence that told her she was right. Her teeth gritted. "Harvey, this is out of hand. John Daelik is going to have our heads when he finds out about this!"

"He's already found out."

Stella jumped at her father's voice, and she turned to see Marcus storming for them, a group of Roses bringing up the rear. But his eyes weren't on her—they were on Harvey, who shrank back a little.

"The Daeliks are on their way here," Marcus snarled. "I told you to stay put tonight, and what do you do? You paint the border red!"

Harvey's jaw clenched. "They were trying to cross—"

"I don't give a shit!" he roared. "I told you to keep your ass at the house! What in the heavens made you think this was a good idea?" He raked a hand through his hair, his unbuttoned suit making him look more disheveled than Stella had ever seen him, but before Harvey could respond, he snapped, "We have to get the bodies cleaned up before Daelik gets here. The news about this has already spread across half the city, and as soon as the sheriff hears—"

"The sheriff hears what?"

Stella groaned as another voice rang out. John Daelik stood a few paces away from the border, his arms crossed and his gray eyes bearing a thunderstorm of rage. Her heart skipped a beat to see Jordan standing to his father's right. He held her gaze, his lips ticking upward for a moment before he saw the carnage at Harvey's feet. Harvey still stood on the Ravens' side of the border, but he seemed unafraid as he looked John Daelik right in the eye, smiled, and licked his knife clean.

"Why bother with cleanup?" he said to Marcus, eyes still on John. "The birdbrains are here. They can take care of their own."

Marcus didn't continue his lecture in front of his greatest enemy. Somehow his expression was colder and angrier than before, and he discreetly reached up to smooth his shirt and button his jacket. Stella and Zoey retreated to their side of the border, Zoey subtly motioning for Harvey to do the same, but he ignored them as he faced the Ravens fully.

"Well?" he demanded. "I know you've got something to say to me. Out with it!"

Thatcher and Half-Daelik appeared beside Jordan, eyes widening as they took in the bodies. Jordan was doing a good job of keeping his expression neutral, but John glared at Harvey with everything he had.

"The sheriff is on his way," he said softly. "I'd like to see you talk your way out of this one."

Harvey licked the other side of his knife. "The sheriff won't do shit to me." He barked a laugh and swaggered forward. "No one will. You're all too rutting scared."

"Harvey," Marcus said, his voice laced with warning.

He only laughed again. "Come on, uncle. Why such a bore? We've got these bastards outnumbered!"

Jordan slowly drew his revolvers as Roses and Ravens alike pressed in from either side. There had been peace on the border since the gala, but tensions were still running higher than ever. Each side was thirsty for blood, and with everyone desperate to prove themselves while Silas was in town, both sides were itching for a fight. Harvey picked up on this with a wide smile as he raised his now-clean knife and pointed it at John.

"Too scared?" he crooned. "Your men are dead at my feet, and you can't even lecture me for it." He spat. "Pathetic. You Ravens are weaker than I thought."

John's eyes blazed. "Get back on your territory, Rook."

Harvey just laughed. "Make me."

Silence fell over the Barter Streets for a precious second.

Then John Daelik lifted his gun, and all hell broke loose.

CHAPTER 44

The Barter Streets descended into a roar of gunshots and shouting. Jordan got a glimpse of the panic on Stella's face before Harvey Rook lunged for his father, the two of them hitting the ground in a tangle of limbs. Before Jordan could even turn to help, the Roses charged, and the Raven heir found himself knee-deep in war.

He shot the first Rose that reached him, then turned and emptied his other revolver on the approaching army. He picked them off one by one, positioning himself in front of his father to keep him as safe as he could. Not that he was much help; John shouted curses as he struggled to keep Harvey's blade away from his face. The Rose enforcer hadn't stopped smiling since John threatened him. Jordan stepped in to help, but a female shout from behind him had him whirling.

Three of his own Ravens had surrounded Stella. She was putting up a hell of a fight, her long hair swinging as she lashed out with her elbow, catching one in the face. He saw a gun in another's hand and lunged, throwing himself in front of Stella.

"She's mine," he shouted at the Ravens. "Go help John!"

They rushed to aid their leader, and Jordan turned to Stella. For a moment, the battle seemed to slow. Her eyes were wide, panicked, and Jordan was struck with a sudden urge to sweep her into his arms and shield her from the bloodshed raging around them.

And then Stella punched him in the face.

He spluttered, stumbling back with a dazed look. Stella lunged again, but this time she grabbed his arm and yanked him close.

"Quit gaping, feathers," she hissed. "We need to keep up appearances."

Right. Their fathers were here, along with a good portion of their gangs. It would look suspicious if the heirs didn't face off. Jordan threw Stella's arm off and mimed a punch that she easily blocked.

"You're not dressed for this," he noted, marking her blouse and dress boots.

Her face scrunched as she aimed a kick at him that he barely felt. "This wasn't what I planned on doing tonight."

He yanked her forward. "So much for our meeting. The sheriff will arrive any second."

"I didn't ask to be here," she growled, dancing around his next blow. "Harvey started this."

Jordan risked a glance over his shoulder. He didn't see Harvey, but he could hear him laughing, and he noted with relief that his father was on his feet and mostly unharmed, trying to fight his way towards Marcus. Everyone was still fighting, the battle raging over the red line that marked the border, but Jordan's eyes picked out a clear path through the crowd, leading into Raven territory.

He looked back at Stella. "This is for the birds. What do you say about skipping out before the sheriff gets here?"

Stella paused with her fists raised. "You're serious?"

They didn't have time to discuss it. Jordan shoved Stella, driving her towards the path he saw. She picked up on what he was doing and retreated several steps, feigning defensive maneuvers as he rained down pretend punches. Their acting was horrible, but amid a battle where everyone was occupied with their own fight, nobody noticed the two heirs play fighting as they slipped to the edge of the commotion.

Jordan glanced around to make sure the coast was clear before launching into a sprint, dragging Stella with him. They cleared the line of buildings and kept running. He heard voices up ahead and tugged her into the nearest alleyway. They ducked under an arch and kept moving, slipping through crevices and narrow walkways until the street sloped down and they found themselves standing in an alley so small and disused that neither the light of the moon nor the street lamps reached them.

Stella gasped for breath. "Good heavens, did we really do that?"

"Yeah." Jordan slumped against the wall. "And I think we got away with it, too."

Her eyes glittered in the dark. "That was genius."

"I wasn't going to stay there and keep fighting when it would have ended in at least one of us hurt. And once the sheriff showed up, we would have been stuck there for at least another hour." He inhaled, still trying to catch his breath. "I don't care if we spy on Silas tonight or not, but I would rather do anything than fight your people when your cousin's running around like a maniac."

She cringed. "Zoey tried to stage an intervention and it went south."

He cocked a brow. "I see."

Voices echoed in the distance, prompting Jordan to draw deeper into the shadows. Stella trailed after him.

"Now what?" she asked.

That was a good question. It was so dark that Jordan could just make out Stella's silhouette, her white shirt ghostly in the shadows. Before he could stop himself, he reached out and caressed her face.

Her brows flattened. "What are you doing, feathers?"

"Enjoying my night." He cupped her chin and kissed her. "What about you?"

She angled her head. "I suppose I'm doing the same."

He kissed her again. Each movement was lazy and slow, as if time couldn't reach them in this alley, as if there weren't threats circling overhead, eyes pointed on them as they prepared to strike. For a moment, Jordan let himself bask in the feeling, in the fantasy he'd woven around them. He let himself think of a world where they didn't have to sneak off every night, where they didn't have to pretend to fight each other to keep up appearances, where they didn't have to give in to the violence and bloodlust and strict rules of their gangs.

He wished he could hold on to that. A world where love ruled instead of loyalty and lust.

But that was a ridiculous thought, and Jordan let it slide from his mind as Stella kissed him back.

Her arms draped over his shoulders. The kiss turned into something deeper, something *more*, and Jordan's blood raced through his veins as his hands slid down, moving down her shoulders and arms to grip her waist. He didn't remember moving, only that Stella's back hit the wall and they were still wrapped in their embrace, no one but the shadows for company.

Stella's hand slipped into his hair, and he nearly melted at the touch. His heart thrummed and a shiver ran down his spine, but all he could think of was the want for more, more, *more*—

"Someone's back here!"

Jordan ripped away as a voice cut through the roar in his ears. Stella gasped, but he was already turning away, pulling her with him as they sprinted in the other direction.

"Shit!" the voice spat. "They're running!"

They were indeed. Jordan took the first turn he came across, dragging Stella behind him. He didn't know exactly who was chasing them—either a Raven patrol or a group John had sent to track down any Roses lingering on their territory—but what he did know was that being caught tangled up with Stella Rook in a dark alley was a death sentence. So he kept running. He risked a glance over his shoulder to gauge how far back the patrol was, only for his eyes to catch on Stella's face instead. She grinned at him.

"Bloody hell, Rook," he hissed, taking another sharp turn. "If I didn't know any better, I'd say you were enjoying this."

A gun was fired, but Jordan didn't see where the bullet went. Stella only grinned harder, and for a split second he was struck with how similar she looked to Harvey.

"Admit it," she said to him. "You like this."

Another gunshot. Jordan sucked in a breath as he dove into another alley. The street sloped down, and the two of them skidded down the hill before ducking under an arch and heading east towards the Harbor. "I don't like getting shot at."

Her lips curved. "Slipping away from a fight to steal a kiss, only to be chased by your own people? This is our kind of danger, feathers."

Jordan couldn't help but return her grin. "I do think you're right, little thorn. Cover me?"

He spun on his heel, drawing both revolvers in unison. He couldn't afford to let his people see him, so he fired before they rounded the corner, knocking out every street lamp he could see and plunging them into darkness. There was a thump and a muffled curse, but Stella was already tugging Jordan down a side street, leaving their pursuers behind.

"Good heavens," Jordan gasped the moment they were away. "This has been quite the night, hasn't it?"

He'd brought them to the cliffs. Jagged rocks jeered up at them like crooked teeth, the ocean frothing around them. The only thing keeping them from going over the cliff and plunging to certain death was a rickety iron rail that had been in disrepair for as long as Jordan could remember. Uncle Dan had always told him that if you looked hard enough, you could see the bones of the countless people who'd jumped the railing and met their fate on the rocks below. Declan had once ventured out to the cliff edge to see for himself, but after a gust of wind had nearly taken him over, they'd stayed firmly on the safe side of the rail.

Stella leaned against it without fear, tipping her head back to look at the stars visible through rips in the clouds. Her hair cascaded down her back. It took some effort on Jordan's part to keep his hands to himself and not kiss her again, but he just didn't think the rail would hold up if they both leaned against it.

She caught him looking and arched a brow. "Well? What now?"

He looped his fingers through his belt as he stared out at the ocean. "As much as I hate to say it…"

"Don't," she hissed.

"We need to check in on Silas," he finished with a wince. "We haven't exactly had much luck concerning him, but I don't know of anything else to do, so the best thing right now is just to keep our eyes on him for as long as we can."

Stella groaned. "Can't it wait?"

Jordan pushed on the rail to test it, then gingerly leaned against it, cringing as the ancient metal groaned. "I mean, we don't have to go tonight. I just… I have too many questions about that man that I need answered. Too many worries keeping me up at night. As much as I enjoy this"—he laced his fingers through hers—"I can't fully enjoy it when I know there's this huge threat looming over the city."

She stared at their hands, then glanced up at him. "We're going to figure it out, Jordan. All of it."

He smiled and gave her hand a light squeeze. "Damn straight we will."

She looked over her shoulder at the ocean just as a sliver of moonlight filtered through the clouds, shining silver light down her face. Her fair skin turned ghostly in the light, and with her dark hair framing her face, her bright eyes titled out towards the ocean, her full lips curved just so, forming the slightest of smiles... Jordan was struck with the sudden urge to draw, to pick up his sketchbook and pencil and preserve her image on paper. But then she looked back at him and the moon disappeared behind the clouds and a twinge of disappointment wormed its way into Jordan's heart.

"Come on," she said. "If we're going to stake out Silas, then we'd better get on it instead of loitering here all night."

He forced a smile as he offered her the crook of his elbow. "Right this way, m'lady."

CHAPTER
45

The sky was dark with the threat of rain as Jordan followed Silas and his father through the heart of the Ravens' territory. The two held an amicable conversation about trade in the city while Jordan did his best to avoid Celia. Seeing her made his vision go red. He didn't like what she was doing to his mind, and her insistence on talking to him every chance she got made it worse .

She walked beside her father now, her light hair twisted up in a sleek knot, a slim pink dress swirling around her knees. She smiled, a pretty display, trying to get them to lower their guards. And it worked—John smiled back every time their gazes met, elbowing Jordan hard in the ribs until he also smiled at the Tradow heir.

He hated every second of it.

The four of them—five counting Tobias—made a complete round through the Ravens' half of the city. Silas said he wanted to get a scope of the trade systems in Lochridge. He'd been ecstatic ever since his gala. For good reason, too; the daily border skirmishes had dwindled down to early-feud numbers. Aside from the bloodbath a few nights ago—which, as far as he knew, Silas had been kept in the dark on—there were exactly two incidents Jordan had been made aware of, an argument between a Rose and a Raven that ended peacefully and a fistfight between two drunkards that just so happened to be on the border. Harvey Rook's antics aside, it was unusual to see the gangs getting along so well.

Though he couldn't help but think it had something to do with his improved relationship with the heir of the White Roses.

He'd met with her every night, either to discuss things with Silas or to feel her lips against his—usually both. The information they found... It was concerning. Jordan hated the idea of Lochridge falling into someone else's hands. He just didn't know how he was supposed to convince his father *and* Marcus Rook of that, especially since both of them were spitting mad after the fight at the border the other night. Schode had to drag himself out of bed to deal with it, and both gangs had been subject to a drunken reprimand that had lasted an hour. Jordan had been away with Stella at the time, but Declan had complained enough about it that he felt as if he'd attended Schode's rambling lecture himself.

Jordan glared at the back of Silas' head. Silas was oblivious as he continued to pepper John with questions, inquiries ranging from the names of business owners to how many employees they had to how far their trade reached. He was blatantly digging for information, and both Marcus and John went with it because they were trying to impress him. They weren't pushing any questions themselves, weren't testing his limits as they usually did.

Which meant it was up to someone else to do it. If Jordan could get Silas uncomfortable, it might reveal his true colors.

He put on a burst of speed, catching up to the others and wedging himself between Silas and John. "Mister Tradow," he said, keeping his tone light and conversational, "perhaps you would like to visit the Red Harbor once more? I heard a rumor that someone made an offer to buy it out."

This was news to John, who raised his brows. "Really?"

Jordan nodded solemnly. "Two men were discussing it in the Broken Bottle the other day."

Silas' eyes narrowed at the name of the bar. He exchanged a look with his daughter, their twin eyes flashing. Triumph flared through Jordan. Leave Silas to wonder how the information had gotten out.

"I'm quite tired," Silas said. "Perhaps I should return to my hotel."

Jordan's fake smile turned genuine. "If we go just one more street over, we'll pass by the Harbor on our way back to your hotel. It will only add five minutes to our trip. I know how much you are interested in the Harbor."

Silas studied him, as if trying to determine how much he knew. Jordan held his gaze with a wide smile that made his jaw ache, refusing to look in Celia's direction as she examined him with an alarming level of scrutiny.

Then Silas relented with a nod of his head. "Alright then."

They reached the Red Harbor in record time. Harsh winds gusted off the ocean, forcing Jordan to squint against the onslaught. The Harbor was as busy as ever, sailors rushing to get their work done before the storm hit. Tarps were thrown over the crates of merchandise to protect them, the sails of the ships were drawn up, and before long, the Harbor would clear out completely. A good Lochridge storm often tossed up massive waves that had washed people clean off the docks in the past.

"Any idea who's trying to buy the Harbor?" John asked Jordan, his voice raised to be heard over the crash of waves against the nearby rocks. "A Rose in disguise, you think?"

"I think they're from out of town," Jordan shouted back. "From up north somewhere." Silas hadn't talked any more about the Harbor on his nightly outings. Jordan had taken care to hang around the docks more than usual, keeping an eye out for this Ritton character. He glanced at Silas, feigning curiosity. "Perhaps you know him. I think they mentioned he was from the Stokes area."

He didn't care if Silas answered; the offhand comment was more about planting a seed in his father's mind. John Daelik was a smart man. If anyone could make the connection, it would be him.

"I'd have to hear the name to know," Silas said mildly.

Smart move. Jordan pretended to screw up his face in concentration. "It was hard to hear. The name started with an R, I think. Rider? Rylick? Richards?"

"Ramsey?" John suggested.

Jordan snapped his fingers. "Ritton. I think that was it."

Save for another look exchanged between the Tradows, Silas and Celia kept their surprise hidden. "I don't know anyone by that name," the former said.

Liar.

Jordan faked his next smile. "I didn't expect you to. It's a big world."

Silas cautiously returned his smile just as the first drop of water landed on Jordan's head.

A bolt of lightning cleaved the sky in two. There was a brief moment of stillness, then the people of the Red Harbor sprinted for cover. Rain pelted down, assaulting Jordan's exposed arms as he ran to his house. John shouted a farewell before sprinting off as well.

Did he feel bad about purposely delaying Silas so they were caught in the rain? Not at all, especially when Celia let out a little shriek, hiked her dress up to her thighs, and sprinted like a madwoman.

Jordan laughed so hard didn't even care that he was soaked by the time he tumbled inside. It was worth every second.

Lillian gaped from the doorway as her husband and son stumbled into the kitchen, dripping wet. Jordan grinned like a fool.

"You're getting water all over the floor," she tutted. "Lana, get some towels!"

Lana rushed into the room a minute later with an armful of towels. Jordan and John dried off the best they could before Lillian ushered them into their rooms to change clothes. Jordan was still ecstatic from his small victory by the time he returned downstairs, his hair wet from the rain. Lillian shoved him in front of the fire with a mug of steaming tea and ordered him to stay put until she was sure he wouldn't catch a cold. He pulled out his sketchbook to pass the time. Lana came and snuggled up against his side, watching him work.

He loved moments like these, quiet minutes with his sister and his sketchbook, her watching him work with fascination while the two of them sat with quiet contentment.

As far as Jordan knew, his father hadn't tried to rope Lana back into the gang yet, but he knew it was only a matter of time. He doubted he'd get to sit with Lana like this once that happened.

He paused his sketching for a moment to wrap his arm around his sister, drawing her close. "I love you, Lanabug," he murmured.

She blinked. "I love you, too."

She gave him a strange look. Platitudes were few and far between among their family. Jordan saying that he loved her was enough to make her think he was buttering her up to ask for a favor. He fought back a wince as he returned his gaze to the sketchbook in his hands. Lana stared at him for a few more seconds before letting her gaze drop as well.

Jordan kicked himself and didn't press the matter any further.

Day slipped into night. Jordan dried out in front of the fire and felt great by the time Lillian announced dinner was ready. The Daelik family gathered around the dining room table, and for the first time in a long time, Jordan realized everyone seemed content. Happy, even.

It was such a rare occurrence that he leaned back in his seat to bask in the feeling.

Mateo elbowed Jordan as he slid into the seat next to him. "How'd the tour with Silas go?"

He lifted a shoulder in a shrug. "We got rained out." He struggled to keep his expression neutral as the memory of Celia running for her life resurfaced. "Otherwise uneventful."

"It went well," John agreed from the head of the table. "I'm taking it as a good sign that Silas is spending more time with us than the Rooks."

The Rooks. Jordan choked on his roasted vegetables. He was supposed to meet Stella tonight. They had agreed to stay home whenever it rained, meaning tonight's meeting was off, but he was upset with himself for forgetting.

"Do you really think we've got this in the bag?" Uncle Dan asked.

John chewed thoughtfully. "I think we have a winning chance. If I'm going to be honest, I thought this would be over sooner than this. Silas is holding out."

Declan snorted. "It's Celia who's holding out. She's had eyes for Jordan ever since she stepped into town."

Jordan glared at his cousin as Dan let out a chuckle. "He'll be smart to take that up," his uncle said, pointing his fork at Jordan. "Celia is what we like to call a fine specimen. In these parts, the only people that can rival her have a last name that starts with an *R* and ends in *ook*."

"I think Stella Rook is really pretty," Lana agreed.

Jordan's knee slammed into the table. "What is wrong with you people?" he stammered.

She blinked. "What? Stella's pretty. I know she attacked me and everything, but I've always wished that I had hair like hers."

Declan let out a sigh. "If only she wasn't a Rook. She's the one reason I would like to be a Rose."

John cleared his throat.

He lifted his hands in surrender. "I'm not serious. But you have to admit, there are some fine Rook women. You've seen Zoey, right? That dress she was wearing at the gala—"

This time it was Dan who cleared his throat, the sound rather aggressive. Declan's mouth snapped shut. Jordan and Mateo exchanged a look before Jordan nudged his sister under the table, a silent warning not to get involved.

A beat of awkward silence passed. Lillian plastered a smile on her face and struck up a loud conversation about gossip in town that John was quick to latch onto. Jordan let his gaze wander as he half-listened.

If only she wasn't a Rook.

Stella and Jordan had long since agreed that their relationship—if they could even call it that—was doomed. Eventually, the wrong person would find out, a rumor would spread, and both of their families would look into the situation and realize what was happening. If John were to find out, he would disown Jordan faster than he could blink.

Jordan picked at his food. Whatever was going on between him and Stella… He wanted it to last. It was unreal how badly he wanted it, needed it. He craved her presence—the same person he couldn't stand to be around a few weeks ago he now couldn't live without.

It wouldn't last. They both knew that.

He looked past the dining room to the window in the foyer. Rain dripped down it in crooked lines, the droplets not falling as hard as before. The storm had lightened up enough to make travel possible. He could brave the wet and sneak out if he wanted to, but Stella wouldn't be there to greet him.

Unless he tracked her down.

Jordan shoved the last of his food into his mouth and muttered an excuse before escaping upstairs to his room—and the window that served as his exit.

CHAPTER 46

It was with a sigh that Stella shed her day clothes and tugged on an ivory-colored nightgown, the silky material soft against her skin. After a day spent rushing to complete her errands in town before the rain fell, she was ready for some much-needed beauty sleep.

Her continued search for a contact had turned up nothing. She'd sent out requests behind her father's back, asking his spies to find someone, anyone, who knew about the situation in Stokes. She expected to hear from them any day. Jordan was right—it was strange that nobody in a city as big as Lochridge had ever visited Stokes. There was something off about the whole situation. Stella had known that from the moment she laid eyes on Silas, but now she had to prove it.

She took up a position in front of her vanity and combed through her long hair. Rain pattered against the glass doors that led to the balcony, a steady yet gentle beat. She was supposed to have met with Jordan tonight; she had debated for a while if she could brave the rain and try to meet him, but the idea was shot down quickly. They'd taken too many risks as it was. Sneaking out for a midnight rendezvous was unwise.

Not that it mattered to Stella. Every moment was a blessing in disguise; every secret feeling, every hidden pleasure, every kiss stolen under the moonlight. It did not matter how she knew she was supposed to hate Jordan, how he had once killed someone she loved, nor did it matter that their parents would likely murder both of them if their secret was spilled.

Stella set down her comb with a sigh. This was quite the mess she'd gotten herself into.

Something thumped against the glass doors. Stella whirled around with a bottle of perfume in her hand, aiming it at the noise like a gun. It sounded again—a distinctive thump against the glass, not at all like the soft patter of rain. It sounded like a knock. She tried to tell herself it was a tree branch scratching against the window, but she knew for a fact there weren't any trees close enough to this side of the house to be disturbing her window at this hour.

Abandoning the perfume in favor of an actual gun, Stella crept towards the doors and flung open the curtains. She gasped aloud as she beheld the shadowy figure standing on her balcony—a man, tall and muscular, revolvers gleaming on his belt.

Then she realized who it was and bit back a curse as she unlocked the door.

"Jordan Daelik, what in the bloody hell are you doing here?" she hissed, tugging him inside. His brown hair was plastered to his face, a shit-eating grin playing across his lips. Water dripped off of him as he shucked off his jacket and smirked at Stella.

"We had a meeting tonight," he drawled.

"I thought our meetings were canceled whenever there was rain!"

"Keep your voice down before you attract unwanted attention, little thorn."

"Keep my—" Stella pinched the bridge of her nose. "Jordan, you snuck into my room in the middle of the night. How did you even get past the guards?"

"I climbed over the gate in the back." He probed a hole in his shirt. "Nearly impaled myself on the fence, but it was worth it. From there I just climbed up the trellis to your balcony."

She planted her hands on her hips. "And how did you know which room was mine?"

"Research? My father has debated assassinating you in the past. I was charged with figuring out the rooming situation of Marcus Rook and his closest family." Jordan winced. "That was a year ago, but I assumed you hadn't moved since then."

Stella could only gape at him. He snuck into the house of his greatest enemy in the dead of night just to uphold a meeting with her.

Jordan must be crazy, she thought. Aloud she said, "You're getting water on the floor."

Jordan glanced down at the puddle of water that was indeed forming beneath his boots. "You know, it might be good for me to get out of these wet clothes." He gave her a roguish wink. "It's a shame your clothes aren't wet, too."

"You can't stay here," Stella insisted in a whisper, even as heat rose on her cheeks. "If someone comes in here—"

"I might suggest that you lock the door."

She glanced over her shoulder to ensure that the door *was* locked, then went as far to shove a chair in front of it. "You need to leave *right now*," she said.

Jordan blatantly studied her bedroom. "Why? I just got here."

"If we get caught—"

"Then we'll deal with the consequences," he finished, meeting her gaze with enough seriousness to make her step back. "Stella, I got halfway here when I realized just how big of a mistake this was. This is stupid in so many ways, but for whatever reason, I am completely unable to stay away from you. You drag me in with that irresistible charm and I can't say no." He ran a hand through his hair. "Whatever this is between us… it won't last. Because I know I will continue doing stupid things like this just for an opportunity to see you, to hold you, to get to know you. It will get us caught and killed one day. But until then, I want to enjoy every damn moment."

It felt like being punched in the gut, the way he was looking at her, his brown eyes clear and full of longing. Stella realized there was no way she'd be able to just toss him out the door like that.

Triumph flared in Jordan's expression as she locked the balcony doors and pulled the curtains shut.

Stella warned, "If we get caught, I'm shooting you and making it seem as if you were trying to murder me in my sleep."

"I would expect nothing less," he crooned, sitting down to pull off his wet boots.

Stella's cheeks burned as she returned her gun to its place on the nightstand. Her hand trembled with a mixture of nervousness and excitement.

If they were caught—

Jordan came up behind her and wrapped his strong arms around her, the raven tattoo on his wrist dark against his tan skin. The water soaking his shirt seeped through her thin nightgown, sending a shiver down her spine.

"I feel the need to say that this is ridiculously stupid," Stella whispered.

She felt him smile against her cheek. "It most definitely is," he agreed.

She twisted to face him. "What are we even doing, Jordan? Meeting at the beach was one thing, but sneaking into my house—"

"I wanted to see you."

"My family—"

"Is full of idiots." His eyes smoldered. "I am sick and tired of every conversation we have revolving around our families. We've dedicated everything to the gangs. Why can't we have one part of our lives that *doesn't* concern them?"

"Because we were born and raised to be their heirs to the gangs," Stella said. "The feud keeps our families in business. To them, not upholding the fight is spitting on family values."

Jordan grunted. "Violence should not be a regular part of a family."

"You're right," she murmured. "But what are we supposed to do?"

"I don't know," he murmured, his hand coming up to brush her hair out of her face, "but I think we're on the right path."

Stella wanted nothing more than to continue down that path, but she forced herself to lean back, putting herself outside of Jordan's grip. "We need to talk about this, Jordan," she said, her voice soft but firm. "I don't know what this is, and that is going to get us in trouble. We need to figure out what we are doing together and why, because otherwise…"

He lifted a brow, a silent question.

Her throat bobbed. "If this is just a fling, a way to get a thrill out of defying our parents, then we need to end it now before someone gets hurt."

He angled his head to the side. "And if it isn't?"

"Then we should try harder to make it work," she breathed. "But that still leaves the question."

He was so close to her, only a breath away. "What question, little thorn?"

Stella wasn't sure she was breathing. "Is this a fling, or is it something more?" She swallowed. "Is this a thrill, or is it love?"

The moment the words left her mouth, the air in the room went still. Jordan's eyes hardened, an unreadable expression on his face.

"What's your answer?" he asked.

"I—" Stella struggled to find her voice, weighed down by his gaze. "I don't know. I shouldn't want you. The entire world has told me that. My mind says I shouldn't because of what happened between you and Liam three years ago. I swore to get revenge, and now it feels like I'm betraying him." His eyes darkened at that, but Stella forged on. "It's driving me crazy, all the thoughts in my head about you. I can't get you out of my mind. Despite everything that's happened between us, between our families, despite everything we've done to make us hate each other…"

She choked a little. Liam—she didn't want to think about that. She'd always viewed Jordan as a monster, a killer, the cocky bastard over the border. But… that wasn't him. That wasn't the Jordan she knew now. This was a boy burdened by his father's orders, one who protected his little sister and sketched when no one was looking.

This was the person who killed Liam, and yet, it wasn't.

"I don't hate you, Jordan," she said. "I think…"

"What?" he pressed.

"I think I love you," she whispered.

Once again, that stilled silence filled the room. Jordan's lips parted, but the words died on his tongue as he stared at Stella, as he held her in his arms.

Good heavens, Stella thought. *I've messed this up*. If only she'd kept her big mouth shut and let this end peacefully, but now she'd complicated everything—

"I love you, too," Jordan said.

The words crashed into Stella. She slumped against Jordan, burying her face into his sodden shirt. He gripped her tightly, one hand playing with her hair, the other pressed firmly against her back.

It felt nice, and yet, Stella felt like she'd just signed her death warrant.

"What are we going to do now?" Jordan asked softly.

She choked on what might have been a laugh. "I have no rutting clue."

Jordan chuckled. "I guess that means we have to stick with my plan, then."

"Which was?"

He kissed her.

Stella drew back enough to say, "I like this plan."

The corner of his lips tugged up into a smile. "Indeed."

CHAPTER 47

Two things happened at Rook Manor the following day.

Well, three if you counted Jordan slipping off in the early hours of the morning, the water dripping from the roof masking his footsteps as he made his escape, leaving Stella alone in her room. She changed into a creamy white dress with sandals, tucking her gold locket away, her fingers shaking a little. She'd allowed the heir to the Ravens into her home. Nevermind the nature of their relationship; Marcus would kill her for that alone.

Which is why he could never, under any circumstances, find out.

The second thing that happened was a knock on the door while the Rooks were sitting down for breakfast. Marcus himself opened it, blinking in surprise when he saw Sheriff Schode on the threshold.

"Sheriff," he said, his voice betraying his surprise. "You aren't here to arrest anyone, are you?"

Schode smiled as if it was a joke, his muddy brown eyes crinkling at the corners, but Stella knew her father was dead serious. "Not this time, Marcus. I have news."

Marcus stepped aside to let him in. Schode removed his hat, and Stella was surprised to see he was sober, for once.

"This isn't welcome news, I'm afraid," he began, "but please don't shoot the messenger." Stella's eyes narrowed as he continued. "The Red Harbor has changed ownership."

Everyone blinked. Stella sucked in a breath. "To who?" Marcus demanded.

Schode drew in a deep breath as if bracing himself. "A man named Micah Ritton. I don't know much about him, just that he's from the north and that he's got a lot of money behind him. The deal was made official last night, and Ritton has asked me to inform the leaders of both gangs that he is now refusing work with any known affiliates of the White Roses—"

A cry of outrage arose.

"—*or* the Ravens!" Schode shouted. "He's cutting off *both* gangs."

That did little to appease anyone. Stella started to panic.

Ritton—that was Silas' friend. The one who was going to buy out the Harbor. She and Jordan *knew* this was going to happen.

But they were too late.

"That is ridiculous," Marcus spat. "We've got dozens of people employed there. You can't just let them all lose their jobs!"

"From what I heard, many of them stayed," Schode said, his voice solemn. "They were offered deals if they left their gang, and most took it. The Harbor is as full as ever, but anyone that refused to let go of their affiliation was fired."

Deals. Schode didn't specify, but Stella didn't need him to. Those contracts Silas passed around the Red Harbor had paid off.

"This is bullshit," Harvey snarled. "The Harbor is neutral ground!"

"Yes, it is!" Schode shouted, raising his voice to remain heard over the shouting. "Even more so now. I've heard the accusations about bribing sailors on both sides. Now it can't happen because neither of you have ties to the Harbor anymore." He spat on the ground. "I am all for this idea. It is *happening*. Any attempt to threaten or bribe Mister Ritton will result in punishment. Understand?"

He swept a gaze over the room. Marcus' jaw clenched, but he said no more.

"Good." He spat again. "Now if you'll excuse me, I have to go have this conversation with the Daeliks."

The moment the door closed behind him, the room erupted. Evelyn's face scrunched with worry. Harvey looked pissed, and the other Roses glanced around in anger and confusion. Stella couldn't blame them. It had come out of nowhere. She and Jordan were too late to stop it now.

She watched Marcus storm off to his office, no doubt to write some strongly-worded letters to his allies about the change in the Harbor, and her chest pinched.

"I can't believe this," Zoey said. "He can't just sweep in and take members of our gang away—"

Stella glanced at her. "He can and he did."

"This Ritton character… Where did he come from, anyway?"

"Stokes," Stella answered grimly.

Zoey's brow flattened. "You don't know that."

"I'm fairly certain."

"You think Silas is behind this?" Her voice was amused, but also incredulous. "Stella, I don't know what kind of conspiracy this is, but what would Silas want with the Red Harbor?"

Stella whipped around to face her. "I don't know, Zoey. What does he want with Lochridge? He said the first time we met he was interested in the Harbor, and now it's been bought out by a mysterious third party from the north. Unless I've had my map turned upside down this entire time, Stokes is north of us."

Zoey gave her a condescending look. "You don't know any of this."

"Don't I?" she snapped, pushing by her cousin and stalking out the door. But she slammed into someone else, cursing under her breath as she looked at the messenger she'd knocked over.

"Miss Rook!" he said, jumping up. "This is for you."

He handed her a letter, wrinkled from his fall. She recognized the name on the front and ripped it open, her eyes widening as she read its contents.

"What is it?" Zoey asked, coming up behind her.

"A conspiracy," Stella snapped, shoving it into her pocket and storming outside.

Jordan Daelik wasn't a fan of ass-kissing, but desperate times called for desperate measures.

He'd thought a lot about what Stella said the other night about sucking up to Celia to get information. He remembered what she had done the first night they worked together. All it took was undone hair and an unbuttoned shirt, and she'd gotten the owner of that pub to bow at her feet. Jordan couldn't do that, exactly, but he could certainly take a page out of her book.

The clerk recognized him when he strolled into the hotel on the far side of town. He raised a finger to his lips, warning her to remain quiet as he swaggered upstairs to room thirty-two. He wore all black as usual, once of his nicer shirts with the sleeves still intact. His hair was purposely mused, his revolvers in their usual spots as he leaned against the doorway and knocked three times.

Tobias answered. He glowered down at Jordan, his beady eyes glinting, and it was then Jordan realized he'd never heard the man talk outside of that one conversation he eavesdropped on. He swallowed and said, "I'm here for Celia."

"Daelik? Is that you?" Celia appeared at Tobias' side, wearing a pink dress so dark it was nearly red. She smiled as she took in Jordan, leaned against the doorframe with his arms crossed. "What a pleasant surprise! Whatever can I do for you?"

He mustered a smile of his own. "I was hoping you would join me for a walk."

Her eyes gleamed. "Of course."

Tobias glared after them as Jordan offered Celia his arm and led her downstairs. The clerk wisely looked away as the pair sauntered outside.

"No rain today," Celia remarked, squinting up at the sunny sky.

"Right," Jordan agreed. "A perfect day for a walk."

A few ravens flitted over the sky, casting their shadows on the street below as the pair strolled through White Rose territory, sticking close to the ocean. Normally it would get him in trouble with the border patrols, but nobody dared to stop him when Celia was at his side. He considered it to be one of the few perks to having her around—as long as he wasn't causing trouble, she granted him safe passage through Rose turf.

Celia glanced at him, amused. "Is there a particular reason for this walk? From what I understand, you haven't been interested."

Jordan shrugged. "I realized there's a pretty girl wanting my attention, so I might as well take advantage of it." She raised a brow, and he added, "And my father might have made me come."

She chuckled. "He wants you to get close to me so that he can get close to my father."

"That's the plan, yes."

"Do you want to be here?"

He shrugged again. "Like I said, pretty girl. Might as well."

Celia smirked. "Don't worry, Jordan. No matter which way this goes, I won't mind keeping you around. I rather like you."

A chill raced down his arms, but Jordan matched her smirk with an easy smile. "And what way do you *think* this is going to go?"

"It's up to my father."

"You have sway, though."

"I do."

They fell silent for a few minutes. Jordan breathed a sigh of relief as they crossed onto Raven territory. He brought them to a halt by the railing overlooking the cliffs. His mind drifted to the other night, when he and Stella had stood in this exact spot. He'd been in much better company that night, and as Celia braced her arms on the rail, it took a lot of effort to resist the urge to push her over.

"I'm worried, is all," he said at last, putting as much emotion into his voice as he could. "Even if my side wins this alliance, I don't know what it means for Lochridge. Trace wants to *revolutionize* it. What does that even mean?"

"It means we're going to make it better," Celia said promptly.

Jordan looked at her, the wind whipping his hair over his brow. "That's not an answer."

She looked up at him, pale eyes glinting. "Are you worried, Daelik?"

"Yes."

The answer was honest. Celia tilted her head. "You shouldn't be. Not as long as this"—she gestured between them—"stays good." She leaned in, her lips parting into a sensual smile. "I like what I see, Jordan Daelik. And as long as you keep your head down and count on me to sway my father, I can do big things for you."

Jordan stilled. Celia's lips brushed his cheek, the ghost of a kiss. And then she was gone, sauntering back the way they came.

Jordan felt cold as he shoved his way back into his house that evening. He'd found himself unable to shake Celia's words, to rid himself of the feeling of her lips against his face. If there was ever a time he had a bad feeling about the Tradows' presence in town, it was now.

Mateo was in the living room when he walked in, his arm slung over Jasmin's shoulders where the two were cuddled up on the couch. He noted the look on Jordan's face with raised brows. "Something the matter?"

"Everything's the matter," Jordan bit out.

He didn't give Mateo time to reply before spearing for the stairs. Between the news about the Red Harbor this morning and Celia's insinuation earlier, his mind was reeling. Declan would be at his usual place in the bar by now, so Jordan had every intention to raid the stash of moonshine his cousin kept under his bed to clear his mind of the thoughts plaguing it.

But his foot was still on the first stair when his father called from behind him, "I need you."

Jordan whirled. "For what?"

John's eyes narrowed as he leaned against the wall. "Don't use that tone with me, boy."

He forced his shoulders to relax. "Sorry. It's been a day."

His father, thankfully, let it drop. "I've questioned all the men that dissented from the gang in favor of working at the Harbor. They'd been paid to keep quiet about the nature of their deal."

Jordan knew what that meant. "I will not interrogate our own men."

"They aren't our men anymore. They made their decision."

"I will not interrogate our *former* men," he snapped.

John's eyes slitted. "I'm not asking, Jordan."

That was his cue to shut his mouth and carry out his orders. But Jordan was in a pissy mood, so he turned to his father and snarled, "And I'm not doing it."

His eyes widened. "Jordan—"

"I already know about the deal," he snapped. "This is Silas' doing. He got them to sign contracts to join the Workers' Union—"

The blow came so hard and fast that Jordan didn't have time to block it. Pain burst across his cheek as John raised his hand, ready to deliver another vicious backhand.

"Shut up," he snarled. "You will not defy me, and you will not question me. We have an alliance to secure, and I will not have you

310

spreading rumors about Mister Tradow."

"It isn't a rumor!"

"*Silence!*" John roared, striking him again.

Jordan fell back, his face throbbing, his tongue stuck in his throat.

"You have crossed the line," John hissed. "You will learn not to push back against me, not to blatantly defy me. If you value your place as my heir, then you will get a rutting grip on yourself, march your ass down to the warehouse, and interrogate those men like I ordered you to." He bared his teeth. "Do I make myself clear?"

The commotion had drawn attention. Lana hovered in the doorway, her eyes wide as she took in the bruise rising on Jordan's cheek. Lillian appeared and hurried her away, but he saw her hands shaking. Mateo and Jasmin came from the living room, more of Jordan's family poking their heads out to watch the spectacle.

It was a struggle to control his breathing. To not reach for his revolvers.

Jordan looked his father in the eye. "Crystal."

John's face was so, so cold. "Good. Now get out of my sight."

CHAPTER 48

Stella's heart raced as she darted through the darkened streets of Lochridge. She crossed over the border without a backwards glance, pressing into the shadows as a Raven patrol wandered past. The moment they were out of sight, she burst into motion, putting the Barter Streets to her back as she sprinted towards the Daeliks' house.

She skidded to a stop just short of the house, daring a peek around the corner. There were guards, of course, and this early in the evening everyone would still be awake. Stella had forced herself to wait this long before coming to Jordan; the letter she'd shoved in her pocket seemed to burn through her clothes, scorching the skin beyond. Trying to sneak into his house now would be risky, but she comforted herself in the fact that she had waited until it wasn't broad daylight out.

Stella stepped towards the house, but just then the front door opened. She dove back into the shadows. Her brows raised as she recognized the lone figure that stalked onto the street. It was Jordan, but she knew immediately something was wrong by the set of his shoulders, the way his hands fisted at his sides.

She trailed after him. She took little effort to mask her steps, hoping he'd hear and turn around, but whatever was on his mind consumed him so greatly that he was oblivious to her presence until she followed him down a side street and grabbed his shoulder. "Feathers."

He whirled, his revolvers flashing in the moonlight. Stella scrambled back. She didn't like his look—wrathful, angry, the shadows twisting him into something cruel. But the moment he laid eyes on her, his face slackened.

"You gave me a heart attack," he muttered, shoving his guns away. "What are you doing here?"

"Trying to find you." She studied his face. "What's the matter?"

"Nothing."

"Bullshit."

"Nothing that concerns you," he corrected.

Stella's eyes narrowed as she noted the bruise on his face. That hadn't been there this morning. "Who hit you?"

"Nothing that con—"

"Jordan," she snapped.

He raked a hand through his hair. "Trust me when I say that you don't want to know."

Stella stared at him for a long moment.

Then she handed them the letter wordlessly.

Jordan stared. Took a deep breath. Fought for his composure. "I can't read, Rook," he said flatly.

Stella felt her cheeks flush, and she was quick to snatch it back.

"My father's spies found a woman whose brother lives in Stokes," she said. "She lives in the neutral territory where our monthly meeting happens. That's why we haven't been able to find her—she's not affiliated with the gangs."

"Your father's spies?"

"He's unaware I used them. And I paid for their silence."

Jordan nodded distantly. "Do you think she knows something about Stokes?"

"If she doesn't, she should be able to point us to her brother, who will definitely know." She folded up the letter and shoved it back into her pocket. "Where are you going?"

He'd been walking out with a purpose—headed somewhere. But he just shook his head. "It's nothing that can't wait. Let's go."

She pulled up her hood and mask and let Jordan lead the way. With her wearing all black and her face covered, she looked nothing more than a Raven loyally following her leader, meaning the two of them could walk freely through the Ravens' territory. Jordan's eyes were distant, and his fingers kept brushing his revolvers as if he itched to draw them.

Something was on his mind.

"Is it your sister?" she asked, breaking the silence.

"What?"

"Something's the matter with you. Is it Lana?"

"No." He shook his head. "That's over."

"Silas?" she pressed.

He shrugged. "I met with Celia today. She didn't tell me anything useful, but she certainly didn't lead me to believe she has peaceful intentions." His mouth twisted in distaste. "That's not my problem, though."

Stella hummed under her breath. "Heavens, I don't know what could be worse than a meeting with Celia Tradow."

Jordan grunted under his breath.

Stella nudged him. "You're not going to be all moody on me, are you?"

A muscle in his jaw ticked.

She sighed dramatically. "It's a shame. I was just starting to like you, too."

His brown eyes slid to her. "I'm not in the mood."

"You aren't?" Stella gasped. "However could you tell?"

Jordan looked away. He was silent for a long moment, and when he finally spoke his voice was quiet. "Has your father ever made you do something that you didn't want to do? And I'm not talking about cleaning your room or eating your vegetables. I'm talking... stuff related to the gang."

Stella studied him. "Do you know how many times Harvey has gotten himself into a fight that I had to break up? He's a maniac. Most people who step between him and his idea of a good time don't live to tell about it." Her fingers brushed a faint scar on her neck. "One time he got so angry over it he came at me with his knife. If Father hadn't been there to intervene, we wouldn't be having this conversation." She dropped her hand. "I wanted nothing to do with Harvey after that. But the next time he got into a fight at the border, do you know who Father asked to deal with it?"

Jordan clenched his jaw. "But you did it."

"Yes," Stella agreed.

"Why?"

It took her a moment to find an answer.

"Loyalty," she said at last. "It's my family. My gang. My father is in charge of both, and it's my duty to listen to him." She shifted her gaze away. "But it's not always the best course of action. I guess we're both learning that now."

"But it's family," Jordan said. "If my father tells me to do something, I should do it. Out of loyalty."

"You're not doing that now," she pointed out gently. "Being with me goes against your family in about a thousand different ways."

"This is different, though. We're stopping a threat against the city. They just don't know it." He glanced at her. "This other thing... it's not the same."

Stella bit her lip. "I wish I could help you, Jordan."

It was a quiet invitation for him to confide in her, but he just turned away with a slight shake of his head. "I wish you could too, little thorn."

The conversation drifted off as they entered neutral ground. They passed by the bar that served as the meeting place and kept going, heading into the slum district. Stella had taken advantage of the day by pouring over a map until she was sure of the route, so Jordan let her take the lead.

The heirs found themselves standing in front of a ramshackle townhouse. The streetlamp next to them flickered, the glass cracked and fogged and hardly providing any light. Below it, ravens picked through rubbish thrown carelessly aside, and Stella's nose wrinkled as a rat scampered across the street. The parts of Lochridge outside of the Roses and Ravens' jurisdiction had a habit of falling into disrepair, plagued by black market dealers and illegal drugs and smaller gangs vying for territory. Their disputes weren't typically as bloody as the main feud, but things could get pretty damn violent. It didn't help that none of the smaller gangs actually cared enough about the city to put any effort into its upkeep, leaving the slums trapped in a cycle of violence and neglect with no one to promise them better. This part of town had been crumbling for the better part of the last decade.

Stella's heart wrenched as she looked at the townhouse once more. Curtains had been drawn over the windows, but she could see candles burning inside.

"What are you thinking?" she asked Jordan. "Both of us go inside and risk being recognized, or just one?"

He considered. "We might as well do both. I'm tired of playing games."

And that was that. Jordan knocked on the door, three short raps. The curtains fluttered, a lock was undone, and then an older woman with curly red hair peered out at them.

"Can I help you?" she asked, her eyes darting between them.

Stella tugged down her hood. "Poppy Wekins?"

She opened the door a bit more. "That's me."

Stella flashed her prettiest smile. "We were hoping to speak with you about your brother."

Poppy's eyes widened. "Jasen?"

She nodded. "It's important."

Poppy's gaze shifted from her to Jordan.

Then she stepped aside, letting them in.

The two heirs exchanged a glance as they stepped inside. Poppy led them to a small but comfortable living room and gestured for them to sit down on an overstuffed couch with burst seams. Stella swept a critical gaze over the area, taking in the candles burned down to stubs, the peeling wallpaper, the scraggly carpets. Poppy drew a shawl over her shoulders as she hovered in front of them. "Would you like some tea?"

"We're good, thank you," Jordan said.

Poppy eased into an armchair. "I haven't spoken to Jasen in months. I don't know what you could want with him."

Stella leaned forward. "Jasen lives in Stokes, doesn't he?"

She nodded. "Wretched town."

A perfect segue. "What's so bad about it?"

She laughed humorlessly. "It's horrible. Or it is now, at least—I grew up in Stokes before moving to Lochridge. It was a nice city back then. But then the Workers' Union swept in and took over everything. Wrecked the major industries, put hundreds out of jobs. Jasen stayed behind to run our parents' mercantile, but after the Union came through, it got shut down." Her mouth twisted. "They've ruined Stokes. Last I heard, Jasen barely had enough to make a living, much less reopen the mercantile. I've offered for him to stay with me, but he's determined to uphold our parents' legacy."

Jordan shot Stella a look. Poppy read it with narrowed eyes. "You aren't here about Jasen, are you?"

"We're here about the Workers' Union," Stella said. No point in beating around the bush. "A representative of the Union has been in Lochridge for the last couple of weeks with intentions to bring this city under their wing."

Poppy sucked in a breath. "You can't let them."

"We don't intend to," Jordan said. "But we were hoping to know more about the situation in Stokes and the other towns the Union has taken over, so we can know what to expect."

"We're convinced this is a threat," Stella added. "The representative... we don't trust him."

Poppy pulled her shawl tighter around herself. "You shouldn't trust anyone from the Union."

"Tell us about it," she prompted gently.

But the woman shook her head, a few strands of fiery hair shaking loose of their knot. "I wasn't there when the Union took over. I only know what Jasen told me." She pressed her lips together. "But I know it wasn't pretty. There was a man—Stephen Trace."

The leader of the Union. Stella nodded for her to keep going.

"He grew up in Stokes. I knew him—he came into the mercantile a few times. He worked in the coal mine just north of town. It was small, barely providing any jobs, but it kept people afloat until a collapse killed a worker and left the rest injured. The sheriff closed the mine down. Stephen and the other miners were put out of a job. They weren't compensated for their work or for the injuries they received in the collapse. The sheriff refused to let the mine reopen, and eventually the owners packed up and moved away, leaving the miners with nothing.

"Stephen took matters into his own hands. He formed the Workers' Union alongside the others. They went to every business in Stokes and convinced the employees to join, and once they were big enough, they went on strike, demanding better wages and compensation for when accidents happen."

"That doesn't sound too bad," Jordan remarked.

"It wasn't," Poppy agreed. "It was a good thing in the beginning, which is why so many joined. The strike ended in a few days because employers caved. Upped the wages and added compensations into their contracts. Stephen still didn't have a job, but he had a purpose. More people joined the Union after the successful strike, and Stephen began charging each member a fee to cover his lack of income. He started more strikes, demanding more each time. Businesses started closing their doors because they couldn't find employees."

Stella angled her head. "Like your brother?"

"Like Jasen," she said quietly. "Stephen killed the jobs in Stokes by promising better. And he delivered—as businesses started shutting down, he was able to take them over, using the funds he reaped from his members. He re-employed the people he convinced to go on strike in the first place, starting them off with high wages and good hours, but as time went on, Stephen got greedy. His fee for being a part of the Union went up while wages went down. But by the time people noticed, he owned every major business in Stokes—and the people, too. It got violent. Those who tried to leave were found dead in the morning. Jasen was approached by Trace himself and asked to join the Union. He refused, but he was scared that Trace would come after him because of it." Her throat bobbed. "Or that's what his last letter said, anyway. I haven't heard from him since."

A tear slipped down her cheek, and Stella's heart wrenched. She put a hand on Poppy's arm.

"What about the other towns?" she whispered.

She shook her head. "I don't know much about those. I know Trace likes to turn people against each other. In Stokes he turned employee against employer and used the tension to insert himself as leader. I do think he had good intentions at the start. He was wronged, and he wanted to make sure others didn't get the same treatment he did. But..."

"Power corrupts," Stella murmured.

Poppy nodded. "Power corrupts. Even the best of men can't refuse."

Stella and Jordan exchanged another look. He gave a slight nod.

"Thank you for your time," Stella said. "You've been a tremendous help." She pulled a handful of gold from her pocket and pressed it into Poppy's hand. "We would appreciate you keeping quiet about this conversation."

Her fingers curled around the coins. "Don't let Stephen ruin this city, too. I've already lost a brother to the Union."

"Don't worry," Jordan said, rising to his feet. "We won't let that happen."

CHAPTER 49

"This is bad."

Stella and Jordan sat on the rocks of Jordan's hidden beach, staring out at the ocean. Stella's long hair whipped in the wind, but the chill running down her back had nothing to do with the breeze. She looked at Jordan. "Poppy said Trace's goal is to turn people on each other. That's exactly what he's doing here. Silas is just his puppet for doing so."

"He's almost there, too," Jordan muttered. Smoke rose from the cigar dangling between his fingers, and he watched the thin haze climb towards the sky. "What now?"

"We have to take this to our fathers. If they don't believe us, then we tell them to investigate Stokes or any of the other towns the Union has a grip on. Tell them to send someone down there and see if that's what we want Lochridge to look like. This isn't about *revolutionizing* the city; it's about taking it over to profit a man with a vengeance."

"That isn't going to work," he said miserably.

"Jordan, we don't have any other options!"

He glared at her. "My father and I are not on good terms at the moment. I don't even know if he will give me the time of day to speak to him, much less listen to what I have to say."

Stella paused. There it was, that look in his eye again. Her gaze traveled down to the bruise darkening his cheek.

"He was the one who hit you," she realized aloud.

He looked away. "I've had worse."

"Jordan."

"He's not going to listen to me," he snapped. "You can try your father if you want, but convincing my family is pointless." He kicked the ground, sand flying everywhere. "*I'm* pointless."

"That isn't true," she said softly. She came to sit next to him, her hand slipping into his even as her nose wrinkled at the smell. "He'll come around."

Jordan let out a humorless laugh. "I'm sure."

Stella didn't think she'd be able to get through to him when he was being like this. But she thought back to their conversation earlier and realized he was right. Whatever fight Jordan and his father had gotten into, it was doubtful that John was in a mood to listen to anyone, much less his own son.

"I'll talk to Father," she said finally, unsure of what else to do or say. "Meet you back here tomorrow?"

Jordan nodded, already standing up. Stella grabbed his arm.

"We'll put a stop to this," she promised. Her lips brushed his cheek. Jordan squeezed his eyes shut and leaned into the touch, angling his head so the next kiss was right on the lips. She slid her arm around his neck, and he shuddered, his hands gripping her face as if afraid she would pull away.

But in the end, it was Jordan who pulled back first.

"Thank you," he whispered. "I couldn't do this without you."

"We're in this together," she murmured.

He pressed a final kiss to her forehead. "I'll see you tomorrow."

Then he dropped his hands and walked away.

Knock. Knock. Knock.

Stella's stomach did a flip as Marcus called for her to enter. She gathered her courage and pushed open the office door. Her father sat behind his desk as usual, barely looking up as Stella closed the door behind her, squeezing her hands together to keep her nervousness in check.

She had one shot at this.

"Have a seat," Marcus said, putting his pen aside. "What is it?"

Stella didn't sit, opting instead to lean against the desk, facing her father with her shoulders squared. "We need to talk," she said. "About Silas."

Marcus tilted his head.

Stella took this as a good sign and forged on. "I know I've said before that I don't trust him—"

"You've made it perfectly clear."

"—but I don't think I explained my reasoning well," she finished, eyes narrowing at the interruption. "This Workers' Union—I've looked into them. Stokes is not a good city. What they did to it cannot be repaired. They destroyed the city, took the power out of the hands of the citizens and gave it to one person and one person only: Stephen Trace, Silas' boss. All he wants is to do the same with Lochridge. He doesn't want to revolutionize it; he wants to claim it as his own. This won't end with an alliance with one gang. He's going to get rid of everyone."

Marcus folded his hands in front of him. "Knowing you, you no doubt have a slew of evidence to back up this claim, correct?"

She blanched. "My word isn't good enough?"

"Stella, I trust you completely. But Silas is offering is the deal of a lifetime. I've spent countless hours with him, and I trust him."

"More than me?" she demanded. "Father, I have tried to warn you about Silas. Why can't you see it? He's the one behind the change in ownership of the Red Harbor. This Ritton character is from Stokes. He's friends with Silas and Trace. The deals our gang members made to continue working at the Harbor? They were contracts to join the Union." She braced her hands on the desk and looked her father dead in the eye. "You have always been a man who does his research before agreeing to anything. Why has that changed? You are blinded by your desire to get revenge on John Daelik, and it's causing you not to see the problem right in front of your face."

He leaned back in his seat. "I trust you more than anyone. But I also think that you're misguided on this subject. I talked to Ritton yesterday to establish a connection. He's from Lancaster, not Stokes. He and Silas don't know each other. As for the contracts, I have yet to find anyone willing to talk about them, but I have been assured that the deals were made fairly. If Silas is behind it—which I highly doubt—then there will be no bad blood between us as long as I am under the impression that nobody was forced into a deal." He shrugged, already turning back to his paperwork. "If some Red Harbor scrubs want to leave the Roses, I will not be happy about it, but I will not force them to stay. We're better off without them if they wanted out so badly."

"But—"

"*Stella.*"

She reared back at the intensity in his voice.

"Enough," he hissed. "I am tired of hearing your conspiracy theories. Zoey is sick of it as well."

She bristled. "You've been talking to Zoey about this?"

"She came to me because she's worried about you. I've got enough on my hands at the moment with weapon shipments disappearing left and right. I don't need my daughter obsessing over Silas Tradow."

"I am not the one with the obsession," she snapped.

Marcus ignored her. "Is this about Celia? I know you haven't gotten along with her, but if a dislike for her is the reason for this, then it needs to stop."

"This isn't about Celia!" she shouted. "This is about you having your head so far up your ass that you're oblivious to the problem at hand!"

She knew the moment the words were out of her mouth that it was the wrong thing to say. Marcus rose from his seat.

"Don't ever," he growled, "speak like that to me again. Do you understand?" When Stella didn't answer right away, he roared, "*Do you understand?*"

Stella jerked back. "Yes," she squeaked out.

Her heart pounded as his eyes blazed. She had seen her father angry, but she wasn't used to seeing him angry at *her.* "Get the hell out of my office, girl. And if you bring up Silas one more time, I will put you on guard duty and let Harvey take your place as heir." He pointed at the door. "Out."

Stella didn't need to be told again. Her throat bobbed as she backed towards the door, her shaking hands fumbling the knob.

She didn't know where she was going, only that she had to get out of here. The walls closed in on her, so she lunged for the back door, escaping into Evelyn's rose garden. The sweet aroma of the flowers lured her deeper. She tore down the beaten dirt paths, the roses blurring into a mesh of white and red and pink around her.

When she was five years old, Marcus had tied a rope swing to the oak tree in the backyard. That's where she went now, plopping down on the worn wooden seat with a sigh. She raked a hand through her hair, upsetting the curls, unable to stop the light tremor that went through her hand.

Stella didn't know at what point she had convinced herself she was no longer intimidated by her father, but now she knew better. Marcus Rook was an imposing figure, and nobody, not even her, was immune to it.

"Stella?"

Her head jerked up to see Zoey hovering at the end of the path. She edged towards Stella, toying with the hem of her thin white shirt.

"I heard yelling from the office and sort of listened in," she said awkwardly.

Stella glared at her, rushing to fix her hair. "I am not in the mood to be lectured about my conspiracy theories."

She bit her lip. "It didn't sound like a conspiracy."

Stella blinked.

Zoey kicked off her shoes and sat on the ground next to the swing, running a hand through her short hair. "This Ritton character…" she said. "You really think he's friends with Silas?"

"I know so."

"How?"

"Because I heard Silas say it."

Her eyes widened. "You've been spying on him."

Stella lifted her chin.

Zoey shook her head. "That's where you've been going every night." She laughed under her breath. "I thought you had a secret lover."

"No secret lover," Stella said. The lie felt sticky on her tongue, but even with Zoey's love and appreciation for forbidden love, she didn't think her cousin would take it well if she told her who she was really seeing.

Zoey leaned forward, her amber eyes stark in the sunlight. "You're sure?"

"Positive."

"Heavens, Stell." Zoey blew out a breath. "What are we even doing?"

"I don't know," she admitted. "I'm not going to pretend that I know everything about Silas. He's… strange. But I do know that he can't be trusted. The Union takes over entire towns and tears them down so they can rebuild them to their suiting. I won't stand to see that happen to Lochridge."

"What are we going to do about it?"

"*We*," Stella said, "aren't going to do anything. *I* will continue doing what I've been doing—find information on him, the Union. Something to convince my father that what he is doing is wrong."

"I doubt you'll have much luck," Zoey said, watching Stella stand up.

She gripped the rope holding the swing aloft. "Perhaps not. But I have to try."

What other choice did she have?

CHAPTER 50

Jordan's bedroom wasn't particularly small, but it felt suffocating now. He paced back and forth, twirling a pencil in his hand, shooting glares at his sketchbook, which sat on his desk opened to a blank page. He had tried to get his feelings out on paper, but the picture hadn't come to him as it normally did.

Jordan, we don't have any other options!

Stella was right. Silas would make his decision any minute. Time was not a luxury they had, and it was clear that Stella and Jordan sneaking around on their own was not doing much good. They had to take action. Getting their fathers involved was an obvious first step, but the thought of presenting himself before John after their last conversation made Jordan want to throw up.

He'd interrogated the dissenters. Three of them. None had broken. Jordan hadn't felt like pushing the matter any further, so he'd killed all three and dumped their bodies on the Harbor as per John's instructions. Neither father nor son had deigned to be in the same room as the other since their argument, so a very unhappy Declan had been appointed as a go-between.

There was a light knock on the door. Jordan wrenched it open, his anger subsiding as he realized who stood in the threshold.

"Lanabug," he said, blinking in surprise. He held open the door and Lana squeezed through. Her pink dress was at odds with the watery light coming in through the windows. "What's the matter?"

"That's what I was going to ask you," she said, her gray eyes filled with concern. "I could hear you pacing from my room."

"Sorry I bothered you."

"I don't want you to be sorry, I want you to tell me what's wrong." She bit her lip. "Is this about the fight with Pa?"

It was more than just that fight, but Jordan nodded, all too aware of the bruise on his face. "Pretty much."

She hugged herself. "He hasn't apologized, has he?"

Jordan let out a humorless laugh as he kicked the door shut. "He never apologizes for anything. I don't see why he would change now."

"He should."

"But he won't," Jordan snapped. He sighed. "Sorry."

Lana wrapped her arms around his waist. "You should talk to him," she mumbled into his chest. "Make things better."

Jordan slid his arm around her shoulders, holding her close. "I don't think that's going to help."

"Maybe not, but you at least have to try." Her eyes met his, full of that childlike innocence Jordan had tried so hard to protect all these years. "Right?"

Lana didn't know half of what was bothering him, but she'd cut right to the heart of the problem. Jordan knew any conversation he had with John would not go well, but he owed it to Stella to try. If she was brave enough to go to Marcus, then he had to go to John.

Jordan forced a smile as he ruffled Lana's hair. "I'll talk to him."

Lana beamed. "You've got it."

"And I've got *you*," he replied, squeezing her into a hug. She yelped, swatting at his arm until he released her. Jordan's heart ached as he watched her scamper down the hall.

His gaze trailed to the stairway. His father would be in his office now, toiling away at paperwork, working to keep his empire afloat. Jordan squared his shoulders and marched downstairs, not allowing himself to pause as he walked into the office without knocking.

John stood at the bookshelf, sorting through ledgers and folders. "I'm busy," he called without turning around.

"We need to talk," Jordan said.

If John was surprised to realize it was him, he didn't show it as he glanced over his shoulder, surveying Jordan with that critical gaze he knew all too well.

"I'm busy," he said again, but there was more of an edge to his words this time.

Jordan slammed the door. "I realize that, but you're going to take a moment and listen to me. We have a problem on our hands."

John set down the ledger. "I will give you five seconds to shut your mouth before I come over there and shut it for you."

"Silas is trying to take over Lochridge—"

"Five."

"He's behind the change in the Harbor—"

"Four."

"This isn't a coincidence—"

"Three."

Jordan started to panic as his father walked towards him. "I've heard him talk! He plans to kill everyone in the city—"

"Two," John snarled.

"Pa, you've got to listen to me—"

"*One!*" he roared in his face.

Jordan's mouth snapped shut.

John stared at him for a long, long moment.

"You're getting to be quite the rebel, aren't you?" he asked.

Jordan's hands shook, and he couldn't find an answer.

John smiled, but his eyes remained cold. "There's a Rose that needs to be questioned," he said softly. "I was going to have someone else do it, but since you can't get it through your thick skull that *I*'—his voice raised, causing Jordan to flinch—"am in charge here, then you will do it instead." His eyes blazed. "Take care of it now."

Jordan's hands trembled with rage. "Yes, sir," he gritted out.

John glared after him as he slipped through the door, stomach churning. He made it to the kitchen before he snapped, grabbing the first thing in sight—a glass of water someone had left on the counter—and hurling it across the room. Glass twinkled as it smashed against the far wall. Mateo had been sitting at the kitchen table, books and notes spread across the surface, but now he jerked so hard that he nearly fell out of his seat.

"What the hell?" he demanded.

Jordan's vision went red as he sent a bowl of fruit crashing to the ground.

"Whoa, whoa, calm down!" Mateo grabbed his arm before he threw something else. "What's the matter?" he demanded, his gray eyes—so similar to their father's—wide with concern. "What happened?"

Jordan's chest heaved. "Pa happened."

He tried to pull his arm away but Mateo held firm. "What did he do?"

Jordan dropped his gaze. "Nothing. He did nothing, as he always does."

Mateo dropped his arm. Jordan pivoted away, jaw clenched as he surveyed the mess he'd made.

"He won't listen to me," he said, rubbing his arm. "Won't give me the time of day. Just tells me to interrogate another person and expects me to follow through. He *knows* how much I hate it, and he makes me do it anyway."

"Maybe he doesn't—"

"Don't justify him," Jordan snarled, whirling to face him. "Don't you *dare.*"

Mateo raised both hands in surrender. "Alright, alright. Let's just calm down and think about this."

"Think about what?" he demanded. "I have every reason to believe that we're in danger, but he won't even give me the time of day to express my concerns. Instead he asks me to make the problem worse by abducting Marcus Rook's men and beating them half to death!"

He crossed his arms. "Then why do you do it? Why not just tell him no?"

"Because—" Jordan spluttered. "Because he's my father. I'm supposed to be loyal to my family, right?"

Mateo watched him pace around. "He might share your blood," he said quietly, "but he isn't acting like your family, Jordan."

Jordan stopped and looked at him. Mateo would know better than anyone what that felt like. John was his father, yes, but he barely spared him a look unless he needed something. The only reason he kept up any kind of relationship with him was because he needed all the men he could to keep the feud with the Rooks going. Mateo and John shared blood, but John wasn't his father in the true sense of the word.

Mateo must have known what he was thinking, because he gave Jordan a rueful smile. "I know what it's like. You can't keep letting him push you around like this. You're his son, not his servant, and the sooner he realizes that, the better off your relationship will be." He rubbed his arm. "That's what I had to do. I realized pretty quickly that nothing I can ever do will please him, so I took to staying out of sight. Your situation is a little different, but nothing will change if you don't speak up."

Jordan sat down, burying his face in his hands.

"I know," he whispered. "But..."

"But what?"

"I can't."

"Jordan—"

He barked a laugh. "Mateo, I can't even go in there and tell him what I think about Silas. What makes you think I can march into his office and tell him off for being a terrible father? I wouldn't be able to get the words out!"

"You haven't even tried—"

"I have tried!" he snapped.

Mateo crossed his arms. "No, you haven't. You've gotten cold feet and backed out, but until you decide to stop being a coward and actually talk to him, things are going to continue just the way they are. I don't think you want that."

Jordan rose from his seat. "Call me a coward again."

"Don't you take this out on me."

He bared his teeth. "I dare you."

Mateo looked him dead in the eye. "You're a coward. And the more you argue with me about it, the more you prove it. Either go back in there and give it to him, or quit bitching and do as he tells you." He turned away. "Just leave me out of it if you choose the latter."

He snatched up his books and stalked out of the room. Jordan's shoulders sagged as he sat back down. He didn't want any part in the risky game his father was playing, but what other option did he have? His nightly outings with Stella were betrayal enough—if he started defying John's every order, what kind of son did that make him?

He scrubbed a hand over his face. He couldn't afford to be on John's bad side, not with so much about to go so wrong. That meant going to the warehouse tonight, no matter how much it killed him to do so.

He was the heir to the Ravens. It was time he started acting like it.

CHAPTER 51

Jordan didn't show.

Stella waited at the beach for an hour past their usual meeting time before heading to the hotel, thinking Jordan might have gone straight there. But he was nowhere to be found, and she hated to think that he had blown her off. He was probably otherwise occupied—his family was just as busy as hers was—but she couldn't stop the twinge of disappointment as she sat alone on the rooftop, staring at the hotel like it might give her answers.

"You're pathetic," she muttered out loud, trying and failing to squash the feeling.

The door opened. Stella perked up as Silas walked out, followed by Tobias and Celia. Their expressions were stern as they turned, catching Stella by surprise by heading deeper into neutral ground rather than going into Rose territory as usual. Her eyes narrowed as she watched them disappear between two buildings. "You missed a good one, feathers," she whispered.

She pushed off the roof, tugging her hood low over her eyes as she ran after them. Clouds blotted out the moon, making it hard to see in the shadows between the street lamps, but Stella knew this city like the back of her hand. She leapt from rooftop to rooftop, agile as a cat, every movement accompanied by the practiced elegance she'd mastered over the years. Down below, Tobias and the Tradows remained oblivious to her presence.

The trio didn't travel far. Stella skidded to a halt as Silas entered a warehouse. The building had been abandoned for longer than Stella could remember, so filthy and degraded that Marcus had deemed it useless and never attempted to expand his turf to include it. But Silas must have found a use for the ramshackle structure, because he cast a wary look around before ducking inside.

Stella waited until the three of them were safely inside before dropping to the ground. She approached the warehouse with cautious steps, ready to flee at a moment's notice. Everything was eerily quiet, however, making the hairs on the back of her neck stand on end.

Going through the front would be too risky, so she circled around the block and slipped through the back door. Her breath hitched as she heard voices from deeper within. A trill of laughter reached her, and she tensed as she realized she didn't recognize it. Silas wasn't alone—another meeting with his comrades from Stokes? Stella resisted the urge to sigh. She wished Jordan was here; she'd grown so accustomed to his presence that it felt strange not to have him here. As much as it irked her to admit, she felt better when he was around.

Stella crept down the hall. The closer she got, the clearer the voices became, to the point that when she reached a narrow doorway, she could catch snatches of a conversation. Silas' nasally voice was easy to pick out among the din.

She held her breath as she eased open the door, offering her a sliver of a view. But when she peered through the crack, the sight beyond was enough to make her eyes go wide.

The main floor was full of people, dozens of men standing around. Tables had been set up along the back wall—right next to the door Stella now peeked through—and they were laden down with weapons, so many guns and boxes of ammunition that Stella couldn't hope to count them all.

Silas stood in the center of the room, holding a conversation with a small circle of people. Celia stood next to her father, her cool gaze watching everything. Tobias was nowhere to be seen, but Stella realized that every person present wore a dark garb not unlike what the bodyguard usually wore. These people were dressed for battle—and it didn't take long for Stella to guess what battle that was.

She stared at the weapons, and then her eye caught something discarded underneath the tables. Crates—many of them bearing the Ravens' symbol on the side.

Stella felt her blood go cold. The *Ravens* had been supplying Silas? That didn't make any sense—

This is a strange question, but has your gang been stealing weapons from us?

I've got enough on my hands at the moment with weapon shipments disappearing left and right.

She fought back against a string of curses. Both Jordan and her father had mentioned weapons disappearing—she hadn't read much into it at the time, but what if...?

She drew back into the shadows as Silas finished his conversation and addressed the group as a whole.

"We have an important mission," he called. Everyone fell silent and circled around him. Stella opened the door a touch more so she could see the entire room. "Mister Trace has assigned me to oversee the take-over of Lochridge. I am putting my trust in all of you to make sure it goes smoothly. We have no room for error. These people are dangerous, and we need them out of our way. But to do that, we must keep the citizens of Lochridge in the dark until we are ready to strike. What I need from all of you is—"

"Father," Celia interjected.

Silas frowned at the interruption, but Stella felt her entire body go cold as Celia's pale eyes settled directly on her.

"We have company," she said.

Stella jerked away from the door. The room erupted into shouting, but she was already sprinting in the opposite direction.

Celia's voice cut through the noise. "Get them!"

Stella lurched for the back door. Something thudded to her left; she risked a glance over her shoulder to see a knife embedded in the door frame.

"The next one goes through your skull," Celia growled from behind her.

Stella didn't turn around, even though her face was covered enough that she was sure she wouldn't be recognized. She ducked through the doorway and kept running, arms pumping at her sides as she struggled to keep ahead of Celia. She didn't dare look back, but she could hear Celia's whispered curses as she gave chase.

A sharp turn came up. Stella grabbed the corner of the building and swung herself around, the rough surface of the brick digging into her hand. Celia hurled another knife that missed her by an inch.

Stella gritted her teeth. This was not going as planned.

The street sloped down. She skidded down it, barely keeping her balance. Celia was close behind, but she wasn't prepared for the slick spot at the bottom of the slope, where runoff from recent rain made a section of the cobblestones as slick as ice. Stella, being a Lochridge native, was used to the city's raging thunderstorms and what spots on the street liked to hold water, so she skirted around it with no trouble. A grin spread across her face as she heard the unmistakable sound of a boot sliding across wet stone—and a grunt as Celia Tradow hit the ground in a very unladylike manner. By the time she got back to her feet, spitting curses, Stella was gone.

Stella was still breathing heavy when she stumbled onto the hidden beach. She didn't know who to be mad at—herself, for getting caught; Celia, for being a bitch as usual; or Jordan, for not showing up. His absence hadn't bothered her at first, but now she was pissed.

Was it that hard to show up? He'd done it every other night—why not tonight? Could he not have at least sent word he wasn't going to make it? Stella kicked the ground, spraying sand everywhere. She shouldn't be upset over this, but seeing Silas' army had messed with her head, and Jordan blowing her off on top of it was doing terrible things to her mind. She needed him—she needed someone to talk to, to rant to, someone to assure her that she wasn't the only one seeing the problem. Zoey was perhaps on her side now, but her cousin didn't even know half of the details. Jordan was the only one who knew everything, the only one she trusted to have her back against Silas.

She glared at the rock he usually sat on. If he didn't want to show, fine. She would find him.

Stella turned on her heel. The Daeliks' house was in the heart of Raven territory, but she was wearing all black with her face covered. Marcus always said that the key to getting into places one wasn't supposed to go was to pretend that they belonged, so instead of keeping to the shadows like usual, Stella walked down the middle of the street with her head held high. Indeed, even though she spotted several Ravens lurking on the streets, their sleeves pushed back to display their tattoos with pride, none of them stopped Stella as she marched past.

Idiots, she thought to herself, her mask hiding her smirk.

The house was dark when she approached. Stella slipped past the guards and shimmied up the drainpipe, taking the same path she had when Jordan snuck her into his house to scare Lana. His window was dark, the curtains drawn so she couldn't see inside. She rapped her knuckles on the glass. When he didn't answer, she fought back a growl and pried the window open.

But Jordan wasn't inside. Stella studied his bedroom in the faint moonlight. The bed was empty, the covers rumpled. His desk was a mess, sketchbooks and pencils and loose pages strewn about. The drawings hung on the far wall were crooked, a few of them ripped or missing altogether, like someone had torn them apart with their bare hands.

Alarm shot through Stella. Something wasn't right.

She heard voices down the hall and eased open the door, this time taking care not to open it so far that she could be spotted. She made out Thatcher and Half-Daelik at the end of the hall, their heads bowed together. Mateo's expression was hard, filled with a brotherly concern that had Stella's brows raising. Whatever he was saying, Declan listened hard, his jaw clenched.

She tried to lean closer to hear better, but the conversation ended as Declan shook his head and stalked into another room, leaving Mateo alone in the hallway. She didn't know why, but she had the distinct feeling the pair had been talking about Jordan.

Her eyes narrowed. If Mateo knew something...

She closed the door, hard enough that it could be heard from the end of the hall. "Jordie?" Mateo called. "You back?"

Stella pressed herself against the wall as he gently knocked on the door, then cracked it open.

"Hey," he said, pushing his way into the darkened room. "Listen, I'm sorry about earlier. I wasn't trying to be an ass."

Stella waited until he was firmly inside the room before kicking the door shut and launching herself at Mateo's back. He grunted as she slammed into him, but she had her gun pressed to his temple before he could get a word out.

"Fancy meeting you here, Half-Daelik," she purred in his ear. "One move, and it will be your last."

He went still. "What do you want," he growled.

She shushed him. "Not so loud. Don't make me have to pull this trigger." The gun dug into his temple. "Tell me where Jordan is."

"I'm not telling you anything," Mateo hissed.

Stella hated to beat up Jordan's brother, but worry was gnawing at her gut, threatening to rip her in two. She grabbed a handful of Mateo's thick, dark hair and yanked his head back. His breath rushed out as he found himself staring up at the ceiling, the gun still at his head.

"I didn't ask," she snarled, careful to keep her voice soft. Thatcher was just down the hall, and she couldn't take on both of them at once. "Tell me where he is."

"Why do you want to know?"

"I don't see how that's any of your business," she said flatly.

"You made it my business when you pointed a gun at my head!"

"Keep it down," she snapped.

She could feel his irritation bleeding through. He hadn't thought to arm himself within his home, where he thought he would be safe. It was a mistake on his part that Stella was more than happy to exploit.

She hummed to herself. "I suppose I'll have to end this if you aren't willing to cooperate."

She cocked the gun. Mateo tensed. "You won't make it out alive, Rook. The house is surrounded by guards."

"Yes, I know. I waved to them on my way in." She tightened her grip. "I'm going to ask you one last time. *Where is Jordan Daelik?*"

Mateo let out a frustrated hiss. "The warehouse on Dawson Avenue, interrogating one of your men. And if you dare to go over there, he'll do the same to you."

It felt like a bucket of cold water had been dumped over her head. Stella's blood turned to ice as Mateo finished speaking.

"I see," she managed, struggling to get the words out. "I thank you for your time, Half-Daelik. You've been a pleasure to work with."

She released him. Mateo spun around, fists raised, but she slammed the butt of her gun against his temple. He crumpled to the floor. Stella made sure the door was locked before stepping over his prone form on the way to the window.

She paused long enough to make sure he was still breathing before clambering through the window, slipping off into the night without another sound.

CHAPTER 52

She couldn't get her hands to stop shaking.

I'll make it up to you later. Deal?

Deal.

Stella turned onto Dawson Avenue. There weren't any guards out front, so she marched right in. She didn't know how much time she had before Half-Daelik woke up from his little nap and raised hell, so she had to make this quick.

This building had been used for interrogations for years. Stella had never stepped foot inside, too afraid of where her mind would go. This wasn't where Liam had died, but he had spent his final hours in agony here. Her throat constricted, and suddenly she couldn't breathe.

"Get it together, Rook," she whispered.

She stalked to the back of the main floor, where curtains hung haphazardly off of metal hooks attached to the rafters. She ripped them open, bile rising in her throat at the sight before her.

A man slumped in the wooden chair in the center of the space, the ropes holding his legs and wrists too tight for comfort. His face was a mess of bruises, but that was nothing compared to the bullet hole in his skull. Stella's gaze skipped to the corner, where a familiar sandy-haired man sat with his back against the wall. His face was buried in his hands. She felt a pang of sympathy for him, but it was quickly replaced with anger.

"I suppose people don't change, do they?" she said. Her voice rang through the warehouse, cold and crisp.

Jordan's head jerked up, and the hollowness in his eyes took her aback. "Stella. What are you doing here?"

She ripped her mask and hood away. "You didn't show up for our meeting."

His face blanched. "I forgot all about it. Pa—"

"Silas has an army," she interrupted.

His brows rose.

Stella gestured around her. "A room bigger than this one, full of men and enough weapons to supply them all. I'm guessing that's where all those missing weapons have gone. I didn't get to hear a lot of his plans before Celia realized I was there and chased me out."

"The weapons…" he murmured, then let out a low, filthy curse. "Of course. That's why we couldn't figure out who was taking them—it was Silas."

"He probably paid off some grunts to do his dirty work." Stella's mouth twisted. "There's plenty of low-level criminals who would have taken the job for nothing but a cigar and a shot of whiskey to wash it down with."

Jordan groaned. "We found booze and other stuff in the wagon they used to take one of our shipments with. All those purchases on his ledger—he was using material goods to pay those rats to take our weapons. That's why we never found the Victory or the other things. They were going straight into someone else's hands."

She crossed her arms. "We would have figured this out an hour ago if you'd bothered to show up."

"I'm sorry—"

"I thought something happened to you," she said, talking over him. "But instead, I find out that you're right back here, stringing up my people for fun."

Jordan's jaw clenched. "That's not what I'm doing."

"That's what you did to Liam."

He shot to his feet. "No, it isn't. Not even close."

Her lip curled. "Then why are you still here?"

"Because it's my job! It's what my father wants me to do, and as his heir, it's my duty to uphold his wishes." He stalked towards Stella. "You don't get to come in here and act all high and mighty, Stella. Just because I killed someone close to you doesn't mean that you're innocent." He turned away, shaking his head in disgust. "You've got enough blood on your hands to know."

"Yes, I kill people," she seethed. "But I don't torture them to death!"

He whirled to face her. "Do you really think I enjoy this?"

"You've rubbed Liam's death in my face enough times to suggest that you do."

"I did that because you were my enemy! Because I was supposed to hate you, and Liam was the easiest thing to get under your skin! But I swore to you that I wouldn't do it anymore, and I have kept my word. So why the hell are you mad about it now?"

"Because you're doing it again!" she shouted, jabbing a finger at the dead Rose.

Jordan's eyes narrowed. "You are as much of a monster as I am, Stella Rook. I've seen you pull the trigger without a moment's hesitation. You have *no right* to come in here and lecture me on my morals."

Anger pulsed through Stella, lighting her blood on fire.

"I thought you were different," she hissed. "I thought that since I'd gotten to know you, I'd stripped away the layers that made up the Jordan Daelik I was familiar with. I actually thought you weren't as bad as I made you out to be all these years." She stepped forward until she was only an inch away from him, both of their chests heaving. "But you're not," she whispered. "You're the same vile rat that I've known my whole life. You tell me you won't bring up Liam anymore, that you're sorry and that you didn't want to do it, but then you turn around and do to someone else exactly what you did to him. Preach all you want about your father making you be here, but John Daelik does not own you, Jordan. He does not dictate your life. It is *your* decision to be here, and it's a poor decision indeed."

Jordan laughed, but it was void of any warmth. "You're scared of pissing off your father as much as I am. If he asked you to do this, you would have. Without hesitation." She opened her mouth, and he shook his head. "Don't even try to deny it, Stella. We both know it's true."

"It's not," she said, but she couldn't hide the slight tremor in her voice.

He just shook his head again. "You Rooks," he said, disgusted. "This is what you lot are best at. Strutting through this city, pretending you're so damn superior to everyone else, refusing to acknowledge that you're just as messed up as we are." He spat at her feet. "At least the Ravens have the decency to admit that they're flawed."

She gritted her teeth. "Don't talk down to me."

"Then stop acting like a prissy brat who has never gotten her hands dirty!"

Her eyes narrowed to slits.

"Do not," she growled, "call me a prissy brat."

He looked her dead in the eye. "Prissy. Rutting. Brat."

Stella bristled. "Mature."

Jordan sneered as he walked around her. "I'm not the one making a big deal out of something that we've discussed several times already."

"Liam is *dead*." She glared at him, twisting to keep him in view. "That isn't something that goes away just because we have a discussion about it."

"You're right—Liam *is* dead. Has been for over three years now, and arguing with me won't bring him back. Do whatever you have to do to get over it, but stop coming after me. I can't change the past, Stella. I would take it back if I could, but getting mad at me for something I did years ago isn't going to help you get over him."

Her teeth gritted together. "We can't change the past, but we can control the present. Have you ever stopped to think about what would happen if you quit doing this?" She gestured to the dead Rose. "Perhaps you should stop doing things you'll regret in the future."

"I have thought about it," he snapped. "And I know that if I stop, my father will disown me. Hell, he might even kill me."

"Are we sure that's such a bad thing?" she snarked.

Jordan's eyes flashed. "I am being loyal to my family."

"You're being a coward."

"And you're being condescending." He curled his hands into fists, the muscles in his arms pulling taunt. "Loyalty is the most important thing in this city. I haven't *changed*, Stella. There's not a hidden side to me that you discovered. I've been the same person this entire time, the same person I was before we started working together. The same person I was the night Liam died. All you saw was me being nice to you because I was in love with you."

Her fists clenched. "If you were so loyal, you shouldn't have started working with me to begin with."

"Maybe it was a lapse in judgement."

"Maybe it was," she snapped.

Something like pain flashed in his eyes, gone as quick as it came. It felt like being stabbed through the heart, but Stella couldn't stop the next words that came out. "You're a filthy, two-faced rat, Daelik. A man who is too afraid to stand up against something he hates and knows is wrong is not a man that I care to be around."

She turned on her heel, fighting against the tears that threatened to spill over. "That's it?" Jordan called after her. "You're just going to walk away?"

"I can't stand to look at you a second longer," she said.

He laughed. "I think that makes *you* the coward."

Her head whipped around. "Excuse me? I'm not the one so scared of daddy that I'd rather *kill people than tell him to back off*"

He bared his teeth. "You're a hypocrite, Rook! A bloody hypocrite who thinks that she is *so* much better than everyone else! Look around you! This is Lochridge, and you are the heir to the White Roses. So many of my men have died at your hands that it would be impossible to count. You throw around your looks, knowing it will earn you favors. You're as violent and manipulative as they come, and yet you think you can come in here and call me the killer. I might have killed Liam, and I might have bragged about it, but that does not justify all the lives that *you* have ended, all the people that *you* have hurt." His brown eyes bored into hers, full of more rage than she'd ever seen out of him. "No, I don't want to do everything my father says. But he is family. He raised me and gave me a roof over my head. I am his *son*, and this thing with Silas has already made me make so many mistakes that I don't know if we'll ever have a decent relationship again. And he doesn't even know about this thing with you yet."

Her nostrils flared. "So you're calling this a mistake?"

"It's not a good thing!"

The tears she had been trying so hard to hold back finally spilled over. "I gave you a chance—"

"You fell in love and ignored the problems," he seethed. He looked down, his anger fading. "We both did."

Stella hugged herself. For a moment, silence reigned throughout the warehouse, and she found herself staring into the blank eyes of the dead Rose.

"This was doomed from the start," she whispered.

Jordan's jaw clenched. "I guess it was."

She struggled to get her breathing under control. "Jordan—"

"Just go," he said, his voice weary. He turned his back to her, untying the Rose with rough movements. "Leave."

"I—"

"This was never going to work," he snapped.

The Rose's corpse slumped to the floor. Stella stared at the trickle of blood that seeped across the floor, so bright and red it made her sick. "It might have."

He paused, gripping the arm of the chair so tight his knuckles turned white. "Stella, it's over. Just go. Please."

"What about Silas?"

"Silas can go to hell."

"Jordan, he's got an army. We can't just ignore that." She rubbed her arm. "It's why we worked together to begin with."

"And that worked splendidly, didn't it?" He glanced over his shoulder and beheld her expression, then sighed. "I'll figure something out."

Her gaze darkened. "Is that so? *You* will figure it all out?"

"Unless you'd rather continue this conversation."

She scoffed. "That's how it's going to be, then."

"The hell is that supposed to mean?"

"It means I'm done. Do it all yourself, if that's how you want to play it. But when Lochridge is in ruins, don't come crying to me for help."

Stella turned away. Her hand trailed up to the locket around her neck. Suddenly its weight was too much to bear, pulling her towards the ground, so she ripped it off and chucked it on the floor as she stormed away.

She expected Jordan to call after her again—who was she kidding, she *wanted* him to. But he remained silent as she stalked out the door, leaving him alone with the corpse on the floor.

CHAPTER 53

Jordan wanted to murder someone.

That seemed awfully counterproductive, given that him killing that Rose had triggered the entire argument to begin with, but it didn't stop the itch in his hands, begging him to draw his guns and feel the thrum of power as he fired them again and again, to listen to the gunshots and see the destruction and know he was in control of it all.

There had been plenty of destruction back in that warehouse. It couldn't be seen, but Jordan could feel the echoes of it in his chest, a stifling pressure that made it hard to breathe. There wasn't a damn thing he had control over when it came to Stella Rook. Her golden locket burned a hole in his pocket. He'd scooped it up after disposing of the Rose's body, but he hadn't been able to find the heart to open it. He was a little scared to find out what was inside—the fact that she'd discarded it after their fight led him to believe that whatever was inside had something to do with him, a fact that both horrified and broke him.

He threw open the front door, letting it slam behind him so forcefully that it no doubt woke up everyone in the house. It was only then that he noticed people were already up—there were lights on, voices coming from the kitchen. Declan lurched through the doorway, his green eyes wide, his rifle in his hands. His expression was enough to set off warning bells in his mind.

"What happened?" he demanded.

"That's what I was about to ask you," he said, looking him over. "We were about to come and get you."

He stopped short. "Why?"

"Stella Rook jumped Mateo upstairs. Demanded to know where you were, then knocked him out."

Jordan was moving before the words were out of his mouth. Mateo sat at the kitchen table. Lillian stood behind him, holding a handful of ice wrapped in a cloth to his temple. John, Dan, and the rest of the family gathered around, all of them holding weapons and murderous expressions.

John's eyes narrowed on him. "Were you attacked?"

Jordan had a split second to come up with an answer to that question. "Yes," he lied. "But I got away. I don't know what Rook's deal was, but she wasn't acting right."

"She clocked me with a gun," Mateo said, wincing as he probed the knot forming on his temple.

Jordan's hands fisted at his sides. "I'm sorry."

He was sorry for Mateo—but more so, he was furious at Stella. How *dare* she lecture him for killing someone when she had just gotten through knocking his brother unconscious? The rutting *hypocrite*. His hand slipped into his pocket, curling around her necklace. He was going to chuck the damn thing into the ocean the next chance he got.

"You're sure you're alright?" Lillian asked, studying his face. "After what she did to Mateo just trying to find you, we thought you'd be in trouble."

Declan nodded as he fingered his rifle. "We were about to slaughter that bitch."

Jordan shrugged. "She's delusional. Whatever she wanted, I don't think she'll be bothering me again."

He cracked his knuckles for emphasis. Lillian bit her lip. John and Mateo relaxed; Declan merely huffed as he sat down his rifle.

"I wish she'd bother us again, if only so I could give her a piece of my mind," Mateo growled.

Declan scoffed. "You don't mean that."

"I do—"

"It's sweet to think you'd want revenge," he said, patting Mateo's back.

John muttered something about ugly Rooks interrupting his sleep before stomping upstairs. Lillian ensured Mateo was taken care of and

Jordan was unharmed before trailing after her husband, wringing her hands in worry. The rest of the family was quick to clear out after that, leaving Jordan alone with his cousin and half-brother.

"Are you alright?" he asked Mateo.

He winced. "I'm going to be sore for a few days, but it's nothing that won't heal." He frowned. "I'm more worried about you, to be honest. She seemed desperate to find you."

"Like I said, she wasn't acting right. Whatever her deal was, I don't think I was the answer."

Declan and Mateo exchanged a weighted look. Jordan read it with lowered brows. "Don't do that."

"Do what?"

"Look at each other like that. I'm fine."

"You seem off, too," Dec said. "Like, not right in the head."

"I just got attacked by Marcus Rook's daughter—"

"You were acting like this before that," Mateo said gently. "I think it has more to do with Pa than it does Stella."

Jordan gave him a dirty look. He felt bad Mateo was hurt, but that didn't stop him from remembering the conversation they had just a few hours ago. Jordan had a feeling that Mateo and Stella would get along nicely.

"I'm fine," he said curtly. "Just tired and pissed off. I'll see you two in the morning."

He walked out the door before either of them could reply. He impressed himself by holding it together until he got to his bedroom, but the moment the door was locked behind him, he let out a little growl of anger as he kicked a chair out of his way. *Bloody hell.* Stella—

No. Just thinking her name made him mad. He searched for something to throw, something to break, something he could rip apart with his bare hands to vent out his anger. In the end he pulled Stella's locket out and threw it across the room. The gold flashed as it hit the far wall, knocking down one of his drawings and pissing him off further.

"Rutting hypocrite," he whispered. "Bratty little rutting bitch."

He kicked the chair again. Then, feeling quite childish indeed, he shoved it into its proper place behind the desk and sat down on the end of the bed, burying his face into his hands.

And that's where he stayed for the rest of the night.

He didn't feel like facing his family the following morning. The night had been torturous, his mind swirling with anger and sadness and bitter resentment. By the time he gathered up the courage to go downstairs for breakfast, his head pounded and it felt like someone had carved his heart out of his chest with a dull knife.

Declan and Mateo both gave him a look as he walked in. Mateo's head was bruised, but otherwise he seemed alright. Jordan ignored them both as he stalked for the cabinet that held the coffee mugs. He watched them out of the corner of his eye, the two of them holding a silent conversation consisting of mouthed words and pointed looks before Dec jerked his head at him, causing Mateo to sigh before heading in Jordan's direction.

He sat down the mug with a thump. "I think I'll go out for breakfast."

"We'll come with you," Mateo volunteered.

Jordan lunged for the front door. "I'd rather go alone, thanks."

The two of them caught up to him before he could make it out. Mateo grabbed one arm while Dec grabbed the other.

"I think we'll go together," Dec said through gritted teeth.

Jordan yanked his arms away. "I don't need an intervention."

"This isn't an intervention," Mateo corrected. "This is a peaceful talk in which you tell us what in the heavens is wrong with you."

"Still not interested."

Dec slid between him and the door, blocking his way out. "Jordie, I know we don't like to talk about our feelings, but something is seriously wrong with you. All we're asking is that you tell us what. Is it just your Pa? Celia? Someone else?"

Jordan gave them a bitter look. "A lot of things are bothering me, but currently you two are at the top of the list."

Mateo said softly, "Don't be like this."

"Then get out of my way."

"You're bitchy," Dec noted.

Jordan leaned right into his face and snarled, "I'm livid. And if you don't get out of my way, then I will show you just how mad I am. *Move.*"

Declan and Mateo held his gaze for a long, long time.

Then they stepped out of the way.

"Thank you," Jordan snarked.

He ripped open the door—and crashed right into Celia, her hand raised, primed to knock. She let out a small grunt as Jordan pushed her away.

Not her. Anyone but her. Hell, he'd rather fight with Stella again than make small talk with a Tradow right now.

"What are you doing here?" he demanded.

She smoothed her hair. Stella had mentioned that she and Celia almost fought last night, but if Celia was bothered by it, she didn't show it. "Fancy seeing you, Jordan. I was coming to visit."

"It's not a good time," he said, shoving past her.

Celia frowned as she watched him descend the steps. "Are you alright?"

"I'm *dandy*."

Her heels clicked against the ground as she dashed after him. "Something is bothering you."

Jordan was not in the mood to have this conversation again. "Now is not the time, Celia."

She laid an arm on his shoulder. "Perhaps I can be of assistance." Her lips curled into a sensual smile as her hand trailed up to his face. "I would hate for anything to impede our fathers coming to an alliance, so if someone is bothering you, I would be more than happy to take care of it." Her grip tightened. "Think of it as a favor."

Jordan grabbed Celia by her wrist and pulled her hand away from his face. "Get your hands off of me," he snarled, squeezing her arm hard enough to leave a bruise. "I don't want a favor from you, Celia, because I don't enjoy being around you. Whatever game you're playing, I don't want any part of it."

Declan and Mateo stepped forward, uncertain if they should help or not. Celia's eyes flashed. "Careful."

He yanked her forward, his other hand coming up to wrap around her throat.

"Stop," he hissed. "All of it, just *stop*. No more flirting, no more threats. I don't give a damn about the deal with your father. You're a lying brat with an attention problem. I'm not interested in being with you *or* working with you, so get that through your pretty little head before

347

you come at me again."

Her expression turned to ice. "You don't mean that."

He snarled right in her face. "I would love nothing more than to see you burn in hell, so leave me alone before I send you there myself."

Celia jerked away. He released her arm, and her eyes narrowed as she stared him down, backing up a healthy step as she did.

"I will give you one chance to take all that back," she breathed. "Or you will regret it."

Jordan sneered. "Tell your father to get the hell out of my city."

He turned on his heel and stalked away, giving Celia a vulgar gesture over his shoulder.

CHAPTER 54

"Stell?"

Stella buried her face into her pillow. It was midday, and she was still in bed. The sheets were rumpled from hours of tossing and turning. She didn't want to know what she looked like at the moment—her cheeks red from crying, her hair still in last night's braid, her nightgown twisted around her legs. The knocking at the door drilled into her head, and she pressed her face deeper into the pillow, trying to make her cousin go away by sheer will.

"Stella!" Zoey called from the other side of the door. "Answer me, or else I'm going to assume you're dead and force my way in!"

"I'm alive," she groaned.

The persistent knocking paused. "Are you alright?"

"I feel sick." It was close enough to the truth that Stella didn't feel guilty for the lie.

"Anything I can do?"

"Just leave me alone. I need rest."

"Uncle Marcus said to get everyone in the parlor. Silas is here, and apparently he has news." Zoey paused, and Stella imagined her chewing on her lip as she did when she was nervous. "It seems important."

Stella raised her head. "That doesn't sound reassuring, Zo."

"Try to come down if you can. But if you're ill, I can tell Marcus—"

"I'll be there."

She forced herself out of bed, teetering on unsteady legs. The memory of Silas' army crashed into her, upsetting her balance. Whatever he wanted, she doubted it was good news, and as much as she would have loved to stay holed up in her room all day, wallowing in her own self-pity, she knew she had to get down there and figure out what Silas wanted.

She grabbed the first dress she came across and tugged it on. Her hair was indeed a mess, and she didn't have enough time to brush it, so she settled on pulling it into a messy knot at the top of her head. She slapped on makeup to mask her blotchy cheeks, perfume to cover up the fact that she hadn't bathed last night, and a forced smile she hoped would hide the hollow feeling in her chest.

Silas sat in an armchair in the parlor, his jaw clenched as he gazed out the window. Celia stood next to him, and the fury burning in her pale blue eyes took Stella aback. Both of them seemed pissed off—which meant something had happened.

Stella halted in the doorway. Her fight with Jordan had almost made her forget Celia chasing her through the streets last night. She hadn't thought she'd been recognized, but what if Celia had put everything together?

Marcus noticed her presence. "Stella, how nice of you to join us."

His tone was clipped. He sat with Evelyn directly opposite Silas. Harvey and Zoey stood behind them, their arms crossed in matching positions as they stared down Celia warily. A knot formed in Stella's stomach as she claimed the seat beside her father. Evelyn's gaze narrowed as she took her in. Her mother had always been able to guess when something was bothering her. She no doubt picked up on the storm of emotion coursing through her, but thankfully she didn't speak up about it as Silas crossed one ankle over his knee.

"I've been in Lochridge for a few weeks now," he said. "And I must say, this city has impressed me. The power structure here is extremely unique, and I have enjoyed seeing the balance between the Ravens and the White Roses."

"It's been a pleasure having you around," Marcus said.

Good heavens, Stella thought. *Does he seem... nervous?*

Silas dipped his chin. "As per the agreement we made when I first came into town, I have pledged to ally with one gang and work with them to revolutionize Lochridge and bring upon it the power and prosperity that only the Stokes Workers' Union can provide. Deciding which gang to pick has been difficult, for both sides are so evenly matched. Each has their advantage, but it has been hard to decide which group will be most beneficial for Lochridge's future." He met each of their gazes evenly. "But as of this morning, I have made my decision."

Stella felt every drop of blood in her veins go cold.

"The White Roses."

The breath rushed out of Marcus. Harvey let out a low laugh, he and Zoey exchanging a grin, and Evelyn's shoulders relaxed ever-so-slightly.

Stella, however, remained rooted to the spot, staring at Silas.

"You're allying with us," she said, not quite believing it.

Silas nodded. "Yes. It took an incident with the Daelik family this morning to make it clear what the right choice was."

Alarm shot through her. "What kind of incident?"

"One involving the heir," Celia spat. She tossed her hair over her shoulder. "Let's just say that I look forward to seeing them taken care of." Her mouth twisted. "Ungrateful bastard."

Silas pressed his lips together. "Jordan Daelik has shown us that his family might not be the most... agreeable to work with." He gave the Rooks a tight-lipped smile. "But fortunately for you all, that is something that you have excelled at."

"Thank you," Marcus said, standing up. "I promise, this is the best decision you have ever made."

Silas stood as well and shook his hand. "I look forward to it."

Was Stella the only one who picked up on the ominous tone in the room? "What about the Ravens?" she interjected. "What happens to them?"

He adjusted the lapels of his coat. "The Ravens will be dealt with immediately. I will require the assistance of the able-bodied men of your gang, whoever is willing to fight. You are more than welcome to help, Miss Rook. I hear you are a force to be reckoned with."

She rose to her feet. "That's it? We're just going to kill them?"

"That's the plan. The entirety of the Ravens will be gone by the end of the week."

"All of them?" she demanded. "Or will we spare some?"

Silas checked his watch with a slight frown. "I was under the impression you wanted all the Ravens dead, Miss Rook. Your father told me that someone very close to you was murdered by the Ravens' own heir."

Her heart beat faster. "That heir has a little sister who is only thirteen years old and has never been involved with the gang. Are we going to kill her?"

"Stella," Marcus warned.

"What about the other women and children who have the misfortune of knowing someone from the Ravens?" she forged on. "Shall we slaughter them as well?"

Silas raised a hand. "That is a discussion I would be more than happy to have, Miss Rook. If you feel that those not directly involved in the gang should be spared, I will consider it."

Consider it. Stella fisted her hands as Lana Daelik came into mind. She'd put her life on the line to help Jordan keep his sister out of the gang. Jordan had been right when he said that she had killed people, but she never laid a hand on children. *Never.*

"Do that," she said. "*Consider* it."

Her entire family stared at her. Stella folded her arms over her chest and edged out of the room. Tears blurred her vision, making it hard to see the ornate rug in the hallway as she leaned against the wall for support. She was completely and utterly wrecked, but she couldn't afford a breakdown. She had to get herself together *fast*.

But Jordan…

She couldn't abandon him. As much as she hated him, she didn't want Jordan dead at Silas' hand. He was about to send his army after the Ravens, and she knew the Daeliks' house would be the first stop. All those people from the warehouse, marching in on the family while they were unaware, because Stella severely doubted that Silas had stopped by their house first to announce his decision to them. They would have no warning of the impending attack.

Not unless she gave them one.

"Rook."

Celia followed her out of the room. Stella didn't feel like being around her—didn't feel like being around anyone, for that matter—but she paused long enough to allow her to catch up.

"What did Daelik say to piss you off?" she asked, looking her up and down.

Celia's eyes flashed. She wasn't upset about the incident last night; whatever Jordan had done was fueling her fire now. "All he did was make it clear that he had no interest in working with me or my father." She sniffed. "If he's not interested in us, then why should we be interested in him?"

"Sounds like he decided for you."

A tight smile. "You could say that."

Stella smirked. Jordan had been handling things by himself for less than a day, and already he'd put a target on his gang by insulting Celia Tradow. Part of her was pleased that she'd been proven right, though that didn't stop her heart from aching at the thought of Silas' army coming after Jordan.

"You know," Celia said, sauntering closer to Stella, "Daelik is actually what I came to talk to you about. You've got quite the vendetta against him, don't you?"

"You could say that," Stella said stiffly, throwing Celia's words back at her.

Celia hummed to herself as she walked around Stella, a shark circling its prey. "I don't take lightly to being humiliated, especially by someone I've tried so hard to be friendly with."

Stella stepped to the side, keeping time with Celia. "I get it. The Ravens were your first pick because you wanted to hook up with Daelik. But he wasn't interested and the plan fell through, so now you're turning to the next best option by enlisting someone who you think hates Jordan Daelik as much as you do."

Both of them came to a stop.

"You're clever," Celia said.

She pursed her lips. "No, you're just easy to read. I might have a thousand problems with Daelik, but unfortunately, I think I like you even less."

"Is that so?"

"I would watch your back if I were you." Stella's voice dropped to a whisper. "People in this city like to watch from the shadows, waiting for a moment to strike. It sounds like Daelik has already marked you as a target. I wonder how many others have done the same." Her smile broadened. "I wonder how many people right here in this house would like to see you dead."

Celia tilted her head. "Are you one of them?"

"I know you want me dead. That's good enough reason to return the favor."

"I never said that."

Her voice dripped with poison. "Haven't you, though?"

Celia narrowed her eyes.

Stella turned away. "Watch the shadows," she called over her shoulder. "You never know who's listening in."

CHAPTER 55

A knock on the door drew Jordan from his thoughts. "Go away!" he shouted.

The door opened anyway. Jordan expected it to be Declan or Mateo, so he choked when John poked his head in. A slight frown creased his features as he took in the drawings on the wall, many of them askew, but he was quick to return his attention to Jordan.

"I'm busy," he said irritably, flipping through his sketchbook. By *busy*, he meant he had spent the last few hours staring at the page, unable to find the motivation to put the pen on the paper. The entire day had been wholly unproductive, and Jordan had no one but himself to blame.

"Whatever you're doing can wait," John said.

Jordan scribbled on the blank page, trying to appear busy. "If you're wanting me to interrogate someone—"

"A Rose has left a note for you."

Jordan froze.

John pushed into the room and dropped a red rose on Jordan's desk. A square of paper had been attached to its stem with a white ribbon. "This came in for you. The messenger who brought it said someone from the Roses' side left it at the border." He scratched his chin. "I don't know what it means, so I was hoping you could shed some light on the situation. Why are the Roses sending you messages?"

He pushed the note towards Jordan, whose irritation spiked. "I can't read, Pa. What do you expect me to say?"

John blinked, then cleared his throat as he retracted his hand. "Right."

He shook out the page and read it aloud.

> *Jordan—*
>> *S is coming.*
>> *Get out of there before you end up like the knight.*
>>> *—LT*

Jordan went still. The knight—?

They picked up their swords and killed the young knight in their rage. The princess screamed and dropped the rose. It landed on the body of the young knight and soon became stained with his blood.

Jordan's eyes trailed to the red rose sitting on his desk, and the realization slammed into him.

"Silas," he whispered.

John narrowed his eyes. "What does he have anything to do with this?"

"He's coming. He made his decision." Jordan realized with no small amount of horror that it had probably been his doing—him treating Celia as he did the day before. She'd been livid. And now... "He's coming for us, Pa."

"How do you know?" John pressed. "Who's LT?"

Little thorn.

Jordan scrambled for anything else to say. The first name that came to mind with those initials put a pain through his chest, but he blurted, "Liam Turner."

John frowned. "That sounds familiar."

Of course it did. John had been the one to order Liam's interrogation and death three years ago. "He's a spy who is sort of close to the Rook family," Jordan lied. "Friend of mine. This is a code to tell me that Silas made his decision. He must be allying with the Roses."

His father stared at the note. "Is he telling the truth?"

His throat bobbed. "Yes."

John stared at him for a long moment. "So Silas—"

"Is coming for us," Jordan finished. He stared at the letter, wishing he could read the words for himself. "We need to get out of here."

His jaw clenched. He mulled over the realization for a few long moments, leaving Jordan to squirm in his seat until he looked down and said, "We've got time. The Ravens are the biggest gang in Lochridge. We can set up a defense—"

"We won't be going against just Silas' people," Jordan said. "Silas has an army that's already here in Lochridge, and that army is now allied with the Roses. Are you really going to tell me that we have more people than both of those combined?"

"An army," John repeated.

"Yes!"

"Already in Lochridge?"

"Well, that's what I've heard—"

"Where would Silas Tradow have stored an entire army without me finding out?"

Jordan opened his mouth to answer, but the words died on his tongue. The simple truth was that he didn't know—Stella had told him about it, and while he trusted her enough to know that she wouldn't have lied, she hadn't mentioned where Silas was holding court.

He swallowed. "I don't know. But you have to trust me on this." He jabbed a finger at the note. "We have no idea when they're coming, but I do know it's going to be soon. We have to get out of here."

"We have to defend our territory," he replied, eyes flashing.

"Pa, there will be nothing left to defend!"

"Are you in charge?"

"No, but—"

"Then your opinion is just that—an *opinion*. One that isn't worth listening to." John turned away. "We will set up a defense centered on the house. I'll send out messages and get our men ready for battle." He cracked his knuckles. "Silas had his chance to be on my good side, but he chose wrong. It's about time we let him know it."

"Pa, wait!"

But John ignored him as he walked out of the room, his mind made up. Jordan stared after him, a sinking feeling in his stomach, bile rising in his throat. His gaze traveled to the rose on the desk. Stella had warned him. *Warned* him, even after their fight last night.

Get out of there.

His jaw clenched. That didn't heal the rift that had sprung up between them, didn't erase the argument they had, but despite it all, Jordan knew he still trusted her.

"Dammit," he whispered.

He stuffed Stella's locket into his trousers, then grabbed his guns and raced downstairs. John had already gathered the rest of the family, shouting instructions from halfway up the stairs. Jordan waited until he was done and everyone had scattered to do their assigned duties before slipping downstairs.

He found Lillian pacing back and forth in the kitchen.

"This isn't good," she said, her voice strung high. "John promised me that we would be the ones to get the deal—"

He put a hand on her shoulder. "It's going to be alright, Ma."

"Is he really going to defend this place?" she whispered. "He's not even going to send Lana away."

Jordan went still. "He isn't?"

Lillian bit her lip. "I can't have her here, Jordan. If something happens to her because of all this—"

Get out of there before you end up like the knight. "Then take her and run. Get out of the city if you have to."

"John wouldn't let me leave."

Jordan let out a growl of frustration. "Then I'll take Lana."

Lillian stared at him. "You would?" She grabbed both of his hands. "Yes. Do that. Get out of here and take Lana with you. I trust John's judgment, but just in case something goes wrong, I don't want my children to be caught in the crossfire." She squeezed his hands. "Please?"

He squeezed back. "Alright."

"She's in her room. Go, and I'll keep John distracted so you can slip out." She pulled him into a hug. "Keep safe."

"I will."

Jordan took the stairs two and three at a time. Lana hovered in her doorway, watching the flurry of movement as members of the Ravens poured into the house, waiting for instructions from John. Jordan was impressed that his father had managed to get everyone organized so quickly, but he didn't think it was enough.

"What's going on?" she asked. "If Mister Tradow is coming, shouldn't we leave?"

"That's what you and I are doing," he said, grabbing her hand. "Come on. We don't have much time."

Lana didn't protest as they slipped down the stairs, taking the hallway to the back of the house. The street out back was empty, so Jordan pulled Lana along, his heart pounding as they made a run for the next block.

It was quiet. Jordan didn't like it.

He caught a glimpse of the Ravens gathering out front. Two familiar faces caught his eye. He was annoyed with them too, but they had an unspoken pact to stick with each other, and he couldn't leave them behind. "Stay here," he said to Lana, tugging her into a shadowy corner. "I'll be right back."

Declan and Mateo stood in the center of the throng, helping John get everyone situated. Jordan elbowed his way to them, and after casting a glance at his father's turned back, grabbed both of them by the back of their shirts and hauled them back.

Dec spluttered. "What the hell, Jordie?"

He leaned in close. "Do you trust me?"

They exchanged a look. "Yes," Mateo said slowly.

"You know how I've been a little worked up lately?"

"A *little* is an understatement," Dec muttered. "But sure."

"Well, this is why." He glanced between them. "The street is about to run red. We need to get the hell out of here."

They looked at him, then at John, then at the rest of the Ravens. The ones that were here were ready for battle, but the full gang had yet to arrive. If Silas' army showed up now, even without the help of the Roses, they'd be outnumbered.

"You're sure about that?" Dec asked.

"Positive."

They swapped another look. Then Mateo nodded. "Let's go."

The three of them turned and slipped away as subtly as they could. They circled around back to Lana, and the moment they were out of sight from the house, Jordan broke into a run, pulling the others along with him.

"Any particular reason we're going rogue?" Declan drawled. "Or is it just for kicks?"

Jordan paused, looking this way and that to ensure the street was clear before crossing. "I've got an informant within the Rooks that's seen the size of Silas' group. He's got an army that was already in Lochridge before he made his decision." He glanced over his shoulder. "Pa is planning a defense he can't make with time he doesn't have. I tried to tell him, and he won't rutting listen to me, so I'm not staying around to see it play out."

"Are Ma and Pa going to die?"

Jordan glanced down at Lana, gaping up at him in horror.

He fought back a curse. "No! No, they're going to be fine. I mean— Um— Pa knows what he's doing—"

He trailed off as Lana's dove-gray eyes filled with worry. "Why are we leaving them behind? If Mister Tradow wants to kill us, why isn't everyone running?"

Jordan didn't know how to reply. But Mateo knelt down and tapped Lana's nose. "We're pretty certain Pa can fight him off. But just in case, we're getting you somewhere safe, alright?"

Lana nodded. Jordan pulled her into a hug as he gave Mateo a silent nod of thanks.

"We're going to be fine, Lanabug," he whispered.

And that's when the gunfire started.

CHAPTER 56

Lana screamed. Jordan looked her over to make sure she wasn't hurt before slapping a hand over her mouth.

"What the hell?" Declan hissed. He glanced at Jordan. "Is that—?"

"Let's go," he said roughly, dragging Lana away.

Mateo's face went slack. "You weren't kidding when you said we didn't have time."

"*Move!*"

They started running. Jordan didn't know where to go, so he picked the first safe house that came to mind and headed there as fast as he could. But the smell of smoke reached them as they turned the corner, and Jordan skidded to a stop.

"Bloody hell," Mateo whispered.

The building was on fire. A group of men stood outside of it. Jordan didn't recognize most of them, so he assumed they were Silas' people. But two of them…

Raven tattoos on their wrists. Worse yet, Jordan knew who they were—sailors who signed contracts with Silas the night he and Stella followed him to the Red Harbor.

It was never about taking over the Harbor, he realized. The contracts were to get people from both gangs into Silas' pocket; the income from the Harbor was just a bonus. The Ravens weren't just being attacked—they were being hunted, flushed out, sold out by their own members.

"New plan," Declan muttered. "Let's get the hell out of here."

Too late—they'd been spotted.

Mateo cursed. Jordan swore under his breath as he whipped out his guns.

"Close your eyes," he ordered Lana.

Then he fired.

The two ex-Ravens fell first, then he turned his sights on the rest of the group. His guns thundered in his hands, powerful and destructive, and he couldn't pretend that he didn't like the feeling.

Only once the entire group was bleeding out on the street did he lower his weapons.

"Shit," he breathed.

Declan slowly unstrapped his rifle. "What the hell is going on? How did they—"

"There!"

Jordan whirled as more of Silas' men appeared, drawn by the gunfire. He scrambled to reload his guns as he positioned himself between Lana and the attackers, but Declan leapt in front and rained down bullets. Mateo drew his own weapon and fired; Jordan got both revolvers reloaded and threw himself into the fray, yelling at Lana to run.

They were outnumbered, no doubt about it, but Jordan wasn't Lochridge's sharpshooter for nothing. His eyes scanned the group, picking out the one with the air of authority, the one the others looked to as he shouted orders.

Jordan's eyes narrowed as he lifted a gun and put a bullet through their leader's right eye.

He tumbled, and the group dissolved into chaos. Jordan advanced step by step, jaw tight and guns blazing, the coppery tang of blood mixing with the smell of gunsmoke. Declan and Mateo fell in step behind him, the trio holding firm until every last one was dead and they were alone on the street.

"Safe houses are out," Jordan said, lowering his revolvers as he watched the pillar of smoke reach for the sky. It wasn't alone—smoke obscured half the Lochridge skyline, at least half a dozen buildings up in flames. The entirety of the Ravens' territory was under attack. It had all happened so fast that Jordan's head spun.

If Dec and Mateo had doubted him before, they sure as hell didn't now. "Where do we go?" Mateo asked. "Out of the city?"

Lana saw the coast was clear and scrambled to Jordan's side. "We can't leave! Ma and Pa are still here."

"We could try Rose territory," Declan mused. "With all their men on this side of the border, no one will expect *us* to be over *there.*"

"And then what?" Jordan demanded. "Where do we go from there?"

Declan didn't have an answer for that. Jordan sighed and turned away, a pang in his chest as the distant gunfire grew louder.

Those were his people dying. He wasn't deluding himself into thinking they stood a chance against Silas and the White Roses combined.

He racked his brain, trying to think of somewhere to go. There was only one place he could think of. It was the last place he wanted to go after everything that had happened there, but he didn't really have another option.

He sighed again. "I know a place. Come on."

It was a bloodbath.

The air stung with the reek of blood and smoke. There were bodies everywhere. Broken glass glittered on the ground, reflecting the light of the burning buildings, chaos rampant all around. The Raven gang was bleeding red, and Stella Rook stood in the middle of it.

Blood dripped from a cut on her cheek. Her hair was twisted into a sleek tail, but a few strands had fallen loose, sticking to perspiration that shone on her face. She adjusted the grip on her pistol, the roar of gunfire driving every thought out of her mind. Her Roses were everywhere, their telltale white clothes separating them from a sea of black. Why Silas' people had thought to wear the Ravens' color into battle against them was beyond her, but she seemed to be the only one to have a problem with it. Marcus hadn't even batted an eye when Silas showed up at their house this morning with his people in tow. So many of them... So many fighters, so many weapons. Stella had waited to see if her father would notice that they carried the same weapons reported missing from their storehouses for over a week now, but he paid them no mind as he rushed to Silas' side to go over the plan one last time.

Stella's breath quickened as she surveyed the Ravens fighting like hell to defend the Daeliks' house. She hadn't thought she could get the warning out in time. It had taken her long enough to decide if she even *wanted* to warn Jordan; in the end, her heart made the decision, the part of her that still clung to what they had before their fight. Even so, it had been difficult to write the words, to sneak out and leave it at the border for one of the Ravens' guards to pick up.

Silas and Marcus had spent the entire morning with their heads bowed together, plotting the attack. Harvey was beside himself with excitement over it. Stella had just watched from the doorway, listening to the conversation without really hearing it. Silas had left and returned with his men in tow, and when she'd been asked if she wanted to join them...

She had to say yes. Had to see if her note had reached the Daeliks in time or if they would catch them by surprise. She didn't really know which outcome she wanted.

But she hadn't expected this.

Movement flashed in the corner of her vision. Stella ducked as a Raven came at her, swinging a knife and screaming up a storm. She shot him before he could get a step closer, running before his body even hit the ground. Half of the Ravens were gathered around the block that held the Daeliks' house. Of all the things Stella expected to see when she got here, of all the possibilities she'd thought up, seeing them make a stand against Silas and Marcus hadn't been one of them.

They weren't supposed to fight back. They were supposed to have run, to have gotten out of town while they still had the chance. Stella thought Jordan had known that—hell, she'd instructed him to in her note!

She broke through the crowd with a growl. She had to get to their house to see if Jordan was there or not. Once the Daeliks' homestead fell, the rest of Raven turf would go with it, which is why Marcus had focused his attacks here. She dodged a knife and for a brief second, she got a view of John Daelik standing in the doorway to his house, a gun in his hand and world-ending wrath on his face. Then someone slammed into her and the world tilted sideways.

Stella hit the ground, grunting as her injured shoulder took the brunt of the impact. She rolled away before a killing blow could land, rising to her feet with feline grace. The battle raged on around her. She gave herself a split second to look around, to search for any familiar faces among the throng, but she saw someone coming for her and launched into a sprint, using her agility to her advantage as she wove through the battle.

Jordan was nowhere in sight. Neither was Thatcher or Half-Daelik. Strange—why weren't they here, fighting alongside the rest of their family?

"Stella!"

Her head whipped to the side to see Zoey and Harvey, standing shoulder-to-shoulder. Harvey, to no one's surprise, was bathed in blood, a murderous grin on his face.

"Little help over here?" he called.

She dove for them. Zoey exchanged a look with her, reading her expression with a light frown. Her cousin had been wary around Silas ever since Stella confided in her about her suspicions, but that hadn't stopped her from being excited about taking out the Ravens. This was what the entire Rook family had wanted for years. Even Stella, as conflicted as she was on the subject, couldn't help but feel a twinge of satisfaction as she watched Harvey plow over some Raven grunts that got too close.

He and Zoey had positioned themselves so they had a straight shot towards the Daeliks' house. It would be tricky to get over there, given the battle raging in between, but with three of them...

Harvey cocked his gun, his knife in his other hand, his smile as bloody as his hands. "We can make it if we go fast. Let's move."

He took off without another word. Zoey and Stella exchanged a look before charging after him.

As it turned out, it was a lot easier to get through a crowd when a bloodthirsty, knife-wielding maniac led the way. People cleared out before Harvey could reach them, making Stella roll her eyes as she and Zoey followed from behind. Those who got in Harvey's path were met with the business end of his beloved knife, leaving the girls to skirt around the bodies. They skidded to a stop at the foot of the stairs that led up to the house, where John Daelik glowered down at them.

"Rook rats," he hissed, raising his gun. "I will make you pay for this."

Stella dove out of the way as he fired, blowing a hole in the cobblestones where she stood only a moment before. She caught a glimpse of Harvey, his face alight with fury at being shot at.

Then John fired again. Zoey spun out of the way, but not before the bullet grazed her side, ripping her shirt and eliciting a sharp hiss of pain from her. Stella looked up just in time to see a deadly cold entering Harvey's eyes.

When Harvey Rook was harmed, he got mad.

But when his sister was harmed, he went ballistic.

"Good luck," Stella told John, grinning.

And then Harvey tackled him to the ground.

Zoey rushed to aid her brother, but Stella skirted around the fight and burst through the front door. None of the Ravens were inside, it seemed, but other members of the Daeliks might be. Lillian and Lana were still around somewhere, and Stella wanted to get to them before anyone else could.

The house was still. Echoes of the fight outside drifted through the halls. It had been a long time since Stella had seen the inside of this place in the daylight, and although it looked as normal as any other house, a chill gripped her as she eased down the hall.

She lifted her gun. Jordan could be in here, too. The thought of seeing him again made her stomach churn.

The first few rooms were empty. There was no one in the kitchen or the living room. She thought she heard movement down the hall and made her way there, fingers curling around the handle of the gun as she threw open the door to the office.

She expected an ambush.

What she didn't expect to see was Lillian Daelik, her shaking fingers holding a gun.

"Get out," she said. The barrel of the gun quivered as she pointed it at Stella, who blinked as she came to a halt. "Get out of my house! Leave my family alone!"

Stella had never thought of Lillian as a particularly strong woman, but even she had to admit that it took courage to do such an act. Lillian's brown eyes—so similar to Jordan's—were stretched wide, but there was no mercy on her face. Her grip on the gun was all wrong, her arms shook like leaves in a harsh wind, and her thick dress would slow her down in a proper fight, but she was making a stand, and Stella respected her for that.

But she didn't feel like getting shot, so she rushed Lillian, slapping the gun out of her hand and pointing her own at her head. Lillian gasped and fell back against the bookshelf.

"Leave my family alone," she whispered.

Her finger froze on the trigger. What was she doing? After giving Silas a hard time about sparing the women and children, was she really going to shoot Jordan's *mother?*

Stella let out a growl of frustration and dropped her arm. "Get out of here. Take Lana and run."

She wouldn't have much time before the rest of Stella's family made it inside the house. But Lillian just shook her head. "I'm not abandoning my family."

Lillian lunged, taking Stella by surprise. She managed to get a hand on Stella's gun before she grabbed her wrist, twisting her arm away.

"Listen to me," she hissed, holding her gun out of reach. "You won't have another chance. Take your little girl and get out of here while you have the chance."

Lillian paused, her gaze searching Stella's. "You're serious."

Stella released her. "I mean it. *Go.*"

"Lana's already gone," she said. "And I am not leaving."

"Standing your ground. Brave, but stupid." She shoved her towards the door. "You seem like a nice woman, and I know you're still friends with my mother, but if you don't get your ass moving, I will shoot you myself."

She blinked in shock. Stella supposed it made for a strange sight—the daughter of her husband's greatest enemy, the girl who'd swore time and time again to kill her son, someone who *should* have shot her on sight, giving her mercy. This was a side of Stella that few people had seen since Liam died.

Stella pushed Lillian into the hallway, aiming for the back door, but the two of them stopped short as they realized they were no longer alone.

Shit.

Harvey grinned as he twirled his knife around his fingers. "Look what we found."

CHAPTER 57

Lillian tensed as Harvey sauntered closer. Zoey was right behind him. Stella might have been able to get past the two of them—Zoey might have even helped—if it wasn't for the group of Roses at the end of the hall, headed by her father.

Stella fumbled her gun before pointing it at Lillian. Marcus nodded his approval before signaling to the Roses. "Fan out and search the house. Their spawn must be around here somewhere."

The Roses dispersed. Stella's breathing came faster as Marcus stepped forward, grabbing Lillian's arm and pulling her with him, ignoring her small whimper.

"What are you doing?" she blurted.

Marcus paused. "Taking her outside with the rest of them."

"The rest?"

She trailed her father through the front door, reigning in a gasp. The fight was over—all the Ravens were dead or on their knees. Including their leader, who knelt in front of his house, eyes downcast. Harvey had done a number on him. His hair fell in his eyes and blood dripped down his face. His dark suit was ripped, the tie discarded, one sleeve ripped completely away to reveal the raven tattoo adorning his wrist. Marcus smirked as he shoved Lillian onto her knees next to John, the two of them exchanging a panicked look before glaring up at them.

Marcus shook his head, a smile tugging at his lips as he looked down on his nemesis. "All great things must come to an end. Eh, John?"

John glared at him. "Go to hell."

He just laughed. "You'll be going there first, old friend."

John spat in his face. Anger flickered in Marcus' eyes, and he delivered a swift but brutal blow that had his head snapping to the side.

"Do you really want to test me?" he snarled. "Do you not see that you have lost?" He threw his arms out, gesturing to the carnage around them. "The Ravens are no more!"

"They aren't yet," John snarled.

Stella jerked back as he lunged. Marcus snarled as John grabbed him by the legs and drug him to the ground. Punches were exchanged; Stella hissed as blood splattered on her boots. John seemed oblivious to the half-dozen guns pointed at his face, or maybe he was aware of them and didn't think anyone would shoot him with Marcus so close. Or perhaps he simply did not care anymore, which Stella thought was the most probable option as she beheld the storm raging in his eyes.

"You bastard!" he screamed. "You traitorous, lying piece of filth!" He punched him in the face. "Do you feel superior now?"

Marcus spat at him. "At least my gang isn't dead in the street!"

"You're a murderer!"

"Better to be a killer than the killed!"

No one seemed inclined to step between the two, but Stella had seen enough. She shoved John away and hauled her father to his feet. He stepped forward, making like he was going to continue the fight, but Stella pushed him back.

"You have your win," she hissed in his ear. "Let it rest."

"Excellent advice, Miss Rook."

Silas materialized beside them, looking ever so prim and proper in his striped suit. Stella's blood boiled as she watched him look over the battlefield, taking in the blood-splattered streets with a look of approval. Silas himself hadn't bothered to join the fight. No, he'd just ordered his men forward before slipping off to watch from afar.

Celia stood next to him. She wore a loose blouse over a pair of dark trousers. To anyone watching, it looked like a comfortable yet practical outfit, not unlike what Stella usually wore, but she alone recognized the dark leather pants—the same ones Celia wore when she snuck out at night. Celia had seen some action, perhaps changing her shirt before presenting herself before the Rooks. Stella's eyes narrowed on a stain on her hand that looked an awful lot like blood.

"This is excellent work," Silas said, drawing her attention. He nodded at John, who snarled up at him. "It went quicker than I expected."

Marcus cracked his knuckles. "We know what we're doing."

Celia swept a gaze over the assembled crowd. "Where are the rest?"

He frowned at her flat tone. "The rest?"

"The heir is missing."

"So are Half-Daelik and Thatcher," Zoey said, stepping through the front door. "The house is empty. No sign of the Daelik children."

In the corner of her eye, Stella saw Lillian slump in relief. John just muttered something under his breath and looked away, jaw working.

"What do you mean?" Marcus demanded.

"I mean, there's no one there. I've got people searching the block, but I think they ran for it." She shrugged. "They could be halfway across the city by now."

Silas cleared his throat. "That's a bit of a problem."

"Of course it's a problem!" Marcus snapped.

"We have to find them."

"How?"

"You know this city better than I do…"

Their voices faded into the distance. Stella blew out a breath, trying not to let her shoulders slump and give away her relief. Jordan wasn't here. He'd taken off with his sister in tow.

And it was the right choice, Stella thought, staring down at John and Lillian.

"Enough of this," Harvey snapped, interrupting the conversation. "Who cares if the Daelik runts made a run for it? We've got the one that matters right here, so let's kill him!"

This was met with a roar of approval from the Roses. John's face blanched. Marcus and Silas exchanged a look as if to say *fair enough* before turning on John.

"You can have the honors," Silas invited.

Stella had never seen her father smile so wide as he cocked his gun and pointed it at John's head. Lillian squeezed her eyes shut. Harvey leaned forward in anticipation. A deadly silence fell over the group as his finger slid to the trigger.

"*Wait!*"

All eyes turned to Stella.

"Wait," she panted, desperately searching for something to say. "We can't kill them yet!"

"Why not?" Marcus demanded.

"Yeah, why not?" Harvey echoed.

She racked her brain. "Because we need them as bait. If Jordan and the others are still out there, we need to bring them in, right?" She glanced at Silas, who nodded in confirmation. "Well, if we kill everyone, they have no reason to stick around. They'll skip town and never be seen again. But if we keep some of the Ravens alive…"

"He might be tempted to come back and rescue them," Celia finished, eyes gleaming. "I like this plan."

Celia wanted Jordan dead more than Stella ever had. She suppressed a shudder and turned to Marcus. "Well?"

His jaw worked as he stared down John, weighing in his options. But in the end, he lowered his gun.

"That's the smart thing to do," he admitted, giving Stella a rare look of approval. "But I want them rounded up quickly." He jerked his head at John and Lillian, the latter clutching her chest and struggling to breathe. "Tie them up and bring them to the house. Harvey, you're in charge of guarding them. If a Raven tries to free them, I want you to take care of them personally."

He grinned. "That's my kind of job."

Stella glanced at Silas. "How about you?"

He straightened his suit. "I am agreeable."

Marcus began barking out orders. "I'll search the house again," Stella volunteered before Marcus could give *her* a task. She marched back inside, grateful for the excuse to get away from everyone and have a minute to herself. A few of Silas' men loitered around downstairs, blatantly going through the Daeliks' stuff. She skirted around them and headed to the top floor, the steps creaking underfoot as she pushed open the attic door.

Jordan's bedroom looked different in broad daylight. She folded her arms over her chest as she edged inside. The drawings on the wall hung at crooked angles, pinned on top of one another, the walls holding years of work. Her fingers brushed over a drawing of a raven in flight, the details on the feathers so intricate that it felt like it would burst from the page and fly away any moment.

She reached the desk. It was lined with pencils and charcoal and thick pages good for drawing on. Her eyes landed on a single red rose lying on the desk. Next to it sat a piece of paper with familiar handwriting—*her* handwriting. She snatched the rose up and shoved the warning note in her pocket before anyone else could see the evidence.

His sketchbook was on the desk, too. Stella had only seen Jordan draw for a minute when he sketched the rose she later put in her locket, but she could easily imagine him hunched over the desk, that same concentration in his eyes as his pencil whizzed across the page.

The sketchbook was heavy in her hands as she picked it up and flipped through it. These drawings were rougher than the ones on the walls, doodles and half-finished sketches. But they were still beautiful, still intricate. It was a hard task indeed to find beauty in such a filthy city, but Jordan had done it. Stella imagined he was drawn to a pencil and paper as much as she was drawn to the piano, her fingers itching to play every time she heard music floating through an open window, every time she heard the birds sing or someone humming a tune. She imagined him seeing the sparkle of sunlight over the ocean or a raven spreading its wings or a roaring thundercloud racing for land, seeing something that caught his eye and made him want to capture it on a page.

She imagined *him*, and it felt like her heart was tearing in two.

A tear slipped down her cheek. Stella wiped it away and snapped the sketchbook closed, her teeth clenched together.

"Are you alright?" Zoey asked from behind her.

Stella jumped, whirling around. "I—I'm fine. What about it?"

Her cousin stepped into the room, tugging at a rip in her cropped shirt. "You don't seem fine. Did you get hurt?"

"No, I'm alright."

"Stella, I've known you long enough to know when you're lying to my face." Her eyes trailed around, taking in the room. "Who's room in this?"

"Jordan's." The words came out in a whisper, and Stella was quick to tack on, "I think."

Zoey met her gaze again, and her next words were soft. "Is this about Liam?"

The words hit Stella like a blow. This was about Liam, in a way, and yet it had nothing to do with him. Her heart twisted, and for lack of a good explanation, she shrugged.

"I'm fine," she said again, the words hollow to her own ears.
Zoey stared at her, eyes narrowed.
"If you say so," she said softly.
Then she walked out.

CHAPTER 58

Jordan was going insane.

It was everything about this place. He hadn't been back to the hidden beach since his fight with Stella, unable to face it after he'd let her in. His traitorous eyes kept drifting to the shore, to that small stretch of beach where they had curled up on a blanket and watched the sun rise while Stella told him a fairytale. He had stared at it so much that Declan became convinced there was something over there and inspected the spot several times to see what the problem was.

"This sucks," he said now, kicking the sand.

Jordan sat on his usual rock, his face buried in his hands, trying to ignore the lash of water against the cliffs, as vicious and stormy as the thoughts raging in his mind. Lana sat next to him, curled up against him and staring blankly at the ocean.

She was shaken. Jordan couldn't blame her, not after everything that had happened. They'd come across three other groups on their way to the beach and were forced to fight their way out. Jordan's ankle throbbed from falling during a fight, Declan had a nasty gash along his cheek, and Mateo had nearly gotten his hand blown off by a stray bullet. Lana had seen more violence today than she had her entire life. The gunfire halted a few hours ago, the smoke fading with time, but he didn't know whether to be relieved or horrified at the silence that now reigned over Lochridge.

"This is my fault," he whispered.

"No, it isn't," Mateo said distractedly, following Lana's gaze out to the distant horizon. He had no idea if Jasmin was alright—she had been across town when the attack started, and although her family weren't true Ravens, they were close enough to the Daeliks to be potential targets.

Especially considering the precedent Jordan had set when it came to killing lovers.

"Yes, it is," Jordan snapped. "I'm the one who pissed off Celia and set this in motion."

Mateo fixed him with his full attention now. "Celia had that coming." His voice was quiet but firm. "And Silas was already planning this. He told us that from the start."

"Pissing off Celia didn't help, though," Declan muttered.

Mateo ignored him. "You aren't to blame, Jordan. You're the one who said to be careful around Silas from the beginning, so I don't see why you should feel guilty. Regardless, let's stop wallowing over that and focus on the present. We need to find out who's still alive"—his voice hitched a bit—"and get out of the city."

Jordan's head jerked up. "We can't leave."

"Silas isn't going to stop. We need to get out of here."

"Exactly," he growled. "Silas isn't stopping—not with us. He doesn't want an alliance. He wants a slaughter." Mateo raised a brow as he stood up and started pacing. "The Roses are next."

"So let them die," Declan yawned.

"I don't want the whole city exterminated!"

"Your parents are probably dead. Do you want to be next?"

"They aren't dead yet."

A new voice cut through the air. Jordan whirled, guns flashing, only to stop short when he saw who it was.

Stella Rook leaned in the entrance to the hidden beach, a leather satchel at her feet. There was no telling how long she'd been standing there. Jordan dropped his arm when he saw her expression, the set of her jaw, the hardness in her eyes.

Bloody hell. He hadn't been expecting a confrontation so soon. She tilted her head, meeting his gaze with that same intensity he'd gotten so used to. The world faded, leaving just the two heirs staring at each other over the rift that had formed between them.

Then Declan cursed, and Jordan remembered they weren't alone.

"Bloody Rook," he snarled, grabbing his gun and leaping forward, Mateo right behind him. Lana squeaked and ducked behind the rocks.

Stella's hand flashed towards her gun—

"Stop!" Jordan shouted, his raised voice scaring off the ravens nested at the top of the rocks.

Declan gave him an incredulous look as he positioned himself between them. "What the hell?"

"She's friendly," Jordan said.

Mateo stared at him like he had grown an extra head. "It's rutting Stella Rook."

"We're all aware," Stella said dryly.

They both glared at her. "She is not *friendly*," Declan hissed. "She's a vicious little monster who's here to kill us."

She picked at her nails. "Oh, yes. That's why I snuck up on you, completely alone, no weapon in hand, and announced my presence rather than shooting you in the back." She threw the satchel at him. "Open your eyes, Thatcher. Who do you think sent that warning to your house?"

Declan caught it before it could smack him in the face. "You're lying."

"She isn't," Jordan said.

He glanced between them, the realization dawning in his eyes. "No. Hell no. Jordan, tell me you didn't."

"You really believe her?" Mateo asked, and Jordan couldn't tell if it was a question or a threat.

Stella just crossed her arms. "Open the bag."

"Make me," Declan snapped.

She arched a brow. He huffed and ripped it open.

"Food," she said, nodding towards the contents. "And weapons. And if it's information you're looking for, I have that, too." She glanced at Jordan. "Your parents are alive. I convinced Silas and my father it would be beneficial to keep them alive and use them as bait to lure in the rest of the Ravens. They're at my house with Harvey watching over them." She gave them a sharp look. "Don't fall for the trap."

"What about the rest of the gang?" Jordan asked.

She pressed her lips together. "Some escaped."

He didn't dare inquire about the ones who didn't. "What do we do?"

"We figure out what the hell is going on," Dec said. "Why is she helping us? What's her angle?"

Stella answered before Jordan could. "I don't trust Silas. I have it on good faith that after he is through with your gang, he will turn on mine.

He wants the entire city dead, and nobody in charge seems inclined to stop him."

"We've been working together for a while," Jordan admitted, fighting back a wince. They *were* working together—it felt strange now after what happened, but Stella was here, and they must still be allied to some degree, even if the tension between them was as taunt as a string pulled nearly to its breaking point. "She's here to help."

"Purely for selfish reasons," she said. "I don't want my gang to look like yours right now."

Declan lunged, but Jordan restrained him.

"But you've tried to kill us, even after Silas came," Mateo said. "You attacked Lana just a few days ago."

Lana popped up from behind the rocks. "Yeah! You were in my bedroom!"

Stella raised a brow at her, her expression softening. "I wasn't trying to hurt you, Lana. Jordan told me that he was scared for you to be part of the Ravens because he was afraid you would get hurt. So he asked me to scare you away *before* that could happen."

Her eyes went wide as saucers as she swung an accusing gaze to Jordan. "You *told* her to attack me?"

"I told her to scare you," Jordan corrected. "And I'm glad I did it, too."

Stella glanced at Mateo. "As for trying to kill you, just know that appearances are important." Her gaze slid to Declan. "But I will hurt you if you don't get that gun away from me."

Mateo gaped at them. At some point Dec had passed the satchel to Mateo and resumed pointing his rifle at Stella's face, but Jordan pushed the barrel towards the ground. "Stand down. I know you don't trust her, but trust me."

"You're playing with snakes," he hissed.

"I would suggest learning how to handle them before you get bit." He turned back to Stella. "How do you suggest we go about this? You're the closest to Silas right now."

She took a seat on her usual rock, prompting the others to retreat a few steps, eyeing her warily. "The first order of business will be to see what forces we're working with. Silas has his men combing through your territory, looking for stragglers. You need to do a search of your own and round up any Ravens that escaped the slaughter. I imagine they'll be ripe for revenge by the time you find them."

"And then what?" Declan demanded.

"Then we attack." Her expression was grim. "We have to act before Silas turns on my father. No one in my family sees it coming." She paused. "Zoey, perhaps. But the others are too far into this to realize there's a problem. If Silas wipes them out like he did your family, then we're going to have a hard time organizing any kind of counterattack."

Jordan scratched his chin. "We'll need time to find our people."

"That's why I brought supplies. I'll bring more the next time I get a chance. The main thing will be for all of you to remain hidden—Silas won't move on until he's sure the Ravens are taken care of. With the heir still at large, you're still a problem for him to get out of the way before he can continue to the next step of his plan."

Mateo tilted her head at her, eyes narrowed. "You really are helping us."

She huffed. "Is that so hard to believe?"

"Yes," Dec said flatly. "The heartless bitch, working with the guy who killed her lover. A touch unbelievable, if you ask me."

Rage flickered in her eyes. "Don't mention him, and we won't have a problem."

Jordan cleared his throat and forced himself to meet Stella's gaze. "Give us a minute."

He grabbed Dec and Mateo and steered them away, going as far away from Stella as the small stretch of beach allowed.

"What is wrong with you?" Declan hissed. "Need I remind you of all the reasons we don't like her?"

"I trust her," he said.

His green eyes were stark in the light as he gave Jordan a flat look. "You asked the heir to the White Roses to *scare* your sister. I'm thinking you're insane, Jordie."

"It's messed up," Mateo agreed.

"I trust her," Jordan said again. "I never would have let her into the house if I didn't."

"You let her into the—" Declan pinched the bridge of his nose. "I love you like a brother, but you are being awfully idiotic right now. Do you not see the way she is looking at you? She wants your head on a platter."

"Because we fought," he said irritably. "The last time we saw each other was not pleasant. But before that, we were getting along fine, trailing Silas every night to see what he was up to. We were *getting somewhere*—both with Silas and with the feud." He glanced over his shoulder. Stella sat on the rock, quietly speaking to Lana, who had inched closer to her. "She's no more messed up than we are. One thing I can say for certain is that she cares about this city. We can trust her on this." He met both of their gazes. "Besides, what other option do we have? If we want to see the others again, she is our best shot. Ma, Pa, Jasmin, everyone else. We need her. And she needs us."

Declan narrowed his eyes. "Are you sure?"

"Positive."

Mateo studied Jordan's face. Declan clenched his jaw and looked away.

"I trust you," Mateo said at last. "And you're right; we don't have any other choice." He fingered his gun. "But I'm keeping my eye on her."

"I wouldn't expect anything less," Jordan said. "Now let's get down to business."

CHAPTER 59

Stella and Jordan spent an hour hashing out the details with Dec and Mateo, telling them everything that they had seen during their nightly outings. Jordan was careful to keep the nature of their relationship—their past relationship, that is—under wraps, and to his immense relief, Stella did the same. They were allies. No more, no less.

By the time they finished, the sky slipping from day to night, Declan and Mateo seemed less wary around Stella. Lana even ventured out far enough to sit on the rock next to her.

"So we've got to find a way to kill this asshole before he kills us," Declan said, scratching his chin. "Easy enough."

"He's got an army," Stella said flatly.

"So do we!" He winced. "We just have to find it."

She glanced at the sky and rose to her feet. "I need to be going. I told my father I would hunt for Ravens—which, technically, I did—but he's going to get worried if I'm out too long."

"How thoughtful of him," he deadpanned.

Stella gave him a simpering look. "Watch it, feathers. I might be helping you, but don't forget who has the power right now. One word from me and you lot will be dead by morning."

Declan leaned back, giving her a lazy smile. "Is that supposed to help me trust you?"

Stella gave him a vulgar gesture that had him grinning before walking away.

Jordan wrestled with himself for a moment before ignoring his better judgement and jogging after Stella. "Wait."

She paused. "What."

Jordan stopped in front of her, out of sight of the others, just the two of them alone. "I wanted to talk."

"About what?"

He lifted a brow. "Don't play dumb."

Stella crossed her arms. "We don't have anything to talk about, Daelik. Nothing that we haven't already discussed."

"Listen, I know we aren't on good terms—"

"Jordan, stop."

His mouth snapped shut.

Stella sighed, running a hand through her hair. "I'm sorry. I am really trying not to let what happened between us get in the way of what we're trying to do here. Silas is the priority right now. You and I... It's not going to work, Jordan. We both know that. The damage has been done, but if we spend time trying to repair it rather than focusing on Silas, then there will be nothing left *to* repair." She blew out a breath. "We're still working together. All that bravado you had about doing it yourself, that's over. If it wasn't for my warning, you would be on a wagon headed to the graveyard with the rest of your family. The only reason I'm still here is because I need you to take down Silas."

Jordan looked down. "No, I understand. Trust me, I'd rather be in any other situation than this." He hesitated. "I was just going to say thank-you for sending the warning."

"Right." She toed the ground. "No problem."

The two of them stood there, not meeting each other's gaze.

"How did you know I would be here?" Jordan asked at last.

She shrugged. "Your hidden sanctuary. You said yourself that no one else knows about it. It was the only place I could think of that you would go."

"You know me too well," he said listlessly.

Her jaw clenched. "That's not a good thing."

"No, it isn't."

They fell into an awkward silence once more.

Jordan let out an angry breath. "You should leave."

"I never should have come in the first place, really. I'm dead if anyone finds out."

"That sounds like your problem," he said irritably, then regretted it.

Stella glared at him. "Big words coming from someone who has an entire army hunting him down."

"Like you aren't next. Celia will slit your throat the moment I'm out of the picture."

"Is that a threat?"

"Did it sound like one?" he retorted.

They glared at each other.

"I'm leaving," Stella said.

Jordan sneered. "Good. I'm tired of looking at you."

"Fine!" she snapped.

"Fine!"

Stella turned on her heel and stalked away, leaving Jordan to glare after her.

But his shoulders sagged as soon as she was out of sight. He couldn't afford to lose Stella's help, not with everything else going wrong. Their relationship was in shambles, but they were still working together. As much as he hated to admit it, Stella Rook was the only help he had right now. He *needed* her. Reverting to their old arguments would not help anything.

Jordan sighed and rubbed a hand over his face. "This is a mess," he whispered to himself.

"Damn straight it is."

Jordan choked as Declan strolled past the rocks. "What are you doing?"

"Eavesdropping on your conversation," he said cheerfully.

He eyed Mateo as he followed Declan out. "And why are you eavesdropping on my conversation?"

"Because you're obviously up to something with someone who is *so* not good for you." Dec leaned against Jordan, mischief dancing in his eyes. "You slept with her, didn't you?"

Jordan spluttered. "Of course not!"

"He slept with her," Mateo said.

"Definitely," Declan agreed.

He felt his face go hot. "That's insane. Why would I—"

They both fixed him with a flat stare, and Jordan's argument died on his tongue.

"Fine," he muttered. "I did."

Declan whooped and threw an arm around Jordan's shoulders. "My man! I *knew* there was something there!"

"It doesn't matter now," Jordan said, shoving him off. "It's over. *We're* over."

He pushed him so hard he hit the ground. Declan just looked up at him with a sloppy grin. "*That's* why you've been so moody lately."

"I have not been moody!"

"You have," Mateo said, chuckling under his breath. "But we get it. There's been a lot of shit going on behind the scenes that you didn't tell us about."

"How did that even happen?" Declan asked. "Stella Rook? What made you think that was a good idea?"

"It wasn't a good idea. That's the point."

He picked himself up off the ground. "Apparently you thought it was at some point in time."

Jordan's gaze wandered further up the beach where Stella had walked away. "My mistake."

But he didn't know which part he regretted.

Stella braced herself as she pushed open the front door. Her father believed she'd been hunting Ravens all day, but she had nothing to show for it. She speared for the stairway, hoping to escape to her room before anyone saw her, but Marcus called her name from the parlor, making her cringe as she turned around.

"Did you have any luck?" he asked.

He sat with Silas and Celia, the three of them enjoying tea. *Tea*. Half of the city was dead or dying, and her father wanted to have a tea party with the man who caused it.

Stella plastered a smile on her face. "Not as lucky as I'd hoped, but I caught a few."

"And?"

"And, I took care of them," she responded dryly, examining her nails. "What else?"

It wasn't a lie; she *did* take care of them. Marcus nodded his approval. "Very good." He gestured to the empty chair. "Why don't you join us? We're discussing the next step."

Silas smiled up at her. Stella struggled to keep her expression intact as she crossed over to the piano and opened up the lid, the polished wood smooth under her hands. She played a soft song so as to not disturb the conversation, choosing to ignore Celia as her face twisted at the music.

Celia will slit your throat the moment I'm out of the picture.

Her hand slipped, hitting the wrong key and causing her to wince.

"Back to what we were saying," Marcus said, "I think we give the bait plan a week. See if the Ravens are dumb enough to fall for it."

John and Lillian were being held in the basement with Harvey leering over them. The thought of being helplessly tied to a chair with her cousin looming over her was enough to send a shiver down her spine. If Stella was being honest, she would have preferred death over such a situation.

Silas let out a sigh. "I don't know if we can wait that long."

"Patience is a virtue," Stella said mildly.

He adjusted the collar of his jacket. "Yes, but I'm afraid we just don't have the time. The weight of my decision caused me to fall behind schedule. I can't afford to lose any more time."

Her lips pressed together. "It sounds like you dallied around too long, and now you're going to get in trouble with your boss over it."

He angled his head. "It's something I'd like to avoid, yes."

Celia perked up at her passive-aggressive entrance to the conversation. Stella twisted in her seat and looked Silas dead in the eye. "We need to wait. Your *plan* isn't going to work unless Jordan and the others are out of the way. I believe everyone in this room wants them dead, so how about we slow down and tie up every loose end before moving on? Your boss would rather it take longer and be a job well done than to rush things and have it fall apart in your hands."

Silas narrowed his eyes. Stella held her breath, refusing to back down. She had to stall for time; the next step of Silas' true plan would be to subject the Roses to the same bloodbath they just put on the Ravens. She had to delay that as much as she could, had to give Jordan time to round up the remnants of his gang and stage a counterattack. A week might not even be enough time.

She held Silas' gaze for a minute before he nodded. "You're wise for your years, Miss Rook. We shall give it a few days."

Stella hid her relief. A few days was better than nothing. She would make it work.

Or else, they were all doomed.

CHAPTER 60

Never had Jordan been so nervous walking through his own territory. But, he realized with a jolt, it wasn't *his* anymore. Silas had conquered it; the White Roses now claimed it. He could only hope that some of his men were still hiding in the woodworks.

"This is creepy," Declan muttered.

The trio made their way down the street. It was dark, moonlight filtering through the clouds. Jordan had a revolver in each hand, ready to shoot and run if an enemy presented themself, his entire body tense. Declan and Mateo were on either side of him, the former with a finger on the trigger of his rifle, the latter scanning the buildings on each side.

They were not making good progress. It had taken them an hour to go two blocks, and Jordan was a nervous wreck about leaving Lana behind at the hideout. More than that, he was worried about finding the rest of his gang. A lot of them were dead, if the bodies lining the streets were any indication, but he couldn't be sure that everyone who was still alive hadn't fled the city already. He had to find them and convince them to fight—a feat that would prove difficult given the fact that Silas' army was as strong as before.

He blew out a breath. "What are we so nervous about? This is our turf. Let's act like it."

Declan dropped his voice to a whisper. "We're nervous about the big-ass army chasing us down."

Mateo glanced at a nearby building. "I am ninety percent sure that is blood, but we are not sticking around long enough to find out. Move."

Jordan didn't have time to inspect the stain on the bricks before Mateo was shoving them forward. "This is ridiculous," he growled.

"Desperate times call for desperate measures," Dec said. He paused, grabbing Jordan's arm. "The bar's still intact."

The Broken Bottle, Declan's favorite bar, was still standing. One window pane was broken, but it had been like that since Declan threw a guy into it last year. Otherwise the place seemed untouched.

Jordan glared at him. "This is not the time for a drink."

"It is most definitely time for a drink, but that's not what we're here for." He checked to ensure the street was clear before jogging across. "C'mon."

The bar was never this quiet at this time of night. It was abandoned; the owners had been Ravens, no doubt slaughtered along with the rest. Chairs and tables were flipped, lights smashed, and there was a dark mark on the floor that looked like it had been burned. The shelf of bottles behind the counter had obviously been raided. Jordan's boots crunched over broken glass. Declan seemed oblivious to all of this as he hopped the counter and rummaged around the shelf of liquor.

"What did we just say?" Mateo hissed. "No drinking."

Declan gave him a dry look. "Have a little faith."

There was a soft click as he hit a switch. The entire shelf swung inwards, revealing a hidden doorway.

Jordan blinked. "Oh."

Declan glared at both of them as he grabbed a bottle of whiskey from the shelf and sauntered down the stairs. "*Now* it's time for a drink, assholes. Let's go."

They trailed him down a flight of stone steps. The place smelled of moss and stale whiskey, but Jordan was fascinated all the same, having been unaware that the Broken Bottle had a basement.

But he really perked up when they hit the end of the stairs and heard the drone of voices from deeper within.

"Gentlemen!" Declan drawled, sauntering into the basement. "Your saviors are here!"

Jordan sucked in a breath. The room was so full it was nearly bursting, every person present bearing a raven tattoo on their wrist. They reached for weapons as the trio entered, but quickly relaxed upon seeing who it was.

A grizzly old man shoved his way to the front. "Thatcher! You're a sight for sore eyes."

"Holden," Declan said with a grin, shaking his hand. Jordan recognized him as the owner of the bar. "Trust me, it's the other way around."

Holden glanced at Jordan. "I don't suppose you know what's happened with your old man? Last I saw 'im, he was fightin' a losing battle."

"He's alive, but being held hostage by the Roses." A cry of outrage rose at that, and Jordan winced. "But it's not the Roses we have a problem with. It's Silas Tradow."

Holden spit on the ground. "Sneaky bastard. I knew I didn't trust 'im."

The other Ravens were gathering around. "This is ridiculous!" one called. "I told you we should have run!"

"We should fight!" another cried.

"No, we should run!"

"Yeah, we have to get out of the city while we still can!"

"But they've got the boss!"

"Who cares? We have to save our own necks!"

Jordan cringed as the basement dissolved into a buzz of voices. This wasn't what he needed. He couldn't have half of what little remained of his gang ready to flee. They had to *fight*.

He glanced at Mateo, who was scanning the crowd anxiously. "No sign of Jasmin," he murmured. "Or her family."

He swept a look over the room. The West family was nowhere in sight. He squeezed Mateo's shoulder. "We'll find them. "

"We can't abandon our gang," one Raven yelled.

The one who spoke first raised his voice to a shout. "What choice do we have? Half our people are dead, and look who's in charge now." He flung a hand at Jordan, Mateo, and Declan. "The heathen, the bastard, and the drunkard."

They bristled. "Watch it," Declan growled, lowering his bottle.

The Raven's lip curled. "You're no saviors, Thatcher. What you are is a bunch of young grunts who don't know what's going on any better than we do." He raised a hand. "I say we skip town while our heads are still intact. Who's with me?"

A murmur ran through the crowd. Jordan tensed. This was all wrong. What he wanted was for these Ravens to be ready to fight, not preparing to run with their tail between their legs.

He had to do something.

He grabbed a barstool and set it in the middle of the room. Declan and Mateo hung back as he stepped up on it, one foot on the seat and one in the railing underneath, making him a head taller than everyone else.

"Listen up!" he shouted.

The room fell quiet. Jordan didn't let himself show any sign of weakness as all eyes turned to him.

"My father is being held hostage by the White Roses," he said, his voice carrying. "But it isn't the Rooks that I have bad blood with right now. It's Silas Tradow and his Workers' Union. They're the ones orchestrating this slaughter. They're the ones who encouraged the Roses to hunt us down and kill us, and they're the ones who plan to turn on the Roses once we are done with. Silas don't just want one gang dead; he wants the entire city bleeding out in the streets. But do I intend to let them? Hell no!"

He twisted, meeting all of their gazes. Rallying the gang was typically John's purview. But John was gone, and that left Jordan in charge.

And if he was in charge, that meant he was doing things his way.

"I have an ally in the Rook family who is keeping tabs on Silas," he said. "They have people combing the streets, looking for any Ravens that survived the slaughter. We don't have much time, but I intend to make every second count." He raked a scathing look over the crowd. "Do we forgive someone who has killed our own in cold blood?"

A murmur went through the crowd. "Hell no," Declan said, raising his drink.

Jordan looked directly at the ones who had suggested they leave the city. "Do we flee when we still have family and friends and allies who might be here?"

"No," Mateo said, this time joined by a few others.

He raised his voice. "Do we run when there is a fight to be had?"

"*No!*" they shouted.

"Then let's *fight!*" Jordan roared. "Let's get our revenge! Our people are dead, and there's nothing we can do to bring them back, but we can avenge them. We can protect those who are still alive. We protect *ourselves*." He rose to his full height, teetering on the stool. "We're going to gather up everyone who is still alive and in the city, and we are going to fight tooth and nail until we get our turf back. They might have won the battle, but there is still a war to be fought, and I intend to go in with my guns blazing." He drew one of his revolvers for emphasis and raised it over his head. "Now who's with me?"

The Ravens cheered. Jordan grinned as he looked down on them all. *His* people. *His* gang.

His army.

Declan grinned and pulled him down to the ground, knocking the barstool over in the process. "Now *that's* a speech."

Mateo appeared on his other side. "Now we should probably get them to be quiet before someone hears. It's going to be hard to stage a counterattack if we all get caught."

Jordan raised a fist, and the Ravens fell quiet. "Alright. Now that we're all on the same page, let's discuss the plan."

It was past midnight by the time Jordan, Declan, and Mateo slipped out of the bar and made their way back to the beach. It had started raining, soaking the three of them to the bone, but Jordan felt like he was walking on air.

"That went about ten times better than I was expecting," he admitted.

Dec clapped him on the back. "You're made for this, Jordie. Aside from the lapse of judgement we will refer to as Stella Rook, I'd say you're a natural leader."

And just like that, Jordan's high was shot down like a bird from the sky.

Mateo read his change in expression with a laugh. "He's not wrong."

"It wasn't a lapse in judgement," he grumbled.

"Wasn't it, though?"

"It was…" Jordan searched for the word. "Nice. While it lasted, of course. It's strange even just talking with Stella about the feud and our fathers. Being sort of friendly with her rather than us trying to kill each other every time we turn our heads." He fiddled with the holster of his gun. "I liked it."

Declan slung an arm over his shoulders. "I wouldn't count it out just yet. She still came around after you fought."

"Because she wants Silas dead, not because she likes me." Jordan glanced at him, squinting to see him through the rain. "Besides, I thought you didn't like her."

"I don't like her," he agreed, "but I'm here solely for the drama. The thought of you two having a thing going is hilarious. Imagine what the feud is going to look like once all this Silas shit is over. You have *history* now."

He blanched. "I'm hoping it won't be the same."

Mateo nudged him from the other side. "All this aside, you did a great job back there. I don't think Pa could have rallied them that quickly. He should be proud of you when it's all said and done."

Jordan snorted. "No, he'll just lecture me for not doing it to his liking and give me a list of dirty work to get done. There'll be plenty of Roses to interrogate after this is over."

He sucked on his tooth. "Well…"

"What?"

"Pa isn't here right now, is he?"

"No."

"So he's not in charge right now, right?"

"Right," Jordan said. "I'm in charge."

Mateo shrugged. "He's the one who came up with a bad plan and got himself caught. You're the one who escaped and is planning to set things right. I don't see how he could say a damn thing about what you did wrong after he screwed up so badly." He shook his head, flinging water everywhere. "Stop taking shit from him, Jordan. As much as this whole situation sucks, one good thing is that you know that you don't have to listen to everything he says, because he can be wrong a lot of the time. I mean, just look at yourself compared to him. He likes to interrogate Roses while you make alliances with them, and look at who's in the better situation right now." He shrugged again. "His way isn't the only way. Yours works, too."

"John isn't the boss of you right now," Declan said, almost gently. "He didn't listen to you when it mattered, so why should you give a shit about what he thinks when he isn't even here to tell you?"

Jordan glanced between the two of them. They were right. None of this would have happened had it not been for John's insistence to do things his way. Silas wouldn't be here if it weren't for his refusal to listen to Jordan's distrust. The Ravens might have had a chance at surviving if he hadn't insisted on fighting.

And the fight with Stella might have never happened if John hadn't sent Jordan to interrogate that Rose.

He wiped water out of his eyes. "Thanks," he said softly. "I needed that."

Declan elbowed him. "You're welcome, idiot."

They reached the beach, where Jordan was relieved to see that Lana was safe and sound, tucked under a rock to keep out of the rain, snuggled up in a blanket Stella had brought. Declan and Mateo were quick to settle down in hopes of catching a few hours of shut-eye before morning, but Jordan found himself unable to even try to sleep.

John wasn't here. Jordan was in charge.

The weight of that crashed into him. He was in charge of the gang, yes, but he was also in charge of *himself.* There was nobody forcing him to interrogate Roses or enforce gang rules. He didn't have to participate in the feud and the fighting if he didn't want to, because who was going to stop him?

His hand slipped into his pocket. Stella's locket was warm between his fingers as he pulled it out, the chain coiled in his hand like a tiny golden snake. He hadn't had the courage to open it yet, a little scared of what he would find inside. But now he was gripped with a vicious urge to open it up and see.

He slid his fingernail under the latch and popped it open, his breath catching.

It was the rose. The drop of blood that he'd drawn over before giving it to Stella.

She had put it in the locket.

Jordan's gaze traveled north. He had a thought, wicked and thrilling. His father would disapprove, but as Declan so eloquently put it, why should he give a shit about what John thought right now? John had gotten himself into this mess; Jordan was digging him back out.

Who's going to stop me?

He closed the locket and slipped it back into his pocket, then leaned down and nudged Mateo. "I'll be right back. I have an errand to run."

CHAPTER 61

Stella had never thought of her father as a happy man, but he had been downright chipper for over twenty-four hours, and it was worrying her.

It started when he whistled a tune as he helped Evelyn prepare breakfast, causing Stella and Zoey to exchange a wide-eyed look. He played with Melonie's twins, listened raptly to Stella on the piano, and almost hugged Zoey when she announced she had a new man. He went out with Silas to do a sweep through Raven territory, returning with a smile on his face, the sight so rare that Stella asked if he was ill.

"I'm not sick," he said. "Just cheerful. Once we take care of Daelik's kids, we'll have reason to celebrate."

Stella took to avoiding him by midday, his cheerfulness so unsettling that even Harvey gave him a funny look. She aimed instead to find Zoey and talk with her about her suspicions. She'd been playing with the idea of telling her everything—she only knew a little about Stella's distrust of Silas. Everything about his plans was still in the dark, and Jordan...

Stella had no idea how she was going to tell Zoey about Jordan, but she felt that she had to try. Her cousin deserved to know the truth, and Stella desperately needed another ally.

But the entire day passed with Stella unable to single out Zoey. She planned to steal her away come evening, but Zoey had already left by suppertime, heading to a bar with a few friends to celebrate the defeat of the Ravens. Stella vowed to wait for her, but Zoey didn't return until after high moon and Stella had nearly fallen asleep in the hallway.

"You didn't wait up for me, did you?" Zoey asked, brows raising.

She wore a short dress that accented her slender frame, a pair of heels dangling from her fingers, her hair wet from the rain, much at odds with Stella's lacy dressing gown. She made sure the coast was clear before pulling Zoey into her room and locking the door behind her.

"I have something to tell you," she said breathlessly.

Zoey's eyes widened. "Ooh, let me guess! It's Mystery Boy!"

Stella blinked. "What?"

"Mystery Boy!" She all but sang the words. "You've been so high-strung lately that I assumed you've been meeting someone in secret. You had this lovey-dovey look in your eyes for a few weeks there, and then you've been moody as hell, so I figured you two had broken up, but there *was* a guy at some point, right?"

Her mouth fell open. "Why—Why would you assume that?"

"I mean, I didn't want to outright say it because of everything with Liam I figured it would be a sore spot. But you've been sneaking out every night—"

"To keep tabs on Silas!"

"You came back wearing a man's shirt—"

"My clothes got ripped and I needed something to wear!"

Zoey gave her a look. "Girl, you aren't fooling me. Spill."

Shit. Zoey knew her better than she thought.

Stella opened her mouth with every intention to tell her the full truth, but the words died on her tongue.

Abort mission.

"There was a guy," she said vaguely. "But we're over now."

Zoey squealed—actually *squealed*—before pulling Stella into a hug. "I knew it! I rutting knew it!" She pulled back with a gasp. "But did you break up? Please tell me I was wrong about that, it's not like I *wanted* that to happen, but you had that day where you said you weren't feeling well and I thought I heard you crying and—"

"It's over," Stella said. "Which is why I don't want to talk about it."

Her eyes gleamed. "That tone suggests it isn't over."

"Zoey—"

"Do I at least get his name?"

"No."

"Is he tall? Dark hair or light? And what color are his eyes?"

"No," she hissed.

"Then what's the point in telling me?" she whined.

"I—" Stella felt her face go hot. "I don't know. But it's over. We would have never worked out."

Zoey looked her up and down. "Stella, I love you, but you are so dense sometimes."

"Excuse me?"

She sighed dramatically. "The fact that you refuse to talk about him means you're embarrassed. You and Mystery Boy obviously had a thing, and the way you're being so…"—she waved a hand—"*hissy* about it suggests that the *thing* isn't over yet. Now you are going to tell me one way or another." She sat down on Stella's bed. "Do you want to do this the easy way or the hard way?"

Stella glowered at her. "Get out of my room."

Zoey smirked as she stood up. "The hard way, then."

She was almost to the door when there was a knock—not at the bedroom door, but at the balcony doors. Stella blinked in confusion as she threw open the curtains, revealing a dark figure standing behind the rain-streaked glass.

"Is there someone on the balcony?" Zoey asked, drawing a knife.

Oh, shit.

She yanked the curtains shut before Zoey could get a look, her cheeks burning.

"Get out," she whispered.

Zoey's eyes went wide. "Stella. I can't believe you're going to make me ask this, but why is there someone on your balcony?"

Not a *someone*. Stella knew exactly who it was, but she couldn't fathom why he would be there. "Zoey," she said slowly. "Do you remember what you just said about it not being over?"

"Of course I do. Why—" She sucked in a breath. "Oh. My. Heavens. Is that Mystery Boy?"

Stella glared at her. "*Zoey.*"

"Fine, fine, I'm leaving!" She raised both hands in surrender as she opened the door. "But you better promise to tell me everything!"

"First thing in the morning," she agreed. That would give her time to think up a convincing lie.

She waited until Zoey was gone before flinging open the balcony doors. Jordan's hair was plastered to his forehead, water running down the bridge of his nose, his hands shoved into his pockets. He looked cold and wet and a little miserable, but that didn't stop Stella from shoving him back as she stepped onto the balcony, pulling the doors to behind her.

"What are you doing here?" she hissed, her voice rising with every syllable. "Unless you are in mortal danger—"

"I wanted to talk to you," he said.

Stella positioned herself so she was underneath the tiny awning over the doors, leaving Jordan to fend for himself in the rain. "How did you even get past the guards?"

"I hopped the fence like last time."

"There should have been guards back there."

He glanced over his shoulder. "Well, they weren't very good."

Stella pulled her dressing gown tighter around herself to fend off the chilly night air. "Jordan. I don't know if you realized, but this house is currently the setting for a very elaborate trap, the sole purpose of which is to kill you. There is half an army squatting on this property, waiting for *you* to come and rescue your parents. You are going to get *caught* and jeopardize everything we're trying to do!"

He shrugged. "I'm not here to rescue them. I'm here to talk."

"Well, it had better be good," she snapped. "You're going to get us killed."

Jordan winced. "Just… hear me out. Please?"

Stella folded her arms over her chest.

He blew out a breath. "I realized something today. My father is not in charge of the Ravens right now. I am. But more than that, he is not in charge of me. I have spent my entire life trying to please him. This thing with Silas has been the first time that I've blatantly defied him, but even then, I've been doing it all in the shadows because I'm scared of what he would think. I have spent the last few weeks terrified of what he will do to me if he found out that not only was I going against his orders concerning Silas, but that I was doing it with Marcus Rook's daughter. And that's not even mentioning everything *else* I was doing with Marcus Rook's daughter."

Stella pressed her lips together. "I suppose this is where you tell me you're sorry about Liam and that you only did it because daddy told you to, but daddy isn't around to tell you what to do anymore, so now we can be peachy?"

"Well, yes." He cringed. "But there's more to it than that. The thing with the interrogations... I was acting on Pa's orders. I was doing what I was told because that's what a loyal son does. That's what a loyal member to the gang looks like. And that doesn't excuse what I've done, because I've realized that being a loyal son to John Daelik isn't a good thing. Our gangs were formed with the sole purpose of fighting each other. The way we've fought all these years, Stella... It's not because we actually hated each other. Not because *we* had strife. We were just carrying on our fathers' fight. I feel that if we truly hated each other, we would have taken one of the hundred opportunities we've had to end the other. All this talk about maintaining balance between the gangs is bullshit. Our entire conflict is merely an extension of Marcus and John's conflict. I killed Liam because my father wanted to hurt a member of Marcus' family. Not because I wanted to, or because I enjoyed it, or even because I wanted to hurt you. I had no idea that he was with you."

"I know that," she said.

Jordan nodded to himself. "The same goes for all the others. That Rose I interrogated the other night? Pa told me to. And that's not an excuse, it's just the truth. I was still clinging onto this idea that John Daelik's loyal son was what I wanted to be. But I've realized that my father is not a respectable man. He and Marcus have taken a disagreement between two friends and scaled it to all-out war. And for what? What good has come out of the feud?" He shook his head, sending water droplets flying. "I don't want to be part of this anymore. I love my gang, I love my family, and I love Lochridge and its atmosphere. I wouldn't change it for the world. But I am tired of fighting for no reason. I am tired of blood being shed because two men can't put aside their pride long enough to see reason. I am tired of trying to be loyal to someone that I can no longer respect." He laughed to himself. "You were right. I'm a coward when it comes to my father. But I don't want it to be like that anymore. I don't want to be known as just John Daelik's son. I want to be someone better than he is. I want to keep fighting, but I want there to be value in it. When I spill blood, there needs to be a *reason*." His throat bobbed. "I am not asking you to forgive me for what happened with Liam. I just want you to know that it won't happen again, because I don't want to be that person anymore." His eyes found hers through the rain.

"I'm *not* that person anymore."

Jordan fell silent, the only sound being that of the rain falling in sheets around them. Stella stared at him, unable to form words, unsure of what she would say even if she could. Jordan searched her gaze, looking for a response she didn't have.

Then he dropped his eyes.

"That's what I came to say," he murmured. "We found the hideout of some of the Ravens that escaped the carnage. It's quite a group, and I've got them searching for more, so whenever you're ready to take on Silas…" He scuffed his boot on the ground. "You know where to find us."

He turned away, boots splashing through puddles as he grabbed the trellis and prepared to climb over the balcony railing. He was almost there when Stella finally found her voice and choked out, "You were right, too."

He went still.

"I killed some of your Ravens," she said softly. "When Silas attacked the other day, I grabbed my gun and marched out with the rest of them. I told myself I was doing it to keep up appearances. I had to, or else Silas would catch on. In my head, I was doing the right thing." Jordan turned to face her, and she wiped her cheek. "But I still pulled the trigger. I still ended lives. You aren't the only person who has killed people because that's what their father wanted."

Jordan dared a step closer to her. "Someone once told me that we can't change the past, but we can control the present." He shook his head. "Why are we doing this? Why are we letting *them* get the better of us? Silas is winning because John and Marcus can't get their shit together. Why do we have to be the same?"

Jordan extended his hand towards Stella, and she didn't miss the slight tremor in his fingers.

"I don't want to be your enemy, Stella Rook," he whispered.

Stella stared at his outstretched hand.

Then she ran right past it and kissed him.

The rain beat down on her face as pressed against him, as he angled his mouth over hers, as she threw her arms around his neck, as his hands came to grip her face. The world slipped away and it was just the two of them surrounded by rain, no one but each other for company.

Stella pulled away, breathless. "I love you."

He tucked her hair behind her ear. "I love you, too."

She noticed his teeth were chattering. "Perhaps we should get inside and warm up."

"Perhaps," he said, his lips curling into a sloppy grin. "We can plan our revenge over some hot tea."

A laugh burst out of her. She tugged Jordan with her, his lips finding hers once more as they tumbled through the doors that had been left cracked open, dripping water all over the bedroom floor, but Stella could have cared less about it.

Until Zoey drawled from behind them, "So *this* is Mystery Boy?"

CHAPTER 62

Jordan's hand flew to his revolver as he ripped away from Stella. Zoey Rook sat on the edge of Stella's bed, watching the pair with gleaming eyes. She wore a wine-red dress that was short enough to show off her tan legs and low-cut enough to show off the rest. A pair of heels dangled from her fingers. Her makeup was smudged and her hair was damp from the rain, suggesting she'd been out recently.

And now she looked between the two of them with wide eyes.

"What are you doing in here?" Stella demanded, her voice carrying that lethal intensity Jordan had only ever heard used on him.

Zoey picked her nails. "You said Mystery Boy was on your balcony, and since I had so many unanswered questions, I stuck around to see who it was."

"You eavesdropped on me."

Zoey gave her a flat look as she rose to her feet. "You've done worse, cousin."

Stella's eyes narrowed to slits. "This was none of your business."

"You were just handsy with the guy everyone in this house is trying to kill. I daresay it *is* my business."

Jordan's hand was still on his revolver. "I—"

Zoey snapped her fingers at him without taking her eyes off Stella. "Shush. I'll get to you in a minute."

His mouth snapped shut.

Stella tossed her hair over her shoulder, somehow keeping up an intimidating elegance despite wearing nothing but a rain-soaked dressing gown. "Jordan and I have been working together for weeks to stop Silas."

Zoey raised a brow. "And that explains why you were kissing him?"

Her cheeks flushed scarlet. "We've come to the realization that we do not want to take part in our fathers' feud."

"Oh, I heard that little speech out there." She glanced at Jordan. "You're a smooth talker, by the way. You should see about joining the theater." She turned back to Stella. "As for you, I'm giving you one minute to explain your reasoning for this"—she gestured in Jordan's general direction—"before I raise hell."

Stella put her hands on her hips. "Silas is planning on turning on the Roses once he gets the Ravens out of the way. We've known for a while that he's planned on taking out both gangs, we just didn't know which one he would start with until he made his decision. We've looked into what his Workers' Union has done in Stokes and other cities and discovered that his boss has essentially stripped everyone of any power and assigned it to himself. They aren't interested in an alliance with Lochridge. They want to kill everyone in it and take it for themselves. Since Jordan and I have a mutual interest in keeping this city and its assets safe, and since both of our fathers were so wrapped up in the feud to see the problem with Silas, we took matters into our own hands and tried to stop him on our own. Currently I'm stalling for time while Jordan gathers up what's left of the Ravens to stage an attack against Silas before he turns on the Roses." She shot Jordan a wry look. "Did I cover everything?"

He sucked on his teeth. "And Celia's a knife-wielding bitch who wants to assassinate you."

"Right." Stella turned back to Zoey. "Celia's a knife-wielding bitch who wants to assassinate me."

Zoey blinked several times. "Seriously?"

Jordan deemed it was time for him to talk. "Taking out the Ravens was just the first step. We've heard Silas talk. His operation won't work if the gangs are still at play here, so he's been feeding off of the conflict to take out both of them."

"A divided house cannot stand," Stella quoted. "Silas has taken that to heart."

Zoey looked between them. "Bloody hell, you are serious."

Jordan clenched his jaw. "Unfortunately so."

Her mouth fell open. "Holy shit. I mean, holy *shit*. Does anyone else know about this?"

"Thatcher and Half-Daelik are in on it," Stella said tiredly. "And Jordan's little sister. But only after Silas' attack. I sent Jordan a warning beforehand—that's why he wasn't there when he got to his house." She glanced at Jordan, almost shyly. "Other than that, it's just us."

"You didn't think to tell *me*?"

Stella winced at the hurt in her voice. "I didn't know how you would take it."

Zoey huffed. "Well, I wouldn't have taken it a lot better if you had just told me instead of making me find out like this."

"To be fair," Jordan said icily, "we didn't ask for you to eavesdrop on us."

Her gaze swung to him. "I didn't say you could talk yet, feathers."

He crossed his arms, deciding it was safe enough to remove his hand from his revolver. "It's a good thing I don't follow orders from you."

Her eyes narrowed as she sauntered up to him. "You've got quite the mouth for someone standing in the middle of enemy territory."

"Perhaps. But the fact that you haven't already sounded the alarm tells me you're okay with it."

Zoey stared at him for a moment before turning to Stella. "Are you completely certain about everything you're saying? You're *sure* Silas plans to turn on us?"

"Yes," she said.

Zoey jabbed a finger at Jordan. "And you're sure he's not going to kill you in your sleep?"

Her lips twitched. "He's had plenty of opportunities to do so. The fact that I'm still here is a testament to how much I trust him."

"I wouldn't hurt her," Jordan said, meaning every word. "I'm done playing into the feud. It's brought nothing but grief to everyone who's involved."

She snorted. "My brother would disagree."

Stella moved so quickly that Jordan almost missed it as she grabbed Zoey by the shoulders.

"Do not," she hissed, "breathe a word of this to Harvey. I don't give a shit if you trust Jordan or not, but I know you trust *me*, and I'm telling you that this situation with Silas is important. We need the Ravens if we want to make it out alive. But we're all dead if Harvey finds out."

Zoey arched a brow. "Do you really think I'd tell him about this? The psycho would paint this room red." She shook her head. "Trust me, I'll keep my mouth shut."

Stella released her. "Good."

Zoey stepped back and looked between the two of them. Jordan shuffled his feet, all too aware of the fact that he was leaving a puddle of water on the floor. Stella was no better, beads of water clinging to her dark hair. He caught her gaze and angled his head, and the ghost of a smile flitted over her lips.

She cleared her throat. "As much fun as this has been, Zo…"

Zoey coughed. "Right. You and Mystery Boy have a breakup to make up for." She pivoted towards the door. "I'll leave, but you have to promise me you won't keep any more secrets from me. If you're scheming with the enemy, I would love to know about it."

"Deal," Stella said. "And no more eavesdropping."

"No promises!"

And with that, Zoey vanished through the door.

Stella made sure it locked behind her before slumping against the door. "I am so sorry about that," she whispered, burying her face in her hands.

Jordan ran a hand through his damp hair. "It could have gone worse."

"It could have," she agreed. "Zoey was the only one in my family I thought we could trust with this. I tried to tell her earlier, but I just couldn't get the words out." She laughed under her breath. "I'm kind of glad she found out."

"It's hard keeping secrets. I certainly feel better now that Dec and Mateo know."

Stella rubbed her arm. "It is nice to have it off my chest."

Her eyes flickered up to his. Jordan couldn't help but smile as he pulled her into a hug. She leaned her head against his chest with a soft sigh.

"I missed you," she whispered.

"I missed you too, little thorn," he murmured into her hair.

Her arms slid around his waist. "We're going to end this. And afterwards…" She pulled back, looking him in the eye. "Afterwards, we make our own path. Screw our fathers. We're the ones trying to fix things."

He had no words, so he pulled her closer, letting out a long breath as she laid her head against his chest. Heavens above, he'd missed this. He didn't know at what point she had stopped being his enemy, but he knew now that he could never go back.

How had their fathers done it? How had two men gone from the closest of friends to the worst of enemies?

Jordan laughed under his breath. "You know, this went a lot better than I was expecting it to."

The corners of her lips ticked upwards. "I imagine."

He tucked a wet strand of hair behind her ear, wincing as he did so. "I should go. I don't need to be here, and I imagine you're ready to get out of those wet clothes."

Stella frowned at herself, then at the puddles left on the floor. "Are you unable to visit me when it's not raining outside?" She shook her head. "In any case, you need to wait. I think you slipped through at the top of the hour when the guards by the fence rotated out. They'll change out in another three hours, and you can leave then."

"It'll be morning by then."

"But it will still be dark out, especially with the cloud cover from the rain."

He bit his lip. "I don't know."

She grabbed his hand. "Trust me. I think it's very reckless for you to be here any longer than you have to, but I also don't want you to get caught on your way out." She studied his clothes. "Harvey's downstairs guarding your parents. I'll grab some clothes from his room."

Jordan choked. "You're going to steal clothes from the family maniac?"

Stella just winked at him before slipping through the door.

Jordan gaped after her, then shook his head and shoved his hands into his pockets. His fingers brushed on something, and he pulled out Stella's locket. When she returned with an armful of clothes, it dangled from his fingers, swinging back and forth in a lazy arch.

Her mouth fell open. "I can't believe you kept it," she said, double-checking to make sure the door was locked.

He shrugged. "I couldn't bring myself to throw it away."

She grinned as she slipped the thin chain around her neck, trading the locket for the clothes. Jordan turned away, grateful to shuck off his wet clothes and put on some dry ones, even if he couldn't help but notice that the shirt had a bloodstain on the sleeve. He was so used to wearing dark clothes that it felt strange to wear white. By the time he turned back around, Stella had pulled on a fresh nightgown, her wet hair loosely braided and the scent of her flowery perfume covering up the earthy smell of fresh rain.

Her lips curved into a teasing smile. "A white shirt. I guess that makes you a Rose now."

He tugged at the sleeve. "My father would kill me if he saw this."

The smile turned into a grin. "Come on," she said, folding back the covers on her bed. "We've got time before the guards rotate out."

After a moment's hesitation, Jordan slid into bed beside her. She threw the thick comforter over them both and snuggled up next to him, her head resting in the crook of his arm, the candle on the nightstand making shadows and light dance across her face.

"You know something?" he whispered into the silence.

"What?"

"I'm glad this thing with Silas happened."

She tilted her head. "He's trying to exterminate your family."

"True," Jordan agreed. "But he's also opened my eyes. If it weren't for him, you and I would have never started working together, because he never would have had a common goal to work towards." He trailed a finger down her arm, causing her to shiver. "I don't like him in the slightest, but if all of this was the only way that you and I ever got to know each other… I would do it again."

"That's one way to look at it, I suppose."

A beat of silence passed.

"I'm worried," Jordan said.

"We both are," she murmured. "But we can't let it show."

"That's not making me feel better."

She pinched him. "It wasn't supposed to."

Jordan chuckled and slid an arm around her. Bloody hell, he had missed this. The banter, the secret-keeping, the kisses in the night. He pressed a kiss to her neck in a silent thank-you for allowing him to be lucky enough to win her back.

All he had to do now was hold onto it—and to survive long enough to make it last.

CHAPTER 63

The rain was gone by morning, leaving a layer of dark clouds to press down from above. A cool wind played with the ends of Jordan's hair as he stepped around a puddle, the water reflecting the stone-gray sky.

Stella and Zoey trailed after him. It felt strange walking with Stella down a public street in broad daylight—made even stranger by the fact that her cousin was with them—but Raven territory had been deserted since the attack. There were still some Ravens hiding out, and of course the Roses and Silas' men patrolled the streets to catch them, but the girls had extensive knowledge of when the patrols would come through, allowing the three of them to walk in peace.

"This makes me nauseous," Zoey said.

Last night's dress was gone in favor of more practical attire, a sleeveless shirt that was cropped to show her stomach and a pair of tight-fitting trousers slung low on her hips. Her short, dark hair whipped in the wind as she squinted at the same bloodstain Mateo had pointed out just a few hours ago.

"It makes *you* nauseous?" Jordan responded icily. "At least it isn't *your* territory."

She gave him a haughty look. "Technically, it is ours now. The Ravens are gone."

"You little—"

"Enough," Stella cut in. "If you two are going to bicker like children, do it somewhere else."

They fell silent, but that didn't stop Zoey from sticking her tongue out at him the moment her cousin's back was turned. Jordan responded with a vulgar gesture that had her grinning like a fiend.

Jordan and Stella had fallen asleep on her bed, completely missing the guard rotation and forcing them to wait. Stella had enlisted Zoey to cause a distraction while she helped Jordan make it over the fence. They hadn't counted on her following them after, claiming that she wanted to talk over the plan more. Jordan had been against it, but Stella agreed.

"I owe it to her," she murmured to him. "She's annoyed that I kept all of this a secret, and I did promise I would keep her updated." She turned pleading eyes up at him. "We need her help."

He hadn't been able to refuse, and now here they were.

They turned the corner and walked down the hill towards the beach. Jordan felt extremely vulnerable walking with his known enemies in an area that was swamped with his *actual* enemy. It wasn't that he was scared of any Ravens finding out; he honestly didn't care if they knew or not. He had already confessed to the people at the Broken Bottle that he was working with a member of the Rook family. Besides that, he was in charge—what were they going to do if they found out Stella was the one he was with?

But it felt weird all the same.

Jordan slipped through the rocks first, motioning for the girls to hang behind. Declan, Mateo, and Lana were munching on the food Stella brought, but they perked up when they saw Jordan.

"Well, the prodigal son returns," Dec said dryly. "We would have waited for you to come back before we ate, but you just disappeared."

"I had an errand."

"Some errand."

"You said you'd be back in a few minutes," Mateo said around a mouthful of food.

"It took longer than I expected." Jordan crossed his arms. "But are you ready for some company?"

They exchanged a look as Stella and Zoey walked in, the latter lifting a dark brow as she took in the beach. Jordan's sanctuary was becoming rather crowded these days, especially as Dec grabbed his rifle and slowly rose to his feet.

"You brought another Rook?" he hissed at Jordan.

"There were four of you and only one of me," Stella said. "I figured we'd even the odds a little."

He narrowed his eyes on Zoey. "Her brother is a maniac."

"Which is why he doesn't know about this," Zoey said tartly.

Stella picked her nails. "You Ravens act like we aren't aware that Harvey is difficult."

"*Difficult*," Declan repeated.

She dropped her hand. "Fine. He's insane."

"Psychotic," Mateo muttered.

"Maniacal," Jordan added.

"Bloodthirsty," Declan put in.

"Crazy," Lana chimed.

They all looked at Zoey.

She threw her hands up with an exasperated sigh. "Yes, yes, he's all of that. Now can we stop talking about my brother and start focusing on the problem at hand?" She waved at the Ravens. "Don't we have another psychopath trying to kill us?"

Declan sat aside his gun. "You better not be sleeping with her, too," he said lowly to Jordan.

Jordan raised a fist as Stella sat down and crossed her legs. "Yesterday you said you found some of your men," she said, interrupting Jordan before he could clock Dec in the head. "How many?"

"Not enough," Declan growled.

"It's a solid group," Jordan said. "But he's right. It isn't enough."

"Enough for what?" Zoey asked. "Taking on Silas? I don't think you'll ever have enough Ravens for that. Half of your gang is dead, and who knows how many have fled the city." She leaned back. "Don't give me that look."

Jordan, Dec, and Mateo were all glaring at her. "No need to be so crude about it," Mateo hissed.

She shrugged. "What? It's the truth. We're going to need more than the remnants of a gang that Silas has already conquered."

As much as Jordan hated to hear it, she had a point. The Ravens had already lost the battle. Even if they found every single member that survived the slaughter, it wouldn't be a match for Silas' people, much less the Roses, too.

He glanced at Stella. "She's right."

Her face remained impassive. "We'll find a way."

"We need more than the Ravens," Zoey said.

"So get the Roses," Declan said angrily. "You're the heir, Rook. Tell your people to get their asses moving and overthrow this bastard before he kills *them*!"

Stella's expression was pained. "It's not that simple. Father is still in charge. If I give orders that go directly against his wishes, he will intervene." She shook her head. "Jordan might be in charge of the Ravens right now, but I am still just the heir to the Roses. I have sway, but not that much."

He threw up his hands. "Then get your father out of the picture! These Tradow assholes are trying to take over our city. I am not going to sit here and twiddle my thumbs while I watch them do it!"

His outburst was met with sullen silence. Jordan looked away, his hands fisted. Mateo stared at the ground. The Rook girls shifted uncomfortably.

"We're going to try," Stella said at last. "Trust me, we don't want to see Lochridge fall any more than you do—"

"Our side has already fallen," he snapped. "You two just sit up there in your castle like spoiled princesses—"

Stella and Zoey shot to their feet, the former reaching for her gun, the latter snarling, "Don't you dare—"

Jordan threw himself in front of them before the fight could escalate.

"Enough!" he shouted. "We may not know what the best course of action here is, but getting into it with each other sure isn't it." He glared at Declan. "Stop insulting them. You know better." He turned to Stella and Zoey. "Quit taking the bait. We're all better than this."

Stella's expression softened, but Zoey and Declan continued glaring at each other. That is, until Mateo thumped Declan on the back of his head, breaking up their staring contest and the tension in the air.

"We're going to continue searching for more Ravens," Jordan said, trying to steer the subject back into a positive direction. "We've only found one group. I refuse to believe that *everyone* else is dead or gone. They have to be around here somewhere, and I know they will be ready and raring to fight."

"The group we found was definitely thrilled at the prospect of putting it to Silas," Mateo said.

Declan snorted. "They were thrilled at putting it to the Roses." He sprawled on the beach, propping his legs up on a rock. "Silas is just a bonus."

Stella played with the sleeve of her blouse. "I might be able to steal a few Roses to help us without my father noticing. But if I can pull that off, we can't have them getting into it with your people." She glanced between Zoey and Declan. "If the five of us—"

"Six," Lana interjected from where she hid behind Jordan.

"If the *six* of us," Stella corrected, "can't get along for more than a few minutes, then I don't see how we can expect entire groups to. The feud had put so much tension between us that all it takes is one spark, and we've got an inferno on our hands."

Zoey pressed her lips together. "It won't do us much good to get some Roses on our side if all they're going to do is fight with the Ravens."

"My point exactly."

Lana peered around Jordan. "Then don't fight."

Her bland tone made Jordan laugh. "It's not that simple," he said, ruffling her hair.

She scowled at him. "Yes, it is!" She gestured to him and everyone else. "If you don't fight, then you're setting a good example for everyone else. You're getting along with Stella, and everyone else here is following suit." She glared at Declan. "For the most part. If we're fighting…"

"Then it's an excuse for everyone else to do the same," Mateo murmured.

"But if we show a united front, it might send the right message," Stella finished. She gave Lana a nod of approval. "Not too bad, feathers."

Lana beamed.

"But the first order of business will be to gather a group big enough to take on Silas," Zoey said. "How much of Raven territory have you covered?"

"Not a lot," Jordan admitted.

"It's rutting scary," Mateo said.

Stella pressed her lips together. "Well, if you three don't cover it, then Silas' people will. They're weeding out more Ravens every day. The longer you wait to gather them up—"

"The less we'll have," Jordan finished with a sigh. "Yeah, we get it."

"We can't do anything to help on that front," she reminded him. "They wouldn't trust us even if we tried."

He sighed again. "We'll get on it." He glanced at Dec and Mateo. "As soon as it hits dark."

Mateo gave a firm nod. Declan lifted a bottle he'd nipped from the bar in salute.

"Good." She glanced at the position of the sun. "We need to get back before someone notices we're gone." She looked at Jordan. "See you again soon?"

He caught her by the arm before she could turn away. "Come back as soon as you can. Keep us updated."

She squeezed his hand. "Of course."

She gave Declan, Mateo, and Lana a nod of farewell before leaving. Zoey just glanced around and said, "See you around, bitches," before sauntering after her cousin.

Declan gave Jordan a slow look from his position on the ground. "You made up with her, didn't you?"

"What makes you say that?"

"Well, you two looked a lot less like you wanted to kill each other and a lot more like you wanted to fu—"

"*Do not*," he growled, "finish that sentence."

He gave a pointed look in Lana's direction. Declan just crossed his arms. "I'm not wrong."

Jordan sighed for a third time. "You're not wrong."

Declan and Mateo smirked at each other. Jordan shook his head as he stared out at the ocean.

Everything was moving so fast, yet not moving at all. Jordan was stuck, hoping and praying that Silas didn't root out his gang before he could make it to them, silently pleading that there were enough of them left to pose an actual threat against the Union. His stomach churned. What if this was all for nothing? What if he led the Ravens in an attack against Silas that ended with nothing but more bloodshed?

He clenched his fists. *No.* He couldn't—*wouldn't*—let that happen.

But he couldn't help but think to himself that this might be out of his control.

CHAPTER 64

Silas was impatient.

He didn't come out and say it that morning, but Stella could tell by the set of his jaw, the way his hands fidgeted and how he kept glancing at the front door like Jordan Daelik would come bursting through it at any moment. Tobias was a dark thunderstorm behind him, glowering at anyone who dared meet his gaze. Celia wasn't much better, pacing around like a changed animal, her hand reaching for a weapon that Stella couldn't see. Marcus must have picked up on it, too, because that afternoon he announced he would do a sweep through Raven territory and invited the Tradows along with him.

The last thing Stella wanted to do was hunt down the people she was trying to rally, but she was determined to keep eyes on Silas, so she volunteered to go along. At first the trip went smoothly. They didn't see a single soul as they walked through the deserted Raven turf. Stella wondered how many Ravens Jordan and his crew had tracked down last night, if any. She planned to take them some more food and supplies tonight, and she hoped she would be met with good news.

"The Ravens might have fled town," Stella said, breaking up the silence in their group. The Tradows, Zoey, and Harvey were present alongside her and her father. They all shot her a questioning look, and she shrugged, feigning nonchalance. "We've always said they're cowards. Looks like they actually lived up to it."

Celia narrowed her eyes on the street ahead. "No, I think Daelik is still around here somewhere. I can feel it."

Stella snorted. "Please. He's the king of the cowards. The rutting bastard wouldn't know bravery if it slapped him in the face."

She gave her an amused look. "You really think they all ran?"

Of course not. "It's a possibility."

"For now I want to assume that all the Ravens are still in Lochridge," Silas cut in. "The ones that matter, at least."

Stella gave him a haughty look. "You know what they say about assuming. It makes an—"

She trailed off as a flash of movement caught her eye. She wasn't the only one who saw it; Harvey perked up, already drawing his knife as he stalked towards it.

Stella's heart leapt into her throat. If it was a Raven—

She couldn't let Harvey get there first. She exchanged a look with Zoey, and the two of them drew their guns and charged, darting right past Harvey and to the figure that was now making a run for it. Stella couldn't see his face, but it was definitely a man, broad-shouldered and dark-haired and smart enough to run for his life when Harvey was present.

He rounded a corner. Stella and Zoey skidded around just in time to see him disappearing into a house at the end of the street. The girls swapped another look as they came to a halt, and by the time Harvey caught up to them, the man was nowhere in sight.

"He disappeared," Stella said.

"Vanished," Zoey agreed.

Harvey scanned the street. "Bullshit. He's in one of these houses."

Stella gritted her teeth. "Let it go."

"No! These Ravens deserve to die, and I'm not going to let them run from me."

He stalked to the first house on the street and tried the door. It swung open, and Harvey looked around before moving onto the next. Every door was thrown open, Harvey holding his knife, a feral look in his eyes.

Stella forced herself to look as he reached the house the man went into. And when he tried the door...

"Locked," he said, jangling the knob. He grinned. "We found them."

He kicked the door in. There was a scream from inside—a girl's scream. The man wasn't alone. Stella squeezed her eyes shut, breathing through her clenched teeth as the scream was cut short.

Zoey stared at the ground. "Shit."

Harvey reappeared in the doorway, dragging a girl out by her hair, which was the same dark color as the man's. Only Stella didn't think the man was alive anymore judging by the blood dripping from Harvey's knife.

"The whole family's in there," he said, still grinning as he threw the girl to the ground. "They were trying to hide from *me*!"

Stella's eyes widened as the girl looked up at them, her deep blue eyes wide with panic. She knew who that was—Jasmin West. Not a Raven, but her family had close ties with the Daeliks. Last she heard, Jasmin herself was being courted by Mateo Daelik.

Shit.

Harvey pulled the rest of the family out, including the limp body of what Stella could only assume was Jasmin's brother. Her eyes widened as she saw him, tears spilling down her cheeks.

Harvey hadn't stopped smiling. "I'd say this was a productive outing." Jasmin whimpered as he grabbed her chin, forcing her to look at him. His knife slid up to caress her throat. "My, you're a pretty little thing, aren't you?"

"Enough," Stella hissed.

He ignored her. "The Daelik rats might not care about their parents, but I'd wager they'll come to rescue Half-Daelik's whore." He swiped his tongue over his teeth, eyeing up Jasmin up and down, a hungry look in his eyes. "You and I can have a little fun while we wait for them to come rescue the damsel in distress."

"Harvey, knock it off," Zoey said.

"I bet we can have a lot of fun together—"

"*Harvey!*"

He slowly turned to look at Stella. "Can I help you?"

Her breath was ragged. "Leave her alone," she seethed.

He stroked Jasmin's cheek, his knife still angled under her chin. "Why? The Ravens are all but dead. I don't see any harm in keeping one to play with."

Stella realized she wasn't getting through to him, so she looked to the person in charge—her father. "Are you really going to allow this?" she demanded.

"It's a good idea," he said. "The West family can serve as additional bait—"

"Not that!" she said shrilly. "Don't let Harvey near her!" She forced her voice to lower. "If a man did that to me right now, would you stand by and allow it? Or would you put a bullet through his skull?" She jabbed a finger at Harvey. "I will not sit here and watch him take advantage of her like this. End it. *Now.*"

Marcus sighed. "Harvey, enough."

Stella loosened a breath. "Thank you."

Harvey glowered as he released Jasmin. His knife had left a bloody streak across her throat. He smirked at it as he stood up, prowling around the West family, silently begging someone to act out so he could take care of them.

"Take them back to the house," Marcus said. "Tie them up with the others."

"You think this will speed things up?" Silas murmured.

"It's worth a shot."

Celia just smirked. "I, for one, would love to see how this plays out."

Her eyes were on Harvey, who was still eyeing Jasmin. Fed up, Stella marched over and hauled Jasmin to her feet, Zoey coming up to flank her other side. The two held Harvey's gaze until he dropped his eyes, admitting defeat.

But Stella knew it wouldn't last long.

"I cannot believe this."

Zoey watched from her bed as Stella paced her room. Her cousin's bedroom was a lot messier than hers was, clothes and jewelry scattered everywhere. The covers of the bed were wadded up on the floor, and Stella couldn't recall the last time she'd actually been able to see the top of Zoey's dresser through all the junk piled on it. The mess made her pacing difficult.

"He's sick," she spat.

"I know," Zoey said tiredly.

They were supposed to be meeting Jordan and the others right about now, but the plan had changed. Jordan might not care about rescuing his parents right away, but Stella had a feeling that the same wouldn't apply to the Wests. From what she remembered, Mateo and Jasmin had been going steady for well over a year. She might actually work as bait.

And not to mention Harvey, who had gladly occupied his guard post in the basement, now watching over both the Daeliks and the Wests.

"This isn't good," she whispered. "If the Ravens try to break them out..."

"They don't have to know," Zoey said. "If they don't know the girl is here, then there's no reason for them to fall for the trap."

"I can't do that. I have to tell them."

"It's not that big of a deal. We don't know how much they actually care for each other. Half-Daelik might not give a shit."

"Well, I do," she said irritably. "I don't care who she is, I'm not going to leave her down there with Harvey for a moment longer than I have to."

Zoey sat up. "Are you suggesting we break her out ourselves?"

"Do you want to leave her down there?"

"Of course not, both for her sake and for Harvey's. He doesn't have a lot of dignity left, and if he does something to that girl, he'll destroy it all."

"I don't give a rat's ass about Harvey's dignity," Stella snapped.

Zoey raised her hands in surrender. "Alright. I get it. And for the record, I am all for breaking her out, I just don't know how you plan to do it. We have to remember that *Harvey* is the one guarding her. We'll never make it into the basement."

Stella rubbed her temples. "I'm working on it."

She sucked her tooth. "I could cause another distraction—"

"He won't fall for it. Jasmin *is* his distraction right now."

Zoey bit her lip. Stella let out a frustrated sigh and sprawled out next to her cousin.

"We have to think of something," she murmured. "I don't feel good abou—"

There was a thump downstairs. It was soft, perhaps someone stubbing their toe on a table in a dark hallway, but it was enough that Stella and Zoey fell quiet and sat up.

There was another thump, and Stella lunged for the door.

She raced down the stairs, her and Zoey both in their nightclothes, only stopping long enough to collect their weapons. The house was dark, but Stella's mind whirled with possibilities. It sounded like someone was breaking in. Could it be Jordan? Or maybe some of his other Ravens? Had word spread that fast?

They reached the bottom of the stairs, realizing with a jolt that the sounds were coming from down the hall. The hall that led to the basement—Stella sucked in a breath. Maybe it wasn't someone breaking in, but rather someone breaking *out*. She wondered if it was possible for John and the others to have overpowered Harvey.

They came around the corner and skidded to a halt.

Not a break-in.

Not a rescue attempt.

Not an escape.

Just Harvey, a smile on his face as he pressed Jasmin West to the wall, his knife at her throat and his hand fisted in her hair and the front of her shirt ripped open.

He was too occupied to notice Stella and Zoey standing there, their twin eyes narrowing at the sight. But Jasmin saw them over Harvey's shoulder, her blue eyes wide and pleading. Begging for help.

And it was that look, that silent cry for help, that had every thought draining out of Stella's mind as she lifted her gun over her head and brought it crashing down on the back of Harvey's skull.

He crumpled. Zoey caught Jasmin before she fell, and Stella was quick to pick the knife out of Harvey's hand. She checked his pulse to make sure he was still alive before turning to Jasmin.

"Are you alright?" she demanded in a whisper.

Jasmin nodded, her eyes wide. She was lucky, so damn lucky that Stella had been awake to hear the noise. Otherwise, who knew how far this could have gone.

"Thank you," she whispered. She trembled so hard she could barely get the words out.

Stella glanced at Zoey. "No rescue attempt needed. Harvey brought her right to us."

Jasmin swallowed. "What does that mean?"

"It means we're getting you out of here," Zoey said gently. "Come with us."

CHAPTER 65

"You truly know where Mateo is?"

Stella had taken five minutes to change into her dark clothes, to give Zoey her extra set to wear, to hand Jasmin a fresh shirt to replace the one Harvey ripped. The poor girl was pale and shaken, edging away from Stella and Zoey even as they slipped past the guards and through the hidden gate in the back. Once they were off the property, Stella explained in a hushed whisper that she was on her side, and only then had she relaxed.

"We're taking you to him now," Stella confirmed. She checked to make sure the street was clear. "This way."

They stole across the street, their shadows long in the light of the street lamps. It felt eerie, sending a shiver down Stella's spine as they snuck across the Barter Streets and into the deserted Raven territory. The three of them were all but running, going far too fast for proper stealth, but they couldn't afford to be out any longer than they had to be. Harvey would be livid once he awoke. He didn't know Stella had been the one to knock him out, but she had his knife tucked in her belt, and she had no qualms about telling him that she'd freed Jasmin.

But she had to get her to safety before Harvey started his hunt.

"What about the rest of my family?" Jasmin asked. "And John and Lillian?"

Stella pressed her lips together. "We're working on it."

"Will—"

"Jordan and the others will explain more, I promise. For now, we've

418

got to keep quiet."

Jasmin loosened a shaking breath and nodded. Stella didn't even want to imagine what she was feeling right now. The thought of Harvey putting his hands on *her* was enough to make her nauseous.

They were about to cross the next street when a flash of movement caught her eye. She jerked everyone back, her heart rate shooting into the sky.

"Someone's there," she hissed. They had to slow down—their rush was making them reckless. Stella peered around the corner and cursed when she saw the figure was heading in their direction.

"This way," she snapped, pushing Jasmin and Zoey back. They went for the first door they came across—the entrance to a glass shop. Zoey jimmied the lock and they tumbled inside, snapping the door shut just as the figure came into view.

Shit.

She herded the other two towards the back. "Go out that way and head for the beach. I'll keep them occupied."

"You sure?" Zoey asked.

"Positive. If that's Harvey…"

Jasmin's face blanched. Zoey nodded and pulled her into the back room.

The doorknob turned. Stella pressed herself against the far wall, tucking herself out of the moonlight as the door swung open and a lone figure stepped into the room

Her breath hitched. It wasn't Harvey.

It was worse.

Celia Tradow's platinum hair gleamed white as she surveyed the shop, her eyes skipping over Stella's hiding spot. "Come out, come out," she sang, flipping a knife in her hand. "I know you're in here."

Stella's hands curled into fists. It wouldn't take long for Celia to assume they'd escaped out the back. She had to distract her enough for Zoey and Jasmin to get away.

So she tugged her mask into place and stepped into the light.

Celia angled her head. "Oh, it's you. I wondered when you'd make your next appearance."

Stella remained silent as Celia began circling her. She moved as well, keeping time with her, the two of them moving around shelves of glass dishes and ceramic figurines, all of it glittering in the moonlight.

Celia smiled. "Cat got your tongue? That's a shame. I was hoping you'd tell me who you are." She raised the knife. "I guess I'll have to find out."

Stella threw herself out of the way as Celia hurled the knife, smashing a ceramic pot that had been directly behind her. By the time she straightened, Celia was *right there*, two more blades in her hand.

She sidestepped the attack. Harvey's knife was heavy in her hand as she drew it, bringing it up just in time to deflect Celia's blade. Metal bit against metal. Stella wasn't a bad fighter, but she wasn't used to the weight of Harvey's favorite weapon, and Celia obviously had training, driving her back step by step.

She gritted her teeth and went on the offensive, knocking aside Celia's arm and aiming for her face. Celia pivoted at the last moment, sheathing her knife and grabbing Stella's arm in one smooth motion. Stella didn't have time to prepare before she yanked her forward and sent her crashing into a display of wine glasses.

The glasses shattered against the floor, the metal shelf smacking against the ground. Harvey's knife tumbled from her hand. Celia kicked her in the knee, eliciting a yelp of pain from her, then grabbed her braid and jerked her head back.

"Let's see who's been such a pain in my side," she crooned.

Stella's mask was ripped away. Celia's eyes went wide.

"*You*," she breathed.

Stella snarled. "That's right, bitch. *Me*."

She slammed her head into Celia's face, the crunch of bone telling her she made contact. Stella whirled, grabbing Celia by the front of her shirt and shoving her backwards into another shelf. Celia let out a grunt as an entire shelf's worth of little glass trinkets rained down on her.

Stella wrapped a hand around her throat. "I heard you wanted to kill me. I'm just returning the favor."

Celia snarled and kicked off the shelf, knocking Stella off-balance. The two of them slammed into the floor, pain shooting through Stella's backside as Celia landed on top of her.

"Oh, I never liked you," she murmured, using the tip of a blade to trace Stella's jawline. "I thought you were suspicious. Father told me to wait before taking any action against you." The knife dug into her skin, drawing blood. "But the wait has made this even more satisfying."

Stella bared her teeth. "You won't get Lochridge."

She smirked. "Thank the heavens that isn't a decision you get to make. Lochridge is *ours*, and there's not a damn thing you can do about it."

Celia had made the mistake of leaving her hair unbound, her white-blonde locks long enough for Stella to get a good grip. She yanked on her hair *hard*, and Celia went with it, her head smacking against the corner of a nearby shelf. It distracted her long enough for Stella to shove her off and make it to the top of the fight.

"I know all about your plan," she snarled, noting the blood staining Celia's pale hair. "You're going to turn on my gang and render it as helpless as the Ravens are now." She punched her in the face. "I don't intend to let you."

Celia's eyes gleamed. "You think you're oh-so-clever, don't you? There isn't a damn thing you can do to stop it. You're alone. You're weak." She grinned. "And you're an unworthy opponent."

Stella noticed the shard of glass gleaming in Celia's hand just before her arm shot up. She jerked her head back, and the glass—aimed for her eyes—sliced open her cheek. Blood poured down her face, but Stella barely noticed as she punched Celia again and grabbed her arm, squeezing her wrist until the glass tumbled out of her fingers.

It disarmed Celia, but the movement cost her the top of the fight. Celia twisted, throwing Stella off of her and sending her crashing into the broken glass on the floor. She was shaking by the time she made it to her feet, bloody and bruised, her mouth set in a snarl.

Celia tossed her hair over her shoulder as she stood up. "Had enough?"

She shifted into a better stance. "Never."

She twirled a knife. "You're brave, I'll give you that."

Stella saw her fingers shift, and she leaned to the side as Celia threw the knife. It flew past her head, and Stella smirked.

"Missed me," she drawled.

Celia grinned.

And then she lunged.

Bloody *hell*, she moved fast. Stella tried to sidestep, but her foot slid on broken glass, leaving her wide open for the vicious elbow Celia sent

421

flying towards her face. Her head whipped to the side and she stumbled, crashing into a shelf and giving Celia all the time she needed to draw her remaining knife.

"Like I said," she snarled, stabbing Stella in the same shoulder she had during their first encounter in the streets, "you are *weak*."

Stella cried out. Celia yanked the knife out and prepared for another blow, but Stella let her knees go weak, sending her to the floor just as Celia lunged. The knife flashed above her head, giving Stella the opportunity to push off the shelf and slam into Celia. She crashed into a table, her weight breaking the fragile wood.

"You *bitch*!" she screamed.

Stella ducked as she hurled the knife. She grabbed the first thing within her reach—a little glass angel that was rather pretty—and chucked it right back. Celia avoided it with practiced ease as she scooped up Harvey's knife and threw herself at Stella.

Unarmed and unsure of what to do, Stella could only raise her arms in a meager attempt at blocking the attack. Celia's momentum sent them both to the ground. She snarled and raised the knife above her head; Stella threw up her arm, catching Celia's wrist before the knife could go through her.

"I am going to kill you," Celia whispered.

The tip of the blade quivered right above Stella's right eye. She gritted her teeth, her arm straining to keep the knife away from her face, but it was hard when Celia was putting a considerable amount of weight down on her. "You haven't yet," she panted, gathering up the last of her bravado. "What makes you think you're going to now?"

Celia grunted and pushed the knife down another fraction of an inch. "You're pathetic, Rook. It wouldn't matter if you knew every fine detail of my father's plan. You can't stop it. Trace has had his eye on Lochridge for years, and when he wants something, he damn well gets it." Stella's arm shook under her weight. "All of this? You're only delaying the inevitable."

"And what's that?" Stella gritted out. "What's your plan here? To kill an entire city and rule over the ruins? You're shooting yourself in the foot."

She laughed. "No. We're going to build it up again with people that actually listen, people who don't act like vigilantes who can save it. Your

gangs have ruined this city, but my father is going to make it shine again."
Her teeth gleamed white, and the knife tip came so close that it was all
Stella could see. "Lochridge is his prize. It is *my* prize. And I will not let
it slip between my fingers."

"Your prize, but my home." Stella reached out with her other hand
searching for something, *anything*, to help. "If you think we are going to
sit back and let you destroy everything we've worked for, then you're
dead wrong."

She hummed to herself. "That's exactly what you've done so far.
Does the Raven gang ring a bell? They're dead, darling."

"Not all of them," Stella whispered. Her hand closed in on something.
"But you are."

She moved her head to the side as she let her arm drop. Celia's weight
sent the knife crashing down into the floor right next to her, the blade
sinking into the floorboard. Stella's arm shot up, the ceramic paperweight
she'd grabbed a comforting weight in her hand as she brought it crashing
against Celia's temple.

Celia went limp. Stella let out a scream of frustration and shoved her
off. She staggered to her feet, gasping for breath, soaked in blood and
sweat. Her entire body throbbed, but she ignored the pain as she limped
around Celia.

"Who's unworthy now?" she sneered.

She nudged her with her boot. Anger got the better of her and she
delivered a swift but vicious kick to her face, but aside from her head
jerking back from the force, she didn't move. Celia was out cold, her
platinum hair forming a pale halo around her head. Stella fingered the
gun still holstered at her side. She hadn't used it out of fear that the noise
would attract more unwanted attention. As much as she wanted Celia
dead, a gunshot wouldn't do her any good.

She yanked Harvey's knife out of the floorboard and pocketed it.
After a moment's thought, she positioned herself next to one of the
shelves and pushed, sending it and all the glass figurines on it crashing
down onto Celia.

There. She wouldn't be moving anytime soon, if ever again. Stella
paused long enough to spit on Celia's prone form before stalking out of
the shop.

CHAPTER 66

"Wake up, feathers."

Jordan opened his eyes to see Zoey Rook standing over him, hands on her hips.

He bolted upright. "What's the matter?"

Declan and Mateo stirred, the former sleepily reaching for his rifle. But Mateo's gaze traveled past Zoey and to the dark figure standing behind her, her face pale in the moonlight...

"Jasmin!" he shouted, scrambling to his feet. He crashed into her, and she buried her face into his shoulder. "Are you alright?" he demanded, trying to get a look at her face. "Are you hurt? Where's your family?"

"She's unharmed," Zoey said, "and her family is locked up with your father." She made a face. "Harvey found them out on patrol today."

"Winston's gone," Jasmin said numbly. "He killed him."

Jasmin's older brother. Jordan let out a curse.

"That's the least of our problems," Zoey said lowly. She nodded at Jasmin. "I think there's some food in that sack over there. Why don't you get something on your stomach?"

She nodded and shuffled over to where Zoey indicated. Something was wrong—Jordan could tell just by her expression. Mateo picked up on it too and tried to follow, but Zoey grabbed his arm and hauled him past the rocks, gesturing for Jordan and Declan to come.

"What happened?" Mateo demanded. "Something's wrong with her."

Zoey's face was grim. "My brother just tried to force himself on her. If me and Stella hadn't been there..."

Oh, shit. Mateo's face went lethal, his eyes narrowing with anger that Jordan rarely saw from him.

"What do you mean," he growled, "that your brother tried to *force himself*—"

Zoey slapped a hand over his mouth. "*Quiet.* She's traumatized enough. Stella knocked Harvey out, but the minute he wakes up, he is going on the hunt. You lot have to stay *hidden.*"

"How in the bloody hell do you expect me—"

"Quiet, Daelik."

"No, he's got a point," Jordan snapped. "That bloody son of a bitch just tried—"

Shit, he couldn't even say it. Zoey had the good sense to look ashamed, and Mateo glared at her as he pushed past her and ran to Jasmin's side.

"That bastard deserves to die," Declan said flatly.

She pressed her lips together. "I have a feeling he's got it coming." She glanced at Jordan. "That's not all. We got spotted by someone trying to make it here, and Stella hung back to take care of them."

Alarm shot through him. "Who? Where?"

"I didn't get a good look at them, but it was on this side of the Barter Streets. I haven't seen her since. We even hung back for a few minutes to see if she would catch up. I thought maybe she'd gone a different way and got here first, but…"

"Shit," Jordan said. This night was *not* going as planned. They'd spent two hours looking for Ravens before the number of patrols made it impossible to do so. Their search had turned up nothing, and since they were rationing the food, Jordan hadn't had a proper meal since heaven knows when. He was already tired and irritated and hungry, but the idea of Stella being in danger…

"Show me where," he demanded.

She raised a brow. "You need to stay here. If Harvey—"

"Screw Harvey. Where's Stella?"

"Here."

Jordan twisted to see Stella stumbling down the hill towards them. She had a hand pressed to her shoulder, blood dripping through, her face stained with bruises. Jordan was moving in an instant, his arms around her before she could fall.

"Who did this?" he demanded.

"Celia," she rasped. "But she's taken care of." Her eyes glinted. "That bitch won't be bothering me again anytime soon."

Zoey shoved Jordan out of the way to get a look at Stella. "How bad are you hurt?"

She examined her shoulder. "I'm going to need stitches. But I don't think it's as bad as the last time."

She squawked. "There was a *last time*?"

Jordan elbowed his way past her. "We've still got the medical supplies you brought. We'll get you patched up in no time."

Stella gave him a grateful smile. He tried to help her sit down, but Zoey wedged herself between them, overtaking the operation.

"*I've* got her," she said pointedly.

He stopped short, his eyes narrowing. "Excuse me?"

"I'm her family, I can take care of her."

"Well, I'm her—" Jordan fumbled the next word. He was her *what*, exactly?

"Both of you, knock it off," Stella said, pulling out of Zoey's grasp and sitting down of her own accord. "Jordan knows how to do stitches. Let him do it."

"I know how to do it!" Zoey yelped.

Stella gave her a flat look. "I watched you attempt to sew up a hole in your favorite shirt last week, and it ended with you spitting mad and the shirt thrown into the fireplace. Let Jordan do it. I need you to go back to the house and control Harvey." She winced as she moved her arm. "I can't deal with Harvey like this. I need to rest."

Zoey huffed. Jordan smirked at her and came to Stella's side.

"Go," Stella said to her cousin. "I mean it. I'm surprised we haven't seen Harvey yet."

She looked between them. "Are you sure?"

"Positive. Now hurry up."

Zoey bit her lip and nodded. "Fine. I expect you back tomorrow, though." She jabbed a finger at Jordan. "And if anything happens—"

"You'll put a bullet through my skull," he finished dryly. "Yes, yes, we get it. Now get out of here."

She sighed and walked away. Jordan turned back to Stella, searching her face. "Where is Celia now?" he asked, digging out the right supplies.

"Dead, hopefully." She probed a bruise on her cheek. "She saw my face. If she *isn't* dead, then she knows exactly who to blame."

"If that's the case, we'll deal with it," he assured her.

"I can't believe that brat did such a number on you," Declan said, blatantly surveying Stella's injuries.

"You haven't seen her fight," Jordan said.

"I get that, but still." He shook his head. "She's messed up."

Stella let out a dark laugh. "That's one way to put it."

Jordan found the gauze right as Mateo appeared at Stella's side and pressed a handkerchief against her shoulder.

"We've got to stop the bleeding," he said quietly.

Quiet rage bled from him. It didn't show in his face, but Jordan could tell from the set of his shoulders, the brutal precision in which he moved. He hadn't seen Mateo this angry in a long time. Stella's brow furrowed as she looked him over. "Are you alright?"

"I'm fine," he said. "But Jasmin's not." He glanced over his shoulder, where Lana now sat with Jasmin, who had barely said a word since she arrived. Mateo's jaw clenched as he turned back to Stella. "Thank you. For saving her."

Her expression hardened. "I'm glad I got there in time. Harvey—"

Mateo's eyes iced over. Jordan cringed. "Might be best not to mention his name," he advised Stella. "Especially around Jas."

She bit her lip but wisely kept quiet. Mateo kept pressure on her wound as Jordan prepped the needle and thread. She hissed through her teeth as he made the first pass, and he gave her an apologetic look. He rarely did this while the person was awake—usually patching up Declan long after his cousin had passed out under the weight of all the liquor he'd consumed. He knew it hurt, but the pain of the needle was better than the fate that awaited her if he left her to bleed out.

"You're right," he said, finishing up the last stitch. "This wasn't nearly as bad."

"Smaller knife," she managed through gritted teeth.

He studied his handiwork, then he and Mateo carefully wrapped up her shoulder, Stella hissing and cursing under her breath. Once her shoulder was squared away, he moved on to the rest of her injuries, because while they weren't fatal, they sure didn't look like they felt good.

"If this is how bad you look, I can only imagine what kind of shape

Celia is in," he remarked.

He rinsed out the handkerchief using a canteen of water and used it to clean off her split knuckles. She looked at the ground, suddenly somber.

"If she's alive…" she whispered.

Jordan's movements turned rough. "She's dead."

"I didn't make sure."

"Then it's not your problem."

"I could have," she said, almost angry. "She was unconscious. I could have slit her throat. I *should* have."

Jordan looked up at her. "No, you shouldn't have." His voice dropped to a whisper. "That would have meant you were doing the same thing you were mad at me for doing." The words caught in his throat, but he forced them out. "If she was unconscious, then the fight was over. No sense in kicking a person who's already down, right?"

Stella stared at him for a moment.

Then she snorted. "I did kick her, actually. Right in the face."

An unexpected laugh burst out of Jordan. A smile twitched on her lips, and she took the handkerchief from Jordan's hand and wiped her face.

"I'm glad I did it," she added. "That bitch had it coming."

Declan sauntered over and plopped down next to Stella. "Don't tell me you're staying here."

She arched a brow. "You don't have to sound so enthused."

He groaned. "This place sucks. This situation sucks. And you're sitting on my favorite rock."

She waved a hand at her bandaged shoulder. "I promise I'm worse off than you."

"You'll be even worse if you don't *move*."

"Dec," Jordan said, exasperated, but he had already shoved Stella out of the way so he could kick back, making himself as comfortable as possible on the weather-beaten stones. "She's injured. Leave her alone."

Stella glared at him as she rose to her feet. "He's lucky I'm injured, or else—"

"Or else, *what?*" he asked, raising both brows. "You're going to kill the only help you've got?"

She looked him up and down. "I wouldn't *kill* you. Just maim or seriously injure."

"I'm *helping* you!"

"You're helping no one by sitting around," she retorted, crossing her arms. She looked at Mateo, and then Jordan, silently extending her lecture to them both. "All of you. We've got a situation on our hands and I'm doing my damn best, but you three are going to have to do more than just sit on your asses and complain."

"Do you think we *want* to be doing this?" Mateo demanded.

Anger leeched off of him. Jordan intervened before anyone could take it any further.

"We are trying," he said. "We went out tonight, but the patrols were so heavy that we didn't make any progress. You said yourself that the best thing we could do was stay hidden." He gestured with both hands. "That's what we're doing."

She blew out a breath. "It's not enough. None of this is. We're running out of time."

"She's right."

They all turned to look at Jasmin as she rose to her feet.

"She's right," she said again, ignoring Mateo as he rushed to her aid. "That man. Silas. I heard him talking to his daughter when they were taking us inside. He made it clear he doesn't want to wait any longer." She cast a pleading look around. "They're going to kill the rest of my family, aren't they?"

"We won't let it come to that," Mateo said, but the words were hollow.

Stella nodded in agreement. "We're going to stop him *before* anything else happens."

"How?" she demanded.

Stella opened her mouth, then closed it. Jordan knew exactly what that meant.

She didn't know.

None of them did.

CHAPTER 67

Stella's entire body ached by morning. Everything hurt, her shoulder throbbing something fierce, but all she cared about was being able to cover up her injuries. She told Jordan it was because she didn't want Silas catching onto what she'd done, but deep inside, a small, extremely vain part of her was clinging to the idea that she wouldn't be beautiful with her face marked up, that she wouldn't be graceful with her bruised knee threatening to give her a limp.

It was silly, she knew. But that didn't stop her from groaning inwardly as she touched the bruise on her temple.

Jordan sat down next to her, the weak light from the rising sun gilding his light hair. "How are you feeling?"

"Sore." She rubbed the bruise. "And ugly."

He studied it. "You're still pretty. Now you've just got battle wounds."

Declan made a gagging noise from behind them.

Stella shot him a look. He sat next to Mateo, who hadn't strayed from Jasmin's side since last night. Lana was on her other side, the two holding a gentle conversation that was too quiet for Stella to hear.

She felt bad for both of them. Jasmin, for everything that happened yesterday, and Lana, for forcing her to stay in such a poor location. The beach provided an amazing hideaway, but it lacked resources, and Stella had forgotten to bring her stash of extra supplies in her rush to get Jasmin away from Harvey last night. Not to mention that the tiny stretch of beach was starting to feel claustrophobic with so many people taking up space. She was surprised the boys hadn't torn down the rocks in their desire to get out of here.

Jordan shot Declan a glare before turning back to Stella. "Do you think you'll go back to your house soon? I know you were going to get Zoey to cover for you, but you can only stay away for so long. Especially with Har—with You-Know-Who seeking you out."

Stella ran a hand through her tangled hair. "I need to. I'll be the best one to handle damage control, and it's going to look even more suspicious on my part if I don't show."

She didn't want to go back. Even though she was in pain, even though she didn't sleep a wink all night, she'd rather stay here on the beach with Jordan and the others than return home. At least here Silas and Celia weren't hovering over her shoulder, Harvey wouldn't corner her to exact revenge, and Marcus couldn't give her a disapproving look for allowing someone to get a blow to her face.

It sickened her that she felt more at home on the wrong territory than she did in the house she grew up in, but that was her new reality.

"Do you think—" Jasmin swallowed, then started again. "Do you think *he* will be mad at you for helping me?"

Stella fought back a sigh. "It's not a matter of *if* he will be mad, but rather *how* mad he will be."

She hugged herself. "I appreciate what you did."

Stella gave her a weak smile, but she was uneasy. Harvey wasn't going to just be *mad*; he would be livid. Stella had not only stopped his sick idea of fun, but she'd injured him, and Harvey Rook never forgave those who drew blood on him.

She rose to her full height. "I'm going to handle it. Everything is going to work out."

Declan gave her a skeptical look. "Who are you trying to convince here?"

Herself, she realized. She gave her head a small shake. "I need to go."

Jordan caught her arm. "Be careful, alright? If there's trouble, get out and regroup. Don't get in over your head."

"I'll be careful," she promised.

Jordan pressed a kiss to her temple, but his expression was still concerned. Stella forced a smile as she turned away.

The first step was to get inside the house.

Stella thought it would be hard. She was still wearing her night clothes, and the black attire would raise questions if she was seen, which meant she had to make it through Rose territory, across the Rook property, into the house, and safely inside her room without being spotted. Making it across her territory proved easy when she knew every shortcut and dark alley like the back of her hand. And when she slipped through the hidden gate at the back of her father's property, ready to make a run for it through the rose garden, the one ally she had on this side of Lochridge greeted her.

"I thought you'd come this way," Zoey said, eyeing her up and down. "How are you feeling?"

"You'd rather not hear the answer to that," Stella said with a grin.

Zoey returned it, but it quickly faded. "Harvey's pissed."

"I knew he would be. Has he figured out who it was?"

"He suspects it was you. I've played dumb on the whole situation because I didn't know how you wanted to spin it. But it's going to be hard, especially with you being gone this morning." She cringed. "He's ready for blood."

Stella eyed the pathway through the garden. "I'll handle him as soon as I make myself presentable."

"That's not all of it," Zoey added, crossing her arms. "Harvey rose hell when he woke up, and Silas went to tell Celia and discovered she was missing. He and Tobias went into town about two hours ago to look for her."

The breath whooshed out of her. "That's good, actually. They won't be lurking around while I deal with Harvey."

Zoey plucked a rose from a nearby bush and began picking the petals off one by one. "I'm not liking the energy today. Something feels off."

"Everything is off."

"This feels different. It's like we're on the edge of a cliff, and everyone but the two of us is ready to jump."

Stella didn't know how to respond to that. "Make sure I've got a clear path," she said quietly. "No one can see me like this."

Zoey nodded and walked away, dropping a handful of red petals on the ground behind her. Stella gave her two minutes to cause a distraction before launching into a sprint, streaking up the path through the garden and to the trellis on the side of the house. She was up it in five seconds flat, tumbling into her bedroom a moment later, her face flushed and hair wild.

Back in the safety of her room, Stella loosened a breath she didn't know she was holding. She caught a glimpse of herself in the vanity mirror and winced. She was an absolute mess in every sense of the word. Her hair was tangled and hanging in her eyes. The bruise on her face was an ugly purplish color. Her clothes were ripped, and if they were any color but black, they would show the bloodstains that had dried overnight, leaving her feeling icky all over. Sand clung to her boots from trampling all over the beach, and there were dark circles under her eyes that she didn't recall being there before.

Cursing under her breath, she stripped off her clothes and shoved them under her bed. The bandage over her shoulder was still holding firm, so she washed up the best she could using the basin in her room and threw on loose trousers and a cream-colored blouse. Her scalp ached from where Celia pulled her hair. Brushing it was a painful experience, but Stella kept the cursing to a minimum as she wrangled her hair into a semblance of its usual style. A little makeup helped with the state of her face. She couldn't erase the bruising entirely, but she covered the circles under her eyes and lightened her features enough to suggest that she'd rested well and hadn't spent the night in a catfight with Celia Tradow.

Her family was in the kitchen when she descended the stairs. "You should drag her ass home right now," Harvey was saying. Marcus stood on the other side of the table, his arms crossed, and Stella didn't have to ask to know she was the topic of the conversation. "She can't get away with this!"

"You don't know that Stella was the one to hit you," Evelyn said calmly.

"Oh, I know it. That brat is going to answer for it, too."

"Someone's in a mood," Stella drawled, leaning against the doorframe.

Harvey stood up so fast his chair flipped over. "You little bitch," he snarled, lunging for her.

His hands reached for her throat. Stella raised her arm, positioning a knife against his throat before he could make contact.

His amber eyes narrowed to slits as he realized it was his own blade. "I knew it was you," he growled. The words were low, guttural, deadly. Harvey was the kind who could make a person run for their life with just a look, but Stella refused to be intimidated.

She angled her head. "What?"

"Don't play dumb. You knocked me out!"

"Yes," Stella snapped, "because you were trying to force yourself on that girl."

"She was a prisoner," Marcus said, coming to Harvey's side. "One that you allowed to escape, didn't you?"

Stella gave them a sharp smile. "I personally escorted her to a safe location. That poor girl had been through enough. You killed her brother right in front of her, locked her up, and tried to take her innocence. I wasn't going to stand idly by and watch it happen."

Harvey gritted his teeth, refusing to back away from the knife primed to slit open his throat. "Those Ravens forfeited their lives long ago. She deserved it."

"*She wasn't a Raven.*"

"She was Daelik-adjacent," Marcus said.

"So that's the standard now?" Stella demanded. "We're not going to stop with the Ravens, we're going to kill anyone who's had a connection to them?" She raked an icy glare over the room. "Lochridge doesn't have much in the way of innocent civilians, but you're going to kill them too?"

Marcus pinched the bridge of his nose. "The Wests are our ticket to trapping the rest of the Ravens. We were using Jasmin to get to the Daeliks."

Her blood boiled. "Just like what they did with Liam?"

The words cut through the air like a knife. Evelyn flinched; Zoey sucked in a breath; Marcus averted his gaze; even Harvey had the good sense to back up an inch.

Stella's voice trembled with rage. "You both make me sick."

She threw Harvey's knife down at his feet and stalked away. Behind her, she heard Evelyn say, her voice gentle yet firm, "She's right. We don't condone such actions, not in this house. Your fight with the Daeliks should not extend to the entire city."

Despite herself, a smile tugged on Stella's lips. Evelyn didn't put her foot down often, but when she did, Marcus usually respected it. Perhaps some good would come out of this situation after all. Her steps were a little lighter as she aimed for the stairs

But then the front door burst open and Silas stormed in, his icy eyes alight with rage.

"Somebody attacked my daughter," he said.

CHAPTER 68

Tobias carried Celia in while Evelyn rushed to track down the family doctor. Stella felt her blood go cold as she took in Celia's limp form. Still alive—the faint rise and fall of her chest was a testament to that. She looked worse in the morning light, the cuts and bruises on her face making her skin seem ghostly pale. Stella warmed with pride at seeing the Tradow heir in such a dismal state. Beside her, Harvey cocked a brow at her dark attire, and Marcus paused for a split-second to frown at her before ushering Tobias into the house.

"Who did this?" her father demanded, coming to Silas' side.

Silas looked one step away from killing someone. "I don't know, but I intend to find out."

Stella had to do something. "It was probably the Ravens," she muttered. "I don't gamble, but if I did, my money would be on Jordan Daelik."

"Mine too," Zoey said.

"That bastard was definitely behind this," Harvey agreed, face lighting up as he took in Celia's injuries. The doc arrived and did a quick inspection before ordering Tobias to bring her to the sick room. Silas remained rooted to the spot, his face ice-cold as he watched his daughter be carried away.

"If those Ravens are behind this," he said softly, "then they shall pay with their lives."

He turned in the other direction and stalked down the hall. It took Stella a moment to realize he was heading for the basement—the basement where the leading Raven was being held hostage.

"Wait!" she cried, lunging after him.

Silas was quicker than she gave him credit for. By the time she reached him, he was already through the basement door, standing in front of John Daelik with fire in his eyes. John had seen better days; he hadn't been given an opportunity to clean up after the battle, meaning his clothes were ripped and stained with blood. His light brown hair hung in his eyes as he glared up at Silas, the ropes tying his wrists to the bar behind him the only thing keeping him from lunging.

"Your son attacked my Celia," Silas snarled. "Tell me where he is!"

John spat on the ground. "If I knew where that coward ran off to, I'd track him down and kill him myself. He probably fled."

"Then who attacked my daughter?"

"It could have been any of the Ravens," Stella said, positioning herself between them. "Just step away. He's been down here this whole time, so how could he know anything?"

Silas didn't take his eyes off John. "I'd wager that he knows where his spawn slunk off to."

"I don't know anything!"

"Maybe *she* knows, then." He turned to Lillian, who reared back. "Tell me, Miss Daelik. Where is your son?"

Her voice trembled. "I don't know."

Silas shrugged. "Perhaps this will change your mind."

He drew a gun and pointed it at her face. Stella's heart dropped. She had expected Celia to be mad over the attack; what she hadn't counted on was *Silas* getting in a frenzy. She had to defuse the situation before it went too far.

"What are you doing?" she demanded, pushing the gun away. "We can't kill them yet! We haven't caught Jordan!"

His finger tightened on the trigger. "Jordan Daelik refuses to fall for our trap. I am done waiting. We kill them, and the others will make themselves known in due time." He cocked the gun. "These two are a liability that I refuse to let live a second longer."

This was not good. Stella scrambled for something to say.

"You're taking out your anger on the wrong people," she snapped. "You're furious your daughter was attacked, so you're going to kill someone who had nothing to do with it? Leave them alive to serve as bait so that you might catch the real culprit."

"The real culprit refuses to show his face."

"So force his hand," Marcus said from behind them. "We will *make* him show himself."

Silas tilted his head thoughtfully, still eyeing John. Stella's breath hitched as she slowly positioned herself in front of the gun, wrapping both hands around the barrel. She hoped John wasn't so dense as to not realize that she was actively helping them, doing everything in her power to keep them alive as long as possible. She was vaguely aware of Lillian trying to get as far away as she could, of the West family trying to do the same on the far side of the basement. Once John and Lillian were out of the way, they would be next in line, and they were well aware of that fact.

Silas' eyes cleared, and Stella knew he had made a decision.

"Tomorrow," he said. "High noon. Everyone will gather in the middle ground of the Barter Streets, and when the sun reaches its peak, I will start killing." He swept a gaze over the entire room. "Spread the word. Make sure those Ravens hear about it. If they don't show their faces by high noon, *everyone dies.*"

She didn't miss John's throat bobbing. But Silas had already turned away, storming up the stairs while he shoved his gun back into its hidden holster. Marcus trailed after him; Harvey and Zoey exchanged a look before following suit. Stella swept a warning gaze across the room of prisoners before dashing after them.

"That's your plan?" she demanded of Silas. "Execute everyone at high noon?"

"Yes," he said through gritted teeth. "The Ravens will meet their end. And if the rest don't show, then we will resume our hunt with renewed vigor."

"And if they try to attack while we're there?"

"My army will be there to stop them. Alongside the entirety of your gang."

He turned away. Stella made to follow him, but Zoey grabbed her arm and hauled her into the parlor.

"Everyone dies," she hissed.

"I heard that part," Stella snapped. "We have to act fast before Jordan's parents —"

"No, Stella. Everyone dies. *Everyone*—and he wasn't just looking at the Daeliks when he said it."

Wait—Silas had swept a look over everyone present, her and Marcus and the others.

Everyone dies.

The realization slapped Stella in the face.

"He's not just going to kill the Ravens," she breathed. "He's going to turn on us, too."

Everyone would be gathered in one place, the apparent victory causing them to let down their guards—perfect for a shootout.

Stella grabbed Zoey's arm. "Warn Jordan and the others. Tell him to get his Ravens ready to move at high noon tomorrow."

Her brows drew together. "But that's exactly what Silas wants."

The gears in her head whirled, a plan coming together. "I have an idea, but we're going to need more than just the two of us." She explained it as best she could, the words rough and slopped together. It wasn't much, but Stella didn't have the time to think of something better. "Tell Jordan to get the Ravens ready to attack, and I'll handle the rest." Her eyes gleamed. "This ends tomorrow."

Zoey searched her face, then gave her a swift nod. "Consider it done."

Stella didn't wait around to see Zoey off. She turned on her heel and ran after Silas, who was now sitting vigil over Celia as the doc carefully wrapped a bandage around her head. Marcus and Evelyn hovered nearby as a show of support. Harvey was there, but he seemed more interested in inspecting his knife for damage than looking after Celia.

"Your plan is stupid," Stella said flatly.

Silas looked up, eyes narrowing. "Excuse me?"

"The Ravens will never show if you've got your entire army waiting for them," she said. "They simply don't have enough people to make it feasible. If there's anything I know about Jordan, it's that he won't risk his own hide to fight through that many people."

"Then we kill his father and be done with it," he snapped.

"Yes," Stella agreed. "But what if you could kill two birds with one stone?"

He angled his head. "I'm listening."

Stella stepped into the room, avoiding looking at Celia. "If I were in Jordan's shoes, and I heard that my enemy would be gathering in the Barter Streets in its entirety after days of patrols combing through my turf, I would take advantage of it. Raven territory will be free of watchful eyes for the first time in days. The fact that Celia was attacked suggests not all of them are gone, perhaps too scared to make a run for it with so many patrols going about." She shrugged. "If it were me, I'd use the opportunity to get out of the city."

Marcus narrowed his eyes. "What are you suggesting?"

She examined her nails. "I'm not in charge here, but if I was, I would take half of Silas' people and half of the Roses and position them on the outskirts of Raven territory, ready to intercept anyone who tries to flee. With their leader about to die and nothing to be done about it, I'd wager a lot of money that they'll try to run." She dropped her hand. "So be ready to catch them."

Marcus and Silas exchanged a look.

"And what if the Ravens hear about this plan and decide to attack while our forces are weaker?" Silas asked. "Seems an awful lot like setting us up for failure."

"They *won't* attack if you lead them to believe that your full army will be with you." She raised a brow. "Besides, even if they did, I am sure we could handle them. They're weak and unorganized. What damage could they possibly do?"

They exchanged another look. "That could work," Marcus murmured.

"Of course it will work," she snapped.

"You came up with the idea to use John as bait," Silas said. "And that has worked splendidly."

She huffed at the sarcasm. "Because I didn't realize Jordan held his parents to such a low regard. If he's not willing to come for them, then we will catch him with this new plan. And if he *is* willing, then we're prepared for that, too. Either way, we come out ahead." She nodded at Celia. "And it will be a perfect opportunity to avenge your poor daughter."

Stella was rather proud of the bruises she'd left on Celia, but for now she could only hope Celia wouldn't awaken before her plan went into effect. The fact that she was still unconscious was promising, but Stella's luck only ran so far. If she woke up...

She shoved the thought away. "Jordan really did a number on her."

"Just like someone did a number on you," Silas observed, studying the bruise on her face. "Where did that beauty come from?"

Shit. Someone had finally brought attention to it. "Harvey," she lied smoothly.

Harvey scoffed. "I didn't hit you."

"Yes, you did," she deadpanned. "Right before I knocked you out last night." She cocked her head to the side. "You don't remember?"

"The concussion must have given him short-term amnesia," the doctor said without looking up from Celia.

Harvey looked at her, lip curling as if he could taste the lie. Stella held his gaze, but her injuries pulsed with pain, reminding her of exactly how much trouble she would be in if the people in this room discovered the truth.

Marcus blew out a breath. "I think Stella's idea has potential. It wouldn't hurt to set up a patrol on the outskirts of Raven territory in any case."

She was grateful for him steering the conversation back in the right direction. Silas looked at Celia for a long moment before nodding.

"It has merit," he agreed. "I'll assign half my men to watch the southernmost portion of the border. Marcus, have your men block the west side. We'll be at the Barter Streets to keep them from slipping into this side of Lochridge." His expression was cold. "We'll trap them in and pick them off one by one."

As horrific as that sounded, the first step of Stella's plan was working beautifully. "I'll tell our side," she offered, glancing at Marcus. "Since it was my idea. I'll pick out the men and give them their instructions."

He nodded. "Have it done by nightfall." Stella raised her hand in a mock salute and turned to leave, but then Marcus grabbed her arm. "I'm glad you're coming around on this," he said, quietly enough only she could hear. "I know you had your doubts about Silas, but look how it turned out." His eyes were bright. "I was right. We come out on top, always. Remember that."

Stella plastered a smile on her face. "I will."

Her stomach churned as slipped out the door, leaving everyone behind her. Everyone except Evelyn, who trailed her out of the room.

"Can I help you, Mother?" she asked.

Evelyn put her hands on her hips, her voice low. "Harvey was hit in the back of the head."

"So?"

"So, how could he have hit you when all evidence points to you sneaking up behind him and landing the blow?"

Stella pressed her lips together. "We got shuffled around in the fight and I got a lucky hit while he was turned around." Her eyes narrowed. "Though I'm interested as to why you think I would lie about it."

She laughed under her breath. "Oh, Stella. I know you better than you think."

Her fingernails dug into her palms. "Are you accusing me of something, Mother?"

Evelyn shrugged gracefully. "I know you didn't like Celia. She shows up injured, and you arrive limping around." At Stella's expression, Evelyn shook her head. "Don't think I didn't notice you trying to hide it. The others may have overlooked it, but I know my daughter." Her hazel eyes met Stella's. "You're even more cunning than your father is, and I have a feeling that I don't even know the half of it."

Stella held her mother's gaze for a long moment.

"Harvey injured me," she said plainly. "And I did not attack Celia because I was too busy dealing with him last night. So I would appreciate it if you kept your accusations to yourself while I go give orders to my men."

And with that, she stalked away, unable to shake the feeling of Evelyn's eyes on her long after she walked out the door.

CHAPTER 69

Everyone dies.

Jordan heard the words coming out of Zoey's mouth, but he was having trouble comprehending them. *Stella has a plan*, she said. *The only person dying tomorrow is Silas.*

But that didn't stop his heart from racing long after she left.

"This is madness," Declan spat. "We don't have enough people to take on Silas."

"We don't," Jordan agreed. "But if Stella wants us to be there, then we'll be there. We have to try."

"Stella is going to get us killed alongside your parents."

Lana sucked in a breath. Jordan glared at his cousin. "Tone down the doom and gloom, will you?"

"I trust her," Mateo volunteered.

Declan snorted. "You fancy her because she saved your girl."

"She defied her family to save my girl," he corrected. "At her own expense. Which is an act that makes me tend to trust a person."

He turned to Jordan. "The group we have at the Bottle might be riled up, but they aren't enough."

"We have Stella. And Zoey. And however many allies they can gather up by tomorrow."

"Which could be none!"

He let out an angry breath. "What else are we going to do, Declan? Sit here? Search for allies we do not have? I am tired of waiting for a miracle to bail us out. I want to fight—I want my revenge against that

443

asshole. He's killed my people, he's taken my family hostage, he let my brother's girl get attacked by a madman, and he's plotting to kill *my* girl as we speak! This is *our* city. Not Silas', not Trace's. *Ours.* I don't care if it's a losing battle—I am still going to fight it with my head held high, and I'm going to keep fighting until I win or until I'm dead, whichever it may be." He rose to his full height. "I'm sick of hiding. If Stella wants me there at high noon, then that's where I'll be. I don't care if you come along or not."

Dec groaned. "Of course I'll be there. You don't have to be so dramatic about it." He spat on the ground. "I'm going to need something stronger to drink."

"That's the spirit," Mateo deadpanned.

Lana edged forward. "You're going to fight him?"

"We don't have much choice, Lanabug," Jordan said. "It's our only shot at getting Ma and Pa back."

"My family, too," Jasmin murmured.

Jordan's jaw clenched. "The two of you will stay here. There's no way in hell I'm risking you."

"We could take them to the Bottle," Mateo said. "The fellas there will leave their wives and kids behind. It's just as hidden as this place, and at least then they'll be inside and have food and water and supplies. We're stranded out here. But you know, just in case…"

In case we don't make it back. Mateo didn't say the words out loud, but Jordan could read it in his eyes. He nodded, throat working. "Good idea."

Bloody hell, they were really doing this. Jordan rubbed his temples in an attempt to sort through his whirling thoughts. They had one chance—a chance that hinged entirely on whatever plan Stella had concocted in the last hour.

Everyone dies.

Nothing seemed to be going in their favor, but Jordan had played enough cards to know that the odds could change in the blink of an eye. He could only hope that they would change enough today for them to get an advantage tomorrow—otherwise, they were all dead.

"No pressure," he whispered to himself, then let out a short laugh that bordered on hysteria. "No pressure at all."

The middle ground of the Barter Streets was directly in the center of the city, equal distances from the Red Harbor and the western edge of Lochridge. The city didn't have an official town square, but if it did, the middle ground would be it.

Stella's hair was pulled into a ruthlessly tight braid. A white rose rested in her left hand, and she twirled it around, grateful to have something to fidget with. Her eyes narrowed against the onslaught of wind. The sun was shining, but she could see the ominous presence of thunderclouds in the distance, a wicked storm riding in on the ocean breeze. It would be here by nightfall, but for now, Lochridge bathed in an eerie light that had her on edge.

The area was surrounded by Roses and Silas' men, all of them armed to the teeth. She couldn't help but notice that Silas' people were antsy, their hands never straying from their weapons. They were making a good show of surveying the area, looking for trouble, but she could tell that they were keeping careful eyes on the surrounding Roses. Stella herself was no exception; she caught Tobias watching her and held his gaze until a commotion on the far side of the square drew her attention.

It was her father. He walked with his head held high, the gray streaks in his hair catching the midday sun. His white suit was glaringly bright, the rose tucked in his shirt matching the one Stella twirled between her fingers. There was a bounce in his step Stella had never seen before, his eyes alight with triumph. He had been riding high all morning. Twenty years of blood and strife were about to end. A month ago, Stella would have been just as happy if she thought John Daelik and his Ravens were about to meet their demise. But so much had changed since then. *She* had changed. And now...

Now, her stomach twisted into knots just thinking about it.

Harvey walked behind Marcus, grinning as he escorted John and Lillian to the center of the square. More Roses brought in the rest of Jasmin's family, who frantically searched the crowd for an ally but were met with unfriendly gazes. A sleek black motorcar pulled in a minute later, and Silas stepped out, adjusting the angle of his hat as he walked towards the group. He wore his usual green-and-white striped suit, his light hair slicked back. The gun from yesterday was now holstered in plain sight, and although his head was high, there was a hardness in his eyes as he looked over the assembled crowd. Flocks of ravens gathered on the rooftops, their beady eyes watching the scene unfolding below.

Hands tied behind their backs, John and Lillian were shoved to their knees. The Wests were allowed to remain at the edge of the group, guarded by the Roses, but as soon as the Daeliks were gone, they would take their place.

John, to his credit, seemed unafraid. He lifted his chin as he watched Marcus join Silas, the two of them standing shoulder-to-shoulder as they addressed the group.

"It's been a delightful journey to get here," Silas called out. "Over two decades' worth of conflict, all about to end. A new era has begun in Lochridge, and I am glad to be at the head of it."

Marcus chimed in. "The White Roses are eternally grateful for Mister Tradow's help. Without him, this may have been impossible. But now, we have finally triumphed over the Ravens! Victory is ours!"

The Roses let out a wild cheer. Silas' men remained silent, as did Stella. She took a moment to survey the square. Besides Marcus and Harvey, Evelyn and the rest of her family were present. Her mother hadn't taken her eyes off of Lillian the entire time, a sadness in her gaze that made Stella's heart wrench. The two had been friends long before the feud started, and they'd never stopped—the feud had separated them physically, but Stella had a feeling that her mother had never let go of their friendship. And with her one breath away from death, she supposed Evelyn had no problem showing it now.

Stella assessed the crowd, studying the faces. Half of Silas' army was here, just as decided. Half of the Roses were present as well, though Silas' people outnumbered them ever-so-slightly—especially considering that Zoey's face was not among them. Stella searched for her cousin but was unable to find her before the cheering died down and Marcus resumed his speech.

"The Raven gang has almost ended," he shouted. "All we lack is its heir. Once we have him, peace will reign over Lochridge. *We* will be the winners of this war, and there is nothing any of the Daeliks can do about it." He looked down at John, and pain shot through Stella's heart as she looked at her father. For a fleeting moment, he looked like a madman—deranged, driven by fury and the lust of revenge, his life's work amounting to the death of his old friend. "John Daelik, I sentence you to death for your crimes against my family." His lips pulled back, showing his teeth. "And I love to think you will die knowing that I have won."

"That's where you're wrong, Mister Rook."

It wasn't John who spoke.

All eyes swung to Silas as he drew his gun and pointed it at Marcus' head.

"It's high noon," he said softly, checking his pocket watch, the gun never wavering. "And I am pleased to inform you that *I* have won."

CHAPTER 70

Silas' people moved so fast that the Roses were blindsided.

Tobias leapt forward, knocking Marcus' gun out of his hand before he could draw it fully. Stella saw her father being shoved to his knees beside John before two men grabbed her from behind. She whirled, reaching for a weapon, but her wrists were seized and yanked behind her back. She got a quick glance of the rest of the crowd—Silas' men turning on the Roses, relieving them of their weapons before they had time to react, her people disarmed so easily that it ashamed her to be their leader.

Silas had prepared adequately, for he had no less than six people go for Harvey. Even then, her cousin put up a fight that ended with one dead before they got him to the ground, his chest against the cobblestones and his hands pinned behind his back. He snarled, trying to wriggle free.

Then Stella's view was ripped away as she was thrown to the ground next to Marcus. Evelyn was shoved down beside her a moment later. Even with her hands behind her back, Stella clenched the rose, the thorns digging into her palm.

Silence reigned for a few seconds as Silas tucked his pocket watch back into his blazer.

Then John Daelik threw back his head and laughed.

It boomed off the buildings, scaring the ravens into flight. Stella couldn't fathom what he possibly found so funny. Silas apparently didn't either, because he swung the gun around to point at John.

"Silence," he snapped.

John quit laughing, but he still smiled ear-to-ear. Silas' lip curled as he looked at him, then swept a gaze over the others.

"You're all fools," he breathed. "Fools chasing a fantasy that was never meant to be. Blinded by rage, obsessed over a conflict you can't even remember the origins of." He shook his head. "How idiotic you are."

"What is this?" Marcus spat, struggling against Silas' men. "We had an alliance."

"You had an empty promise," Stella said, glaring at Silas. "He never intended to keep it. He's a businessman, and businessmen get what they want. And in this case, he wanted Lochridge."

Silas smirked down at her, and her blood boiled.

"He used the feud to create more conflict than there already was, using the fight to gain the trust of both sides so that he might gain all the intel he needed." Her wrists ached from trying to pull against the men holding her back. "If anyone questioned him, all he had to do was bring up the *deal* to make them back off." Silas kept smiling, and she forged on. "He promised the death of the opposing gang. That was never a lie, and he's done an admirable job at keeping up his end of the bargain. It was the alliance that was a lie—he never wanted to make peace with Lochridge. He wanted to clear it out so that his boss might rule it."

"Smart girl," Silas crooned.

Stella gave him a saccharine smile. "You think you're clever, don't you? Celia thought she was clever, too—right until I smashed a paperweight against her head."

Silas blinked, then his eyes narrowed.

"Bring her here," he barked.

Tobias grabbed Stella by her hair and hauled her to her feet. She hissed through her teeth as he pulled on her already-sore scalp, putting her right in front of Silas, who leveled his gun at her face.

"What did you say?" he hissed. His hand trembled with rage. "Because it sounded an awful lot like you just admitted to attacking my daughter."

Stella bared her teeth in a smile. "Celia is a mean fighter, but she found out the hard way that I'm meaner."

The gun cracked across her face, the blow so hard that Stella felt blood trickling down her face as she looked back at Silas.

"You're pathetic," she whispered, tightening her grip on the rose in her hand. It wasn't time—not yet. "Just like she is."

Silas hit her again. Then again. Stella spat out a mouthful of blood and met his gaze with a bloody smirk.

"Leave her alone!" Evelyn shrieked.

"We had a deal!" Marcus bellowed at the same time. "An alliance! You said you were a man of your word!"

"A man of his word shows it through his actions," Stella panted. "An honest man doesn't have to tell people of his nature."

The next blow sent her head rocking to the side, the only thing holding her upright being Tobias' iron grip. "This filth you call your daughter," Silas said, "is right about many things." He glared at the Roses. "I was sent to eliminate the citizens of Lochridge, anyone that posed a threat to what we were trying to do here. This city is known for its power, its potential. The Red Harbor is the most profitable port on this side of the Great River. We are going to harness it and turn it into something more than the home of a conflict between two deranged men and their bloodthirsty families."

Stella spat on his suit. "Lochridge's power is not something you can *harness*. Its potential resides in its people—if you kill all of us, you kill the very thing that keeps this city running. You can't expect it to be the same."

He shook his head. "No," he said. "I expect it to be *better*. More powerful." He used the barrel of the gun to tilt her chin up, forcing her to look him in the eye. "I can't very well do that if you hooligans are running around, wrecking havoc. So you must go."

"Is that what your boss told the people in Stokes?" she asked. She smiled at the slight widening in his eyes. "I did my research. The first city to fall to Trace's regime was his own hometown. He got screwed over and took out his revenge on *everyone*. And when that wasn't enough, he set his sights on other cities, other places. Lochridge is just the next in a long list of obstacles in his way. What is the master plan here? World domination?"

The words were sarcastic, but Silas shook his head all the same. "Miss Rook, you simply do not understand what we are trying to do here."

"You're trying to kill us," Harvey snarled, still fighting the five people holding him down. It was almost working, too—there was panic in their eyes as they struggled to keep Harvey contained. Stella viewed this as one of the rare instances in which it was beneficial to have a sadistic monster in her family.

"I am trying to revolutionize the world," Silas said. "And if I have to kill people to get there, then so be it."

Marcus scoffed. "You're joking."

"I really don't think he is," John said, eyes narrowing. "You killed my people."

Silas just laughed. "Your people were idiots—reckless, filthy heathens who desired drunken fistfights and gambling halls. They were unorganized and uncivilized. Your son most of all—I don't know what my daughter possibly saw in him, but he was the worst of the lot. And now he's too cowardly to even show his face when the lives of his parents are on the line."

"Tell us something we don't know," Marcus muttered.

Silas' eyes blazed as he rounded on him. "Don't even get me started on your *Roses*. Pretentious, self-absorbed brats, every one of them! You think so highly of yourself when you are just as dimwitted as the rest." He sneered at Stella. "This one is the only one with any brains, and she's put it all to waste working for a man whose ego is so inflated I'm surprised it hasn't burst." He shook his head in disgust. "You all put your trust in me, and it has cost you your lives. What a sorry mistake indeed."

"I never trusted you," Stella said.

He tweaked her chin with the gun. "Is that so?"

Her lip curled. "You're a liar and a manipulator. I knew your intentions from the moment you walked into town." She leaned forward as much as Tobias would allow her. Admittedly, it wasn't much, but Silas still leaned back a hair. "This was all planned. The change in ownership of the Red Harbor? A friend of yours from Stokes. The gang members that quit? They signed contracts to join your Union. You manipulated both sides of the border with nothing but pretty words and a false promise. You've been sinking your claws into this city for weeks now, and everyone has been blind to it—which was exactly your intention all along."

Silas chuckled. "You've got me all figured out, don't you?"

Stella smirked. "I've had you figured out for a while. You're not the only one with a clever scheme. All of this has just been me stalling for

451

time while I wait for reinforcements to arrive." She smiled as she held up the white rose—then unclenched her fingers, letting it fall to the ground. "And here they are."

Silas laughed again. "Silly girl. You—"

He froze at the unmistakable sound of a gun being cocked. And then a voice drawled from behind him, its lethal edge music to Stella's ears.

"Let her go," the heir to the Ravens snarled.

CHAPTER 71

Jordan kept a steady hand as he held his revolver against Silas' skull. Declan and Mateo circled around him, putting themselves on either side of Silas as the rest of the Ravens filled in behind them, all carrying guns and knives and vicious smiles that would make anyone think twice before lifting a finger against them.

"Let her go," he said again. "I don't have to be a sharpshooter to know that a bullet fired from point blank will hit its target."

He would have paid a lot of money to see Silas' expression right then, but instead he settled on Stella's face, which he could just see over Silas' shoulder. She smirked like a cat despite the blood and bruises on her face, Tobias' face a thunderstorm of rage behind her. The rose laid at her feet. That had been their signal to strike—but the fight wasn't over yet.

Jordan leaned down to speak directly into Silas' ear. "Last chance," he whispered. "I stopped playing nice a long time ago."

Slowly, slowly, Silas raised his hands. Jordan plucked the gun out of his fingers, and a small nod from Silas had Tobias releasing Stella. She glared at him as she smoothed her hair.

Jordan handed the spare gun to Mateo and circled around Silas, his revolver never straying from his head. He caught a glimpse of his parents, relief coursing through him as he saw they were alive, if a bit worse for wear. Lillian stared at him with a mixture of anxiety and relief; John just glared. Jordan ignored them as he came to stand shoulder-to-shoulder with Stella, the two of them facing Silas with their heads held high.

Blood dripped down her face from fresh wounds. Jordan didn't know who had delivered the blow, but he knew he was going to kill whoever did it.

Stella was *his girl,* and he wasn't going to let someone lay a finger on her.

Silas let out an unbelieving laugh. "What a nice show of solidarity. But you are still outnumbered."

"Are we?"

Jordan grinned as Zoey's voice rang out. As the Ravens filed in from the south, Zoey appeared from the north, the other half of the White Roses coming in behind her so quietly that Silas hadn't noticed them until it was too late. There were a few hostile looks between the two gangs, but most of the anger was directed towards Silas as both groups fanned out, forming a full circle around the area, completely blocking in Silas and his men.

"Lochridge might have fallen for your trap," Stella said with a smug smile, "but now you've fallen for ours. The Ravens were never going to flee. All I did was get half of your army out of the way while preparing half of mine for the real battle." Her eyes shone. "Surrender now and we'll let you walk out alive."

Silas spluttered. "No—this is not right. You are the heirs to the gangs. Are you telling me that you're working together?" He barked a laugh. "What a ridiculous thought."

Jordan narrowed his eyes. Then he drew his other revolver and handed it to Stella, who cocked it and pointed it at Silas' face, drawing a gasp from someone in the crowd.

He hissed. "Whatever game this is—"

"It's not a game," Jordan snarled. "This city was never yours, and it never will be. Stella and I might not have a lot in common, but we both have an interest in keeping Lochridge safe." He tightened his finger on the trigger. "We might spit in each other's faces every chance we get, but we'll be damned if we're going to let someone else spit in our faces, too."

He could feel John's eyes on him from behind. Betrayal—that had been the look on his face.

Silas curled his lip. "You're still outnumbered."

"Half of your people are squatting on the far side of the city," Stella said flatly.

"And that's exactly where they will stay. We aren't leaving. We aren't giving up just because you put on a show." Silas spat at her feet. "I will give you one chance to pack your things and leave before I kill you all."

"Bold words from a man staring down the barrel of a gun," Zoey called. "Face it, asshole. You're outnumbered."

"Outnumbered," Jordan said, "and outmatched. This is our home, and we will fight tooth and nail to keep it that way."

He snarled. "We're going to revolutionize it!"

"Tough shit," Declan drawled. "You ain't just gonna waltz in here and call the shots." His rifle was about an inch away from poking Silas in the ear. "I would suggest getting out of here while you still have your head intact."

Mateo edged forward. "You're messing with a group of people who don't take lightly to being bothered. If the feud has been any indication, then you know we hold grudges. We're going to have a serious problem if you don't leave."

Silas looked around frantically. All of his men had guns pointed at them, and the Roses that had been detained had gained their weapons back and joined their companions. Marcus and John, still on their knees, alternated between glaring at Silas and each other. Harvey Rook finally broke free as his attackers scattered. He shot to his feet, panting wildly, looking around as if trying to decide who he was supposed to kill. In the end, his feral eyes settled on Silas.

Jordan saw it in Silas' eyes. It was the same look he saw in the interrogation room when a person was a breath away from breaking— the giving up, the silent surrender. He couldn't win here. His people were outnumbered. Any attempt at a fight would end with him dead.

"You're all rats," he hissed. "Rats! Filthy, uncivilized monsters who think they know it all! You think you're clever, staging this little attack. The group I have brought to Lochridge is nothing but a fraction of the resources available to me. Stephen Trace is a powerful man, and when he figures out what has occurred here, he will give me full permission to overtake Lochridge by *whatever means necessary.*" His ice-cold gaze raked over them, sending a chill down Jordan's spine. "You have no idea what you have unleashed."

Declan groaned. "And you have no idea how pissed off I am. There's no use in fighting—right here, right now, this is a battle you cannot win."

"It's a good thing I'm not focused on the battle," Silas said quietly.

"There is a war to be fought, and I intend to win it." He lifted his chin. "But not today."

He raised a hand to signal to his men. Jordan motioned as well, and the Ravens stood down, stepping aside to let Silas through. Jordan and Stella both lowered their weapons, a small sigh rushed out of him.

But then Silas paused and turned around, Tobias coming to his side.

"But first, there is one more matter to be taken care of," he said. "My daughter is in critical condition. The doctor said might not survive. In Stokes, we firmly believe in the saying, *An eye for an eye, and a life for a life.*" His pale eyes settled on Stella as Tobias handed him a small pistol. "So a life for a life, Miss Rook. I hope it was worth it."

The next few moments seemed to crawl by, time warping around Jordan. He saw Silas raise the gun, his finger slipping to the trigger. Stella tensed next to him, but Jordan was already in motion, slamming into Stella and sending them both to the ground as a gunshot split the air.

CHAPTER 72

Stella slammed into the cobblestones, Jordan landing on top of her with a grunt. Her ears rang, and her breath came too fast as she assessed her body and realized she was alright—but something hot and sticky soaked through her shirt. Blood—but not hers.

Her eyes widened as she realized whose it was.

"Jordan!" she screamed, flipping him over. He grunted, blood pooling between the fingers of the hand he pressed against his abdomen. Declan and Mateo were there in an instant, the former dropping his weapon to press his hands against the wound, the latter lifting Jordan's shoulder to get a look at his back.

"No exit wound," he rushed out.

Dec spat a curse. "The bullet's still in there."

No. *No. Nonononononnononononononono—*

"Interesting."

Stella looked up to see Silas standing over them, his head cocked to the side.

"A life for a life is all I said," he murmured. "I guess I didn't specify who."

"You shot him," Stella said numbly.

"That I did." He tipped his hat at her. "I will be taking Raven territory for my own. Anyone who dares to cross the border will be shot on sight, no questions asked. And don't fret. We will come for the rest of Lochridge in due time. I bid you all a good day."

"You son of a bitch," Declan snarled, grabbing his rifle. Stella rushed forward to stanch the blood flowing from Jordan as Declan raised his rifle, but Half-Daelik tackled him to the ground.

"*Hold your fire!*" Mateo roared, even as the Ravens raised their weapons. "They're leaving! Hold your fire!"

Stella was only vaguely aware of Declan still trying to fight past him, of the Roses and Ravens edging away from each other with hostile looks, of Silas strolling away with his hands in his pockets, his people going with him. All she could see was Jordan struggling to breathe as his blood painted her hands red.

"Little thorn," he gasped. "I—I'm alright. I'm—"

"You're shot, you idiot," Declan snapped. "We've got to get you to a doctor."

"The family doc—" Mateo started.

"Is on the side of the city that Silas just walked onto. If he's even *in* Lochridge still." Declan placed his hands over Stella's, applying as much pressure as he could. "We don't have anyone on this side who would help us."

"But we do," Zoey said, running up. "There's a doc at our house."

Mateo shook his head. "We can't transport him that far."

Stella glanced up, frantically searching for options. Her eyes fell on the rose she'd dropped. Horror lurched through her as she saw the white petals were splattered with red. Blood—Jordan's blood. He was *bleeding out* and wasn't there a doctor around here—

Her eyes landed on something in the distance, and she finally found her voice.

"The motorcar," she whispered, then shouted. "The motorcar! Silas left it!"

Mateo's head whipped around. "Yes!"

"We can use that!" Zoey said. "Come on, get him up!"

Stella kept pressure on the wound as Declan and Mateo positioned themselves on either side of Jordan, preparing to lift him up and carry him to the car. But they didn't make it an inch before a towering figure stepped in their path.

"What the hell do you think you're doing?" Marcus demanded of Stella. "That is Jordan Daelik. You are not taking him to my house!"

Her mouth fell open. "He just—He just took a bullet for me!"

"If he's stupid enough to do that, then he deserves to bleed out."

"That is my son you're talking about," Lillian snarled, stumbling to her feet. "Your daughter is alive because of him!"

"No!" Marcus roared. "I won't allow it!"

This time it was Mateo who grabbed the rifle. "That is my brother," he panted, pointing it at Marcus' face. "And he just saved your ass. So either you step out of the way, or I will show you how it feels to take a bullet."

Marcus appeared unfazed by that. His gaze slid to Stella, wrathful and condescending. Every part of her mind screamed to cower underneath that gaze, to give into his intimidation tactics.

No—she was Stella Rook, and she would not give in.

She held her father's gaze, unblinking and unmoving, refusing to back down. Refusing to cower, to step away when she'd worked so damn hard to clean up the mess he'd made.

Stella held Marcus' gaze without a trace of fear, and in the end, he broke first.

"You're going to regret this, girl," he said.

Her eyes were cold. "I have nothing to regret. Now step out of the way."

Evelyn appeared. Amber fire burned in Marcus' eyes as he allowed his wife to pull him to the side. Stella glared at him as they lifted Jordan, who groaned softly. His face was pale as Zoey opened the back door, as they slid Jordan inside. Stella's fingers trembled as she applied as much pressure to his wound as she could.

"I'll drive," Declan said, aiming for the driver's seat.

"No," Jordan rasped. "Don't... trust... you. Let Mateo... do it."

Stella didn't particularly trust Thatcher behind the wheel either, so she was glad as Mateo slid into the driver's seat and started the car. Declan grumbled as he climbed in the back with the others, taking over for Stella.

Her blood-slicked fingers shook as Mateo tore down the street. She didn't think he knew how to drive any better than Declan did, but at least he was sober enough to make a solid attempt at it. He white-knuckled the wheel as Zoey shouted directions.

There was so much blood. Jordan fought to stay conscious, mumbling incoherent things under his breath. Stella's mind flashed back to that night on the Harbor, Liam sprawled out on the ground, struggling to breathe as the life drained out of his eyes—

No. This wasn't Liam. This was *Jordan*.

And he was going to survive, dammit.

Mateo didn't wait for the guards to open the iron gates. He drove right through them and up the dirt path until they were right in front of the manor's front porch. Stella threw open the door and charged inside.

"Doctor!" she screamed.

The doc appeared at the end of the hall. "I'm sorry, Miss Rook. They came and took her—"

Alarm shot through her. "Took who?"

"Celia. Her father's people came and took her away, I didn't think she should be moved—"

Celia was Stella's last concern. "I don't care. I've got a victim of a gunshot wound to the torso that I need you to take care of."

A second later, Declan, Mateo, and Zoey stumbled through the door, an unconscious Jordan hanging between them.

The doc's face paled. "That's Jordan Daelik."

Stella snarled. "And I said to take care of him. Do we have a problem with that?"

Her face paled further, but she shook her head. "Get him in here. Quickly."

She called for another servant for help as they deposited Jordan on the bed Celia had been laying in only a few hours ago. Silas must have had his men transport her in case any of the Rooks escaped and came back to find his daughter still in their home. Stella was glad she was gone, or else she would have slit her throat.

They were ushered out of the room. Stella stumbled into the parlor, her breathing coming much too fast.

"Hey," Zoey said, grabbing Stella's shoulders. "He's going to be alright."

"He pushed me out of the way," she breathed.

"Bloody idiot," Declan muttered.

Stella felt a tear slip down her cheek. "He pushed me out of the way, Zo."

Zoey pulled her into a hug, both of them coated in blood. "I know. But he's tough. He's going to pull through."

"Jordie's seen worse," Mateo affirmed.

Even Declan sighed. "He's an idiot, but he's a tough one at that." He nudged Stella. "And if I didn't know any better, I'd say that he likes you."

Stella choked on a sob. "If he doesn't make it—"

"He's going to," Zoey said firmly. "Jordan is going to be fine. That whole confrontation ended with just one bullet being shot—it went so much better than we hoped." She squeezed Stella's shoulder. "We won, Stell."

She shook her head, slumping down on the bench in front of the piano. "No—Silas is still here. We haven't got rid of him."

"But we saved everyone," Mateo said. "Both families are alive. We did everything we set out to do without a single casualty on either side." He paused. "Well, Harvey killed someone. But other than that, your plan worked. You should be proud."

It had worked, hadn't it? Stella rubbed her cheek. They were right. Silas, who had wanted everyone dead, had retreated with minimal damage. If it was any other battle, Stella would have been beside herself in glee at how flawlessly her plan was executed.

Jordan was hurt. Silas was still in Lochridge.

But everyone was *alive*.

A weak smile rose on her lips. "It did work."

"Hell yeah it did," Declan agreed, patting her on the back. His gaze trailed around the room, soaking it in. Stella winced as he appraised her piano with a cocked brow. "Though all of us standing in Marcus Rook's parlor is not how I expected this to go down."

A broken laugh escaped Stella, and Mateo cracked a smile. Zoey sat down next to Stella, pulling her into another hug, and the four of them grinned at each other.

Stella leaned her head against Zoey's shoulder. Declan plopped down in Marcus' favorite armchair, seemingly oblivious to the fact his hands were coated in Jordan's blood. After a moment, Mateo sat down as well, casting glances towards the doorway the doc had taken Jordan into.

For a few minutes, they sat there in silence.

Then there was shouting on the front porch, and Stella realized that the dust had not settled yet.

Mateo had picked up both of Jordan's fallen guns. Stella took them from him and stormed out the front door. Her father stood at the top of the stairs, the anger in his eyes unlike anything he'd ever seen.

"You are not allowed in here!" he bellowed.

John Daelik and the Ravens stood in front of him. "My son is in there!"

"Your son is a dead man."

"How dare you take him!"

"Take him? How dare you allow your sorry excuse of a child to waltz onto my property!"

"Why, you—"

"Enough," Stella ground out.

Both men ignored her. She tried to shove her way past Marcus, but he pushed her back, too focused on John to notice her vying for his attention.

"Stop it," she cried.

A gunshot cracked the sky. All eyes turned to Declan, who lowered his smoking gun.

"Shut up and listen to her," he snapped.

Stella flashed him an appreciative look before stepping around Marcus. "This is madness." She glared at her father. "Jordan pushed me out of the way of a bullet. I don't know if he's going to make it or not. I'm really hoping he does, because we need him. Silas planned this from the beginning, and if you weren't so damn blind, you would have seen it!" Tears pricked at the corners of her eyes. "I tried to warn you. I told you I didn't trust Silas, told you I'd followed him and figured out his plans. But *you didn't listen*. You *never* do."

"And look where it landed us," John hissed.

Stella's gaze whipped to him. "Don't you even dare. Jordan and I have been working together for weeks now, and I know he tried to talk to you about Silas. But instead of putting aside your ego and listening to him, you assigned him dirty work and ignored a voice of reason." She looked between them. "You both did."

"I had nothing to do with this," Marcus snapped. "This is *his* fault!"

"My fault? I'm not the one who made a deal with that bastard!"

"*Enough!*" Stella screamed.

She lifted Jordan's guns, one aimed at John and the other at Marcus. John seemed used to guns being pointed at his head by a Rook, but Marcus stumbled back, his eyes going wide.

"You wouldn't," he whispered.

"I would," she hissed.

Silence reigned. Harvey edged forward, looking like he would try to wrestle the gun out of Stella's hand, but she glared at him.

"If you value your life," she said, her voice lethally soft, "you will back the hell up."

He tilted his head to the side, eyes gleaming. A grin curled over his lips as he stepped back, watching the scene unfold with growing interest.

Marcus bared his teeth. "Get the gun away from me, girl."

"No." The word cut through the air. Stella's amber eyes blazed. "No, I will not. Both you are so misguided, so driven by a desire to put the other down that you couldn't see the threat right in front of your faces even after your *own children* told you about it. Silas has now claimed half of this city as his own. It was only because Jordan and I put our differences aside that we were able to stop him from claiming this half as well." She gripped the guns tighter. "I don't care about the feud anymore. I don't care about the Ravens or the White Roses or which side of the border I'm on. All I care about is making sure that this city remains a place I can call home. But we can't very well do that if you two won't stop bickering like children every time you lock eyes. So I am laying some ground rules." She looked at John. "Without Jordan and the Ravens, we would not have pulled this off. In return for their help, your gang will be allowed asylum in Rose territory until we get Silas out of yours."

"That's ridiculous," Marcus spluttered.

She whipped around to face him. "No, it isn't. The Ravens will stay off of our property, but they will be allowed to stay on this side of the border with *no* interference from the Roses. Jordan will stay in our house until he is fully recovered from his injuries. And once he does, we will work together as a joint force to clear Raven territory of Silas and his men so that we might restore Lochridge to its former standing. But until then, the two of you will get along." Stella waved the guns in emphasis. "I have plenty of bullets to spare, so unless you'd like to find out exactly how pissed I am at the both of you, I would suggest you do as I say. We let you have your way for weeks, and it did not work, so we are trying something else." She looked at both of them. "Do we have an understanding?"

John's gaze slid past her to Marcus, his eyes narrowed.

"We have an understanding," he ground out.

Stella had expected John to cave. He didn't have any other choice—

with Silas on his territory, his only other option was to leave Lochridge entirely, and she didn't think he was ready to give up so easily. But it was her father she was worried about. She met his gaze, and his lip curled in response.

No more being intimidated. No more backing down. If Jordan could stand up to John, then she sure as hell could put it to Marcus.

Her eyes bored into him, and he averted his gaze. "We have an understanding."

Triumph coursed through her. She lowered both guns, standing a little straighter now. "Good."

She made to walk back into the house, but John grabbed her arm.

"You're going to regret this," he breathed. "Remember what I told you about pulling the trigger? You're a coward, and it will get you killed."

It took a lot of effort to keep a civil head. "Let go of me," Stella said.

John released her, and he exchanged one last glare with Marcus before turning to his men. She saw the hesitation in his step, unsure of where to go.

"Zoey," she called. "Find them a place to hole up for a while, and make sure everyone knows not to mess with them. Any Rose found bothering them will be killed and their corpse thrown into the ocean." She glared at John. "And if the Ravens cause any trouble, I'll do the same for them."

Her cousin nodded with a smirk before slipping down the porch stairs. "Right this way, gentlemen."

Marcus was still glaring at Stella as the Ravens made their way off their property. But Stella didn't have to deal with her father right away—the doctor appeared in the doorway, her lips pressed together.

Her heart sank. "Is he alright?"

The doc nodded. "He's stable. I got the bullet out and patched him up."

A breath of relief whooshed out of her. In the corner of her eye, she saw Declan drop his head, Mateo muttering a prayer under his breath.

He was stable. He was *alive*.

"Can I see him?" Stella asked.

The doc nodded. Stella made her way back up the steps, still holding both of Jordan's guns. Marcus looked away as she passed by him, and it took all of her effort to keep her lip from curling. His pride would kill him one day—she was just glad it wasn't today.

"We'd better go with the others," Declan said, eyeing Zoey's retreating form. "Keep us updated on Jordan?"

"Of course." She handed the revolvers back to Mateo. "I'll be in touch soon."

Mateo glanced at the guns, then shook his head and pressed them back into Stella's hands. "You hold on to these. He'll want them back once he wakes up."

She nodded and wrapped her fingers around their grips. Declan clapped her on the shoulder before bounding after the Ravens. Mateo gave her a soft nod before trailing after his cousin, shooting a glare at Harvey before the two of them jogged off to catch up with the rest. Thunder clapped, and she heard Declan shout a curse as rain pelted down.

A smile tugged on her lips as she turned back to the house, gripping the revolvers.

They still had work to do, but the dust had settled for now.

CHAPTER 73

Jordan's eyes fluttered open, and a soft groan slipped past his lips. It hurt—pain radiated all the way through his midsection, a horrible, throbbing ache that made it hard to think. His throat was dry and his head swam, but he tried to sit up all the same, scanning the room for a glass of water.

He blinked. This was not his house. He hadn't seen this room before, but the gauzy white curtains and hardwood floors, the quilt thrown over him displaying a pattern of white roses… He knew where he was.

"Welcome back to the living."

He rubbed his eyes, his vision focusing enough to make out Stella. She slumped in an armchair next to the bed. The blood had been cleaned away, but her face was still a patchwork of cuts and bruises. Her unbound hair spilled over her shoulders. Her eyes were tired, but despite her marred face, she was so pretty in that moment that Jordan took a minute just to soak it in.

Then reality crashed into him, and he remembered that he'd been shot.

"This is your house," he managed. "Does your father—"

"All of Lochridge knows you're here." Her eyes glinted. "My family is not happy with it, but they can get over it. We have bigger things to deal with."

"Silas?"

"He retreated to Raven turf after shooting you."

Alarm shot through him. "We've still got people over there. Lana, Jasmin, the other women and children. They're still hiding out."

"Zoey said that Declan and Mateo took a group to retrieve them while Silas was getting his people organized. They got out safely, but no one will be going back anytime soon." She sat up, wincing as she moved her injured shoulder. "I convinced my father to let your people stay on our side of the city until Silas is taken care of."

Jordan raised a brow. "Convinced?"

"Threatened," she amended.

A smile tugged on his lips. "That's my girl."

Stella's eyes were distant. He tried not to think too hard on his half of the city—his father's empire, now in the hands of their enemy.

A tickle rose in the back of his throat, and he launched into a coughing fit. Stella grabbed a glass of water from the nightstand and held it to his lips. He drank greedily, lightning bolts of pain racing through him as he sat up a bit more. She positioned the pillows behind him, and he slumped against them with a sigh.

"How long was I out?" he rasped.

"A few hours." She sat next to him on the bed, brushing his hair off his forehead. "It's morning now."

His gaze slid past her to look out the window. The sunrise was breathtaking, a layer of clouds pressing down from above, a sliver of clear sky visible just above the horizon, stained with a single bright color.

"The sky is red," he noted.

She looked over her shoulder. "So it is."

"That's not a good sign."

Her mouth twisted. "I didn't need some sailor's tale to know that we've got bad things coming." She looked down at him, her expression drooping as a moment of silence passed between them. "You pushed me out of the way."

"I did."

"You shouldn't have."

"But I did."

"Declan said you were an idiot, and I'm inclined to agree with him." She searched his face, and he glimpsed tears in her eyes. "Why? What the hell were you thinking?"

"I wasn't thinking," he said honestly. "I saw the gun in Silas' hand, and I just... *acted*." He found her hand and laced his fingers through hers. "I love you, Stella, and I want you to know it."

"Because of your insistence on being the hero, the whole damn city knows it." She squeezed his hand as the tears finally spilled over. "I love you too, but you didn't have to take a bullet for me. You could have died."

He arched a brow. "A few weeks ago, you would have been delighted."

"Things have changed, I suppose."

His lips curled upwards. Stella leaned down and gave him a gentle kiss, her lips no more than a brush of air against his.

"I stood up to my father," she murmured. "I pointed a gun at him and gave him orders."

His eyes narrowed. "It didn't go very well, did it?"

"So far, he's done as I said. But..." She bit her lip. "He's angry."

"Let him be angry," Jordan said. "He should kick himself for not listening to you earlier." He blew out a breath. "I think my father will be even angrier. Did you see the look on his face when I handed you my gun back there? He was livid."

"I pointed a gun at him, too."

Jordan laughed under his breath. "You've been busy."

Stella gave him a half-hearted smile, but it quickly dropped.

"Hey," Jordan murmured, caressing her cheek. "What's the matter?"

"I don't know what the next step is," she whispered, looking down. "The plan worked, but I gave no thought to what we would do if Silas didn't leave Lochridge. I don't know how we're going to deal with him now that he's taken over your territory." She looked at him, her amber eyes stark. "What do we do, Jordan?"

Jordan forced himself to sit up all the way, cupping a hand under her chin.

"First," he said softly, "we heal up, regroup, think about the next step. We gather our forces and make a plan."

He looked out the window, to the sky stained in shades of red. Unbidden, his mind traveled to the bodies of his Ravens on the ground, of fire and smoke staining the sky. He shuddered with the thought of the Tradows searching through his house. Of them claiming his turf as his own. When he looked back at Stella, his brown eyes were hard with determination.

"And then," he said, his voice firm, "then, we take our city back."

ACKNOWLEDGEMENTS

I've never done one of these before, so I'm going to try my best, but there's a good chance that this could turn into the sentimental ramblings of a teenage author instead of a proper thank-you to everyone who helped on this project. But I'm going to give it my best shot, so here we go:

First and foremost, thank you Lord for providing me with the creativity and ability to write. There isn't a day that goes by that I am not thankful for my writing and my stories, and I thank You for giving me such a great talent.

Thank you to my parents, for providing me with such a good life and setting me up for success. I appreciate you guys so much, and although it might take you a while to read this book from cover to cover, I am e-ternally grateful for your love and support. And a special thanks to my mom, who was the one to introduce me to the story of the Hatfield-McCoy feud, which is what inspired *Shades of Red* to begin with.

A huge thank-you to my beta readers for your love and feedback on this project. Beta readers are a really underappreciated part of the publishing process, and I am so thankful to have had so many people who showed an interest in this project when all you knew about it was a vague aesthetic video and a little information about the tropes. Your thoughts and feedback really helped shape this story and I appreciate the heck out of all of you. Especially Haven, who read countless versions of this manuscript and gave me so much feedback and advice that I know this story

469

wouldn't be the same otherwise.

And a special thanks to Eli, who not only helped shape this story from its roots, but was a tremendous help on my other projects as well. She was the first one to read *Diamond in the Rough*, and she has stuck with me no matter how many times I raved about a story idea, showed her a cover for a book I will never write, or shoved yet another half-finished manuscript into her DMs. Thank you for all your love, feedback, and sage advice, and I am so excited to read a book of your own once you write it (o7).

A big thank-you to Ink & Lore Maps for the absolutely stunning map at the beginning of this book. I tried several times to make one of my own before finally breaking down and commissioning one, and it was the best decision I ever made! You took my vision and exceeded my expectations with it. The details on this map are beautiful and make a perfect addition to the story.

And last, but most certainly not least, thank you to everyone who has sup-ported me through this crazy journey to becoming an author. From my first sub-scribers on YouTube to everyone who has picked up one of my books, I am so so *so* thankful for your support. It is so amazing that the story ideas I had when I was fifteen have turned into something this big, and I am in awe of how many people are just as excited as I am over *Diamond in the Rough* and *Shades of Red*. Just know that all of you guys are appreciated, and I look forward to more projects in the future!

ABOUT
THE
AUTHOR

JAYDEN THOMPSON first discovered her love of writing at fifteen years old. Her first novel, *Diamond in the Rough*, was published when she was eighteen. A Kentucky native, Jayden spends her time reading, hanging out with family, watching too many YouTube videos, and daydreaming about fictional worlds.

For sneak peeks of upcoming books and more content, you can check out her website (jaydenthompson.com), her YouTube channel (@jaydenthompsonauthor), and her Instagram (@authorjaydenthompson).